W9-ACR-755

— THE —
RAVEN
RING
A Lyra Novel

Patricia C. Wrede

A TOM DOHERTY ASSOCIATES BOOK

NEW YORK

THE RAVEN RING

A Tor Book
Published by Tom Doherty Associates, Inc.
175 Fifth Avenue
New York, N.Y. 10010

Tor ® is a registered trademark of Tom Doherty Associates, Inc.

Library of Congress Cataloging-in-Publication Data

Wrede, Patricia C.
    The raven ring / Patricia C. Wrede.
        p. cm.
    "A Tom Doherty Associates book."
    ISBN 0-312-85040-9
    I. Title.
    PS3573. R38R38   1994   94-30178
    813'.54—dc20   CIP

First edition: December 1994

Printed in the United States of America

0 9 8 7 6 5 4 3 2 1

— THE —
RAVEN
RING

PROLOGUE

Spring in the Mountains of Morravik was about as predictable as a tired two-years child in a house of wonders, or so it seemed to Gralith as he picked his way between patches of half-melted snow. Today the sun was warm and bright, and he could hear birds singing and water rushing over rock; tomorrow might bring a sky as gray as the stone beneath him, and snow on a bitter wind. He paused to look around, then turned toward a clump of firs on the mountain's shoulder.

As he climbed, his steps grew slower. Not because of the slope; after two years in the mountains, he had become used to long walks and steep ascents. The duty waiting at the end of his journey was the burden that held him back.

He had never met the Salven family, but he had seen other Cilhar receive similar news, and he could predict their reaction. No tears, no horrified denials, no wails of grief; only a short silence and a white look about the lips of the husband or wife or child who offered ale and perhaps a little fruit to the bearer of the unwelcome message. Gralith found that look harder to bear than weeping.

On the far side of the firs, he stopped again, peering about for the next landmark and hoping he would recognize it for what it was when he saw it. He ought to be glad the Cilhar finally trusted him enough to tell him the locations of their homes and the hidden routes to their doors, but he wished they could be persuaded to write things down. A map would make visits such as this one so much easier! But the only maps the Cilhar kept were large-scale ones, fine for tracing a route from Kith Alunel to Ciaron or locating Morlang Isle, but useless for short local trips. He saw a boulder that fit the description he had been given, and started toward it with a long-suffering sigh.

Ten minutes and two landmarks later, he came on the house at last. He saw it suddenly, almost as if it had materialized by magic out of the mountainside while he was not attending. The cliff that sheltered it curved around two sides, blending smoothly into the weathered gray boards. The Salvens probably had a storeroom or two carved into the rock, Gralith thought. Then he blinked and looked at the house more carefully, and his heart sank. The building stood on a stone ledge. Half a flight of wooden steps led up to the door; there was no porch. The windows were narrow slits, and from where he stood to the foot of the steps he could see no stone nor tree nor shrub large enough to provide shelter for a man. This family kept to the old ways; his task was going to be worse than he had thought.

Gralith sighed. There was no point in putting it off. His boots made solid thudding noises against the weathered boards of the steps as he climbed up to the door, and his knock echoed them.

To his surprise, the door opened almost at once. "You

came! I didn't think you'd get here until tomorrow or the day after, at the earliest—" The speaker, a beautiful red-haired woman of perhaps twenty, broke off when she saw Gralith. An eyeblink later a thick-bladed, sharp-looking knife appeared in her hand. "Who are you?"

"My name is Gralith. I'm from the Island of the Moon, now acting as a representative for the Emperor of Ciaron," Gralith said, carefully keeping his hands motionless and in view.

The woman nodded, and the knife vanished. The worried expression on her face remained, and Gralith wondered whether she had some premonition of the reason for his coming. "I've seen you in Calmarten a time or two," she said, motioning him to come inside. "Sorry for the fuss; I thought you were someone else."

"I gathered," Gralith said, entering. The interior of the house was cool and smelled of soap and lamp oil. A row of unstrung bows hung on the wall next to the door, with two empty quivers beneath them; the only furnishings were a table and two wooden stools, a copper pot hanging beside the hearth, and a bed in the far corner. A girl of around fourteen sat at the table, helping a boy a few years younger than herself fletch arrows.

"I have a message for the head of the Salven family," Gralith said, remembering belatedly that among Cilhar it was the guest's privilege to speak first. "Would that be you?"

The woman's face went stiff. "A message?"

Gralith looked away from the fear in her eyes. "I'm afraid so. Are you the head of the family?"

"I'm Eleret Salven." The woman glanced toward the bed in the corner, her worried expression deepening. "But I'm not the head of the family—"

"Not by a bowshot and a half!" said a weak voice from the bed. "I'm not dead yet."

"I know, I know, but you will be if you don't keep quiet long enough for Orimern to get here, Pa," Eleret said.

"What's wrong?" Gralith asked, glad of the excuse to put off his errand for an extra moment or two.

"Nothing catching," Eleret assured him. "He got mixed up in a rock slide two days ago and broke a leg."

"And?"

Eleret looked at him. Gralith smiled slightly. "Orimern's the best healer around Calmarten village. You wouldn't have sent for her if the leg were the only problem."

"You're right," Eleret said with a sigh. "He was unconscious for a long time, even after we brought him home. Now every time he tries to move or sit up he gets sick to his stomach. I sent Jiv down to the next claiming yesterday to tell them we needed Orimern, but I expect it will be two or three days before she comes. We're not close to any of her usual circuits."

"I might be able to help," Gralith offered, glad that for once he could do something positive to offset the news he brought. "The Island of the Moon—"

"Trains people as healers!" Eleret's face brightened.

"Among other things. And we all know the basics, whatever we end up doing. So if you're willing to let me look—"

"I don't hold with takin' charity," the man in the corner grumbled.

"It isn't charity, Freeman Salven," Gralith said truthfully. "I would welcome an opportunity to put my knowledge to use."

"Getting out of practice, are you?" the man said, but he let Gralith come nearer.

Gralith checked the leg first, because it was simplest.

The splint looked well done; rather than unwrap it to examine the leg physically, he muttered the key phrase of a seeing spell and pointed. A cold blue light sprang up around the leg, and behind him the children gasped. He tried to ignore them while he concentrated. The light held steady all along the leg, which meant that the bone had been properly set. Good. Now for the head injury.

He pointed again, and the light swirled upward and settled around Freeman Salven's head. Again it held steady, and Gralith suppressed a sigh of relief. He let the light die and went on to more ordinary tests: feeling the pulse, checking the pupils of the eyes, watching the man's movements as he looked right and left or tried to touch the fingers of opposite hands together at arm's length. Finally, he straightened and turned to the hovering red-haired girl.

"His brain's been badly shaken, but he should recover in a few more days if he rests quietly in bed. If his stomach bothers him again, give him some isi-bark tea."

"That's all?" Eleret said, while behind her the two children exchanged relieved grins.

"Some things are best left to nature to heal," Gralith said apologetically. "Bones and brains are two of them, unless one's an adept-class healer, and I'm not."

"I wasn't complaining," Eleret said hastily. "Really. It's just— I was so worried—"

"Lot of fuss over nothin'," her father said, but he, too, looked more relaxed.

Eleret glowered at her father. "It's a good thing you broke your leg in the bargain, or we'd never keep you there long enough to heal right."

"Don't try to get up too soon," Gralith warned. "It'll slow down your brain's recovery, and if you should have a dizzy spell and fall on that leg again, you could cripple yourself."

The man snorted. "I'm not fool enough to chance that."

"Not now you've been told." Eleret looked at Gralith. "I'm glad you came; he wouldn't have listened to me." She hesitated, then raised her chin defiantly and said in a resolutely steady tone, "What brought you up here?"

"Bad news, I'm afraid." There was no way to say it gently. "Tamm Salven died in the service of the Emperor three weeks ago. The word came to me from Ciaron this morning. I'm sorry."

The man on the bed turned his face toward the wall. No one else moved or spoke, not even the children. The silence was every bit as bad as Gralith had expected it to be. After a moment he could not stand it, and to break it he said, "The Imperial Guard will send her wages on to you in a month or two, when the passes are clear enough for caravans."

"What happened?" Eleret's father said in a gruff voice.

"There was a skirmish on the western border near Kesandir," Gralith said. "Freelady Salven was wounded in the battle, and died a few days later. I'm sorry I don't have any more details."

"Damn it, I told her to duck!" He turned his head away once more, and Gralith heard him whisper, "Ah, *mihaya*," to the shadows beside the wall.

Gralith looked away, pretending not to hear. On the other side of the room, the younger girl laid a half-feathered arrow on the table with unnatural precision. Then, with the same slow carefulness, she reached over and took her brother's hand tightly in her own. Beside them, Eleret shook her head as if to clear it.

"Now what?" she asked in a quiet voice that was not quite steady. "I mean, what happens next with the Guards and—and everything."

"They'll deliver Freelady Salven's pay to you, as I said,"

Gralith told her. "That's all." He paused. "If you'd like, I can send a message to our school in Ciaron, and they'll see that the Guards bring you her personal belongings along with the money."

"No," Eleret said. "I— No. Ma wouldn't have liked strangers going through her things, more than was needed. I'll go and get them."

"That ought to be for me to do," Eleret's father said.

"Well, you can't, not with your leg and your head and all," Eleret replied, her voice strengthening as she spoke. "I can handle it, Pa."

"Tamm couldn't."

The girl at the table raised her head. "Eleret won't be in the army, Pa. And somebody should go."

"The Imperial Guard will send you your mother's things," Gralith said, a little taken aback by this unexpected development. "There's no need for any of you to go to Ciaron to get them."

"Maybe you don't think so," Eleret said, "but we do."

"If this Guard of yours is so willing to help, why didn't they send Tamm's things along with the news?" her father added.

"Climeral could only send a brief message," Gralith said. "It would take a circle of Adepts to actually transport an object." Then, seeing their blank expressions, he asked, "I'm sorry; did you think the news came by messenger?"

"Oh," Eleret said. "But you told us Ma died three weeks ago."

"It took that long for word to get back to the capital," Gralith said, understanding in turn. "Climeral sent it to me this morning, as soon as he was certain."

Eleret shrugged. "It doesn't matter. One of us has to go, and Pa can't. That leaves me."

"It's not an easy trip," Gralith warned. "You'll have to go overland, so it will take at least a month. And even in Ciaron you may run into people who . . . dislike Cilhar intensely."

"Syaski, who'd rather see a Cilhar dead than not, you mean," Eleret said, nodding. "We have trouble with them now and again, in spite of the Emperor's treaty. They're a little more careful about when and how they raid, that's all."

"It'd be harder for them to pull their tricks in Ciaron," Eleret's father put in. "Right there under the Emperor's nose, so to speak. But you pack a full kit anyway, Eleret. Weapons don't do you no good unless you're carrying them."

"Yes, Pa." Eleret looked over at the two children. "Better get those arrows finished tonight, Nilly; I'll take a full quiver with me when I leave, and you'll want replacements."

"You're determined to do this?" Gralith said.

"Any reason I shouldn't be?"

Gralith made a helpless gesture, unable to put his misgivings into words. "There's some wild country between here and the city. You should at least wait for the spring caravans."

"I've traveled wild country before, and I want to see this finished soon."

"Very well," Gralith said, giving up at last. He sighed. "If you have a map, I'll show you the best route. It's the least I can do."

"I'd be grateful for your help," Eleret replied, and gestured him toward one of the stools beside the table.

ONE

Ciaron smelled strange. It wasn't the saltwater smell of the sea, or the fishy tang of the docks, though both permeated the air even at the farthest inland edge of the city. No, Eleret thought, the odor that made her nose twitch came from the mingling of coal smoke with frying onions, stale beer, and attar of roses, and from the reek of hot metal, warm horse dung, and sweaty clothes—and all the other smells of too many people living in the same place. She wondered how the folk passing by her managed not to notice, and whether she, too, would adjust if she stayed long enough in Ciaron.

The noise was almost as bad as the smell. Wagons rumbled past, wheels clattering against the gray stone pavement while their loads of jars and barrels clattered against each other. Men and women called out in singsong voices, praising a confusing array of wares for sale. Shouting children ran through the crowd on mysterious errands, dodging people and horses and carts. If she did not listen too closely, the sounds blended into a continuous hum of activity.

A man in a gray cloak pushed by her and Eleret gave herself a mental slap. Sunset was only a few hours away, and if she didn't get moving she'd have nowhere to spend the night. After three weeks of traveling, she had learned the importance of finding lodging early. She stepped forward, and the fabric of her loose brown skirt wrapped around her calves as she tried to take too long a stride.

Eleret shoved her unbraided hair out of her face and grimaced. She had bought the garment the day before, in a small village some thirty miles east, and she was not yet used to the way it hampered her movements. She was not used to hair in her face, either. But Gralith had insisted that, if she must go to Ciaron alone, she should at least dress in a manner that did not instantly proclaim her Cilhar origins. The idea had sounded reasonable at the time, but she was beginning to wish she had not listened.

After a moment, the skirt unwound. Eleret slipped her left hand into her pocket, groping for the slit she had made in the material. She found it and reached through, to the knife she wore strapped to her thigh. Touching the smooth horn handle reminded her of home and made her feel better. She couldn't stand in the street all day holding a knife under her skirt, though. The thought made her smile slightly as she withdrew her hand. Shrugging the strap of her kit bag into a more comfortable position, she started slowly up the broad avenue inside Ciaron's east gate.

The avenue was at least three times the width of the widest street in Calmarten. Gralith had said there were eight such avenues in Ciaron, radiating out from Castle Hill at the center of the city. Eleret wondered whether they were all as crowded as this one. A bearded man on horseback rode by, passing a wagon filled with water jars coming in and another going out that carried crates with a few wilted vegetables in the bottoms. A dark-haired woman in a brown wool cloak argued with a merchant over the price of a small wooden box, glancing up from time to time to watch the traffic coming through the gate. An elderly porter shuffled from one shop to the next, hoping for work. And all around them, people walked, some briskly, others slowly, jostling each other with a cheerful unconcern that set Eleret's teeth on edge.

The buildings were as oversized as the street. Near the gate most of them were of wood or brick; farther along stood towering structures built of the same dark gray stone as the street. Painted ships and carts decorated a few of the walls, but most were plain. At the far end of the street, the steep sides of Castle Hill rose above the heads of the crowd, with the Emperor's palace perched on top.

A cart rattled by, piled with chairs carefully roped together and padded with coarse cloth. Its driver, a middle-aged woman in a faded green dress, glanced curiously in Eleret's direction and gave a little sniff as she passed. Eleret looked after her, more amused than annoyed. She had done nothing that she knew of to deserve the woman's contempt, and if she had overlooked some local custom, she would find it out soon enough and correct it.

At the next corner, Eleret left the avenue and headed south. "See Adept Climeral at the school first, before you do anything else," Gralith had said. "He'll know the best place for you to stay, and who you'll need to see." Then, Eleret had been skeptical of the need for such guidance, but five minutes inside Ciaron's outer wall had convinced her that it would be more useful than she had thought. Ciaron was enormous; she could waste hours or days trying to find an inn that suited her slender means.

Gralith's instructions were easier to follow than she had

expected. Accustomed to choosing a path based on land-marks, even in villages, she had assumed that Gralith was unused to giving directions when he had said only "two streets, then right; three streets, then left." Now she understood. Ciaron had been carefully planned; the streets ran in straight lines at fixed distances from each other. The narrow alleys at the rear of the buildings were straight, too. It made Eleret even more uncomfortable than the throng of people.

As she drew farther away from the avenue, the crowd thinned. There were still more people on the street than she was used to—a couple wearing matching bright blue capes and hats, a dark-haired woman in a brown cloak, a group of youths swaggering slowly in no particular direction, a pair of muscular men carrying fishnets—but at least now she could walk without bumping into them. She wondered how her mother had felt about the people and the straight streets and square buildings, and whether she had missed the clean quiet of the mountains. But Tamm Salven had been in the army, Eleret reminded herself, stationed out on the western border. She probably had not spent much time in Ciaron.

Preoccupied with her thoughts, Eleret almost walked right past her destination. The Island of the Moon had set up its school in yet another large, plain, square stone building. Eleret had an unexpected attack of nervousness when she saw it. She told herself not to be foolish; a house was a house. Putting her shoulders back, she laid one hand lightly on the hilt of her dagger and went up to the door.

No one answered her repeated knocks. Eleret frowned. This was the official home of the Islanders in Ciaron; *someone* must be in. She stepped back a pace and studied the door. She saw no knocker or bellpull, but at the left side of the door, set in a niche in the stone, was a small brass knob. Feeling foolish, Eleret pulled at it.

A faint chime sounded somewhere inside the building. Eleret smiled. A moment later, a dark-haired girl in a plain gray robe opened the door. She looked as if she might be only a year or two older than Nilly, but she held herself with the stiff correctness of someone much older. "Welcome to our House. What service may I do you?"

"I'm here to see Adept Climeral," Eleret answered, all her uncertainty returning with a rush at the girl's formality.

The girl's eyes widened, and suddenly she looked younger and considerably less dignified. "Climeral? But he's head of the school; he doesn't *do* things for anyone, he just directs everyone else. Are you sure you want to see *Climeral?*"

Eleret repressed a strong desire to deny that she wanted any such thing. "Yes. I have a message for him, from Gralith in the Mountains of Morravik."

"Oh!" The girl gave her a bright, relieved smile. "Then you must be Eleret Salven. He's been expecting you for several days, even though Nijole said you couldn't possibly get here before the end of the week. *He* said Nijole hadn't ever met any Cilhar and didn't know what they could do. Looks like he was right again. Oh, I'm keeping you waiting. Come in; I'm Prill, and I talk too much."

To agree would have been unmannerly, so Eleret stepped inside without speaking. As she crossed the threshold, her uneasiness vanished like smoke in a sudden breeze. The stone walls seemed to radiate peace and solid comfort despite—or perhaps because of—their plain, uncarved surfaces. A bar of sunlight fell through a long, narrow window slit above the door, turning a thin stripe of stone to gold and making the high arch of the ceiling seem to vanish among quiet shadows.

"It *is* something of a mausoleum, isn't it?" Prill said cheerfully, misreading Eleret's expression. "Blame it on the Ciaronese. It's four hundred years since Imach Thyssel fell, or nearly, and they still won't allow decent windows in any building inside the city walls. Even the Emperor's palace has nothing but arrow slits on the first two floors. It's been hundreds of years since anyone attacked Ciaron; you'd think that by this time they'd feel safe enough to allow a few windows. But I was forgetting, you're Cilhar. You probably approve of buildings that are easy to defend."

"They have certain advantages," Eleret replied. She wondered what it would be like to live in a place that no one had attacked for a hundred years.

"Yes, I suppose they do. I'm sorry. I tend to forget that every place isn't as peaceful as the Island. Still, a city doesn't have to be completely peaceful to allow big windows. Look at Kith Alunel."

"Um," said Eleret. Kith Alunel was just a name to her, a city rich in history which she did not expect she would ever see.

"Exactly," Prill said. She threw open a door and announced, "Eleret Salven's come, Adept. And Nijole owes me a tenth piece."

"I'll remind her when I see her, Prill," an amused tenor voice said from the interior of the room. "I'll also remind her about making wagers with the juniors. Come in, Freelady Salven. I am Climeral of the Island of the Moon, as Prill here has neglected to mention."

Eleret stopped dead in the doorway, staring at the white-robed man behind the table at the far side of the room. His hair was silver-white and swept back above an unlined forehead; his eyes were a dark gray-green and tilted upward at the corners. He was unmistakably one of the non-Human, semilegendary Shee, and all Eleret could think was that Gralith might have warned her. It was one thing to know that all four of Lyra's races lived and worked on the Island of the Moon; meeting a Shee magician in person was something else entirely.

"Go on, Climeral won't eat you," Prill said.

"I may, however, mark *you* down for some classes in proper conduct," the Shee Adept said to Prill. "You appear to be badly in need of them."

"I'm taking two next season."

"If Nijole is going to put you on door-duty, you had better start sooner than that," Climeral told her. "Get along with you, child."

Prill made a face at him, gave Eleret a gamin grin, and disappeared down the corridor. Eleret looked at Climeral uncertainly, half expecting him to scowl. Instead, he smiled. "Welcome, Freelady."

"I thank you for your courtesy," Eleret responded automatically. "May your welcome bring strength to us both."

"And defeat to our enemies, yours and mine," the Shee finished. "Though mostly yours, I expect; Cilhar seem to collect them the way Traders collect money. Come in and sit down."

Eleret hesitated, wishing she had thought to question the young doorkeeper before she had gotten into this. However logical she tried to be, however much she told herself that Gralith wouldn't have sent her here if it weren't acceptable, it just didn't seem right to ask a Shee, one of the race of wizards who had raised up the Mountains of Morravik in order to hold back the Melyranne Sea, to give her directions to a cheap inn.

Climeral saw her glance back the way she had come, and misunderstood. "Don't mind Prill. We're very informal among ourselves, and she hasn't been here long enough to realize that some people find it disconcerting."

"It's not that," Eleret said quickly, and then wondered what she would say if he asked her what the problem was. She didn't think she could bring herself to explain that she did not know how to treat a being who had stepped straight out of the oldest and most beloved tales she knew.

Fortunately, Climeral didn't ask. He waited until she had settled herself into the chair, then said, "Gralith told us you were on your way, but the method he used does not allow long messages. You've come to collect your mother's effects?"

"I'm to pick up Ma's things, yes," Eleret answered, relieved by the Shee's businesslike tone. "Where do I go to get them?"

Climeral shuffled through several sheets of paper, then pulled one out and looked at it. "The office of the Imperial Guard. Ask for Commander Weziral. If anyone tries to make difficulties, tell them I sent you." He looked up with a smile. "And don't let anyone talk you into signing up."

"I won't." Tentatively, Eleret returned the smile. "How do I get to the office of the Imperial Guard?"

"I'll give you directions, but it's too late for you to go today. By the time you got there, everyone would be gone."

Eleret stared, her awe of the Shee swept away by astonishment. "Gone? What do you mean? How can you run an army if no one can get hold of the commanders?"

"There aren't many emergencies of that sort in Ciaron," Climeral said gently. "If something *should* happen, there are ways of sending messages to the people who need them. Important as it is to you, though, I don't think giving you your mother's things would be considered a good reason to summon the Commander during his off-duty time."

"Then I'll go tomorrow," Eleret said. The Shee magician might be right, but the arrangement still seemed peculiar. An army couldn't do much if it only fought for a few hours every day, and the people who ran it had to work as long and hard as the soldiers or everything was likely to come to pieces. Of course, Climeral was a wizard, not a warrior, so perhaps he didn't understand. "Can you suggest a place where I can stay tonight?"

"Try the Broken Harp. It's a little farther from the palace and the sights of Ciaron than most people like, so it's not expensive, but it's clean and reasonably comfortable. I'll have someone escort you there, if you'd like."

"No, thank you."

"Ciaron can be a bit overwhelming if you're not used to cities," Climeral warned. "And I wouldn't like to think that anything . . . unpleasant might happen to you. You may not be wearing Cilhar styles, but someone may still guess where you've come from. And you're an attractive young woman; that can be a danger in itself."

For a moment, Eleret was tempted; then she shook her head. She didn't think Climeral could assign someone to be her guide and bodyguard for the whole time she was in Ciaron, so sooner or later she would have to survive the city on her own. It might as well be sooner.

Climeral shrugged. "All right. I'll write you out directions to the inn, then." He reached for the inkpot in the corner of the table.

"No need to waste the paper," Eleret told him quickly, a little shocked by the very idea. "Just say them over; it'll be faster."

"You're sure you'll remember them?"

"Quite sure." Eleret smiled, thinking of the straight, evenly spaced streets outside. The problem wouldn't be remembering the turns; it would be keeping count of them as she walked. She'd have to, though, if she wanted to find the inn. Everything in Ciaron looked like everything else; from what she'd seen, there were hardly any useful landmarks.

Climeral still looked dubious, but he told her. He seemed surprised when she did not ask him to repeat the directions, and even more surprised when, to reassure him, she faultlessly recited what he had said.

"What a remarkable memory," Climeral said when she finished.

"Me?" Eleret said. "You mean because I can say over that little bit? That's nothing. You should hear Siff or Bilet do a telling; they can go on for hours and never miss a word."

"This ability is common among Cilhar?"

"Most people can do it a little, if that's what you mean."

Climeral gave her a long, thoughtful look. "I can see that there is a great deal more to your people than their skill with weapons. Since you have so little difficulty, I may as well tell you now how to get to the offices of the Imperial Guard."

Eleret listened closely to the instructions, and repeated them at Climeral's request. It all seemed simple enough. In another day, or at most two, she should be ready to leave Ciaron. Climeral raised an eyebrow when she mentioned this, but did not comment, and a few minutes later a small boy solemnly escorted her to the door of the school.

TWO

The sounds and smells outside were a shock after the cool quiet of the Islander's school, and Eleret paused for a moment to get her bearings. A wrinkled, sour-looking man passed by, pushing a two-wheeled cart with long handles. On the far side of the street, a dark-haired woman in a brown wool cloak stood tapping her foot impatiently and peering east at the shapes of people walking toward her. She seemed vaguely familiar, but that was impossible. Eleret didn't know anyone in Ciaron except the people at the school, whom she had just met. She frowned and shifted uncomfortably. Something felt wrong.

She looked around once more. The man with the cart turned onto a side street. Three young women, hardly more than girls, came toward the school from one direction, talking and giggling, while a short fat man going the other way glared at them. The dark-haired woman showed increasing signs of irritation. None of them seemed particularly interested in Eleret.

Eleret shook herself and started down the street. It was

only the strangeness of the city that was making her uncomfortable, she told herself. It was all the smooth, unweathered stone, all the tall buildings and straight lines, all the people. Still, she kept her hand near the hilt of the dagger she had strapped to her leg under her skirt. Cilhar did not make old bones by ignoring a warning hunch, no matter how unlikely it might seem.

Despite her worries, Eleret reached the inn without incident. She saw the splintered harp hanging from the bar above the door when she was still two blocks away. The inn itself was wood, not stone, and comfortably shabby, as if it had stood in its place through years of sun and storms. As she set her hand against the faded blue paint on the door, Eleret felt almost at home.

The middle-aged couple who kept the Broken Harp took half a copper coin as an earnest, then showed Eleret to a sunny chamber on the south side of the building. Eleret thanked them and promised to take dinner in the public room. As soon as they had left, she set down her kit bag and examined her new quarters.

The windows were the same long, narrow slits that Prill had been complaining about at the school, but these were set in groups of three, less than a hand's span apart. Built that way, they let in more light and gave the impression of a larger opening, but only a very small child would be able to get into the room through one of them. The door was made of wide pine boards and had two iron hooks on the inside, though Eleret did not see a bar anywhere around. Perhaps the innkeeper could supply one. In the corner next to the door, a wooden frame with rope woven across it supported a straw-stuffed pallet and a couple of blankets. The rest of the furnishings consisted of a glazed clay chamber pot, a small oak table with a pitcher and washbasin on it, and a short, three-legged stool.

The sight of the washbasin made Eleret suddenly conscious that she had been traveling all day and was covered with dust. Upon investigation, however, the pitcher proved to be empty. Eleret picked it up and went out in search of a pump.

As she reached the door to the public room, she heard voices on the other side. The room had been empty when she arrived, and the innkeeper's wife was at the far end of the hall, just going into the kitchen. A customer must have come in while Eleret was looking around. Not wanting to interrupt, Eleret went past the door, toward the kitchen.

The door swung open. "—on the second floor," the innkeeper said. "Will that do?"

"It will be suitable," a woman's voice answered.

Eleret glanced back over her shoulder and froze. The speaker was the dark-haired woman in the brown wool cloak who had been waiting for someone outside the Islanders' school.

Leaning into the shadows, Eleret waited until the innkeeper and his new guest had gone on up the stairs. Then she walked softly back to her room and sat down on the bed to think.

The woman had followed her from Climeral's school. Why? Not to steal; Eleret had nothing worth taking except her knife, and that was hidden among the folds of her skirt. Could it be because Eleret was a Cilhar? It was not so long ago that any Cilhar who left the mountains risked his life against the assassins of Syaskor. The Emperor of Ciaron was supposed to have put an end to that, but could he have succeeded completely in only eight years? But how could the woman have known where Eleret came from? Her knife and her pouch of finely balanced iron raven's-feet were the only things Eleret could think of that might betray her origin, and neither was obvious to a casual observer.

Perhaps the woman was one of Climeral's people. Eleret considered this idea for a moment, then shook her head. She did not think Climeral would send someone to follow her after she turned down his offer of a guide, and if the woman had come from the school without Climeral's knowledge it was not likely that she meant well.

Frowning, Eleret stood up and checked her weapons. She readjusted her skirt slightly, until she was completely satisfied that she could reach through the slit and draw her knife as quickly as possible. Then she picked up the pitcher in her right hand and left the room once more, moving as warily as if she were hunting squirrels in the mountains around her home.

She saw no one but the innkeeper's wife, who filled the pitcher with water and Eleret's ears with a stream of apologies for having left it empty. Eleret seized the opportunity to ask about a bar for the door.

The woman gave her a sharp look, then nodded approvingly. "That's right, you're a pretty one and there's no sense taking chances. We're a respectable inn, we are, but even so, it's better. Here, take your pick." She gestured at a stack of smooth wooden bars, each as thick as Eleret's forearm, which stood against the wall behind the kitchen door.

Eleret examined the bars with care and chose one without knots or cracks that might weaken it. She thanked the innkeeper's wife, picked up the pitcher in one hand and the bar in the other, and returned to her room, keeping a cautious eye on the stairs where the dark-haired woman had gone.

* * *

The public room of the Broken Harp was as agreeably shabby as the rest of the inn. The wooden floor was smooth with years of wear, and the passage of countless feet had ground gray-black paths from the door to the trestle tables. At one end of the room, an open hearth took up most of the wall. Someone had tried to scrub the ancient accumulation of smoke stains from the stone shelf above it, and had given up less than halfway through the job. A row of mismatched small jugs with harps and pipes painted on the side stood on the shelf. Even from the doorway at the opposite end of the room, Eleret could see cracks in two of them.

"Soup and ale, one and a half bits, since you have the room," the innkeeper told her. "There's meat as well, for two bits extra, if you want it. Beer's a half-bit for the first draw, a bit for every one after that. Wine depends on what you're drinking; we don't have many fancy ones, but there are one or two that aren't bad."

The prices seemed high, but she'd been warned that everything would be more expensive in Ciaron. It was a good thing she wasn't planning to stay long. "Soup and ale are fine," she said.

"Sit down and I'll bring it for you," the innkeeper said, smiling. He turned and vanished in the direction of the kitchen.

Eleret seated herself at a table near the inner door, where she could watch the room with her back to a wall. The other two patrons had plainly come for refreshment rather than a meal. From all appearances, they had been refreshing themselves for some time. Eleret smiled slightly to herself.

The kitchen door swung open. "—quite sure you can

carry it, Dame Nirandol?" said the innkeeper over his shoulder.

"It is no trouble," a woman's voice answered, and Eleret stiffened. An instant later, the dark-haired woman entered the room, holding a wooden bowl in one hand and a cup in the other. The innkeeper followed, still looking distressed at the thought of one of his guests carrying her own meal. In one hand, he bore three mugs; in the other, a half-loaf of bread, hollowed out and filled with Eleret's soup.

The innkeeper brushed by the dark-haired woman, muttering apologies, and set two of the mugs in front of the drinkers. Then he crossed to Eleret's table and left the soup and the third mug in front of her. "If there's anything else you want—"

"I'll let you know," Eleret said, only half attending. Most of her mind was concentrated on the dark-haired woman making her way slowly across the public room toward them.

"As you wish," the innkeeper said, and left. Eleret picked up her mug and sipped at the black, bitter brew. The dark-haired woman drew nearer, moving with studied grace. She was at least twenty-eight, Eleret guessed, but no more than thirty-two, and she had the look of someone used to getting her own way. Under the table, Eleret's left hand crept into her pocket and closed around the hilt of her dagger.

The woman reached the bench on the other side of the table and paused. Her eyes studied Eleret with unconcealed interest. "May I join you?" she said just before the silence became acutely uncomfortable.

"There's no dagger in the door to stop you," Eleret replied, shrugging one shoulder.

"A curious expression." The woman seated herself sideways and swung her legs awkwardly over the top of the bench. Her green skirt trailed behind and caught on something; she had to squirm for a moment before she could settle into a comfortable position.

"It's something my grandmother used to say." Eleret made her tone as flat and unencouraging as she could. She lowered her eyes to her meal, hoping the other woman would take the hint. It was not entirely pretense; eating right-handed took considerable concentration. The comforting feel of the dagger's hilt in her left hand was worth the inconvenience.

"I see." The woman hesitated. "I was wondering whether you would be willing to help me."

"Help you do what?" Eleret asked, still wary.

"I am a . . . collector of ancient relics; my name is Jonystra Nirandol. I am on my way to Kith Alunel, and have only a few days to spend in Ciaron. I will not be able to look through most of the shops. I was hoping . . . that is . . . would you tell me if you see anything I might find interesting?"

Eleret tore off a piece of bread and dipped it into the steaming soup. Deliberately, she swirled it to collect the anonymous bits of vegetables that floated in the thick brown liquid. "I have business of my own to attend to," she said, and bit into the sop.

"I do not wish to keep you from it," Jonystra said earnestly. "But I am sure that, wherever your business takes you, you will see things that I will not. All I ask is that you tell me of them, or leave a message."

"What kinds of things?"

"Old ones, preferably small enough to carry easily," Jonystra said. "Scent bottles, brooches, seals, rings—that sort of thing. For the right merchandise, I will pay well. Very well."

Her voice was eager. Too eager. Eleret kept her expression neutral. "I can't promise I'll notice anything you'd like, but I'll keep you in mind."

"Thank you." Jonystra's smile held anticipation and a touch of relief. "Anything small and old, remember—rings, buckles, gloves, anything."

"I'll remember. How long will you be in Ciaron? I wouldn't want to make you miss something just because I waited too long to leave you a message."

"Three or four days. The caravan master isn't sure how long it will take to find the cloth he wants, so it could be longer." Jonystra raised her cup and sipped at it. "How long will you be here?"

Warning-horn calls echoed through Eleret's mind. "Two weeks, at least," she lied.

Jonystra's eyebrows rose. "You are young to have so much business in this city."

"Oh, I should finish my business in three or four days," Eleret said, forcing a smile. "But I've never been in the city before, and I intend to make the most of it."

"Ah. Then you must let me recommend a few places for you to see. I have been here many times, and I know Ciaron well."

Eleret let Jonystra turn the conversation. For the rest of the meal, the other woman described various sights, streets, shops, and amusements that she felt no visitor to Ciaron should miss. Eleret listened carefully, noting each name and occasionally asking for directions so that she could be certain of avoiding the places that moved Jonystra to the greatest heights of enthusiasm. The dark-haired woman might be entirely honest and sincere; the sun might shine someday in the Alimar Caves, too. Eleret wouldn't wager a broken arrow on either one. She escaped as soon as she finished her soup and returned to her room, where she barred the door and went to bed early. She had a great deal to do the next day, and she had the feeling that the sooner she was done with her business and away from Ciaron, the better.

She rose early and breakfasted without seeing any sign of Jonystra, then left, heading for the offices of the Imperial Guard. The streets were just as crowded as they had been the previous afternoon, and they made Eleret just as uncomfortable. Twice, she nearly tripped herself with the folds of the unfamiliar skirt. It was a relief when she finally reached the block of square stone buildings that housed the Guard.

Following Climeral's directions, Eleret went straight to the central building. A middle-aged woman in uniform gave her a questioning look at the main door, but when Eleret explained what she wanted, the woman summoned a boy to escort her to the Commander's staff rooms. They passed several bored-looking guards posted at intervals along the hall before the boy threw open a door and announced importantly, "Freelady Salven for Commander Weziral."

Eleret stepped through the door into a high-ceilinged room, automatically noting a second door in the far wall. The bare floor and stone walls magnified the smallest sound, and she stopped walking as soon as she was inside. As she entered, three men looked up from a litter of paper that all but covered the top of a large square table. The one in the center, a tall man with a face like chiseled rock, said, "To see the Commander? Why?"

"I have business with him," Eleret replied.

"I can imagine," the man on the right muttered, eyeing Eleret. He was the youngest of the three men, and the only one not in uniform. His hair was a greasy brown, and his eyes were small and narrow.

"The Commander cannot see everyone," the tall man

said, with a glance at the previous speaker that should have frozen him where he sat. "We are members of his staff; I'm sure we can handle your business for you."

"Sure," the man on the right said, leering. "We'll be happy to . . . handle you."

"Maggen!" The tall man turned his head. "Your connections obliged me to give you this position; they do not oblige me to put up with insubordination, interruptions, or insinuations. If you wish to continue drawing your outrageously lavish pay, you will confine your remarks to the business of the Guard. Have I made myself clear?"

"Abundantly," Maggen said. He leaned back against the wall, smiling slightly, his eyes fixed insolently on Eleret.

Eleret kept her own eyes fixed on the tall man. "Adept Climeral at the school of the Island of the Third Moon runs said I was to see Commander Weziral," she told him. "He didn't mention anything about staff."

"I see. In that case, I will let him know you are here. What was the name again?"

"Eleret Salven."

Maggen's sneer vanished, and he straightened abruptly. The tall man gave him a warning glance, then nodded to Eleret and went to the inner door. He knocked, waited a moment, and entered, leaving Eleret facing Maggen and his remaining companion.

"You know I, uh, didn't mean anything personal," Maggen said, looking nervously at Eleret.

"Then perhaps you should have been more formal," Eleret said.

"Look, I don't want—"

The third man cleared his throat and glanced meaningfully from Maggen to the inner door. Maggen broke off in mid-sentence. Eleret suppressed both a relieved smile and a strong desire to pace, wondering how much longer the tall man would take.

The inner door opened. "The Commander will see you, Freelady Salven," the tall man said. He gestured her inside and closed the door behind her.

THREE

Commander Weziral was a small, gray-haired man who radiated a cheerful energy that Eleret found immensely appealing. He sat behind a barricade of shelves, books, boxes, and crates that seemed to be taking over the entire office. Dusty sunlight fell through a high, narrow window slit behind him, accompanied by the unmistakable sounds of someone directing an exercise drill outside.

"You're Eleret Salven?" the Commander said as the door closed. "Sit down, sit down, you'll give me a crick in my neck if I have to keep looking up at you."

"Thank you, Commander," Eleret said. She selected the only one of the plain wooden chairs that did not have books and papers stacked on it and seated herself. She looked up to find herself gazing into the shrewdest pair of eyes she had seen since her grandfather had been killed in a Syaski raid.

"Tell me why you're here," the Commander said.

"To pick up my mother's things. She was in the Imperial Guard; her name was Tamm Salven. She died at—" What was it Gralith had said? "—at Kesandir, about six weeks ago. Adept Climeral said I was to speak to you."

"I know all that," Weziral said impatiently. "I mean, why did you, yourself, come to Ciaron?"

"Pa was hurt, and Nilly and Jiv are too young," Eleret said, surprised by the question.

The Commander made an irritated noise. "It's a long, hard trip. We could have sent your mother's things. So why did you come?"

Eleret shrugged. "It wouldn't have been right to let someone else bring them home, once we knew. Ma wouldn't . . . wouldn't have liked it." Her eyes prickled, remembering.

There was a brief silence, then Weziral said gently, "You're very like her."

"Thank you," Eleret managed. She took a deep, shaky breath. "May I have her things now?"

"In a moment. There are some facts you should know first; frankly, I thought you'd gotten wind of them somehow, and that was why you'd come."

Eleret tensed. "What are you talking about?"

"Your mother's death. I'm not satisfied with the reports I've gotten. Tamm Salven was seriously wounded, but she shouldn't have died of it." Weziral's face hardened briefly. "I don't like losing good officers. I especially don't like it when there's no reason for it to happen."

"No reason?" Eleret blinked. "What do you mean? Gralith didn't know the details, but we thought—we thought that she died of her wounds, or perhaps that one of them went bad. Even little ones do, sometimes." All the way to Ciaron, she had been trying not to examine that last possibility too closely. When she was eleven, she had worked with the healers after the Battle of Kilimar Pass, and she had vivid memories of the puffy, oozing wounds, the smothered moans, and the stench. She didn't want to have to picture her mother in the place of those she had helped tend.

"It wasn't wound-fever," Weziral said. "And the healers tell me she was beginning to mend."

"Then how did she die?"

"If I knew that, I wouldn't be tacking across the harbor like this," Weziral said dryly. "All I *know* is that Salven died unexpectedly in the night, four days after the fight at Kesandir, under the care of one of the best healers I have in the field, of clean wounds that had begun to close."

"You think someone murdered her."

"I think the whole thing smells worse than haddock that's been three days in the sun, but I don't have any facts that can tell me why or how. When I find some, I'll see that you're told."

Eleret nodded.

"It's not only your mother's death," Weziral went on. He bent and picked up a plain wooden box from somewhere beside his feet. He set the box on the table in front of him and gazed at Eleret across the lid. "Someone tried to ambush the messenger team who brought me the news of Kesandir. They were amateurs, and unsuccessful ones at that, but that kind of thing isn't supposed to happen in the middle of Ciaronese territory. And since this"—he tapped the box—"arrived three weeks ago, there have been two attempts to break into my office. Draw your own conclusions."

"Ma found something that someone wants very badly," Eleret said without hesitation.

"Exactly."

"Do you know what it is?"

"No. I haven't even opened the box; you can see that the seals are still intact," Weziral replied. "I admit to an enormous curiosity, quite apart from my professional interest, and I would take it as a personal favor if you could see your way to opening it up here."

"Of course." The wooden box was nearly a foot and a half on a side, but from the way the Commander had lifted it there was not much inside. It would be simpler to unload it here, and she would attract less attention carrying a small bundle back to the inn.

Weziral beckoned, and Eleret came forward. She examined the seals briefly, then pulled out her knife and began removing them. Weziral's eyes widened. "Is that a Sadorthan dagger?"

"Yes," Eleret said, working the point carefully under the wax. "Ma gave it to me when I started hunting regularly, so I'd have a good one when I needed to skin something. It cost more than we could really afford, but Ma said it would be worth it in the long run."

"I should think so. Do you have any idea how many people in Ciaron would cheerfully slit your throat to get their hands on that dagger?"

"On my *knife*?" Eleret said incredulously.

"I didn't think you did. You'd do well to keep it out of sight, unless you intend to go looking for trouble."

"Cilhar don't hunt trouble." Eleret kept her face and voice neutral to avoid showing how much the conversation unsettled her.

"Trouble seems to find quite a few of them nevertheless," Weziral replied. "Under the circumstances—"

"I'll be careful."

The last of the seals came loose as she spoke. Eleret wiped the film of wax from the end of her dagger and slid it through her pocket and into its sheath. Then she reached out with both hands and opened the box.

There was not much inside: a worn leather pouch for

raven's-feet, a dagger in an embroidered sheath, and a waterproof kit bag that covered the bottom of the box. Eleret lifted the things out one at a time and set them on the table. Suddenly she stiffened. Under the kit bag, lying crosswise in the bottom of the box, was a thick braid of chestnut hair. A strand of yellow wool wound through the coils, and both ends were bound with red cord. Yellow for honor; red for death in battle. How had the Ciaronese known? Eleret tore her gaze away and looked up, questioning.

"Salven wasn't the only Cilhar at Kesandir," Weziral said. "There aren't many of your people in the army, but they keep track of one another. According to the report, one of them showed up at the medical tent shortly after Salven died and insisted on doing things his way. That was part of it." He gestured at the braid.

"Part?" Eleret said unsteadily around a fist-sized knot in her throat.

"He also demanded that the body be burned." Weziral looked at her sharply. "It was."

Eleret nodded, beyond speech. She was too numb even to feel gratitude for the nameless man who had seen that the death rites were properly performed for Tamm Salven. Slowly she picked up the braid and set it on the table beside her mother's possessions. Her hand brushed the leather pouch. It was flat and empty; her mother must have used all her raven's-feet in the battle. Perhaps that was how she had earned the yellow strand in her braid.

Without thinking, Eleret picked up the pouch and fingered the smooth surface of the leather. Something shifted under her hand, a hard lump in the bottom. The pouch was not completely empty after all. Eleret loosened the strings and tilted it over her right hand.

Silver flashed in the sunlight as a ring rolled out of the

pouch. Eleret recognized it at once, and a wave of anger swept over her. That ring was an heirloom, practically the only one the family had! Tamm should never have taken it with her. What if something had happened, and the ring had been lost? Eleret's mind froze suddenly. Something *had* happened, and it was not the ring that had been lost. Her fingers tightened around the hard, sharp metal.

"What is it?" Weziral asked.

Eleret looked up with a start. Still struggling to control her unruly emotions, she said, "A ring. It's been handed down in the family for generations. I was . . . surprised to see it. I thought Ma had stored it with the rest of the things she left at home."

"May I see it?"

Silently, Eleret peeled her fingers away from the ring and handed it to the Commander. Then she turned away and busied herself with the kit bag. She knew what the Commander was seeing: a band of twisted silver, worn thin and nearly smooth, set with a flat black stone. Etched into the stone, in the manner of a seal, was the tiny, meticulously detailed figure of a raven rising into flight. Eleret remembered reaching out as a child to touch a carved wingtip, while her mother explained that the raven was a symbol of protection for the Cilhar. She scowled fiercely at the ties of the kit bag to hold back her tears.

"Interesting." Weziral's voice drew Eleret's thoughts back to the dusty, paper-strewn office. "It almost looks like Kith Alunel work. You say it's been in your family for a long time? I suppose you don't know how long."

Eleret forced a smile. "Not precisely. Geleraise Vinlarrian, my multi-great-grandmother, brought it with her when she settled in the mountains, right after the Neira sank the Island of Varna. That would be a little over seven hundred years ago. It doesn't go all the way back to the migration, if that's what you're asking."

"Pity." Weziral gestured toward the kit bag. "Did you find anything else of interest?"

"Not unless someone wants Ma's whetstone and comb," Eleret replied.

"Doesn't seem likely, does it? It must be either the ring or the knife they're after, then." The Commander turned the ring over in his fingers once more, then handed it to Eleret.

Eleret thought for a moment, then slipped the ring on her right index finger. If anyone *was* after it, they'd have more trouble taking it from her hand than picking it out of her pocket. It was a little tight, but not uncomfortably so. She studied it, then turned the stone toward her palm, where it would be less noticeable.

Next, she examined the knife, testing the edge against her thumb and tossing it in the air to check the balance. It was a good weapon, perhaps the equal of her own. She reached through her pocket and pulled out her dagger, then set Tamm's in its place. It fit the sheath reasonably well, but she made sure she could draw it quickly before she packed her own dagger in the kit bag.

"One more thing," Weziral said as Eleret picked up the bag. He rummaged under the table once more and came up with two pouches made of heavy canvas. They clinked when he dropped them on the table. "Your mother's regular wages, combat pay, bonuses for special work, and death fee. Feel free to count it, and you're welcome to inspect the registers if you like. We like our people to be certain they've had fair dealing."

"You wouldn't make the offer if this wasn't fair," Eleret said. The bags were heavier than she expected; she was probably holding more money than the whole village of

Calmarten would normally see in a year, unless the Imperial Guard paid in copper bits instead of silver. She frowned, then unwrapped her sash and knotted it around the bags. They made an awkward lump when she rewrapped the sash, but it was better than leaving the money in her pockets or the kit bag. She would find a better way of carrying it when she got back to the inn.

"I'll detail someone to escort you back to your rooms, if you'd like," Weziral offered. "It's a lot of money, even in Ciaron."

"No, don't do that," Eleret said as he reached for a small bell on the corner of the table. "It would only draw attention to me, and you can't very well give me an escort all the way back to the Mountains of Morravik."

"True." Weziral's brows contracted, then relaxed. "Very well, have it your way. But if you change your mind, or if you think of anything else you need, come back and see me."

"I will. Thank you very much for your help."

"It's my job; there's nothing to thank me for. You're sure you don't want someone with you?"

"Quite sure." Eleret picked up the kit bag and slung it over her right shoulder.

"Stubborn Cilhar. At least tell me where you're staying and for how long, so I can send you a message if I need to."

"Send it to the school the Island of the Moon runs," Eleret replied, suddenly wary. "Adept Climeral knows how to find me. I only expect to be in Ciaron another few days." She expected to leave as soon as she collected her belongings from the Broken Harp, and certainly no later than the following morning, but she wasn't going to admit that to anyone. Not after what the Commander had said about the ambush and the attempted break-ins.

"Cautious as well as stubborn." Weziral shook his head.

"Under the circumstances, I can hardly fault you for that, can I? Very well, very well. Good luck to you, Freelady Salven."

"It's under the raven's wings," Eleret said with a shrug as she opened the door to leave. "But thank you for your good wishes."

The Commander nodded, and Eleret left. To her relief, only one man remained in the outer room, the silent one, and he did not even look up as she crossed to the other door and let herself out into the hallway. The boy who had brought her to the office had disappeared, but Eleret was not concerned. The building might be a maze to a Ciaronese used to straight lines and right angles, but the route had not seemed difficult to her.

She started down the hall and turned right at the second intersection, almost without thinking. The strap of the kit bag felt heavy and strange on her shoulder; the raven seal-ring was an awkward, constricting lump against her fingers; the knife lay large and unfamiliar against her thigh. Carrying Tamm's things somehow made her absence, her death, seem less real instead of more.

"Lady Salven!"

Startled, Eleret whirled and stepped back a pace while her hand went automatically to the raven's-feet in her pocket. The door to one of the side rooms was open, and the man called Maggen stood just inside, beckoning.

Eleret took hold of one of her throwing weapons but did not bring it out into view. "What do you want?"

"Just a chat," Maggen said. "Come in, please; you'll be more comfortable."

"I'm comfortable where I am."

"Look, I said I was sorry about that business earlier." Maggen smiled. "But I understand. If you want to stay there where anyone can overhear, go ahead."

"Why should I worry about someone overhearing?" Eleret asked. "Just what is it you want, anyway?"

"I thought that since I, ah, made a bad impression at the beginning, I ought to do something to make up for it," Maggen said.

"Such as?" Eleret doubted that she would be interested in anything Maggen was likely to suggest, but his odd behavior made her curious.

"You, ah, came a long way to get that," Maggen said, gesturing at the kit bag. "It'll be awkward and heavy to carry all the way back, maybe dangerous, even."

Eleret almost laughed. Awkward and heavy? The kit weighed barely as much as a brace of pheasants. "So?"

"So I'll buy it from you." Maggen leaned forward. "The whole thing. I've got a . . . friend who needs outfitting; this way I can get him fixed up and do you a favor at the same time. Money's easy to carry."

"All that's in this is a whetstone and comb."

Maggen's ingratiating smile returned. "Well, I'll pay you three stars. That's more than it's worth."

"It belonged to my mother. It has sentimental value."

"All right, four stars. You can buy a lot of sentiment for four stars."

You could buy a lot of other things, too, even at Ciaron's prices, thought Eleret. Maggen was a fool, and whatever he wanted must be valuable indeed. "I'm still not interested."

"Five, then!"

"Not for five stars nor for twenty-five stars," Eleret replied. "I'm not selling Ma's things." In three quick steps she was past the door; by the time Maggen stepped out into the hallway she was well out of reach. He wasn't likely to try anything in the heart of the headquarters of the Imperial

Guard, especially in a hall where someone might come by at the wrong time.

"You'll be sorry you didn't sell it to me!" Maggen called after her. "Wait and see. You'll be sorry."

"I doubt it," Eleret said over her shoulder, and kept walking. Maggen did not try to follow, and a few minutes later Eleret reached the building's entrance. She nodded to the woman on guard, glanced back one last time to make certain Maggen was nowhere in sight, and stepped out to join the flow of traffic on the street.

FOUR

hree streets down and two over from the offices of the Imperial Guard, Eleret stepped into a doorway and paused to consider. If she kept to the main streets, she was in little danger of direct attack, but among all these people it was impossible to tell whether she was being followed. Having slipped up once already, Eleret did not want to lead any more people back to the inn where she was staying. She might, however, lead them somewhere neutral, somewhere less crowded, where she would have a better chance of spotting them. Eleret smiled and stepped back into the street. At the next corner, she made the turn that would take her to the Islanders' school.

The press of people and wagons lessened as Eleret drew away from the main thoroughfares, and she quickened her step. Each time she turned a corner she managed to glance back along the street, and on her fourth turn she spotted a tall, narrow-faced man whom she was sure she had seen before. He was still behind her when she turned again. Eleret was considering whether or not to let him know she had seen him when a voice behind her called loudly, "That's her! Stop, thief!"

Startled, Eleret looked back. The narrow-faced man had been joined by a woman in the indigo-and-maroon uniform of the City Guard, and the two were heading purposefully in Eleret's direction. Eleret glanced around, unable to quite believe she was the person they wanted. A young man in a scarlet cloak had paused, frowning, on the opposite side of the street; everyone else seemed to have melted into alleys and doorways.

"Stop, thief!" the narrow-faced man called again, and this time it was plain even to Eleret that she was the one he meant.

Mildly puzzled by the man's behavior, Eleret stopped. A flash of irritation crossed the man's face, as if he had neither expected nor wanted her to wait for him. Eleret's puzzlement increased. Theft was a grave charge in the mountains, but Tamm had said once that the Ciaronese did not treat it as severely as Cilhar. She had also said that a false accusation was an even more serious matter in Ciaron than among the Cilhar. Why would the man risk an honor-challenge when he must know that Eleret had stolen nothing?

"Is there some problem?" Eleret asked the guard as the two reached her.

"This man claims you stole that bag from him," the guard answered, gesturing at the kit hanging from Eleret's shoulder.

"It's mine, all right," the man said. He made a snatching motion, and Eleret sidestepped to avoid it. "Watch out! She's trying to get away."

"You've made a mistake," Eleret said to the narrow-faced

man, her temper beginning to rise. "This is my bag, and I've never seen you before in my life."

"Ha! You snatched it from me not half an hour ago on the Northwest Castle Road." The man's eyes blazed with excitement. "It's mine, I tell you!"

"Please, Grand Master Gorchastrin, control yourself," the guardswoman said. "This is my job, not yours."

"Then do it!" the narrow-faced man retorted. "Surely it's not difficult, even for you. There's the bag; take it from her and give it to me."

The guardswoman stiffened. "She is a subject of the Emperor, and there are certain procedures—"

"And as a Grand Master of the Order of Tsantilar of Rathane, I have certain privileges!" Gorchastrin snapped back. "Privileges, may I remind you, that hold even in Ciaron. Now, I want my bag!"

Eleret frowned. Gorchastrin's strategy was clear now; he expected the guardswoman to seize Eleret's kit and give it to him, on his word alone. The guard didn't look strong enough or quick enough to take the kit without Eleret's cooperation, but Eleret didn't want to start a fight in the middle of the street, particularly not with an official. Fortunately, it wasn't a matter of her word against Gorchastrin's; Commander Weziral could confirm that the bag was hers. Provided, of course, that she could convince the guard and the privileged foreigner to walk back across the city to Weziral's office.

"Perhaps I can be of some assistance, my lady guard?" said a new voice. Eleret turned her head. The young man in the scarlet cloak had come up unnoticed during the discussion. As everyone looked at him, he doffed a black cap with a plume dyed to match his cloak and swept a bow. "Lord Daner Vallaniri, at your service and the Emperor's."

"It is a minor matter only, my lord," the guard said, bowing deeply in return. "Grand Master Gorchastrin's bag was stolen, and he says this woman was the thief."

"Unlikely," the newcomer said in a dismissive tone, adjusting his cap carefully over his wavy blond hair. He smiled warmly at Eleret. "So lovely a woman would never be a thief. Her face is too memorable for such a profession."

"Exactly!" Gorchastrin said, but Eleret thought he did not seem as sure of himself as he had a moment previously. "I remember her perfectly."

"I regret that I cannot return the compliment," Eleret said politely. She shifted the kit unobtrusively as far away from him as she could manage, and slipped her left hand into her slit skirt pocket, just in case. "But as I have said, I have never seen the Grand Master before. The bag is mine; it was given to me this morning by Commander Weziral of the Imperial Guard. I'm sure that he will tell you so himself, should you ask."

"Well, then," the guardswoman said, clearly relieved. "That settles the matter, doesn't it?"

"I believe it should," the young lord, Daner, said. Eleret barely kept herself from an irritated frown at the smug undertone in his voice. He hadn't done anything to warrant such self-satisfaction. Then she did frown. Why *had* Daner come shoving his dagger in where it wasn't wanted? Was he after Tamm's kit, too? Or was she seeing shadows on noon snow?

"Not so fast!" Gorchastrin said. "How do you know she's telling the truth? How do you know she hasn't bribed this Commander Weziral to say whatever she wants?"

Eleret stiffened at the implied insult, then saw that the guardswoman looked just as horrified as she felt. Before either of them could speak, Daner's eyebrows rose in haughty disdain. "Bribe a Commander of the *Imperial Guard of Ciaron?* You forget yourself, Rathani."

Gorchastrin's lips tightened. "I meant no insult to your people," he said with effort. "I intended only to express my doubts about this woman." He gestured at Eleret.

So Gorchastrin would apologize for insulting the Ciaronese, but not for the affront to a Cilhar, would he? Eleret wished she could pull her knife and challenge him at once, but that would be poor tactics. Without proof, one way or another, the two Ciaronese might not support her. More important, it would be foolish to start a fight while she was wearing the Ciaronese-style skirt. The wretched thing was hard enough to *walk* in. "If it is a question of *my word*, perhaps Adept Climeral of the Island of the Third Moon will speak for me," she said instead. "I was just on my way to the school to see him, and it's only another block or two."

Even Daner looked startled by this announcement. The guard's eyes narrowed. "In that case, I think this can be settled quickly. Unless Grand Master Gorchastrin chooses to question the integrity of the Islanders as well as that of Ciaron's Imperial Guard." Her tone made it clear that if he did he would lose what little cooperation she was still willing to give him.

"I, ah, wouldn't dream of it." Gorchastrin's voice was full of smothered fury.

"Then we will proceed to the School of the Third Moon and accept the judgment of Adept Climeral," the guard declared. She turned and bowed to Daner in respectful dismissal. "Thank you for your assistance, my lord."

"I believe I'll accompany you to the school," Daner said with a sidelong glance at Eleret. "I was heading in that direction anyway."

"Of course, my lord." The guard bowed again, stiffly.

The young nobleman returned the bow with casual grace, apparently unaware of her disapproval, and stepped to Eleret's side.

Eleret frowned and opened her mouth. Then she saw Gorchastrin's expression, and closed it again without saying anything. Lord Daner Vallaniri might or might not be after the kit bag, but Grand Master Gorchastrin certainly was. Of the two, Daner was clearly the safer companion, however short the walk.

"How is it that you are acquainted with Adept Climeral?" Daner asked Eleret as the little group started down the street.

"We met shortly after I arrived in Ciaron," Eleret answered. "I'm sure he'll confirm what I've said."

"Ah," Daner said in a satisfied tone. "You *aren't* from Ciaron. I was sure I couldn't have overlooked such a jewel among women for long." He gave Eleret an admiring smile.

"Ciaron's a big city," Eleret said uncomfortably.

"Not that big."

Eleret raised her eyebrows and said nothing. Fortunately, they had nearly reached the school, so Daner had no time for further pleasantries. The guardswoman pulled the knob while Gorchastrin shifted from one foot to another and eyed Eleret's bag possessively.

The door opened. "Welcome to our House," said Prill. "What service may I— Freelady Salven! Welcome back. Do you want to see Climeral again?"

"She does," Daner said before Eleret could reply. "As do we all. Unless of course this is confirmation enough for the Grand Master?"

"It is enough," Gorchastrin said, glaring at Prill. "I . . . must have been mistaken."

"Perhaps you should apologize for the inconvenience

you have caused Freelady Salven," Daner said in a voice like silk just as Gorchastrin began to turn away. "And of course there's the matter of a false charge."

"Mistakes happen," the guardswoman said doubtfully.

"And when they are discovered, they must be remedied." Daner stepped back and bowed to Eleret, one hand resting lightly on the hilt of his sword. "My blade is at your disposal, Freelady."

Eleret stared at him, her temper rising as she realized he meant to take her fight on himself. She was neither wounded nor ill nor pregnant, so why was he insulting her with the implication that she could not fight? Her left hand dropped to where her knife should have been, and brushed the heavy wool of her skirt. She paused. Perhaps the man had not intended any insult. Anyone with eyes could see that she was not dressed for fighting; perhaps in Ciaron that was as important as actual fitness for battle.

"Take his offer," Prill whispered in Eleret's ear. "Daner's *good.*"

So it *wasn't* an insult. Eleret looked at Daner and hesitated. She'd rather fight her own battles, no matter what Ciaronese custom was, but she didn't want to return insult for an offer that had been kindly meant. She looked at Gorchastrin.

"I apologize for the inconvenience," Gorchastrin said in a strangled voice. "It was a mistake."

"Even so—" Daner began.

"My lord, please consider," the guard broke in. "The Grand Master is a foreigner, and unused to our ways."

"Well . . . if the lady is satisfied . . . ?" Daner gave Eleret an inquiring look.

"Since the Grand Master has admitted his mistake, I see no reason for you to fight him," Eleret said carefully. *And if he turns up a second time I'll handle him myself, skirts or no skirts. He'll never cry thief at a Cilbar again, once I've done with him.*

Daner lifted his hand from his sword-hilt. "Then I am content."

"If you wish to come to the corner guard post, Grand Master, I can continue investigating the theft of your bag," the guard said.

Gorchastrin transferred his glare to the guard. "I have no more time to spend on this petty matter. You may be sure, however, that your superiors will hear about the bungling treatment I have received." He turned and swept off.

"What was that about?" Prill said inquisitively. "And what are you doing with Freelady Salven, Lord Daner? Aren't you supposed to be helping Nijole translate and classify those scrolls this morning? I don't blame you for dodging her. Last time I saw her, she was in the room just off the library, swearing like a Kulseth fisherman with a knot in his line."

Daner clapped a hand to his forehead. "I forgot."

"That's not going to chip any stone where Nijole's concerned," Prill said. "Now that you're here . . ."

"Yes, I understand." Daner gave Eleret a significant glance. "But I had hoped—"

"I would like to see Adept Climeral," Eleret said. "Privately, if possible."

"I don't think he has any appointments," Prill said. "He was going over the reports from Napaura, and he hates that. He'll be glad to be interrupted. Come on, I'll take you. And you'd better get going, Lord Daner, or Nijole will really have something to say to you."

With a wry smile, Daner swept his hat off and bowed to Eleret. "I shall hope to have the pleasure of meeting you again, Freelady."

Eleret controlled the impulse to reply, *Not if I can help it,* and nodded awkwardly. Daner smiled, adjusted his hat, and strode off down the corridor, his scarlet cloak billowing behind him. Eleret rolled her eyes and turned to Prill, who was looking after Daner and shaking her head.

"He's really something, isn't he?" Prill said, catching Eleret's eye. "Climeral says he's just a little spoiled and too sure of himself, and needs to be taken down a peg or two. How'd you meet him, anyway?"

"It's a long story."

"Oh? That's unusual. Lord Daner's got a reputation for moving fast." Prill giggled. "On some things, anyway. Come on, you can tell me while we walk. Unless you'd rather not."

"He pushed into an argument that had nothing to do with him and then wouldn't go away again," Eleret said, falling into step beside Prill. She didn't want to go into detail; she would have to explain too much. At least Prill's reaction meant that Daner was probably not after Tamm's kit.

"Well, that doesn't surprise me. Once he makes up his mind, he's awfully persistent. You should have heard him pestering Nijole to teach him sorcery last year! She said some really terrible things to him, but he wouldn't go away and he wouldn't go away and finally she gave in."

"Thank you for letting me know," Eleret said.

Prill gave her a puzzled look.

Suppressing a smile, Eleret explained solemnly, "If Lord Daner decides to pester me, I won't try saying terrible things to him to make him go away, since you tell me that it won't work. It will save a lot of time."

Prill laughed. "I hadn't thought of it that way." She stopped and knocked at a door, then opened it and stuck her head inside before there was time for a response. "Adept? Eleret Salven's back and wants to see you. I thought you'd want to know."

"You are an undisciplined minx, but unfortunately for discipline you are also quite right." The amusement in Climeral's voice was clear despite the muffling effect of the partly closed door. "Bring her in."

Eleret nodded her thanks to Prill and went in. Climeral was sitting behind a paper-strewn table that reminded Eleret of the one in Commander Weziral's office. "Welcome, Free-lady Salven," he said as she sat down across from him. "I had not expected to see you again so soon."

"Didn't you?" Eleret said.

Climeral smiled. "Should I have?" Then the smile vanished and his eyes narrowed to slanted slits. "You think so. What is it that you believe I should have known and told you of on your first visit here?"

"Someone has been trying to steal my mother's things," Eleret answered. "Didn't Commander Weziral tell you?"

"No," Climeral said, frowning. "Is he certain?"

"He may not be certain, but I am," Eleret said. "I had some trouble on my way here." Swiftly, she described Gorchastrin's accusation and his attempt to have the kit bag turned over to him.

"You seem to have handled the matter well," Climeral said when she finished.

"Thank you," Eleret said. "But I'm not sure I would be so lucky another time. I don't know enough about the way you do things in Ciaron."

"If you are wise enough to admit that, you will probably manage better than most."

"Probably doesn't suit me. Especially if there's a chance trouble is going to follow me all the way home."

"What is it you want, then?"

"You said when I arrived that you could supply a guide

for me, someone who knew his way around Ciaron. Could you find someone who has traveled a little between here and the Mountains of Morravik? Someone who'd be handy in a fight, and who can leave the city with me tonight or tomorrow? I'll pay whatever is reasonable," Eleret added, thinking of the money tied up in her sash.

"An excellent idea." Climeral thought for a moment, then began to smile. "Payment won't be necessary. I know just whom to send, and if he agrees, paying him a fee would be like giving beer to a brewmaster. Tonight or tomorrow? I'll send someone to the Broken Harp this evening, then. Is there anything else I can do for you?"

"Yes," Eleret said. "I'm worried about my family. If someone's after Ma's things, he might be smart enough to light out for home ahead of me. Gralith said you'd gotten him word of Ma's death without waiting for a messenger. Could you do that again, for a message from me? Just to tell them what's happened, and that there might be trouble. I'd feel more comfortable if I knew that nobody was likely to catch Pa and Nilly and Jiv by surprise."

"Of course I can," Climeral said. "I'll ask Gralith to keep an eye on them, too, if you'd like. He has certain skills—"

"Magic, you mean? No, I don't think so. Pa doesn't hold with mixing up magic in a fight."

"What if his opponents do not feel the same?" Climeral asked skeptically.

"Oh, I'll back Pa against a wizard any day," Eleret said, smiling at the thought. "As long as he knows what he's up against, anyway, which is why I asked about sending him a message. Besides, I wouldn't want your folk to get mixed up in our trouble."

Climeral's eyebrows rose. "I appreciate the consideration, but I hope you are not expecting too much of your family. Forgive me for asking, but have you or your father ever faced magic?"

"Pa ran up against wizards a time or two during the Syaski wars," Eleret replied. "He says they cause a bit more damage than ordinary people, tossing spells around, but an arrow in the right place kills them as dead as anyone else. He'll manage."

Climeral shook his head in amazement. "You have a unique viewpoint. I wish I could in conscience persuade you to stay in Ciaron for a few more days so we could talk, but under the circumstances—"

"I'd rather start back as soon as I can," Eleret told him with real regret as she rose to leave. "But perhaps I can visit your island someday."

"I'll hope so," Climeral said. "Good fortune to you, and may the Third Moon light your path."

"My thanks," Eleret said, wondering briefly how a non-existent moon could light anything at all. She nodded and went out. She found Prill waiting to escort her back to the main door, and persuaded her to take her to a different exit, in case Gorchastrin was still watching the front entrance. In a few moments she was on the street once more. She kept a sharp watch all the way back to the inn, but this time no one followed her or attempted to stop her, and she reached her room without incident.

FIVE

No one occupied the front room at the Broken Harp when Eleret came through it on her way to her quarters. Inside, she inspected the chamber quickly but thoroughly, then barred the door. As she dropped the kit bag on the bed, she breathed a sigh of relief. After all that had happened, she had been half afraid she would find someone waiting in her room.

Eleret shook her head. She had thought that once she collected her mother's things everything would be simple; instead, matters seemed to grow more complicated by the minute. Who was Gorchastrin? Was he working with the unpleasant and overeager Maggen, or did they each have a different reason for wanting Tamm's kit? Was either of them behind the attempts to break into Commander Weziral's office, or was that the work of yet another person? And what, exactly, were all of them after?

Frowning, she opened the kit and dumped its contents on the straw-stuffed pallet. Perhaps if she took a closer look, she would find some clue. She had not had time at Weziral's office to examine everything as carefully as she would have liked.

She began with the kit itself. It was the same one Tamm always carried whenever she left the mountains. The leather was a little more faded and one of the thongs had been replaced, but that was all. It even had the same smell, a blend of trail dust and old leather and the slightly rancid oil Tamm had insisted on using to keep it supple.

The outline of the bag blurred, and Eleret had to pause and blink the tears from her eyes. *Stop that*, she told herself fiercely. *You have a task to finish.* She raised her eyes to the corner of the ceiling and kept them there, forcing herself to think about Maggen and Gorchastrin, until the burning ache of unshed tears subsided. Then she took a deep breath, swallowed hard, and returned doggedly to her work.

An oblong whetstone seemed a safe enough item to examine next; one couldn't get too sentimental over a stone. It looked perfectly ordinary, and Eleret began to feel more composed. There was a depression down the center, where years of metal stroking along it had worn the stone away. Years . . . Eleret remembered her mother sitting before the fire, knives and arrowheads laid ready to hand, telling the story of the duel between Morravik and the Varnan wizard Ilarna del Bifromar, with the hiss of steel against stone as a steady accompaniment. She dropped the stone as if it had turned red-hot in her hand, and reached blindly for something else.

Her hand closed on a wad of wool stockings knotted around something hard. Slowly, she unwound them and found a wooden spoon, short and thick and square, made for eating from rather than for stirring the pot. Her father had carved it to replace the last one Tamm had broken, just before she left. Eleret remembered the two of them laughing about it, and her father's warning to Tamm to take better care of this one. Apparently, Tamm had tried. Eleret stared at the spoon, and suddenly her tears welled up and spilled over.

This time, control was impossible. Wrenching sobs shook her until she could breathe only in harsh gasps. Tears burned her eyes and cheeks. Her mind seemed to split in two, half of it swept away by the unexpected wave of grief, the other half coldly calculating how loudly she could cry without being heard outside the room. She stuffed a fist into her mouth to muffle the sound and rocked back and forth where she sat, while the grieving half of her mind chanted, *Never again, you'll never laugh with her again, she'll never tell stories again, never give you advice you don't want, never, never again . . .*

A long time later, Eleret stopped crying. Her eyes were sore, and the room seemed too bright and sharp to look on comfortably. Her lips tasted of salt, her nose was too stuffed up to breathe through, and her face felt hot and prickly. She wiped her cheeks with the backs of her hands, wondering with a kind of desperation how much time was left before the mid-afternoon meal. If she looked as ravaged as she felt, it might be hours before she could be sure that her face no longer revealed too much.

Eleret swallowed, blinked, and looked down. She caught a glimpse of the scattered belongings on the bed and in an instant was halfway to tears once more. Hastily, she averted her eyes, rising as she turned away. She had to find something else to do, something to occupy her mind for a few minutes while she regained her composure. She reached for the pitcher and washbasin on the table beside the window.

Water sloshed over the lip of the pitcher as Eleret began to pour; the innkeeper's wife had filled it too full. Eleret ignored the puddle on the tabletop and the dampness dribbling down the front of her skirt. When the washbasin was half-full, she set the pitcher down, shut her eyes, and plunged her face into the tepid water. She held her position until her lungs ached for air, then straightened, gasping and spraying water in all directions. In her haste she inhaled a drop of water and began to cough.

When she could breathe freely again, Eleret looked at the soggy mess on and around the table and gave a wavery chuckle. She couldn't have done any worse if she'd dropped the pitcher or tipped the basin over. She brushed dripping tendrils of hair away from her face with one hand and reached for the towel with the other.

Cleaning up the spill did not take long, but by the time she finished, Eleret's skirt was nearly as wet as the towel. She took it off and spread it over the end of the bed, then frowned. The only other clothes she had were the ones she had brought from the mountains. Anyone familiar with Cil-har garb would recognize her full green leggings and soft knee-high boots, even if she pulled her shirt down into a sort of tunic that would cover the top. Eleret shrugged. She had no real choice. She would just have to stay inside, out of sight, until the skirt was dry.

Eleret pulled her own kit out from beneath the bed and started to untie it, then stopped short. The knot was the same one she had used, but it was tied backward. The left-hand thong should have been looped, with the right crossing over and around; instead, the right thong was looped, with the left crossing over and around. Someone had opened the kit while she was out.

Slowly, Eleret untied the thongs and unlaced the flap. The things inside lay just as she had left them, neatly folded and placed to fill the bag as efficiently as possible. One by one, she lifted them out, then shook the empty kit to make certain nothing had been hidden in the bottom. Nothing had. She packed everything up again, wondering whether she was imagining things, then reached for the thongs. No, she would never have tied them that way; it felt awkward and unnatural, and she had to think about every move. Someone else had tied that knot.

Eleret sat back on her heels, fingering the hilt of her knife. Who could it have been? She considered briefly and then dismissed the possibility that the innkeeper or his wife had been snooping; the careful repacking of her kit was unlikely to be the result of casual curiosity. Climeral and Prill were the only people in Ciaron who knew where she was . . . except for the woman who had followed her from the school. What had she called herself? Jonystra, that was the name. And she had asked about small, old things, like seals and rings. . . .

With a muffled exclamation, Eleret opened her right hand and peered at the raven ring. She turned it on her finger so that the stone was outward, as it should be; then she sat staring. The silver gleamed, untarnished, but the black stone seemed to drink up whatever light fell on it, no matter how she turned it. She felt like a fool for taking so long to connect it with Jonystra's cryptic remarks. She stroked the carved raven gently with her fingertip, as if by doing so she could learn what made the ring so important to Jonystra and perhaps others.

What had Tamm told her about the ring? The raven was for protection, she remembered that much, and the black stone was for night and shadow. The silver setting meant something, too, but try as she would she could not remember what. It had been handed down from mother to daughter or granddaughter ever since Geleraise Vinlarrian had come to the Mountains of Morravik seven hundred and some-odd years ago, to settle among the Cilhar. "Our good-luck charm," Tamm had called it, though the luck it had brought her seemed to Eleret to have been of the other variety.

Once more, Eleret turned her hand to catch light on the raven ring; then she shrugged and twisted the ring so that the seal rested against her palm. She wasn't learning anything by looking at it, and she doubted that Jonystra would be willing to explain her interest. Perhaps Climeral would know something about it—no, she was being foolish. She couldn't expect Climeral to have *all* the answers she needed just because he was a Shee and a magician. Eleret sighed. Her curiosity would simply have to go unsatisfied.

Feeling as if she had settled something, however temporarily, Eleret put on her leggings and boots. She was surprised at how much better she felt in her normal dress. She thought for a moment, then went over to the bed and picked up Tamm's embroidered knife-sheath. With a little work, she could adapt it to wear on her right leg, and she was beginning to think that the more weapons she had handy, the better.

Eleret was tying her second spare thong around the lower part of the sheath when someone knocked at the door. Eleret hesitated, wondering whether to pretend she was not there. But anyone who tried the door would realize that it was barred from the inside, and the visitor was as likely to be someone from Climeral's school as it was to be the innkeeper or his wife. "Who's there?" Eleret called.

The knock was repeated and someone mumbled a sentence that did not carry through the door. Eleret frowned and slid the knife out of the sheath she was working on. Holding the weapon so that the opening door would hide it, she eased back the bar and swung the door a handsbreadth out.

From the hall outside, Jonystra Nirandol smiled through the crack. "I'm so glad you're here. I was just passing by, and I thought I'd stop and see how your day went."

"As well as I expected," Eleret replied, staring in undisguised fascination. Jonystra's dark hair was piled on top of her head in a series of elaborate and precarious-looking waves. Her eyes were heavily outlined in kohl, and two brass medallions dangled from her ears. She wore a loose, floorlength tunic made of a dark blue cotton embroidered in brightly colored silk, and her belt was a chain of medallions that matched her earrings. She looked like some sort of doll.

"Have you finished your business in Ciaron?" Jonystra asked, her smile widening.

"No," Eleret lied. "I'll have to go back tomorrow. Something about procedures, they said."

"Ciaron is like that," Jonystra said. "Perhaps I could be of some assistance? I've dealt with the authorities here before."

"I don't think that will be necessary," Eleret said firmly. "And it might confuse them if I brought an extra person along."

"True." Jonystra shrugged, then lowered her head. Light slithered across her waves of hair. "Would you join me for dinner instead? There's a place near here that's very entertaining; I was just on my way there. I'm sure I could loan you something to wear, and with your looks you'd create quite a sensation."

Eleret had a momentary picture of herself dressed as Jonystra was, and nearly laughed aloud. "Thank you, but I'm afraid I can't. I've already made arrangements for dinner."

"The innkeeper will understand," Jonystra persisted. "And if you're only going to be in Ciaron for a week, you ought to see as much as you can."

"I'm meeting someone," Eleret said. One inadvertent

meal with Jonystra had been enough, to her way of thinking; she was not sitting down to another if she had to invent legions of relatives, friends, and admirers unexpectedly encountered in the town.

Jonystra's smile slipped. "I thought you didn't know anyone in Ciaron."

"I thought so, too," Eleret said. "But as it turns out, I do. Another night, perhaps. Tomorrow, or the day after?" If Jonystra thought she had arranged to meet Eleret, she wouldn't suspect that Eleret was planning to leave Ciaron before then. She might even stop pestering Eleret, though that was probably too much to hope for.

"Tomorrow, then." Jonystra did not appear altogether happy, but as long as she left, Eleret didn't care much about the woman's mood. "In the meantime, perhaps—"

"Excuse me," said a familiar voice from the door at the end of the hall. "But could you tell us— Oh, there you are, Eleret! I was going to ask the innkeeper where to find you, only he wasn't around, and his wife said you were just down the hall."

"Hello, Prill," Eleret said, opening her door a little wider and blessing Prill's timing. As long as Prill didn't say the wrong thing, Jonystra would assume that she was Eleret's intended dinner companion. "I was waiting for you. Come in while I finish getting ready."

Prill glanced over her shoulder. A tall figure moved out of the shadows and resolved into Lord Daner Vallaniri. Prill shook her head at him and said uncertainly, "I don't know if—"

"So long as the wait is not a long one, I will be content to stay here," Daner said. "I am sure the results will be well worth it, and the company is charming." He gave Jonystra an admiring glance and swept her a bow.

"All right, then," Prill said. "But don't go complaining about it later."

Eleret stepped back and swung the door open. "Excuse us," she said to Jonystra as Prill walked past her and slid into the room. As she closed the door, she heard Daner say coaxingly, "You will keep me company, won't you?"

"Why did you bring *him*?" Eleret asked Prill, who was looking around the room with interest.

"Lord Daner? Oh, he's going to be your guide, if you'll have him," Prill said.

"What?" Eleret stopped short in the middle of sheathing her dagger to stare at Prill.

"I told Climeral that would be your reaction," Prill said with some satisfaction. "But honestly, Daner's not so bad. And he does know just about every road east of Ciaron; he's been traveling to Kith Alunel or Brydden or Mindaria or somewhere every year since he was fifteen."

"Maybe, but is he any good in a fight?"

"Don't let his mannerisms fool you," Prill replied seriously. "The last generation of Vallaniris lost a couple of sons in duels and stupid brawls, and ever since they've been determined to see that it wouldn't happen again. They're among the best swordsmen in the city, and Lord Daner is the best in the family. And don't forget that he's a magician, too; that could come in handy."

"For what?" Eleret turned away and began stripping off her leggings. She could hear the murmur of voices outside the door, and she wondered just what Daner and Jonystra were saying to each other. It was not a comforting idea.

"How should I know?" Prill said. "It depends on what you run into. Starting fires, maybe. And even if he's not an Adept, he can tell whether anyone is using magic to look for you. If you're worried about being followed . . ."

"You're right," Eleret said, frowning. "I hadn't thought of that." And Climeral *had* chosen Daner; presumably the Shee Adept had good reasons for regarding him as suitable. "I suppose I ought to give him a chance."

Prill giggled. "I'm beginning to see why Climeral said this would be a good idea. And Daner thinks Nijole is bad! I wish I could come with you, just to watch."

"Watch what?" Eleret asked absently as she strapped on her knife. She glanced longingly at the second dagger-and-sheath, but left them lying where they were. Slitting the other skirt pocket would take too much time to do right, and there was no sense in wearing a weapon she could not get at. She pulled on the skirt, which was now only a little damp, and quickly bundled the litter on the bed into her mother's kit bag. "Let's go."

SIX

When Eleret opened the door, she found Daner alone in the hall, gazing toward the stairs with a thoughtful expression. The first thing he said was, "Freelady Salven, how well do you know the woman who was here just now?"

"Better than I'd like," Eleret replied. "Which is to say, not very well. Come in; we can't discuss it in the hall."

"Watch out for her," Daner said, throwing a last glance at the stairs before he turned to enter Eleret's room. "You and your plans were the only things she cared about, the whole time she was talking to me. She didn't want to chat about anything else at all." He sounded faintly indignant, and Eleret could not keep from smiling.

"I'm not surprised," she said as she closed the door behind Daner. "I think Jonystra was the one who searched my room this morning, while I was out."

"Searched your room?" Prill said. "How did you know? Did she take anything? What was she looking for?"

"I'm not sure what she was looking for," Eleret replied.

"I'm not even sure that she went through my things, but someone did. I don't think it was the innkeeper or his wife, and she's the only other person outside the school who knew where I was staying."

"A very unsettling experience, I'm sure," Daner said sympathetically.

"No, it's annoying, that's all. What sort of information was she hunting for?"

Daner blinked, evidently startled by her matter-of-fact reaction to Jonystra's prying, but he made a quick recovery. "Where had I met you, how long were you planning to stay in Ciaron, where were we going for dinner, how long would we be gone. That sort of thing."

So Jonystra hadn't entirely believed Eleret's comments about her stay in Ciaron. "What did you tell her?"

"Nothing, of course. I'm not a fool, and Climeral said it was important to keep your plans quiet. I told her we hadn't had a chance to talk much yet." Daner gave Eleret a long, speculative look. "What *are* your plans? Or would you rather talk after dinner?"

"After dinner," Eleret said. She picked up her mother's kit bag, then bent and retrieved her own from under the bed. "Preferably after dinner and several miles outside Ciaron."

"But—" Daner looked at Prill and then back to Eleret. "I thought you didn't intend to leave until tomorrow. And it's already late; we won't get very far."

"If we leave behind the person who searched my room, it'll be far enough." Without thinking about it, Eleret checked her weapons—throwing-knife in easy reach through the slit skirt pocket on the left, raven's-feet poking sharply through the fabric of the pocket on the right—then shouldered the bags. "I want a head start on everyone, if I can get it. Didn't Climeral tell you I might want to go tonight?"

"Yes, but . . ." Daner's voice trailed off and he sighed. "All right, if you insist."

Prill giggled. "I'll bet you didn't believe Climeral. I'll bet you thought she didn't mean it. Honestly, Daner—"

"I said all right," Daner snapped. The tips of his ears were turning red.

"You don't have to come with me," Eleret said. After his warning about Jonystra, she was willing to admit that Daner had some intelligence, but she was still not convinced that she wanted him for a companion on the trip home. If he backed out, she wouldn't even have to feel guilty about not taking Climeral's suggestion.

"Not come?" Daner's expression went blank in shocked surprise; then his eyebrows rose in insulted indignation. "And let a girl like you travel all alone, with who knows how many villains waiting for you? Don't be absurd!"

"In that case, let's get started," Eleret said, and turned toward the door.

"What about your bags?"

Eleret gave Daner a puzzled look. "What about them?" she asked, indicating the two kits hanging over her shoulder.

"I mean the rest of your things," Daner said gently. "You don't have to leave them behind just because you're in a hurry, you know."

"I'm not leaving anything," Eleret said, still puzzled. "What are you talking about?"

Prill giggled again. "He's talking about his sisters, that's what he's talking about. They can't go anywhere without at least six trunks' worth of dresses and cloaks and veils and things. Freelady Salven's a Cilhar, Lord Daner, not a court lady."

"I'm beginning to think I don't have the slightest idea what that means," Daner said, looking at Eleret's bags with patent disbelief. Eleret thought of Jonystra's dress and almost smiled. Perhaps she wouldn't have to worry about the woman as much as she had thought. Traveling with trunks full of clothes would certainly slow her down.

"He's right about one thing, though," Prill said. "You shouldn't carry your kits out in plain sight like that. Anyone who sees you will know you're leaving."

"Not if they share Lord Daner's opinions," Eleret said. "But I can't be sure they will." She frowned, thinking. She had her dagger and her raven's-feet, and she had the raven ring. The bags of money Commander Weziral had given her were still tied in uncomfortable lumps inside her sash. She wouldn't like to lose the things in the bags, but she could get along without them if she had to. But if she didn't have to . . . She turned to Daner. "Will you carry them? If you drape your cloak a bit more toward the front, you can keep them out of sight a lot better than I can."

"Drape my cloak . . ." Daner sounded as if he couldn't believe what he was hearing. "It'll ruin the line!"

Prill dissolved in laughter. Eleret looked from her to Daner. "The line?"

"The way it hangs," Daner said uncomfortably. "It's cut to fall back across the shoulder, like this. Pulling it forward doesn't look right."

He flipped the right side of his cloak down across his arm. It didn't look particularly odd to Eleret, but it wasn't worth arguing about. She shrugged. "I'll have to take the chance, then. Let's go."

"You— I— Oh, give them here." Daner all but snatched the two kits from Eleret's hand. They disappeared under his cloak, and after a few shrugs and a great deal of muttering Daner pronounced himself ready. Eleret studied him critically to make sure the bags really were not readily visible, then nodded. Daner gave her a dark look, which Eleret ignored, and they left the room.

Before departing from the inn, Eleret hunted down the innkeeper and explained that she had found some friends and would not be returning until very late. She also paid him in advance for three days' lodging, hoping that this would convince him and anyone to whom he might mention it that she was staying in Ciaron.

Outside the inn, Eleret turned to Daner. "Which is the best way out of the city from here?"

"If you want to head directly for the mountains, we should use one of the gates on the east side," Daner said, pointing. "But it'll be quicker if we leave from the north and swing around the outside of the city."

"Why?" Eleret asked. "It doesn't look far."

"Because to get to the east side of Ciaron from here, we'd have to swing north anyway to avoid the tenements. And because I want some travel supplies of my own. There's a trade station by the north city wall where I can pick up the necessary gear. You can't seriously expect me to leave town without money or spare clothes."

It was a reasonable request, but Eleret hesitated, thinking of the sisters and the six trunks. Ciaronese seemed to have more extensive ideas of what constituted "necessary gear" than she was accustomed to. On the other hand, Daner's current attire was not exactly inconspicuous, and with any luck at all he would not consider the scarlet cloak and plumed hat suitable for travel. She nodded. Daner smiled warmly and gestured along the street. "This way, Freelady."

Four blocks from the inn, Prill stopped. "Here's where I turn. Good-bye, Eleret."

"You're not coming with us?" Eleret was not really surprised, but she found that she was disappointed nonetheless.

The small, cheerful young Islander would have been good company, and Nilly and Jiv would certainly have enjoyed meeting her.

"If you have the time, you could join us for dinner," Daner put in persuasively. "I know a nice little place by the Larkirst Trade Station that would—"

"No," Eleret interrupted, though the mention of dinner had reminded her how long it had been since she had eaten. "That's what I told Jonystra we were going to do."

"Jonystra?" Daner gave her a puzzled frown.

"Jonystra Nirandol, the woman at the inn."

"Oh, her."

"So I'd rather wait for dinner until we're out of the city," Eleret said. She turned to Prill. "Tell Adept Climeral good-bye for me. I'm sorry I can't tell him myself, but—"

"He'll understand." Prill smiled, then said seriously, "Be careful, both of you. And good luck!"

With a final wave, she turned down a narrow side street. Eleret looked after her for a moment, then shook herself. She should not be wasting time. She glanced at Daner, who was studying her with an unfathomable expression, and said, "How far is this place where you're going to pick up your gear?"

"About another eight blocks. Up two to the northeast avenue, along it for three, then up two more and over one. It won't take us long."

"Good."

Daner flashed her a surprised look and they started walking once more. Eleret paid him no attention at all; instead, she studied the people they passed, watching for too-familiar faces that might be following them. Daner made two attempts to engage her in conversation, but by the time they reached the northeast avenue he had given up and was walking beside her in sulky silence.

The avenue made Eleret nervous. It was as crowded as every other avenue she had seen in Ciaron, and the press of people made it impossible to get a good look at all of them. Carts and carriages rumbled by, raising acrid dust from between the paving stones and adding to the difficulty of keeping watch. It was a relief when Daner stopped and said, "We cross here. It's not much farther."

As they crossed the avenue and started down the side street Daner had indicated, Eleret saw a small man in a dark hat and cloak coming quickly toward them. His head was down, as if studying the paving required all his concentration; it looked as though only a minor miracle or a major work of magic was keeping him from colliding with everyone he passed.

Eleret nudged Daner and stepped to one side, well out of the man's way. Daner smiled in amusement and stepped to the other side. Like a mind reader or a dancer, the small man made the same move at exactly the same instant and cannoned into Daner head-on.

There was a moment of confusion while the two men struggled for balance and murmured excuse-me. Eleret moved closer, intending to help, and saw the small man's hand slide sideways and curl around Daner's belt-pouch. Forgetting her intentions, Eleret grabbed with her right hand and pulled her dagger with her left. The small man yelped, saw the dagger, and froze.

"Eleret, what are you doing?" said Daner, brushing at his cloak.

"He was trying to steal your pouch," Eleret said. She made a small gesture with the tip of her dagger, which was resting at the base of the thief's throat. A thin red line followed the dagger's path. "Weren't you?"

The thief winced. "Ah, yes, of course, all right, anything you say. Couldn't you move that knife back, just a little? Say, two or three feet? You might slip, you see, and then where would I be?"

"I won't slip," Eleret said, but she lifted the dagger half an inch.

"Thank you," the thief said in tones of heartfelt sincerity.

"Call a guard and turn him over," Daner said. "We're attracting attention."

"No," Eleret said.

Daner stiffened. "Eleret—"

"I knew you were a person of taste and discrimination," the thief said to Eleret. "And you can't think how much I appreciate it. City guards are so . . . inflexible about little misunderstandings like this."

"Be quiet." Eleret glanced around and spotted an alley between two solid-looking stone buildings. It was not much in the way of cover, but it would be better than the street. "Over there, thief. Slowly, and no tricks."

"I wouldn't dream of it," the thief said, rolling his eyes down toward her knife hand.

"We don't have time for this," Daner said as he followed Eleret and her prisoner into the relative shelter of the alley. "And what are you going to do with him, anyway?"

"Yes, what *are* you going to do with me?" the thief said. His hat had slid to one side, revealing an unruly mop of hair the color of a wet fox. "I have a great personal interest in the answer, you understand."

"I'm going to ask questions," Eleret said. She smiled slightly and moved her dagger hand a fraction of an inch, her eyes fixed on the thief. "And you're going to answer them. After that, we'll see."

"Naturally." The thief kept his attention on the dagger. "What was it you wanted to know?"

"He'll only lie," Daner said.

The thief looked indignant. "There's no need to be insulting! What do you think I am, stupid or something? Besides, I have a low tolerance for pain. Particularly my own."

"Prill says you're a wizard," Eleret said to Daner. "Can you put a truth spell on him?"

"A wizard?" The thief looked appalled. "I was trying to rob a wizard? Sweet snakes, I'll never hear the end of this one."

"If you're going to babble, at least tell us something useful," Daner said. "Who are you?"

"Karvonen Aurelico, sometime thief, at your service," the man replied promptly. "I'd bow, but I'd hate for the gentle lady to misinterpret the gesture." He smiled at Eleret over the knife blade, and Eleret almost smiled back in spite of herself.

"You're not a very good thief, from the look of things," Eleret commented. "Why'd you pick us to rob?"

"I don't suppose you'd believe that it was your beauty? The challenge? Something in his attitude?"

Eleret shook her head and wiggled her knife. Karvonen sighed. "I didn't think so."

"This isn't getting us anywhere," Daner muttered.

"It might if you'd stop interfering," Eleret said, annoyed.

Daner stiffened. "Freelady Salven, I am supposed to—"

"Freelady?" Karvonen interrupted, his eyes widening. "You're not—do, please, tell me you're not—from the Mountains of Morravik, are you?"

"Don't tell him!" Daner said quickly.

"That means you are." Karvonen slumped, ignoring Eleret's dagger completely. "You're Cilhar. Oh, shit. I'm going to get kicked out of the family for sure. No, they'll probably kill me first and *then* kick me out. Wizards and Cilhar! Why do these things always happen to me?"

"What are you babbling about now?" Daner demanded.

"He's not Cilhar," Eleret said. "I am."

"Oh. Well, that's something." Karvonen's gloomy expression did not improve noticeably. He frowned, then glanced searchingly up at Eleret's face. "I don't suppose—" His eyes slid past her and widened. "Uh-oh."

"Don't take your eyes off him, Eleret," Daner warned. "He's trying some kind of trick."

Without bothering to answer, Eleret took a tight hold on the thief's tunic and threw herself to one side, pulling Karvonen along with her. They fell against Daner's legs, knocking him out of the way as they went down. An instant later, something whizzed through the space where they had been standing and struck the wall of the building with a metallic clang.

Eleret twisted her shoulders to face the unexpected attack. Three hard-faced men blocked the entrance to the alley. One had a bow; the other two held drawn swords. The bowman had a second arrow already nocked. Eleret let go of Karvonen and rolled, making herself a moving target that would be more difficult to hit. The unaccustomed folds of the skirt tangled her legs and made her clumsy, and in the instant of hesitation, the bowman let fly.

The arrow whispered past Eleret's shoulder. "Stay down, Eleret!" Daner shouted, flinging his cloak back and throwing both kit bags aside as he reached for his sword.

Eleret ignored him. Behind her, she heard a scuffling noise; Karvonen was probably escaping. She finished her roll and came awkwardly to her knees. The bowman was reaching for another shaft, but he was too slow. Eleret flipped her dagger end for end, aimed, and threw.

The bowman dropped his bow and staggered, clutching at his chest. Daner ran forward, sword in hand, to meet the other two, and Eleret cursed mentally as she scrabbled in her pocket for her raven's-feet. The noble Ciaronese idiot was blocking her throwing lines. As she stumbled to her feet, cursing the skirt and Daner impartially, the bowman fell, twitched once, and lay motionless.

Swords rang, scraped apart, and rang again. Daner was every bit as good as Prill had promised, but he was still blocking Eleret's sight lines. She moved left, searching for an opening, and saw Karvonen gliding to the right under the cover of a couple of barrels. At least he was out of the way.

A movement at the end of the alley, beyond the sword-fight, caught her eye. She glimpsed a lean, angular face, half-hidden by the hood of a cloak, and saw a hand rise to point at the combatants. Simultaneously, something pricked sharply at her right index finger, where she wore the raven ring.

Daner stumbled, leaving himself wide open to his two opponents and clearing Eleret's throwing lines. With two quick flicks of her wrist, Eleret threw a raven's-foot at each of the hard-faced swordsmen. The missiles struck badly, leaving a shallow slash across one man's cheek and rebounding off the other's leather shoulder strap, but they distracted the men long enough for Daner to recover. Almost too fast for the eye to follow, his sword flicked up, left, and out, and one of the men was down. The other turned to flee, and Daner ran him through the shoulder. His weapon clattered to the pavement, but the only sound he made was a small grunt of pain.

"Now, sirrah," said Daner as the lone survivor turned and held out his good hand, palm up, in a gesture of surrender, "explain the meaning of this attack."

"*Kovinsuy Cilbar*," the man said, glaring, and spat.

Someone shouted outside the alley, and Eleret glanced toward the entrance. The cloaked man was gone, but she could see people running in the street beyond. "Let's get out of here," she said to Daner. "We've attracted too much attention already."

"My sentiments exactly," said Karvonen's voice from behind them.

Eleret and Daner turned. The thief grinned at their startled expressions and bowed extravagantly, gesturing down the alley. "This way, my lord and lady, if it please you. Shall we go?"

SEVEN

Giving Karvonen a glance of mingled contempt and distrust, Daner turned back to his prisoner. The man had had sense enough to stay where he was, though his eyes were full of hate. Eleret did not bother to return his glare. She was all but certain, now, that he was a Syask, and probably his two companions as well. Hatred was the best a Cilhar could expect from the people who had tried time and again over the last two centuries to forcibly occupy the Mountains of Morravik. But how had they known she was Cilhar? Frowning, she fingered her skirt. She had thought she was being careful.

The shouts in the street sounded closer. Eleret shook off her preoccupation and ran forward to jerk her knife from the dead bowman's chest. She gave the blade a quick but thorough wipe with a corner of the man's cloak, then thrust it into her pocket. A proper cleaning would have to wait for later, when they were safe. "Come *on*, Daner," she said over her shoulder.

"Not before I find out the truth about this attack," Daner said without taking his eyes off the wounded man.

"Then I wish good luck to you." Eleret scooped up the two kit bags, hers and her mother's, from the pavement where Daner had dropped them, and started toward the far end of the alley. If the stubborn Ciaronese nobleman couldn't see that they'd be better off elsewhere, he could stay and welcome.

She had not gotten three steps when a new voice said, "Stand and lower your weapons, in the name of the Emperor!"

With a grimace, Eleret turned. A brown-haired woman and a stocky, long-faced man, both dressed in maroon-and-indigo uniforms, stood at the entrance to the alley, their swords ready and their eyes moving constantly up and down and across the open space, checking for more trouble. Eleret cursed under her breath, but did not try to continue her retreat.

"Your arrival is most timely, guardsmen," Daner said, lowering the point of his sword perhaps an inch. "I am Lord Daner Vallaniri, at your service and the Emperor's, and I wish to lodge a complaint against these three men."

The man glanced down at the pavement and raised a thin black eyebrow, making his long face appear even longer. "Looks to me like it ought to be the other way around."

"What sort of complaint, my lord?" the woman guard asked Daner. She nodded toward the two bodies and added, "Bearing in mind that by the look of things there's only one of them left to answer it."

"This offal attacked me, three to one, without reason or provocation," Daner replied. Eleret stared at him. Three to *one*? Hadn't he noticed her dagger in the first man's chest, or the raven's-feet that had distracted his opponents for a crucial instant when he stumbled?

"No reason," the stocky guard said. "Sure. Happens all the time. People wander the streets every day whipping up fights for no reason."

The woman guard cleared her throat and frowned at her companion, but he took no notice. Daner's face stiffened. "They had no reason that I know of," he said with cold politeness. "And they meant to kill."

"That's what they all say." The man walked over to Daner's side as he spoke. He inspected Daner and the injured attacker with the same air of mild skepticism, then took hold of the prisoner's good arm. With his own sword, the guard nudged Daner's weapon. "Now, you just put that—"

"Sunnar." The woman's voice held a warning note. "He's telling the truth. Don't put your foot in it, or I swear I'll get another workingmate before the day is over."

Sunnar paused. "How do you know?"

"That it's Lord Daner? I saw him in an exhibition match with Reva Dario a couple of months ago. Sword and dagger. He won, too."

"Against Reva?" Sunnar pursed his lips in a silent whistle. "No wonder you remember him. Your pardon, my lord. We hear a lot of tall stories, and most of 'em are no more real than a Rathani whore's jewelry."

"Sunnar!" The other guard rolled her eyes in exasperation.

Daner's angry look vanished and his lips twitched. He bent forward, hiding his face from the two guards, and wiped his blade on the shirt of the nearest dead man. When he straightened, his expression was under control once more.

Both guards watched him narrowly until he sheathed his sword. Then, apparently satisfied that no one would make any more trouble, they put their own weapons in their scabbards.

"So what do you want done with this catch?" Sunnar asked Daner casually, oblivious to his companion's glare. "Two beached and dried, one hooked alive for the pot, and— What about the girl, there?" He gestured at Eleret.

"She's with me," Daner said. "You'd better bring the other man along, though. I'll have a complaint against him, too; he's a thief."

"What other man?" the female guard asked.

Eleret glanced back over her shoulder. The alley was empty. Involuntarily, she looked at Daner, and saw his mouth twist in a rueful response. She gave him a faint smile in return, feeling obscurely pleased. She had almost liked Karvonen, even if he was a thief, and while she'd still had some questions for him, she could not help being glad that they would not have to turn him over to the City Guard.

"He seems to have gone," she said to the guards.

"That's one less to worry about, anyway," Sunnar muttered, barely loud enough for Eleret to hear. He gave Eleret a speculative look that she did not quite like, then turned to Daner and raised his voice. "You'd better come along to the duty hut, my lord, and make your complaint there. It won't take long, I promise you."

Daner scowled. "I have wasted enough time on these scum already. I do not intend—"

"Let's go, Daner," Eleret interrupted.

"What? But I thought you— Oh." Daner followed Eleret's glance and broke off in mid-sentence. A crowd of curious passersby had formed in the mouth of the alley. The throng kept a respectful distance behind the two City

Guards, but Eleret could almost feel the intensity of the gazes focused on her and her companions. There was no hope now of staying out of sight, and no telling who might be concealed among the inquisitive people jostling each other in search of a better view. The safest course would be to go with the guards, and slip away once they had left the crowd behind.

"If you'll come along then, my lord?" Sumner said. "Charis, you take a look around here, and get some of these carp-faced loafers to clear up when you're finished."

"Worry about your own job, and stop telling me how to do mine," the woman guard told him without rancor. "Go along."

Sunnar motioned for Daner and Eleret to precede him. As Eleret moved forward, the prisoner, who had been standing in sullen silence, sprang toward her. The unexpected move broke Sunnar's hold, and the prisoner swung an open hand at Eleret's head. The crowd gasped. Without thought, Eleret took a half-step backward and brought her hands up, catching his wrist and arm. She pulled, using the force of his own lunge to send him stumbling on past her. As he went by, she got one glimpse of the man's face, twisted with hatred, and saw the glint of metal between his fingers; then she released her hold and kicked at the back of his knee.

The man's legs buckled and he went down, landing clumsily on one knee and his injured arm. As Eleret stepped forward and pivoted, bringing her leg around for another kick, his weakened arm gave way. Instead of sending him sprawling onto his back, her foot hit high and awkwardly, knocking him forward onto his face with both hands hidden under his body.

Eleret bounced away from the fallen man and skipped back two paces. Her hands were already in her pockets, feeling for her dagger and her raven's-feet, but it was not necessary. Daner and the guards had their swords out, and their expressions made it clear that the prisoner would not have another chance to attack or escape.

"Eleret! Are you all right?" Daner said.

"Yes," Eleret replied, slightly puzzled by the evident concern in his voice.

"Neatly done," Charis said to Eleret. "Where'd you take your training?"

"At home," Eleret answered. Feeling that something more was called for, she added, "In the mountains."

Charis shot her a startled glance, but returned her gaze almost immediately to the prisoner lying facedown on the pavement. Daner also looked her way, but his expression was more bemused than surprised.

"Now, you," Sunnar said. "On your feet, and no more tricks."

The man did not move. Sunnar exchanged looks with his partner, then stepped closer and nudged the man with his foot. When he still did not respond, the guard motioned to Daner to keep close watch and bent forward. As he seized the man's shoulder, his expression changed.

"The blasted cod's-head's gone and died on us, Charis," he said in tones of deep disgust.

"How? She took him down nicely, but it didn't look to me as if she hit hard enough to break his neck."

"I didn't," Eleret said. "I got a clean strike on the back of his knee and a bad kick on the same side, but neither one would have done more than bruise. I wasn't aiming to kill."

"I see." Charis gave Eleret a long, measuring look.

Sunnar, who was examining the dead man, gave a sudden exclamation. A moment later, he pulled a small metal implement gingerly out of the dead man's hand. Eleret leaned closer to get a better view. It was a narrow band of metal, just long enough to span the width of two fingers. The ends curved up and around the fingers, holding the strip in place. From the outer surface projected two needlelike prongs an inch long, coated with something black and shiny.

"Stupid of him to wear it on the palm side," Sunnar said, grimacing. "Got a bag for this, Charis?"

Daner stared in fascination. "What is that thing?"

"An assassin's weapon called a viper's tooth," Sunnar said, sitting back on his heels. "They wear it like so." He held the wicked-looking object up so that the prongs stood out from the backs of his fingers. "The teeth are poisoned; it only takes a scratch to kill."

Daner stiffened and stepped protectively between Eleret and the dead man. For once, Eleret did not mind. No Cilhar would ever use a viper's tooth, but in the Mountains of Morravik even the youngest children had heard of them. There had been a time when half the Syaski raiders who invaded the lower passes had carried the deadly little tools. She turned away, feeling a need to put more distance between herself and the body of any man who would employ such a weapon.

"This one was a pretty inept assassin," Charis said, handing her partner a leather pouch. "I take it he fell on the thing?"

Sunnar shook his head. "Closed his hand around it when he went down, I'd say. It comes to the same thing. I *said* he was stupid to wear it on the palm side." He turned to Daner. "Who wants you dead, my lord?"

"No one I know of," Daner replied. "And anyway, I don't think he was aiming for—"

"Not now, my lord," Charis broke in loudly. "We'll go over the details at the duty hut, when you make your complaint. Until then it's best not to discuss it."

Daner frowned. "But—"

"Don't bother objecting, my lord. Your father'd have our swords, and rightly so, if we let you leave without looking into this."

"He'd have more than that, now that you mention it," Daner said. "He'd have my hide to patch his mainsail." His frown faded and he shrugged. "Very well. Let's get this over with."

"Come along, then," Sunnar said. He turned toward the crowd and raised his voice. "Clear a way, there. Official business, City Guard. Clear a way."

Slowly, a path opened as the people jammed themselves together in response to Sunnar's wave. Sunnar strode toward it, motioning to Daner and Eleret to follow. Feeling a little nervous, Eleret did so, and Daner fell into step beside her.

"There's no need to look so grim," he said softly as they left the alley. "This really won't take long. We'll have plenty of time to get out of the city before nightfall, if that's still what you want."

"Not now, Daner." Watching the crowd on both sides while following Sunnar kept Eleret fully occupied; she had no attention to spare for conversation.

"I thought you'd change your mind," Daner said, misunderstanding her completely. "In a day or two, the guards will have found out the reason for this attack, and then—"

"*Later*, Daner."

Her tone must have gotten through to him at last, for he fell silent. Eleret gave a quiet sigh of relief and concentrated on the crowd. Once they got away from the alley, the traffic returned to its normal density, but there were still too many people. Anyone could hide among them, anywhere.

Half a block from the alley, Sunnar turned down a side street. Two blocks farther on he stopped in front of a small wooden building with shuttered windows, huddled between two tall stone structures. As he unlocked the door, Charis came hurrying up the street after them.

Sunnar reached for his sword. "Now what?" he asked as his partner reached them.

"Now we take Lord Daner's complaint," Charis answered blandly. She pushed the door open and motioned them forward.

"Sink it in a whirling storm, Charis! Why aren't you seeing to the cleanup, the way you're supposed to?"

"I thought you'd need me here. Don't fuss, Sunnar; Troke and Audellen saw the crowd and stopped. They'll handle things there."

"And we'll owe them another favor," Sunnar muttered, shoving his half-drawn sword back into place. "Why do you always push the messy jobs into someone else's boat?"

"Because if I didn't, we'd never do any other kind," Charis said with unruffled calm. "Inside, Sunnar. We're keeping Lord Daner waiting."

Sunnar looked at Daner and turned the corners of his mouth down expressively. With a final glare at his partner, he marched through the open door. Relieved at the chance to get off the street, Eleret followed. Daner shrugged and did likewise.

The interior of the duty hut was dim and smelled of smoke and stale beer. An iron lantern, flecked with rust, hung on a wooden peg beside the door, just above a narrow horizontal slot in the wall. A willow basket sat on the floor underneath the slot to catch whatever might be put through it. Along one wall, opposite the hearth, stood a table littered with paper and assorted odds and ends—a bunch of keys, an apple core, a coiled bowstring.

Sunnar flung himself onto a large barrel sitting beside the table. Folding his arms, he leaned back and glared at his partner. "All right, Charis, what—"

"You've gotten hold of the wrong end of the oar, Sunnar, that's what." Charis shut the door behind her and leaned back against it. "Those three weren't after Lord Daner. They were trying to kill this girl. At least, that last one was."

"The girl?" Sunnar's long face grew thoughtful, then he nodded. "Sure. I'd have seen it myself if I'd had more time to think about it. So?"

"So I wanted to hear for myself what these two have to say. Your summaries tend to lack detail." Charis turned her head to look at Daner and Eleret. She gave Daner a respectful nod and added, "Now, will you tell us what happened, my lord, so we can start looking into this properly?"

EIGHT

Daner seated himself on the nearest of two sturdy wooden boxes, throwing the right side of his cloak back over his shoulder. "Of course I'll tell you," he said, smiling. "Although I don't have much more to say. They came up behind us and started shooting arrows; it's sheer luck that one of us wasn't hit. And before you ask, no, I don't know why they did it."

"They were assassins." Sunnar spread his hands wide as if to demonstrate how obvious this deduction was.

"No," said Eleret. "They were Syaski. At least, the last one was."

All three of the others turned to look at her. "How do you know?" Charis asked.

"He used a Syaski expression right after Daner disarmed him. And assassins aren't the only ones who use the viper's tooth; the Syaski do, too."

"So they're Syaski assassins," Sunnar said with evident impatience. "The important thing is who hired 'em to kill you, not where they came from."

"I'm afraid you're wrong again, Sunnar." Charis directed her level gaze at Eleret, and smiled slightly. "You're a Cilhar, aren't you?"

Eleret nodded.

Sunnar looked from her to Charis with a baffled expression. "So she's Cilhar. So what?"

"The Syaski and the Cilhar are mortal enemies," Daner said. He looked at Charis. "I think you've got hold of the right line, madam."

"Oh, come on. You're not saying that *that's* the reason those clam-heads started in on the two of you," Sunnar said to Daner. "It isn't enough."

"It's been enough for two hundred years," Eleret said.

"Two hundred *years?*"

"That's how long the Syaski and the Cilhar have been fighting," Daner said. "The only reason they've finally stopped is that eight years ago the Emperor took the Mountains of Morravik under his protection and then pulled his lines in, hard. There's still trouble along the border now and then."

The surprise Eleret felt must have shown on her face, for Daner gave her one of his charming smiles and added, "My family is somewhat involved in the eastern trade, so of course we keep track of politics in the area."

"All right, maybe that shark-bait would have jumped you in the mountains," Sunnar conceded. "But this is Ciaron." He frowned suddenly. "How'd they spot you, anyway? Did either of you recognize any of 'em?"

"No." Eleret would have felt better if she had known one of the men; it would have explained how they had found her. But her one skirmish with Syaski raiders had been an archery battle, and none of the enemy survivors had gotten close enough to see her face. She wished suddenly and passionately for her bow and quiver and the clean, uncrowded mountain forest where she knew the dangers and how to face them.

Daner, too, shook his head. Sunnar's frown deepened. "Well, if they didn't know you, why in the name of the Emperor's backside did they jump you?"

"Sunnar!" Charis sounded thoroughly exasperated. "Beg pardon, my lord. We don't deal with nobility often in this section."

"I take no offense," Daner said. A hint of dry amusement sounded through the formality of his tone.

A fleeting expression of relief crossed Charis's face. Then she smiled and gestured Eleret toward the second box. "Sit down, Freelady . . . ?"

"Salven," Eleret said, taking the seat. "Eleret Salven."

"Thank you, Freelady Salven," Charis said. She turned to Daner. "I think it would be best if we heard the whole story from the beginning now, my lord." She glanced sternly at her workingmate. "So we'll know what questions to ask."

"As you wish," Daner said. "We had just turned off the northeast avenue, when—"

"What were you doing on the northeast avenue?" Sunnar broke in.

"We were on our way to the Larkirst Trade Station," Daner said, raising his eyebrows.

Sunnar nodded, unimpressed. "Go on."

In quick, well-chosen words, Daner summarized their encounter with the fast-talking thief, their withdrawal to the alley, the attack, and the fight that followed. From his description, Eleret could tell that he did not know whether her deadly knife-throw had been the result of luck or skill, and he had not even noticed her raven's-feet or the cloaked and hooded figure at the end of the alley. She concluded that, for all his skill, the young Ciaronese had little experience with real battles. No Cilhar would have been so sublimely unaware of what might be happening around him, nor so oblivious to a companion's help. No wonder Daner had kept getting in the way of her throwing lines.

"Very good, my lord," Charis said when Daner finished. "We'll keep an eye out for the thief, I promise you, but I can't say we've much hope of catching him."

"He's probably halfway to the tenement section by now," Sunnar agreed glumly. "We'll need more than a description to catch up with him there."

Daner hesitated. "He said his name was Karvonen Aurelico."

"*Aurelico?*" Sunnar straightened up so quickly that he almost fell off his barrel. "Are you sure?"

"That was the name he gave us," Daner said cautiously. "I can't tell you whether he was lying."

"He wasn't," Charis said with certainty. "Nobody who knows enough to use that name would lie about it." She frowned, fingering the hilt of her sword. "But look here, Sunnar, he can't have been *the* Aurelico. Not picking pockets on the open street."

"Doesn't matter," Sunnar replied. "I'd settle for a fourth cousin twice removed, if I could catch one. Rot it, my lord, why couldn't you have held on to him until we got there?"

"I had other things on my mind just then, if you recall," Daner said. "Who is this person we stumbled across?"

"Somebody worth catching," Charis said. "The Aurelico family are the best thieves on Lyra and have been for generations. No one knows how many of them there are, or where they're based. They're a tight-knit group, with their own code of honor, such as it is, and they're very particular about certain things. One of which is the use of their name."

Sunnar nodded emphatically. "A fellow down in Drinn stole a ruby from one of the temples a couple of years ago and left a note claiming *the* Aurelico had done it. He probably hoped to throw the pursuit off his trail, but he didn't count on the Aurelicos. Two days after the theft he turned up tied to the high altar like a goat ready to sacrifice, with the ruby lying in the middle of his chest and a note from the Aurelicos underneath it. They didn't like taking credit for things they hadn't done, they said, so they were returning the missing jewel and the man who'd stolen it. They apologized for the irreverence of their method, but said they felt it was appropriate."

"You keep talking about *the* Aurelico," Eleret said. "Who is that?"

"*The* Aurelico is the head of the family," Charis said. "The Master Thief, if you like. More than that, I can't tell you. I wish I could."

"You know, if one of the Aurelicos is working Ciaron, we'd better send word to the palace," Sunnar put in thoughtfully. "And to some of the noble houses, too. Lady Trewisha Povarrella has a diamond necklet that's enough to tempt *the* Aurelico himself."

Charis shook her head. "Sunnar, we're talking about an Aurelico, and we don't even know what he's after. You can't expect everyone in the city with something worth stealing to triple their security."

"No, but when whatever-he's-after turns up missing, it'll be the fault of the palace sentries or the lord's watchmen, not the City Guard."

"True." Charis crossed to the table and began rummaging through the litter. "Where's the clean paper? I'll write a quick note to the head of the Palace Watch now, and we can send the details when—"

With a muffled rattle, a white square poked through the slot beside the door and fell into the willow basket below. The two guards turned as one to look at it.

"Now what?" Sunnar grumbled as he stood up. He plucked the note from the basket, flipped it over, and groaned. Charis turned and glanced at the dark blob of wax, then rolled her eyes.

"The official seal of the Imperial Guard," she said with disgust. "What do they want this time? And why in hell can't those lazy oafs use proper channels for it?"

Sunnar thumbed his ear at the letter, then slid the same thumb under the seal, breaking it. He unfolded the paper and squinted at it. A moment later, his face settled into an official, expressionless mask. "See for yourself, Charis," he said, passing her the note.

As she read the message, Charis's eyebrows rose. "Well, look at this. Another timely warning from the Emperor's high-nosed and most excellent Imperial Guards to us lowly folks who patrol the streets every day. It seems there's a young, red-haired Cilhar woman, name of Eleret Salven, whom they expect will get into some kind of trouble on her way out of the city, maybe today, maybe tomorrow, maybe three or four days from now. We're to keep a weather eye out for her and send her along as soon as we find her. Signed and sealed, et cetera. Idiots. I'll wager they've known about this for a week."

"I don't think so," Eleret said. "I saw Commander Weziral this morning. I'm sure he'd have warned me then, if he'd known anything." Had it only been that morning? It seemed more like days.

The two guards looked at her. "You know the Commander?" Sunnar said at last.

"Not really. It was business." Eleret did not feel like explaining about her mother and the kit bag and the Commander's misgivings. These people were friendly enough, but she had known none of them until today. "It's a long tale."

"I'll bet," Sunnar commented sourly.

Charis refolded the note and tucked it under her belt. "It doesn't matter. Unless you have something to add, my lord, we'd best be going. Idiots or not, the Imperial Guard doesn't like to be kept waiting."

"What?" Daner said, startled.

"Got salt in your ears?" Sunnar said. "That note said to bring her along to the Guard as soon as we found her. That means now."

"But if the note was a warning, surely there's no need for us to go all the way back to the Imperial Guard offices," Daner said, plainly taken aback.

"*If* all the Guard wanted was to warn her, and *if* the warning had to do with the three Syaski who attacked you, you might be right," Charis said. "But we don't know that."

"And it's possible the Commander remembered something he didn't tell me this morning," Eleret put in. *Or that he's learned something more about Mother's death, or discovered why so many people are interested in her kit,* she added silently. "I'd like to find out."

Daner looked at her with an air of mild irritation. "I thought you were in hurry to leave."

"I am. But information is always good to have. The more you know of danger, the better you can prepare for it."

"I'd rather avoid it, myself," Daner said, smiling as he stood up. "Very well, if you're willing, we'll go."

"Thank you, my lord, Freelady," Charis said, and waved them out the door as if she were afraid they might change their minds if she gave them an opportunity.

* * *

By the time they reached the headquarters of the Imperial Guard, it was late in the afternoon. Eleret led the little group straight to Commander Weziral's office, which caused Sunnar to remark caustically on her obvious familiarity with the building. As she did not want to become involved in a comparison of Ciaronese streets and buildings to mountain byways, Eleret let the remark go by without comment. She was a little surprised that no one stopped them to ask their business, but after some consideration decided that the presence of the two City Guardsmen made their party suitably official looking.

The tall officer with the face like chiseled rock was alone in the outer room when they arrived. He remembered Eleret, and went in at once to notify the Commander. A few minutes later, he returned and ushered them inside.

"Good afternoon, Freelady Salven," Weziral said as they entered. "What can I do for you? You haven't run afoul of our city compatriots here, have you?"

"Not exactly."

"Then what brings you back so soon?" The Commander leaned back in his chair, his expression one of polite inquiry.

"I thought you wanted to see me," Eleret said, puzzled by his reaction.

Weziral frowned. "I'm certainly happy to meet you again, but I get the impression you have something more specific in mind. Why?"

Suddenly at a loss for words, Eleret looked over at the two City Guards. Charis stepped forward and bowed. Pulling the note from her belt, she handed it to Weziral and said, "Because of this, Commander."

The lines at the corners of Weziral's mouth deepened as

he read the note. "Have a look at this, Hara," he said, tossing it to the rock-faced officer.

"If we've misunderstood—" Charis said in a formal, apologetic tone, but the Commander cut her off with a wave.

"No, I don't think you did," he said. "Well, Hara? What do you make of it?"

To Eleret's surprise, the officer's lips set in a hard, tight smile. "It's got the right seal and the right wording, sir. Someone here sent it. And I know it wasn't authorized, unless you ordered it yourself, sir—"

"Which I didn't."

"Then there's only one person who could have sent it." Hara's expression grew even more grimly amused. "Birok Maggen, the City Liaison's aide. He's abused his position in small ways many times, but he's been careful not to go too far. Until now."

"By the time I'm through with him, he'll wish he had stayed careful." Weziral drummed his fingers against the tabletop. "Why do you suppose he did this?"

"I expect he wanted to cause a few difficulties for Freelady Salven," Hara said. "He was with Sergeant Giancarma and me when she arrived this morning, and made himself rather disagreeable. I gave him penalty duty afterward, and he's the sort that would blame her for it. Forcing her to make an unnecessary trip back here is just the kind of petty reprisal he would think of."

"It still doesn't explain why he took such a chance."

"Actually, it wasn't much of a risk. Look." Hara held out the note, pointing to the last few lines. "From the way this is written, most guards would assume she was to be taken to the Liaison's office in the east wing. As long as he was the one on desk duty there for the next few days, no one else would know a thing about it."

"Really." The Commander's voice was dry. "We'll have to do something about that, Hara. I can't have minor officials abusing the authority of the Imperial Guard. Especially not civilians." He turned to Eleret. "I'm sorry about the inconvenience, Freelady. It won't happen again."

Eleret hesitated. "I can't be positive, Commander Weziral, but I think it was meant to be more than an inconvenience."

"How could it have been?" Daner said. "There's nothing to show that this person—"

"Birok Maggen," Hara put in.

"—had anything to do with the Syaski who attacked us."

"What attack?" Weziral demanded.

"Three Syaski jumped us in an alley," Eleret said, wishing Daner had not brought it up. "It doesn't matter, and it's not what I meant anyway. I think Maggen was after Mother's kit."

The Commander bit back a comment and sat very still for a moment, watching them with an expression that prevented anyone from adding anything more. At last he shook his head. "Sit down, all of you. That includes you, Hara; I may want a second opinion on this later. Once you're settled, I want an intelligible story out of each of you, with as few interruptions as possible, and none of you are leaving until I get one."

NINE

In the moment's silence that followed Weziral's pronouncement, Sunnar and Charis exchanged a sour look. Then Daner bowed, smiled, and sat down in the chair in front of the Commander's desk. Eleret sighed and gave in. She presented Daner and the two guards to Weziral while Hara went out for more chairs, and in a few minutes everyone was settled.

Weziral smiled at the motley group and leaned back in his chair. "Thank you, Freelady Salven. Now, I would like to hear what has happened to bring you back here so soon and in such interesting company. I would also like to know why you have such decided opinions about Birok Maggen, a man you have met only once."

"Twice," Eleret said. "He was waiting in the hall as I left, and he offered me five stars for Mother's kit and everything in it. That's why—"

An exclamation from Sunnar interrupted her. "Five stars? For a kit bag? What have you got in it, rubies?"

Daner shook his head. "Eleret, five stars is a price for a war horse or a wizard's sword, not a travel pack."

"That's what I thought."

"Are you sure about this, Freelady?" the Commander asked, leaning forward once more. "Can you remember what he said?"

"I haven't had time to forget. It only happened this morning." Eleret thought for a minute, deciding where to pick up the conversation. "He stopped me in the hall as I left and said, 'You came a long way to get that. It'll be awkward and heavy to carry all the way back, maybe dangerous, even. So I'll buy it from you. The whole thing. I've got a cousin who needs outfitting; this way I can get him fixed up and do you a favor at the same time. Money's easy to carry.' I told him I wasn't interested, and he said, 'I'll pay three stars. That's more than it's worth.' When I said it had belonged to my mother, he said, 'All right, four stars. You can buy a lot of sentiment for four stars.' I said I was still not interested, and he said, 'Five, then!' I told him again that I wouldn't sell and started walking away, and he said, 'You'll be sorry you didn't sell it to me. Wait and see.' That's all."

"By the Harp-sung Fires!" Hara said, staring at her. "You can give his very words!"

"That's what the Commander asked for, wasn't it?" Eleret responded with mild puzzlement. She was beginning to get used to the Ciaronese regarding perfectly ordinary things as remarkable, but she still didn't understand why they made such a fuss about it.

"It was, and I thank you for it, Freelady Salven," Weziral said. "The rest of your story need not be so detailed. If I want more than you tell me, I'll ask."

Eleret nodded and gave him a quick summary of the day's events. She left nothing out, from her encounter with Grand

Master Gorchastrin to the arrival of the supposedly official note at Sunnar and Charis's duty hut. At Weziral's request, she explained how she had known that her bags had been searched and the reasoning behind her decision to leave the city as quickly and quietly as possible. She mentioned her suspicions of Jonystra Nirandol, and her worry that someone might have followed her and Daner along the crowded avenue. And she described as clearly as she could their meeting with Karvonen Aurelico and the fight that followed.

"You're sure this thief didn't set you up for the bowmen?" Hara asked when she finished.

"If he had been working with the Syaski, he wouldn't have given us any sign that they were about to attack."

"A good point," Weziral said. "And if he *is* an Aurelico, he can't be the person who tried to break into my office twice last week."

"Why are you so sure of that?" Daner said, frowning. "He's a thief; he said as much himself."

"Weren't you listening back at the hut?" Sunnar demanded before Weziral or Hara could reply. "The Aurelicos are *good*. If one of them wanted to snoop the Commander's office, it wouldn't take him two tries to get in, and except you noticed something missing, you'd never know he'd been there."

"Unless he wanted it that way," Charis added.

The silence that followed was long and thoughtful.

"Maggen's still the more likely culprit," Hara said finally, shaking his head in regret.

"For a break-in?" Sunnar said. "I thought you said he worked here."

"In the building, yes, but not near this office," Hara replied. "Normally, his duties don't bring him around more than once a month, and that's just to deliver a report to the

Commander or me. Come to think of it, he's been hanging about for the past two weeks like a seagull waiting for the cook to dump slops."

"I think we'd better have a talk with Birok Maggen," the Commander said. He picked up the folded note and tapped it gently against the pile of paper that lay on the table in front of him. "Fetch him in, will you, Hara, and let's see if we can find out what he's after."

Hara bowed and left the room, and Weziral turned back to Eleret. "Now, you said something about a person watching your fight in the alley. Did you recognize him?"

"No," Eleret said. "I don't even know for certain that it was a man. All I really saw was the cloak and hood, and a hand pointing, and only for an instant."

"I didn't see anyone," Daner put in.

"I know," Eleret said, nodding. "If he'd had a bow or a throwing knife, you'd be dead. Your right side was wide open from that angle."

Daner sat back, disconcerted. "I was *busy*. Those two swordsmen weren't exactly amateurs."

"They still weren't anywhere near as good as you are," Eleret pointed out calmly. "They only lasted as long as they did because there were two of them. And because you were blocking my throwing lines."

"What? Look, no matter how much you think you—"

"Ahem." The Commander's cough was not loud, but the sound penetrated the conversation easily. Daner glanced at Weziral and fell silent, though Eleret thought the Commander looked more amused than impatient. Still, it was not the right time for a stroke-by-stroke review of the fight, and she should not have begun one while other, more important questions were unresolved. She was a little surprised that she had let herself be drawn so far off the track.

"Thank you, Lord Daner," Weziral said. "Now, did either of you"—he indicated the two City Guards—"notice this person in the hooded cloak when you arrived?"

Charis and Sunnar looked at each other and shook their heads.

"Pity, but not really surprising. If he *was* working with the Syaski, he'd have been a fool to stay once it was clear they'd lost. Freelady Salven, you said he was pointing. At what?"

"Let me think." Eleret closed her eyes, reliving the brief moments of the fight in her mind. An instant later, her eyes flew open. "Daner. He was pointing at Daner."

"Directing the swordsmen?" Weziral asked.

"In the middle of a fight?" Daner snorted. "Hardly. Things change too fast for outside advice to do any good."

"That wasn't quite what I meant," Weziral said mildly. "He could have been signaling them to pull back, for instance. What happened next, Freelady?"

"Daner stumbled," Eleret said. "I threw a raven's-foot at each of the Syaski, but I'm afraid they didn't do much damage."

"Mmmm." Weziral looked at Daner. "You stumbled?" he said in a neutral tone.

"It happens to the best of us, Commander," Daner said. "And it wasn't magic, if that's what you're thinking. I'm no master magician, but I've had enough training to tell when someone throws a spell at me."

"I'm sure you do. Since we seem to have come around to you now, my lord, would you oblige me with your version of the fight?"

Halfway through Daner's description, Hara returned. He was alone. Daner stopped talking in mid-sentence, and Weziral raised an eyebrow.

"He's gone," Hara said disgustedly in answer to the question no one had asked aloud.

"You mean this cod's-head Maggen's run?" Sunnar said.

Hara shook his head. "He's just left for the day. Stelinn's office boy says he nearly always goes home early."

"How'd a dead fish like him get a job with the Imperials?" Sunnar asked the air in front of Weziral's desk.

"I was about to ask that myself," Weziral said, looking at Hara. "Although I'd have phrased it a little differently."

"Connections," Hara said in tones of deep disgust. "Maggen's one of Lord Ovrunelli's relations. His *many* relations."

Daner stiffened. Sunnar pursed his lips thoughtfully, and Charis's eyes widened. Commander Weziral nodded in evident understanding.

"Who?" said Eleret.

"Lord Ovrunelli is one of His Imperial Majesty's chief advisers," Weziral explained. "One of the privileges of that position is the ability to provide one's family and friends with suitably lucrative posts."

"I see." Eleret tried to conceal her shock. If the Ciaronese wanted to let their city be run by people whose only qualifications were greed and a blood tie to a man in power, it was their battle, not hers. As long as they treated the Cilhar fairly and competently, of course.

Her face must have shown some of what she was thinking, for the Commander smiled and said, "It isn't as bad as it sounds. The important positions have to be earned, and even most of the lesser ones require that the holder have certain skills. Since Maggen is only—"

"Aide to the City Liaison." Hara supplied smoothly.

"—I assume he is neither capable nor closely connected to Lord Ovrunelli."

"Third cousin, once removed," Hara said. "And as incompetent as they come. He trims his sails to suit the wind, though, and I haven't had an excuse good enough to get rid of him until now."

"You think that will be enough?" Daner asked, gesturing at the note that still lay on Weziral's desk. "What if he did it at Lord Ovrunelli's request?"

"Then Lord Ovrunelli will no doubt find him some other, equally profitable position when he is sacked out of this one," Weziral replied. "Imperial adviser or not, Lord Ovrunelli cannot force us to keep a man who has abused his post so flagrantly."

Well enough for you, Eleret thought, *but what about me?* If Birok Maggen was in league with his powerful cousin, she was in even more trouble than she had thought. She should get out of Ciaron soon, before Maggen discovered that his trap had been sprung and decided to try something else.

As if he had overheard her thoughts, the Commander said, "True, Hara, but there's Freelady Salven to consider." He hesitated. "I suppose this makes you eager to leave Ciaron, Freelady?"

"It certainly sounds like a good idea. Why do you ask?"

"I hoped to persuade you to stay, at least until we've managed to bring Maggen in for a talk. It might be useful to have you there to help sort out what he's up to; in return, I can provide some protection for you while you're in the city."

"Eleret will be under the protection of the Vallaniris," Daner said with rigid politeness.

"I see. Well, Freelady?"

Eleret looked from the Commander's carefully blank expression to Daner's worried one. They were both thinking more about her safety than about the doubtful help she could give them with Maggen, but it didn't really matter.

Tamm's things were at the bottom of this mess, and since some of it had spilled over onto the Commander, Eleret owed him her aid if he asked for it, no matter what his reasons. Besides, she couldn't see heading for home with an unmeasured string of trouble trailing behind her. She needed information, and questioning Maggen would be a start at getting it. The time would be well spent, especially since leaving the city now would hardly be worth the effort. She couldn't get far from Ciaron in what was left of the day's light, and somehow she didn't think Daner would like the idea of traveling after dark.

"I'll stay the night, at least," Eleret said. Both Weziral and Daner looked relieved. Eleret thought of the Syaski, and Jonystra Nirandol, and Grand Master Gorchastrin, none of whom seemed likely allies for Maggen and his cousin, and all of whom were somewhere in the city, probably hunting for her. She looked down at the kit bags slung over her arm, and anger swept through her. *Ma, how could you do this to me?*

"Thank you," Weziral said. "Now, Lord Daner, I believe Hara interrupted you. If you would finish your story . . . ?"

Judging from the look on Daner's face, he would have preferred not to, but courtesy compelled him to resume his tale. The Commander insisted on a far more detailed account than he had asked of Eleret. He was especially interested in the Syaski style of swordplay, and made Daner give a blow-by-blow description of each thrust and countermove.

After a few minutes, Eleret stopped listening. The sword was not her best weapon, and normally she would have paid close attention in hopes of learning, but the terms the Ciaronese used were unfamiliar. She found it impossible to follow the conversation without interrupting constantly for explanations—what *was* the Pirate's Parry?—and she did not want to break Weziral's chain of thought. So she let the Ciaronese talk, and considered what she should do next.

Returning to the Broken Harp seemed like a bad idea, even if Jonystra was the only one of Eleret's pursuers who knew of her presence there. With Tamm's wages and death fee under her belt, she could afford a room somewhere else, but she didn't like that idea much, either. Inns were a bad place for a defense if it came to real trouble, and if someone had told other Syaski about her, real trouble was sure to come. Perhaps she could spend the night at Adept Climeral's school. Safety was more important than a comfortable bed; she could sleep on the floor in the hallway if there was no other room.

Weziral finished with Daner and went on to Charis and Sunnar. Their story took less time than Daner's, and Weziral seemed less interested in quizzing them about the details. When they were done, he smiled and said, "Thank you both. I won't keep you from your duties any longer. I'm sure I don't need to tell you not to mention what you've learned here."

"Then why did you?" Sunnar asked.

Charis jabbed an elbow at his ribs. "Sunnar! Don't be difficult. We understand, Commander. We'll have to put some of it in our report, of course, but I'll see that it goes through the, um, longest possible official channels."

"Right," Sunnar said, nodding. "It'll be weeks before anyone bothers to look at it."

There was a choking sound from the corner as Hara tried to swallow a laugh. Weziral's lips twitched.

"Very good," he said. "Hara, see them to the gate, would you? And make sure you mark them down for a special commendation and bonus."

Hara paused. "Yes, Commander. Ah, Imperial bonuses

for City Guards are normally handled through the City Liaison's office."

"Not this time." Weziral gave his aide a long look. "Handle it yourself."

"Yes, Commander. This way, please."

As the three left the room, Weziral turned to Eleret. "Freelady Salven, after what has happened today, it seems unwise for you to go back to whatever inn you have been living in, but I'll be happy to help you make other arrangements. I wish I could offer you a cot in the barracks, but they're full right now. Recruits, just before heading out to reinforce the western border."

"I understand," Eleret assured him. "I'll stay at Adept Climeral's school, if they'll let me."

"Nonsense," Daner broke in with great firmness. "You're coming home with me."

Weziral's eyebrows rose almost to his hairline. "*Is* she now, Lord Daner?"

Daner's cheeks reddened slightly. "To my *family's* home. My mother and sisters will be happy to have her, and it's one of the safest places in Ciaron if Lord Ovrunelli has his nets out."

"Ah, yes." Weziral looked suddenly pensive. "That hadn't occurred to me. You're quite right. But—forgive me for asking, Lord Daner—why are you willing to do this?"

To Eleret's surprise, Daner glanced at her and hesitated. "I promised Climeral I'd do my best to see that El—that Freelady Salven stayed safe."

"I see. We'll leave it there." Weziral looked at Eleret and smiled as if his thoughts amused him. "I'll send word tomorrow morning when we've gotten hold of Maggen. Would

you care for an escort as far as the west castle road, my lord?
No, I thought not. Well, you shouldn't have any more difficulties if you stick to the main streets. Give you good day,
my lord, Freelady."

TEN

Once they were on the street again, Daner shook off his preoccupation and led her west, toward Castle Hill. The Emperor's palace was a blurry patch of black against the shifting glow of the setting sun, and the people who filled the streets moved less briskly but with more purpose than they had earlier in the day. The salt-scented breeze off the Melyranne Sea had diminished, allowing the strong odors of cooking fish and warm horse dung to take over the city air. Eleret wrinkled her nose, wondering once again how the Ciaronese stood it.

"You get used to it after a while," Daner said, and for a moment Eleret was afraid she had spoken aloud without realizing it. Then Daner smiled and added, "I always notice the smell when I come back from a trip, but after a day or two I'm not even aware of it anymore."

"It would take me more time than that, and I don't plan to stay so long."

"After the way things have been going today, I can't blame you." He gave her a sidelong glance that she could not interpret. "I wasn't lying to Commander Weziral, you know. My mother really does enjoy having visitors."

Daner seemed to expect some sort of reply, but Eleret had no idea what. She nodded without speaking, hoping he would interpret the gesture as the right response.

"No, really," Daner said. "And I'm sure my sisters will like you."

Still confused, Eleret nodded again. Daner sighed. "Look, it won't be that bad! Father doesn't like formality, so you won't have court manners to deal with. Toricar and Uncle Panasci are with the Emperor's delegation to Brydden, so you won't even meet them. And my mother and my sisters will be happy to have you."

Eleret looked away to hide her smile. Daner thought she was worried about meeting his family! She could not resist saying in a mournful tone, "I'm sure they will."

"It's only for one night!"

"I know."

"Maybe you'd feel more comfortable if you went back to that inn you were staying at," Daner said in tones that made it clear how much he doubted it, "but it isn't safe. You must see that."

"Of course I see that," Eleret said, frowning. "What I don't see is why you're sure your family's home will be so much safer than the Imperial Guard barracks or the school of the Island of the Third Moon."

"It's politics," Daner said, as if that was all the explanation she would want or need.

"That's plain enough," Eleret told him. "What I want is a detail or two."

"Oh. Right. Well, it's because of Lord Ovrunelli . . ."

Daner's explanation took nearly the whole of the walk, and Eleret had to keep prompting him with questions whenever his summary became too general. What it amounted to was that Lord Ovrunelli couldn't or wouldn't interfere directly with another noble household unless he went through a complicated procedure that sounded as if it would take weeks. The Imperial barracks had no such immunity, and, since it was run by foreigners, neither did the Islanders' school. It all reminded Eleret of the sword-sanctuary customs in the mountains, except that those made sense.

As they drew nearer to the palace, the street grew wider and less crowded, and Eleret breathed a little easier. Litters went by several times, all of them with drawn curtains. There were more men in brightly colored cloaks and hats with long feathers, more women in shin-length silk dresses and finely tooled leather boots. Twice, Daner paused to make invisible adjustments to his cloak, though the few disapproving looks Eleret noticed seemed directed more at her than him.

Finally Daner stopped in front of an oak door banded with iron. He rapped once, and immediately a small panel opened at eye level. Eleret caught a glimpse of dark eyes surrounded by deep wrinkles, and then she heard a sharp intake of breath. The panel snapped shut, something scraped loudly along the inside of the door, and then the door swung open.

The weather-worn man holding the door bowed. "Welcome home, my lord. We weren't expecting you."

"I know, Bresc," Daner said, stepping into the small entry room. "It's nothing. This is Freelady Salven; she'll be staying the night. She's to be given full guest courtesy. Pass the word, will you?"

"Very good, my lord," the man said. As Eleret entered, he gave her a look that took in not only the two kit bags but also the places where her skirt hung oddly over her raven's-feet and her unsheathed dagger. Eleret's opinion of him rose.

Then he bowed again and closed the door behind them, and they went on inside.

A narrow, crooked corridor led away from the entry room to another door. Beyond was a stone flight of spiral stairs, dimly lit by the overflow from some stronger light high above. Daner went first, climbing with the unthinking ease of long practice. He did not even scrape his sword against the outer wall as he moved around and around the tight, steep turns.

They climbed past a short, wide door and went on up. Daner opened the next door they came to and went through instead of continuing the ascent. Eleret gave a quiet sigh of relief. The shadows and the closeness of the walls around the stairs made her feel as if she were lost in a cave, with her torch running out and the mountains pressing down above her. She told herself not to be silly, and followed Daner out of the stairwell.

The room beyond was a shocking contrast. Eleret squinted in the sudden light, taking in the tapestry-draped walls and the high ceiling. Bowls of fresh flowers and delicate porcelain statuettes stood on tables draped with lace and surrounded by thin-legged wooden chairs overflowing with embroidered silk pillows. Even the lamps looked fragile, with filigree bases and narrow necks. *What an awful place for a fight*, Eleret thought.

As they stepped into the room, a group of women rose like startled quail from a cluster of chairs in front of the hearth, scattering pillows and bits of embroidery thread across the floor. Three of them, ranging in apparent age from seventeen to twenty-five, rushed forward with delighted cries and crowded around Daner. The remaining two—a short, plump, grim-faced matron and a taller and happier-looking woman of middle years—approached more slowly. All of the women wore floor-length tunics similar to the one Jonystra Nirandol had had on when Eleret had last seen her, but these were of finer materials more elaborately embroidered.

"Girls, behave yourselves," the tall woman said as she drew nearer. Her tunic was a soft blue-gray silk, and the embroidery around the square neckline glittered in the lamplight. "Daner, my love, what a pleasant surprise. And so unexpected."

"Hello, Mother," Daner said, shedding eager young women in all directions as he bent to kiss her hand. "I'm sorry I didn't warn you I'd be home tonight, but I didn't know myself until half an hour ago."

"Then you're forgiven." She looked past Daner, and her twinkling gray eyes met Eleret's. "I don't believe we've met, my dear. I'm—"

"The unfortunate mother of an unmannerly lout," Daner broke in. "Mother, this is Freelady Eleret Salven."

Morravik's death! Eleret thought, *I should have told him not to use that title.* It was too late now, though, and from the various startled looks the ladies were giving her it was plain that every last one of them had identified her as a Cilhar on the strength of it.

"Eleret, this is my mother, Lady Laurenzi tir Vallaniri," Daner went on. "And my aunt, Lady Kistran Vallaniri; my sisters, Lady Laurinel Trantorino, Lady Raqueva, and Lady Metriss."

Eleret nodded in acknowledgment of each name. Lady Kistran was the grim-looking matron; her expression did not lighten in the least as she swept her eyes up and down Eleret like a group-captain looking for a betraying glint of metal before a night foray. As Daner finished his introduction, she sniffed and raised a hand to stroke a necklet of beaten gold that must have cost as much as six workhorses and a sword of Sadorthan steel.

Lady Laurinel—or was it Lady Trantorino?—was a sweet-faced blonde in her mid-twenties who returned a smile for Eleret's nod, then glanced uncertainly at her aunt.

In contrast, Lady Raqueva eyed Eleret with the same open evaluation as Lady Kistran, but with less hostility. Her hair was darker than her elder sister's, and she had a more determined set to her jaw. "Freelady? You're a Cilhar, then?"

"Yes, Lady Raqueva," Eleret said, hoping she had gotten the designation right. From Daner's behavior and their own, she could see that there was a hierarchy among these women as strict as the order of officers in a full assault call-up, but she could not puzzle out exactly how it worked. Why couldn't Daner have told her something *useful* on the walk there, instead of jabbering on about how much they would like her? But that was unjust; after all, she hadn't thought to ask about forms of address any more than he had thought to mention them.

"How interesting," said Lady Metriss, the seventeen-year-old. She carried herself as if someone had stuck a steel-clad arrow down her back, and her tone was one of polite boredom. "Is that what they're wearing in the mountains this spring?"

"Not now, Riss." Lady tir Vallaniri cast a reproving glance at her youngest daughter, then turned to Eleret. "It's a pleasure to have you with us, Freelady Salven. Will you be staying for dinner?"

"She'll be staying the night, Mother," Daner said before Eleret could reply. "I'm sorry to spring it on you like this, but it's necessary."

All five women turned their heads to stare at Eleret with varying degrees of astonishment.

"Necessary?" Lady Kistran invested the word with an amazing amount of skepticism. "And just *why* is it 'necessary'?"

"Politics, Aunt," Daner said.

Curiosity left all five faces like water running out of an overturned bucket. "Very well, Daner," Lady tir Vallaniri said. "You can discuss it with your father after dinner."

"*And* with Baroja," Lady Kistran put in swiftly. "I trust you will be able to satisfy them."

"Cousin Baroja is going to be here tonight?" Plainly, Daner was not much taken with the idea.

"Yes, he and your aunt are staying to dinner," his mother said. Eleret thought she heard a warning note below the casual tone, but she did not know Lady Laurenzi tir Vallaniri enough to be sure. Suddenly she felt as if she stood on rotten spring ice, where a solid-seeming trail might give way underfoot without warning, and she had no way to find the safe path.

Daner's mother turned her head toward her daughters and went on. "Lauri, will you show Freelady Salven to her room? The west corner upstairs, I think. She'll want a few minutes to refresh herself before we eat."

Lady Laurinel, the eldest and friendliest-looking of the sisters, smiled. "Of course, Mother. Freelady?"

A bit uncertainly, Eleret followed Laurinel down the length of the room to the far door. She would have preferred a few moments alone with Daner to get a fast report on the things she needed to know about his family, but that did not look possible. Getting away from the lot of them was the next best thing; she couldn't misstep if she wasn't there.

As they reached the door, Laurinel scooped a small lamp from the table beside it. Holding it high, she led Eleret down a wide hall to another staircase. This one was made of broad oak boards and rose in three short, straight flights to the next floor.

"It's just around the corner," Lady Laurinel said as she stepped into the upstairs hallway. "I'm sure you'll—"

"Mother!" Halfway down the hall, a door flew open. Automatically, Eleret reached for her dagger, then relaxed as a small blue-clad whirlwind rushed toward them. A belated cry of protest followed, and a moment later a tall, gaunt woman appeared in the doorway.

"Drioren, come back here at once!" the woman called. Then she saw Laurinel, and sucked her breath in so strongly that even from where she stood Eleret could hear the soft hissing sound. "My lady! I do beg your pardon, my lady. The young lord is a rare catch today, and no mistake."

"She wants me to take a nap," the small person informed them. "I don't want a nap. I want a story. Will you tell me a story, Mother?" He raised wide gray eyes and smiled winningly.

"Not right now, Drioren," Lady Laurinel said. "I have a duty. But you may come with me, if you like."

Drioren tilted his head, plainly suspicious. "What kind of duty?"

"I must show your grandmother's guest to her room, and see that she is comfortable."

"Oh, *that's* all right, then." Drioren smiled at his mother again. "Yes, please, I would like to come with you, Mother."

"My lady, you should not encourage him to disobey," the gaunt woman said stiffly.

"Should I not?" Lady Laurinel said in a soft, cool voice.

The gaunt woman's eyes dropped. "Beg pardon, my lady, I'm sure."

"Very good," Laurinel said in the same soft tone. "Now, be so good as to fetch a washbasin to the west chamber for our guest. Drioren will be with us when you bring it."

"Yes, my lady."

Laurinel smiled. "You may go." She took her son's hand and started down the hall. As the gaunt woman turned away, a flash of anger, almost hatred, crossed her face. Once again, Eleret had the feeling of unfamiliar hazards lurking below a thin crust of polite formality. It was a good thing she was not going to be here long.

As they walked down the hall, Drioren threw several curious looks over his shoulder at Eleret. Finally he tugged on his mother's hand and asked in a clear, piercing whisper, "Mother, who's she?"

Laurinel paused, then turned. "Forgive me, Drioren, I should have presented you. Freelady Salven, this is my son, the young Lord Drioren Trantorino. Drioren, your greeting."

Letting go of his mother's hand, Drioren stepped forward and bowed. He kept his solemn dark eyes fixed on Eleret's face the whole time, which made the movement awkward, but Eleret managed not to smile. "Welcome, Freelady," he said.

"I thank you for your courtesy," Eleret replied, as she would have in the mountains. "May your welcome bring strength to us both."

"As you will have it," the boy responded, though he was plainly unsure that this was the right thing to say. Eleret smiled encouragingly, and Drioren relaxed. "You aren't from Ciaron, are you? Where do you come from?"

"I'm Cilhar," Eleret told him. Daner's polite introduction had seen to it that the adults all knew her origins; there was no point in hiding them from the child. "I come from the Mountains of Morravik."

"Really?" The boy's eyes grew wide. "Where they have dragons and Varnan wizards and Wyrds and everything?"

"I've never seen a dragon, and as far as I know there are no Wyrds living in the mountains," Eleret said. "We don't have many wizards, either. It takes time to study magic, and none of us have much to spare."

Drioren's face fell. "No wizards?"

"Not now, and not recently. But one of my great-great-grandmothers was a Varnan *and* a wizard."

"Will you tell me about her?" Drioren asked, tucking his hand confidently into Eleret's.

Eleret glanced at Lady Laurinel, who smiled and shook her head. "Not right now," Eleret said.

"First we must show Freelady Salven her room," Laurinel added.

"Oh, that's right. It's a duty." Drioren did not seem at all upset, and Eleret gave an approving nod. Whatever else the Ciaronese did or did not do, this child at least was being taught a proper regard for duty.

Halfway down the hall, Laurinel opened a door and gestured Eleret inside. "I hope this will do, Freelady."

"It will be fine," Eleret said. The chamber was nearly as large as the front room at home, with a wide bed piled with pillows, two spindly chairs and a matching round table, a long, high table underneath a window, and a fireplace set in the outer wall. The air smelled faintly of old smoke and damp stone, like a storage room that had gone unopened for a month. A thick rug covered the floor in the center of the room, and a pair of black iron tongs leaned against the stone wall next to the fireplace. She looked more closely and saw that the handle end was shaped like a bird's head. She smiled slightly, tightening her right hand around the raven ring, and suddenly felt more comfortable.

"Good," said Drioren. "*Now* will you tell me a story?"

"If it's all right with your mother—"

"Are you sure you don't mind, Freelady?" Laurinel said in a worried tone.

"I have two youngers at home, a sister and a brother," Eleret said. "I like children." She set her kit bags on the dainty-looking table where she could see them and gingerly lowered herself into one of the chairs. It was more comfortable than it looked. "What kind of story would you like to hear?" she asked Drioren.

ELEVEN

Drioren gave Eleret a bright smile and plopped down on the rug in front of her. "Tell me an *old* story, please."

"All right," Eleret said. "Long, long ago, when three moons hung in the sky and all the races were one race, there lived a man—"

"That's not right," Drioren broke in. "Old stories are supposed to start, 'A long time past, when the great gray ships sailed east to harbor . . .'"

His mother shook her head reprovingly at him, but Eleret smiled. "Those are your stories," she told him. "Where I come from, the oldest stories begin differently."

Drioren frowned, considering this. "But it sounds funny."

"That's because you've never heard my story before."

The frown lasted a few seconds more, then Drioren nodded. "All right, but if I don't like it you have to tell me another one."

"Oh, no," Eleret said, fighting a desire to laugh. Until he was ten, Jiv had tried the same trick every night to delay his bedtime. It had never worked, but that hadn't stopped him. "You asked for one story, and one is all you get. And all you said was that you wanted an *old* story, so the rest is my choice to tell. Take it or go hungry."

"But—"

"One story, or none at all. Which do you want?"

"One story, please," Drioren said with a resigned sigh. "You're *mean.*"

"Thank you." Eleret suppressed another smile at the boy's startled look, and began again. "Long, long ago, when three moons hung in the sky . . ."

She told the story of Nirrit, who could change his skin to become like any creature on Lyra but who was never satisfied with any of his forms, and his patient son Suranel, who had to find stranger and stranger new shapes for his father to change into. While Eleret talked, Lady Laurinel moved about the room, prodding pillows, looking with disapproval at the cold hearth, and occasionally casting an indecipherable glance at Eleret.

When the story ended, Drioren gave Eleret a wide smile. "That was *good.* Do you know any more stories?"

"Yes, but I am not going to tell them to you now," Eleret said.

"Freelady Salven wants to rest before dinner," Lady Laurinel added. "And you are—"

The door opened, revealing the gaunt woman. She carried an enormous silver washbasin and jug, and she had a towel draped over one arm. She marched in and set her burden on the table below the window, then nodded stiffly to Lady Laurinel. "If there's nothing more, my lady, the young lord and I will leave you now."

"When you pass the waiting hall, send someone here to

lay a fire," Laurinel said, waving at the empty fireplace. "At once."

"I'd rather be left to myself," Eleret said quickly. The room was cool, but not unpleasantly so, and she had been looking forward to having some time alone to think.

"Then that will be all, Jakella. I will come and see you tonight, Drioren, before your bedtime."

The gaunt woman gave Lady Laurinel a sour look, as if she did not approve of giving a child so much attention. She held out her hand and Drioren rose obediently and went slowly to her side. Just before they reached the door, the boy turned. "Thank you, Freelady. Thank you, Mother."

"You're welcome, Drioren," Eleret said, noting that he had not said exactly what he was thanking her for. He was probably hoping to pry another story out of his grim-faced nurse.

As the door closed, Lady Laurinel turned to Eleret. "My thanks as well, Freelady Salven. My son can be overly persistent at times."

"I thought he behaved very well."

"I'll leave you now. Dinner is in an hour; I'll send someone to show you the way." Laurinel smiled. "This old pile has so many levels and cross-corridors that it takes months for new people to learn their way around."

It hadn't seemed that bad to Eleret, but she nodded. There was nothing to gain by contradicting the woman.

"How long will you be staying?" Lady Laurinel went on.

"I'm not sure." One night at the most, but there was no reason to tell Laurinel that, either.

Laurinel nodded understandingly. "I suppose Daner hasn't told you yet. It's just like a man to drag you off to a strange place and then forget to mention how long he expects you to stay. You must try and tie him down after dinner."

"I—" Eleret broke off, not knowing what to say. She didn't want to lie outright, but if she told the woman Daner had nothing to do with her plans, Laurinel was sure to ask again how long Eleret proposed to stay. The last thing Eleret wanted was to give a specific, truthful answer to that question. It was bad enough that everyone here knew she was Cilhar; she didn't want the time of her intended departure to be common knowledge as well. Gossip traveled swiftly, and the three Syaski who had attacked her and Daner that afternoon undoubtedly had friends.

"You needn't speak to him if it makes you uncomfortable," Laurinel said hastily. "It really doesn't matter. I forget sometimes that he's not just my little brother anymore, and of course if you're from the mountains you haven't dealt much with lords."

"True." *And a good thing, too,* Eleret added silently. Had the Ciaronese jumped to this many false conclusions about Tamm? And how had she handled it? But no, Tamm had been on the road with the army, not mingling with the nobility. And the army had gotten her killed. . . . Eleret wrenched her thoughts forcibly back to the conversation.

"I'll speak to Daner myself," Laurinel said. Eleret gave herself a mental order to catch Daner first and remind him to be vague. "Is there anything else you need?" Laurinel went on.

"I can't think of anything."

"Then I'll leave you to your rest." Lady Laurinel moved gracefully across the room. At the door, she paused, one hand on the latch. "I can't help seeing that you haven't brought your traveling cases," she said delicately. "I suppose

— 126 —

Daner was in too much of a hurry to get you here, so I won't ask for more of a reason than that. But if you would like to borrow something to wear tonight . . ."

Eleret barely hesitated. "No, but I thank you for the offer."

"You're sure?" Laurinel said doubtfully. "I'm sure I could find something that would fit you."

"Very sure." She'd had enough difficulty moving in the wide, calf-length skirt she'd been wearing for the last two days; she wasn't about to climb into a straight, floor-length garment that clung closely enough to reveal exactly where she had strapped her knife. Besides, she could hardly slit the pocket of someone else's gown, and after the way things had been going she wanted her weapons easily available, even at a noble family's dinner table.

"As you will have it, then." Laurinel nodded farewell, and the door closed gently behind her.

Eleret breathed a sigh of relief and began stripping off her clothes. She had plenty of time to clean up, and after the fight with the Syaski she needed to do just that. It was a good thing the washbasin was large.

When she untied her sash, it fell to the floor with a muffled thud. *The money from Commander Weziral!* After a few hours, she had grown used to the lumpy weight at her waist, and in the rush of later events she had forgotten it entirely. Well, she had remembered it now. She picked up the sash and tossed it on the bed. As soon as she had finished washing, she would find a better way of carrying it.

To her pleased surprise, the water was lukewarm. Perhaps there were more advantages to living in the city than she had supposed. Or perhaps it was living in a noble household that was the advantage, although she wasn't sure that warm wash water would make up for wearing clothes one couldn't move in and tiptoeing around spindly chairs all day. She finished washing and turned back to the bed.

The knot had tightened around Weziral's two pouches. When she sat on the edge of the bed to work it free, pillows puffed up around her. She made a face and smoothed them down, then began patiently pulling at the folds and bunches in the sash. In a few moments, the knot came loose and the bags tumbled onto the bed.

Eleret picked up the nearest pouch. This was the reason Tamm had left the mountains. "One last time," she had said, and she had been right, though not in the way they all had hoped. Eleret stared bitterly at the pouch, feeling a strong urge to open the window and throw it as far out as she could manage, as if by casting away the money she could bring her mother back. But Tamm was dead, *dead*, and wasting the coin would not bring her back. Eleret's fist clenched around the pouch, and with all her might she threw it against the stone wall.

The impact split the canvas, and a glittering shower of coins rang down the wall to roll across the rug. Eleret stared in disbelief, then dove off the bed and scooped up the nearest. She had not been mistaken. The coin was gold.

Eleret glanced at the door, wondering whether anyone had heard the noise. Probably not; the walls were stone and the door was thick. She stood up and walked back to the bed. With shaking hands, she reached for the second pouch, loosened the ties, and poured its contents onto the pillows. More gold. Everyone knew the Emperor was generous with his soldiers, but this? It *had* to be more than ordinary army pay, even with combat wages and death fees added in. She frowned fiercely, forcing herself to think. Hadn't Commander Weziral said something about special assignments?

Slowly, Eleret raised her head and stared sightlessly into the fireplace.

"Oh, Ma," she whispered. "What were you *doing?*"

The fireplace did not answer. After a time, Eleret bent and began methodically picking up the scattered coins. The pouch was beyond repair, but she still had the empty leather bag Tamm had used for her raven's-feet. She piled the coins on the table next to the washbasin, then went over to the kit bags to get out the pouch. The practical tasks made her feel more like herself.

As she dropped the coins one by one into the pouches, she frowned. She couldn't bring herself to leave this much money lying unguarded in her room while she went off to dinner. Not that she mistrusted Daner's family particularly, but all her life she had been trained to keep whatever was truly important *with* her. If a raiding party broke through or a snowslide threatened, there was seldom time to pack, or even to snatch up a pouch or kit. Certainly no one had time to go back for things. Of course, at home "truly important" meant weapons and tools, mostly, with clothes and water and food next on the list. Money was scarce, but not important; other things were harder to replace. *This* money, however, was different. Tamm Salven had died to earn it, and Eleret was not returning home without it.

But if she kept it with her, what was she to do with it? Eleret looked at the brown skirt lying on the bed and frowned. She couldn't put the pouches in her pockets without making it difficult to get at her weapons, and knotting them into her sash was awkward, uncomfortable, and obvious. If she wedged them into the tops of her boots, they would quickly rub her legs raw. On the other hand . . .

Eleret went back to her kit and began pulling clothes out of it. In two minutes she had donned her green homespun leggings and her good linen shirt. The money pouches went into the deep inner pockets of her deerskin vest, and two rows of raven's-feet slid under thin leather thongs sewed across the front of each shoulder, making lines of deadly decorations. Her knife hung at her right side in Tamm's embroidered sheath. After a moment's thought, she slipped Tamm's death-braid into her inner vest pocket as well. Pulling on her boots, she felt better than she had in several days. She hadn't realized just how irritating that skirt had been.

As she leaned over to pluck the skirt off the bed, her hair fell forward across her shoulder. She glanced down and smiled suddenly. Braiding her hair wouldn't take long, and she'd gone this far already; she might as well continue. She reached for her kit and the colored cord in the bottom.

As she finished the last knot, someone knocked at the door. When she opened it, the boy outside had his fist raised for another knock, and he fell back a pace in embarassment. "F-Freelady Salven?" he stammered. "I'm to escort you down to the family."

"Fine," Eleret said. Habit made her glance around the room one last time, but she already had everything she wanted to take with her. Her weapons were ready, the money was safe in her pockets, and the raven ring still circled her index finger. She opened the door wider and stepped out.

The boy's eyes widened as he looked at her, and he hesitated visibly. Finally he said, "Uh—you're going to dinner, Freelady."

"I know."

"Um—you're going like *that*? Freelady?"

"Unless you refuse to show me how to get there."

From the look on his face, the boy was considering doing just that. Duty, or perhaps fear of the consequences, held him to his task. He swallowed hard and said, "This way, Freelady."

The boy led Eleret back to the long cluttered room she and Daner had first entered. Daner, his mother, and his three sisters were already there, along with a tall, bearded man whose wavy gray hair looked as if it might once have been the same rich blond as Daner's. They all turned as Eleret entered, and the women froze, wide-eyed. Daner closed his eyes briefly, then opened them and stepped forward. "Father, I would like to present Freelady Eleret Salven. Freelady, my father, Lord Breann tir Vallaniri."

"Welcome, Freelady." Lord tir Vallaniri's demeanor was perfectly correct, and the expression on his face was polite, but Eleret thought she saw a twinkle in his eye.

"I thank you for your courtesy," Eleret said. "May your welcome bring strength to us both."

The twinkle grew more pronounced. "And defeat to our enemies, yours and mine," he said, to Eleret's surprise. "Daner has been telling me about you, Freelady. I can see he didn't cover more than half of it."

"I don't doubt it," Eleret replied. "It was a busy afternoon."

Lord tir Vallaniri's eyebrows rose. "*Was* it." He smiled. "The three of us will have to have a long talk after dinner."

Daner caught Eleret's eye and rolled his eyes, while his sisters exchanged glances of astonishment. Beside them, Lady tir Vallaniri gave her husband a long look, then shook her head in resignation.

"I'll be happy to talk to you," Eleret said. "But I don't think I can add much to whatever Daner's already told you." *Or rather, there are a lot of things I don't want to mention.* She had better get to Daner soon, and make sure he understood.

"As you will have it," Lord tir Vallaniri said, nodding. "I'm still curious to hear your side of the story, however. Until then, Freelady." He turned to Daner, and the women moved forward to surround Eleret.

"What a remarkable . . . costume," Lady Raqueva said in a low voice. "And how very daring of you to wear it."

Her voice was not quite low enough; Lady tir Vallaniri heard her and frowned. "Raqueva! Freelady Salven is our guest."

"Yes, and it's a good thing we haven't any others to-night!" Lady Metriss said. "We'd be the talk of the city. I thought you were going to make sure she had something decent to wear, Lauri."

"Lady Laurinel offered me the loan of a gown," Eleret said. "I declined."

"I understand your pride, Freelady," Daner's mother said, and hesitated as if deciding how best to phrase what she wanted to say next.

Eleret gave her no opportunity to continue. "Oh, it wasn't that," she said. "It's because of Lady Metriss here."

"Me?" The girl raised her chin haughtily. "That makes no sense, which I suppose is about what we can expect from—"

"Metriss." Lady tir Vallaniri did not raise her voice at all, but her daughter subsided abruptly.

"But you said you wanted to see what people were wearing in the mountains this spring," Eleret said to Lady Metriss with a bland smile. "This is it."

Lady Metriss's mouth fell open. She looked, Eleret thought, very like a young dog that had poked its nose into a ground squirrel's den, intending to bite the squirrel, and was surprised and hurt when the ground squirrel bit first. Lady tir Vallaniri suppressed a chuckle, while Laurinel smiled and Raqueva gave Eleret a wary look. Before any of them could respond, the door opened once again and Lady Kistran swept in.

"Hasn't Baroja arrived *yet*, Laurenzi? I thought you were going to send someone—" Lady Kistran stopped short, staring at Eleret with an expression of outraged horror. "What in the Emperor's name—"

"Freelady Salven is showing us what's fashionable in the mountains," Lady Raqueva said spitefully.

"Fashionable?"

"It looks very comfortable," Laurinel said suddenly.

"Perhaps it is, for soldiers or guardswomen or women in *trade*," her aunt said with a sniff. "For *ladies*, however—"

"Hello, all! Sorry I'm late, but I hope you'll forgive me," said a new voice in carrying tones.

Eleret turned to look along with everyone else. A young man posed in the far door, head thrown back, eyes half-closed, one arm extended along the frame of the door above his head. A bright blue cloak hung from the arm in graceful folds, displaying a gold-colored lining that looked as if it might be silk. His sword hung carelessly at his left side, and jewels glittered on the pommel and the guard. Remembering Prill's description of the Vallaniri sword-skills and Daner's unexpected competence, Eleret withheld judgment. Jewels could be embedded in Sadorthan steel as well as forge-scrapings.

"Baroja!" Lady Kistran smiled indulgently and stepped forward, her interest in Eleret forgotten. "We've been waiting for you."

TWELVE

Baroja stepped forward and bowed to his mother with studied grace. "I regret that I've inconvenienced you, Mother, but when you hear my news I hope to be forgiven."

"News?" said Raqueva in a tone just short of skepticism.

"I've arranged a treat for us all," Baroja said, sweeping one arm up in a gesture that made his cape swing dangerously close to a vase of flowers on a nearby table. "Now am I forgiven?"

"That depends on what your 'treat' is, Cousin," Daner said dryly.

"Yes, why are you being so mysterious, Baroja?" Metriss said. "What is this treat of yours?"

"A surprise."

"Baroja!" Metriss stamped her foot. "Aunt Kistran, make him tell us what he means."

"Don't tease your cousins, Baroja," Lady Kistran said. "Tell us what your surprise is."

"But it isn't a what," Baroja said with a wide, toothy smile.

"It's who. I've found a Luck-seer; one of the best in Ciaron! And she's promised to come chart the cards for us later on tonight. Now, am I forgiven?"

Daner's female relations were too busy exclaiming with delight to answer him directly. Even Lady tir Vallaniri looked pleased. Eleret wondered why they were all so excited and whether they would expect her to join them. Probably; Baroja's scheme had the sound of something done for amusement after dinner, like a rope-chase or a dice game. She sighed quietly, and resigned herself. She'd have preferred to spend the evening in her room, sharpening her knives and setting her thoughts in order, but she could not insult her hosts by retiring early when there was entertainment planned, even if they had not been the planners.

Daner seemed to agree with Eleret. "My idiot cousin has done it again," he muttered. "I wonder how much *this* notion will cost him?"

"More than he can afford," Lord tir Vallaniri answered in a similar undertone. Raising his voice, he said, "Bring out your Luck-seer, Baroja, and let's have a look at her."

"She isn't here yet, Uncle," Baroja replied. "I told her to come an hour from now, after dinner, since she can't chart while we eat."

"I hope you remembered to warn Bresc," Lord tir Vallaniri said. "I doubt that he'd let her in otherwise."

Baroja looked startled. "He wouldn't? I'd better go tell him, then." He smiled winningly at Raqueva and Metriss. "It wouldn't do to have her sent away after I promised you a treat."

With another bow, he turned and swept back into the stairwell. "Be quick," Lady Kistran called after him. "We've spent enough time waiting for you as it is."

"Yes, Mother." Baroja's words, echoing back from the

stairwell, had the sound of an automatic, meaningless response.

"I think we will go in to dinner now," Lady tir Vallaniri said, waving her daughters toward the door. "Baroja won't be long."

"I have seldom heard more hopeful words spoken with less reason," Daner's father said. "But by all means let us go in to dinner." He nodded at Lady Kistran, then made a half-bow and held out his left hand, palm up, to his wife. Lady tir Vallaniri smiled and covered his hand with her own. Together, they walked slowly down the hall toward the door. Lady Kistran looked after them with a sour expression.

"Eleret!" Daner whispered urgently.

Eleret turned, hating him for one brief, irrational moment because *his* mother was here, walking handfast with her husband through the rooms of her home. The moment passed, and Eleret realized that he was holding his left hand out to her in the same gesture his father had just used. Surprise kept her motionless for an instant, and Daner's brows contracted.

"Come *on*, Eleret," he said in a low voice, his lips barely moving.

Still wondering, Eleret laid her right hand on his. As she did, Lady Kistran gave an audible sniff and turned. "Daner," she said in a commanding tone, "I— Oh."

Daner's fingers closed convulsively around Eleret's as his aunt spoke, and suddenly Eleret understood. Lady Kistran's expression grew even more sour than before, but she made no comment as Daner led Eleret down the hall after his parents and sisters.

As they drew away, out of hearing, Eleret looked at Daner and raised her eyebrows. "What was that about?"

"Family," Daner said. "Aunt Kistran is in one of her

— 136 —

moods, and I didn't want to spend dinner coddling her. Which I won't have to do if I take you in instead of her. No matter how irritated she's feeling, she'd never humiliate a guest by demanding the place you'd already claimed."

Maybe not, thought Eleret, *but I'll bet she'd have taken it without a second thought if I* hadn't *already claimed it.* Which explained why Daner had been in such a hurry. Eleret sighed, wishing she knew more of Ciaronese ways. Or was it knowledge of noblemen's ways that she needed? Well, it was only for one evening, and if she annoyed Daner's family out of ignorance, it would not matter much once she was back in the mountains.

Dinner began awkwardly. When Eleret and Daner had entered the room, Daner's sisters already occupied three of the four chairs placed around the center of the long table. As they approached, Lady Raqueva looked over her shoulder, flushed, and leaned sideways to whisper something to Lady Metriss. An instant later, they rose and moved to the lower end of the table. Lady Metriss sniffed audibly as she passed. Daner, apparently oblivious to the undercurrents, seated Eleret in the chair Raqueva had just vacated and took Metriss's place himself.

On Eleret's left, Lady tir Vallaniri gave her daughters an approving smile. As if in answer to a signal, Lady Kistran swept in, frowning, and took her seat across the table from her hostess. Lady tir Vallaniri's smile flattened slightly; then she turned to her husband and said calmly, "We are all here except Baroja. Is it your pleasure to begin, my lord?"

"It is my very great pleasure," Lord tir Vallaniri replied, and nodded at an unobtrusive man standing beside a side table heavily laden with covered platters. The man bowed.

Picking up the nearest of the platters, he removed the cover and carried the dish to Lord tir Vallaniri. Lord tir Vallaniri examined the contents, then served first his wife, then Lady Kistran, and finally himself.

The man bowed again and moved to Daner's side. To Eleret's surprise and annoyance, Daner proceeded to spoon some of the contents—a pile of finger-length fish that had apparently been fried whole—onto her plate. He did the same for his sisters, then served himself. The servant returned the platter to the side table, chose another, and repeated the sequence. While he made his slow way along the table, a dark-haired girl entered with a pitcher and poured wine into the pewter goblets that stood in front of every place.

The number of dishes and the amount of food amazed Eleret. There were chunks of white fish wrapped in dark green leaves, thick slices of well-browned meat, fresh bread with herb-flavored oil to dip it in, and a whole tray of small birds stuffed with grain. Most of the food was lukewarm, but she still had to remind herself several times not to eat too much. A large meal would make her sluggish.

Daner's sisters chattered almost constantly, but to Eleret's relief they did not seem to care whether or not she joined them. Lady tir Vallaniri, on Eleret's left, directed an occasional remark to her, as if to let her know that she was not being overlooked. None of the comments required a response, and Eleret did not give any beyond a nod of recognition. Eating without bumping elbows with Lady tir Vallaniri was difficult enough; doing so while trying to talk sensibly without giving away too much would be next to impossible. Fortunately, the wine was watered, but even so Eleret drank sparingly.

True to Lord tir Vallaniri's prediction, Baroja did not appear until everyone had almost finished their first servings. He had disposed of his cloak, but he walked as though he still wore it. Eleret could almost see it swirl behind him as he progressed from the door to the dinner table. Daner's sisters pounced on him at once, firing questions at him like a company of archers.

"Tell us about the Luck-seer, Baroja! How soon will she be here, do you think?"

"Will she be able to chart our cards right away after dinner, or will we have to wait?"

"Can she do all of us, or only one or two?"

"Will she let us watch each other's chartings?"

"Where did you find her? Is she very good?"

Laughing, Baroja threw his hands up in a gesture of surrender. "One at a time, if it please you, ladies! And remember that I haven't eaten yet."

"And whose fault is that?" Daner muttered as Baroja took the seat across from him and smoothed an invisible crease from his sleeve. The dark-haired girl materialized immediately to fill Baroja's goblet.

"Have some fish," Raqueva said, signaling the man by the side table. "How soon can we begin?"

"Not until I'm done with dinner," Baroja said with a smile. "Thank you, Cousin."

"Oh, Baroja, don't be difficult," Metriss said. "You can talk while you eat. Tell us about the Luck-seer!"

"Such enthusiasm astounds me," Lord tir Vallaniri put in, taking another piece of fish. "I commend you, Baroja. I haven't seen Metriss so lively since she was four."

Metriss flushed. Across from Eleret, Lady Laurinel frowned. "You shouldn't tease Riss, Father. We're all excited. It isn't everyone who can have her cards charted by someone who really understands how to do it."

"I stand corrected."

"What is 'charting the cards'?" Eleret whispered to Daner as Baroja finished filling his plate.

Daner looked at her in surprise. "You've never heard about charting the cards?" he said in a normal tone.

Heads turned along the table, and Eleret sighed. "No, I haven't. What does it mean?"

"It's difficult to explain," Metriss said. "Baroja—"

"Let your cousin eat in peace, Riss," Lady tir Vallaniri said. "You have the rest of the evening to question him."

"Does that mean you've never had your cards charted?" Raqueva asked Eleret in a speculative tone.

"If I had, I might know what all of you were talking about."

"It's a variety of divinatory magic," Daner said. "Very popular for predicting the future, in spite of its inaccuracy and lack of clarity."

"Inaccuracy!" Metriss's half-shriek of outrage drew a disapproving frown from her aunt. "What about Sivelin's brother? What about Vanery and the horse? What about—"

"Metriss." Lady tir Vallaniri's voice was not loud, but it penetrated her daughter's stream of complaints like a fire-arrow penetrating fog. Metriss broke off, scowling petulantly.

"Riss is very firm in her opinions," Laurinel put in. "You should not tease her, Daner." Despite her words, her eyes were on Eleret as she spoke, and her tone was apologetic.

"It only makes me more curious," Eleret said. Since it seemed that she would have to join in this card-charting, she might as well find out what she was in for. "How does this card magic work?"

"Resonance and imaging," Daner replied. "The pattern of the cards themselves sets up a weak charm over a limited area, so in theory it doesn't even take a magician to use them."

"I presume that is the reason for their popularity," Lord tir Vallaniri put in, looking interested.

"Yes, but without a magician to reinforce the spell, it's a matter of luck whether or not the focus is the one intended," Daner said. "Hence the inaccuracy."

Raqueva gave her brother a sharp look, then said in a bored tone, "And the lack of clarity?"

"It's part of the same problem. Anyone can lay out a pattern of cards, but interpreting it correctly takes knowledge and skill. The knowledge is rare enough; skill is even more so."

"But, Daner, that's the whole point," Baroja said. He smiled winningly as everyone looked at him.

"What is?" Daner asked wearily when Baroja did not continue.

"Why, hiring a Luck-seer, of course." Baroja sat back, his expression smug, as if he had just made an unarguable point. "You see?"

"No."

"Really, Daner!" Lady Kistran frowned at him. "Clearly, Baroja's Luck-seer has both knowledge and skill, or she would not be earning coin by charting cards. How did you find her, Baroja?"

"Oh, one of Toricar's Trader friends presented her to me this afternoon," Baroja said. "And if anyone knows about charting cards, it's a Trader."

"Traders are also remarkably good at spotting an easy catch," Lord tir Vallaniri remarked.

"I think it was very clever of Baroja to hire her," Metriss said pugnaciously.

"And very kind of him to think of us," Raqueva put in.

"It was nothing," Baroja said modestly. "The moment I saw her, I knew you'd want her to do your cards. And knowing that, how could I *not* beg her to come?"

"Will your Luck-seer have time to chart all of us?" Lady tir Vallaniri asked. "We seem to be more numerous than usual tonight."

"I don't see why not," Baroja replied. "She said she'd stay the whole evening."

"This Luck-seer of yours must be a remarkably obliging woman," Lord tir Vallaniri said. "I am becoming eager to meet her."

"Does that mean that you'll have your cards charted this time, Father?" asked Laurinel.

"No, it does not."

"Daner will, though," Metriss said. "Won't you, Daner?"

"Only if you insist," Daner told her. "I'm not interested in trickery."

"Freelady Salven must certainly have her cards charted," Raqueva put in, giving Eleret an indecipherable look. "Especially since she's never done it before."

"Yes, of course you must, Freelady," Laurinel said. "I hope the Luck-seer will let us watch. Charting someone's cards for the very first time is more involved than renewing a chart; it would be so interesting."

"As you will have it," Eleret said with a mental grimace. There'd be no getting out of it now, but then, there had never really been much chance of avoiding the card-charting. She could only hope it wouldn't last too long, or be too dull. Daner's attitude was not exactly encouraging.

"And Aunt Kistran must have a turn as well," Raqueva said. "After all, we wouldn't have a Luck-seer at all if Baroja hadn't brought one."

"By that logic, Baroja should go first." Daner's voice was full of mischief. "What do you say, Cousin? She's your Luck-seer."

"Oh, Daner!" Metriss turned the corners of her mouth down. "Baroja brought her here for *us*."

"Very true," Baroja said. "I'll go last."

"That hardly seems fair," Laurinel objected, frowning slightly.

"Well, but if Aunt Kistran takes the first turn—" Raqueva began.

"I do not intend to have my cards charted at all," Lady Kistran announced.

"Don't you?" Lady tir Vallaniri said with mild surprise. "I shall certainly have mine done. I find it interesting to watch, especially when they get everything wrong."

"It is an amusement for younger folk, Laurenzi," Kistran replied. "I will be quite content to listen to their tales as they come back from their charting."

Daner leaned toward Eleret and said softly, "What she means is that she doesn't want *her* chart chewed over in public. She'll lecture everyone else on what their charts really mean, then corner the Luck-seer privately later on, wait and see."

Eleret nodded without comprehension, and let the conversation flow on without her. The meal ended at last, and the Vallaniris withdrew from the eating room, leaving the servers to clear things up. Eleret trailed after Daner's sisters and his cousin and his aunt, wishing she could slip quietly away and escape to her room. But even if she had been lost to all sense of her obligations to her hosts, she could not have done it; Daner and his parents were right behind her.

Baroja led them back to the long cluttered hall where

they had met before dinner. A servant stood at the far end, waiting patiently; when he saw Baroja, he came forward and whispered something to him.

"Bring her in at once!" Baroja said.

The servant bowed and crossed back to the stairwell door. Baroja smiled broadly at his relatives.

"The best card-charter in Ciaron has arrived!" he announced. He turned and waved with perfect timing as the far door opened. "Mother, Aunt, Cousins, allow me to present Luck-seer Jonystra Nirandol."

THIRTEEN

Eleret had to force her face to remain blank as Daner's mother and sisters moved happily forward to greet Jonystra. *How* had the woman managed this? And why had she bothered? Unless she was a fool, she must know that Eleret would be on her guard. And not just Eleret; Daner, too, watched Jonystra with a face like stone.

While Baroja beamed at his cousins, Eleret slipped across to Daner's side. "Daner," she said in a low voice, "get hold of yourself, or everyone will know something's wrong."

"How did that *creyuda* get a line on Baroja?" Daner said in a savage undertone. "I don't know whether to wring his neck or hers!"

"Try it with either, and I'm gone. If you make a scene—"

"Your aunt and your sisters will demand to know the reason," Lord tir Vallaniri said from behind Eleret.

Without thinking, Eleret spun, one hand on her dagger's hilt. She took control of her reflexes in time to keep from drawing it and cursed herself mentally for an incompetent fool. Bad enough to lose track of someone, even if he was not an enemy, but to let herself be startled into such a strong response was inexcusable. "Exactly my point," she said as calmly as she could.

Lord tir Vallaniri raised an eyebrow at her. "I've been tempted to wring Baroja's neck myself, now and again, but what is it about his companion that provokes such a response in you?"

"That woman—the so-called Luck-seer Nirandol—followed us here," Daner said. "How and why, I don't know, and it would be for Eleret to say even if I did, but I don't like it. Demons take Baroja for bringing her in!"

Eleret was positive that Jonystra hadn't actually followed them, but then, she wouldn't have needed to. Jonystra had heard Daner's name at the inn; tracing a well-known nobleman could not have been hard. And she'd had most of the afternoon to arrange a way of getting inside the Vallaniri household. However she had done it, the result was what mattered.

"Baroja has demonstrated a certain aptitude for innocently doing whatever will cause the greatest inconvenience to whomever he is with," Lord tir Vallaniri said in a slow, thoughtful tone. "It's practically the boy's only talent; I'm pleased to see it hasn't deserted him."

"Pleased?" Daner gave his father a skeptical look.

"Everyone should be good at something."

"Teach him to sleep well." Daner glanced toward Jonystra, then closed his eyes as if the sight hurt him. "Loren's Curse, how are we going to get her to leave?"

"Unless she does something extremely foolish, such as trying to stick a knife into Freelady Salven or kidnapping one of your sisters, you can't," Lord tir Vallaniri said. "Not without mortally offending Baroja and your aunt."

"I don't think Jonystra's a danger to you and yours," Eleret told Daner. "I'm the one she's after." Though she still could not see what Jonystra hoped to accomplish. She might secure a few minutes alone with Eleret, but there wasn't much she could do with them. Unless . . . "Daner, how likely is it that Jonystra knows some magic?"

Daner looked startled. "What makes you think she might?"

"You said at dinner that charting cards works best when a magician reinforces the spell. If she's as good at it as Baroja claims—"

"She probably isn't any better than Metriss and her silly friends," Daner said, frowning. "Baroja believes every seller's speech he hears in the midtown market."

"But you can't be sure."

"No."

Eleret shrugged. She had suspected as much, but it had been worth asking. She started to frame another question, then stopped. A wiry man of medium height had followed Jonystra quietly into the room, carrying a large black-and-red lacquered box with an ornate brass lock. Though he wore no visible weapon, he moved with the wary confidence of an experienced warrior. His thin sandy hair had been oiled flat; combined with a sharp jaw and a face that seemed all flat surfaces and sharp angles, it made his head look like a skull.

"Now what?" Daner said under his breath.

As if she had heard him from across the room, Jonystra glanced back and saw the new arrival. "Ah, Mobrellan!" she said, smiling graciously at the wiry, skull-faced man. "You have all that we shall need?"

The man nodded.

Jonystra turned to Baroja. "Then, my lord, will you say where we are to chart the cards?"

"Where do you want them, Aunt?" Baroja asked Lady tir Vallaniri.

"That depends. What will you require for your work, Luck-seer?" Lady tir Vallaniri said.

"A small room, where we can be private, with a table, so"—Jonystra demonstrated the proper size with her hands—"and two chairs."

"Only two?" Lady Metriss said in tones of deep disappointment. "Can't we watch each other's cards?"

"The influences are clearer if only one questioner is present at a time," Jonystra replied. "If you wish for a true foreseeing, I must chart each of you separately. Afterward, you may discuss the results as much as you choose."

"Why don't you let her use that little room two doors down?" Baroja said to Daner's mother. "The one with all the books."

"No," said Lord tir Vallaniri, raising his voice slightly to carry across to Baroja. "You may have talent, Nephew, but I am not compelled to allow you to exercise it."

Baroja looked over with a puzzled expression. "Thank you, Uncle. What talent did you mean?"

"Never mind. Your Luck-seer can work in the wall chamber."

"But the other room—"

"Is my study. No."

"Oh, very well. This way, Luck-seer Nirandol. How long will it take you and your porter to set up your things?" The closing door cut off Baroja's voice, and Daner's aunt and sisters sorted themselves into chairs to wait for his return. Lord tir Vallaniri escorted Eleret over to join them, then drew Daner aside for a brief conference.

Eleret had no objection to being abandoned. She listened to the girls' chatter with less than half her attention, while the rest of her mind reviewed her previous encounters with Jonystra, trying to see patterns in her actions and words. Clearly, the woman was intelligent, and she seemed to favor indirect methods. She was persistent, too; every time Eleret avoided her, she found a new way to approach her again. Her movements and her dress were not those of a fighter, but that might not mean much. Jonystra Nirandol had as many faces as a shapeshifter: traveling collector of ancient objects; hopeful, friendly dinner companion; well-born flirt; experienced card-charter and Luck-seer. Possibly she was a sneak thief or a wizard as well, though Eleret had no proof that it was Jonystra who had searched her room at the Broken Harp or that she could work magic.

Better to be prepared for the rock that doesn't fall than to be hit on the head by the one you didn't expect. Her mother's voice echoed through Eleret's memory, its tone warm and chiding at the same time, patiently repeating the lesson that had since become an ingrained habit. Eleret choked. *Go away, Ma, and let me concentrate*, she thought, although she knew it was her memories that were the problem, not her mother. Tamm Salven's body had been burned six weeks before; the greatest wizard born could not have raised her blank-eyed corpse from ashes, nor summoned her spirit after so long a lapse of time.

The recollection steadied Eleret, and she forced her mind back to Jonystra. No matter how good a thief Jonystra was—if she were a thief—Eleret doubted that she could steal the raven ring from her finger or her money and other valuables from the inner pockets of her vest. Not without knocking Eleret unconscious first, at any rate, and to do that she would need both surprise and fighting skill. Or magic. Eleret frowned involuntarily, then shrugged. She couldn't do anything about magic except be ready to dodge, assuming dodging would help. *What you can't counter, block; what you can't block, avoid; what you can't avoid, don't fret yourself skinny over.*

Eleret shivered, wondering if the wine at dinner had been as weak as she'd assumed. Her mind did not normally play such unpleasant tricks. What had she been thinking of? Magic. Jonystra. What *could* she do if Jonystra really was a magician?

An arrow kills a wizard as dead as anyone else. Least it does if you're a halfway good shot. This time the remembered voice was a deep male growl, and Eleret almost smiled. She didn't have her bow, but she had plenty of raven's-feet and two well-balanced and finely honed knives. If it came to a fight, she could manage.

"Thanks, Pa," she whispered, then shook her head at her foolishness. Fortunately, Daner's sisters were deeply involved in their discussion, and had not noticed.

"But who's going to be the first one charted?" Metriss asked as Eleret brought her attention back to the conversation.

"I think we should let Freelady Salven go first," Laurinel said. "She's never had her cards charted before, and she's a guest."

Lady tir Vallaniri nodded. "An excellent idea, my dear. Freelady—"

"No, thank you," Eleret said quickly. "I'd rather wait. Let someone else take the first turn." She was tempted to refuse altogether, as Lady Kistran had earlier, but that would be cowardly. Besides, how else would she find out what Jonystra was planning?

"Do the cards make you nervous?" Raqueva said, watching Eleret from under half-lowered eyelids as if she knew exactly what Eleret had been thinking. "Or do you lack belief in them?"

"No," Eleret said. "I'd just prefer to wait." She shifted uneasily, hoping the spindly chair would not give way beneath her. It *felt* secure enough, and it didn't creak or wobble, but the legs still didn't look strong enough to stake spring peas.

"Well, if you're quite sure, Freelady, I think Laurinel had better be the first," Lady tir Vallaniri said. "She is the eldest, after all. We can discuss the rest of the order while she is having her cards done."

Metriss scowled, but her mother's tone forbade argument. When Baroja returned a moment later and announced that the Luck-seer was ready, Laurinel rose and went to meet him. Baroja smiled, offered her his hand, and escorted her out of the room. As soon as the door closed behind them, the remaining ladies returned to their debate on the order in which they should have their cards charted.

Listening in silence to the polite bickering around her, Eleret concluded that the dispute was not really about cards. Lady tir Vallaniri kept her comments to a minimum, but Raqueva, Metriss, and Lady Kistran maneuvered for verbal advantage with the skill of long practice. Daner, who had finished his conversation with his father and come over to join them, seemed to find the procedure amusing. Several times, he dropped an innocent-sounding remark into the conversation that gave new energy to the flagging debate. Finally, Lady tir Vallaniri asked him pointedly when *he* wished to have his cards read. Daner laughed and disclaimed any desire for a chart, but from then on he made no more provocative comments.

By the time Baroja and Laurinel returned, everything was settled. Raqueva and Metriss would take the next two turns, followed by Eleret, Lady tir Vallaniri, Daner, and Baroja.

Lady Kistran continued to maintain that she did not wish to have her cards charted, however skilled the Luck-seer. Her determination was sorely tested when Laurinel reentered the room, her face radiant and her mouth full of praise for Jonystra's skills.

"She said that Domori—Lord Trantorino—will be home soon, and with great success," Laurinel told them happily.

"There's a first time for everything," Lady Kistran muttered, loudly enough for everyone to hear.

"Oh, Aunt!" Raqueva rose and gave Laurinel a quick hug. "Don't mind her, Lauri. And don't forget anything; when I get back, you're going to have to repeat everything you've told them."

Laurinel smiled, and Raqueva left with Baroja. Frowning slightly, Eleret gazed after them. Then she shook her head. Raqueva was a tangle she didn't have time to comb straight. Best to concentrate on Jonystra and her cards, at least for the present.

Fortunately, Metriss was eager to hear all the details of Laurinel's experience, and she flung new questions at her sister almost before Laurinel had time to answer the old ones. Much of the story was obscure to Eleret, for she was unfamiliar with the cards and their meanings and no one stopped to explain them. She had to figure them out from the conversation. It didn't help when Lady Kistran began arguing about the interpretation of Laurinel's chart.

"The Eight of Stones is for *completion*," she said flatly. "It doesn't always mean *success*. I think you're too optimistic, Laurinel, as usual."

"But with the Lady of Shells supporting the Eight—" Metriss began.

Kistran shook her head. "The Lady is one of the least

powerful of the Ruling Cards in the suit of Shells. Now, if it had been the *Sorceress* of Shells, or the Lady of *Flames* . . ."

"It's not the power of the individual card that counts," Laurinel objected. "It's the way it relates to the rest of the cards in the chart."

"Look at the rest of your cards, then," Kistran said with a small sniff. "Only one Major Trump in your whole chart, and that was Silence. And your Minors! The Mountain, Despair, and Taxes! That says it all, as far as I'm concerned."

"The Mountain is a good card," Metriss said uncertainly. "At least, it can be."

"And Despair was reversed," Laurinel added. "And Taxes was in the quarter of Past Opposition. You *can't* pull bits and pieces out of a chart and expect to make any sense of them, Aunt."

"Or rather, you can make anything you like of them," Daner put in. "All you have to do is pick the right bits and pieces. Or the wrong ones."

Laurinel gave Daner a look of gratitude. "Yes, that's exactly what I was trying to say."

"Nonsense. If you want to get the most out of a chart, you must look at *all* the relationships," Kistran said. "You must—"

The door at the far end of the room opened, and Baroja and Raqueva came in. Metriss jumped to her feet at once. "It's my turn now; let's go, Baroja."

"There's no need to rush," Baroja said. He relinquished Raqueva's hand and brushed at an invisible speck on his sleeve. "The Luck-seer has to clear the influences or something between each chart. At least, that's what she said."

Daner frowned. "She did? Are you sure? Baroja, exactly what did she say?"

"I told you," Baroja said in an injured tone. "Something about clearing influences. It's what took us so long."

"Baroja—"

"If you really want to know, Daner, I'll ask when I get there," Metriss said. "Come on, Baroja."

Baroja bowed with a flourish and held out his hand. Smiling, Metriss took it and swept out of the room. Daner looked after them, still frowning. No one besides Eleret seemed to notice his reaction. Raqueva sat down and immediately asked Laurinel about her chart, giving Lady Kistran the chance to repeat her gloomy interpretations while Lady tir Vallaniri watched indulgently.

The new conversation was even more incomprehensible to Eleret than the previous one had been, though she noted that Raqueva chose not to describe her chart for her aunt to explain. Instead, Raqueva guided the discussion into the realm of theory, and the argument quickly became abstract. It reminded Eleret of the talk at Raken's place on the rare quiet summer evenings: first would come a comment about a specific battle; next, a discussion of one commander's tactics, which would develop into an analysis of the strategic decisions that had led to the battle, until finally the argument drifted into a theoretical discussion that ranged freely over wars and centuries, until the cook-fire dwindled to coals and starlight frosted the mountain peaks with silver. She wished Raken were with her now, in Ciaron. His good sense would be as useful as his combat skills.

Eleret's reflections were interrupted by the return of Baroja and Metriss. The girl wore a self-satisfied expression, and lost no time in explaining it. "I am going to be one of the Empress's ladies, and marry a man of great influence and power!"

"How impressive," said Raqueva. "No wonder you look so pleased. Do you have any idea how long it will be before all this happens?"

"Very soon," Metriss said, her smile growing. "The Four of Flames was right next to my crown card."

"That doesn't necessarily mean anything for the long run," Lady Kistran said. "In fact, the Fours usually—"

"A moment, Mother, if it please you," Baroja broke in. "I do apologize for interrupting, but better now than when you're in the midst of an explanation. Freelady Salven, you're next, I think. If you will join me . . . ?" He held out his hand in a graceful, demanding gesture.

As Eleret rose to her feet, Daner stepped forward and bowed to Baroja. "No, no, Cousin, you've done your duty for the evening. Freelady Salven is *my* guest; I'll escort her, and let you join the conversation here."

"Very proper," Lady Kistran said, nodding. "Come and sit down, Baroja."

"You are too kind," Baroja said to Daner. "Fair breezes turn your cards, Freelady." He bowed again and crossed to his mother's side.

Eleret laid her hand on Daner's and accompanied him to the far door. As soon as they were out of the room, she let her arm drop and turned to face him. "What's wrong?"

"If I knew, I'd have put a stop to this nonsense when Raqueva came back," Daner said. "But there's nothing I can sink a hook in, just a feeling that you'd be better off with me standing reserve in the hall than Baroja."

"It was that business about 'clearing the influences,' wasn't it? What does that mean?"

"Nothing, probably." Daner frowned and began pacing along the hall. "She could be just repeating a phrase she's heard, or Baroja may have mixed up what she told him with what little he knows of magic. But if she isn't, and if he didn't, then you may be right about Jonystra after all."

"You mean she's a magician?"

"Maybe."

"Can't you *tell*?"

Daner looked at her in exasperation. "Can you tell just by looking at someone whether he's a warrior?"

"Mostly." Eleret had to smile at Daner's expression. "It's in the way people move."

"Well, can you tell a healer from a scholar or a judge, then? Or a carter from a wheelwright or a sawyer? Magic isn't something that marks you out for all the world to see and wonder at. The only way to spot a wizard is to observe him just after he's done a spell, when the residue of the magic he's been using is still clinging to him."

"Or catch him in the middle."

Daner nodded. "So I simply don't know about Jonystra. I thought that if you didn't want to risk . . . whatever, we could just stand here for a while and then go back. I can tell you enough about the cards to get you past Aunt Kistran."

"Maybe." Eleret frowned, considering. How great was the risk, really? Jonystra had never actually *done* anything but talk. Still, it might be better to take the raven ring off before she went in— No, it was safer where it was. Nothing Jonystra could say would coax the ring from Eleret's finger, and if it did come to a fight, the Luck-seer wouldn't get far against a Cilhar. On the other hand, if Jonystra could work magic . . . *What you can't counter, block.* "If you're standing outside in the hall, will you know if she starts casting a spell? And can you stop her if you notice?"

"I can probably stop her if I notice, but I won't notice

unless it's a powerful spell. Are you actually thinking of going through with this?"

"Yes. I don't think Jonystra will try anything big or powerful in a nobleman's house, but if she does, you'll have all the excuse you need to question her. Won't you?"

"Of course, but—"

"And she's had other chances to do something small, and she hasn't used them." *What you can't block, avoid.* "Still— Is there some way I can tell if she tries?"

Daner pressed his lips together for a moment, then shook his head. "I doubt it, especially if she's pretending to magic the cards. It takes a trained wizard to tell a really good fake from a very subtle spell."

"If it's that hard, what's the difference? Oh, never mind. If things start to look odd, I'll yell, and you can come in and figure out what's going on." She didn't like having to place so much trust in a Ciaronese, but Daner *was* good in a fight, and from what Prill had said, he knew far more about magic than she did. *What you can't avoid, don't fret yourself skinny over.* Well, she'd done what she could to prepare. "Let's go."

"You're sure this is a good idea?"

"No. I just don't have a better one. Let's *go*, Daner."

"All right." Daner shrugged and held out his hand once more. As soon as Eleret took it, he started briskly down the hall.

FOURTEEN

Baroja had put Jonystra in a narrow chamber along the front wall of the house. To Eleret's secret relief, Daner entered along with her, and his presence gave her an extra moment to evaluate the situation.

Partway across the room, Jonystra Nirandol sat on the near side of a rectangular table. Her skull-faced servant stood in the shadows on the far side of the table, straightening the red cloth that draped it. Eleret could not make out many details, for the light was very bad. Although the chamber was two stories above the street, the windows were not much wider than the cross-shaped arrow slits on the ground floor, and since it was well after sunset, nothing showed through them. No fire burned on the hearth, and none of the lamps were lit; the only illumination came from a lone candle at Jonystra's elbow.

"I bring you your next client, Luck-seer," Daner said, bowing.

"I thank you, my lord," Jonystra replied. She lowered her

eyes, then looked up again with a smile. "It is good to see you again. Both of you."

"I'm pleased you remember me," Daner said. He hesitated, then stepped farther into the room and gave Jonystra his most charming smile. "It inspires me to request a favor."

"A favor?" Jonystra's eyes dropped once more, and the corners of her mouth stiffened slightly, making her smile look as if she had pasted it in place. "What sort of favor?"

"May I observe your charting? I'm interested in different techniques, and I don't get the opportunity to watch a true Luck-seer very often."

Jonystra looked up, plainly startled. "You wish to stay to watch this lady's cards charted?"

"If you'll allow me." Daner bowed again.

"I fear I cannot," Jonystra said, visibly pulling herself together. "You will have opportunities enough when your own cards are charted." She paused. "You do intend to have your cards charted?"

"Of course, but it's difficult to pay close attention to technique when one is personally concerned with the outcome."

"And I would appreciate having Lord Daner's opinion," Eleret put in. It was a good idea; she should have thought of it herself. If they could persuade Jonystra to let Daner stay, she'd be less inclined to try anything and less likely to get away with it if she did.

Jonystra shook her head sadly. "Charting the cards is a delicate business. The presence of another person would reduce the accuracy and—"

"Oh, that's all right." Eleret smiled, hoping Jonystra did not know much about Cilhar, and added, "Without help, I won't remember what you tell me anyway."

Daner gave Eleret a startled look, but fortunately Jonystra was not watching his expression and he recovered quickly. "A good point," he said smoothly. "With my mother and Lady Kistran demanding details from everyone, I can see why you are concerned."

It was Eleret's turn to be puzzled; Daner's mother had not expressed any particular interest in the fine points of the charts. The words seemed to carry some meaning to Jonystra, however, for she frowned uncertainly and glanced across the table at her silent servant. "I'm not sure," she said. "That is, I don't think . . ."

"I venture to say that Luck-seer Nirandol is equal even to so difficult a task as my lord proposes," the skull-faced man said, bending his head respectfully. His voice was deep and mellow, a complete contrast to his appearance, and he spoke with a trace of an accent that Eleret did not recognize, though it seemed vaguely familiar.

Jonystra blinked, as if this was not the response she had been expecting. "Thank you, Mobrellan. We shall try it, then." She smiled at Daner once more and gestured toward the end of the table. "If you will stand there, my lord, you may watch, but do not speak or move suddenly during the charting. It would be distracting for both of us."

"My gracious thanks to you, Luck-seer." Daner, his expression one of admiring interest, took up the position Jonystra had indicated.

"Now, Freelady, if you will sit here, we may begin."

With a twinge of misgiving, Eleret tugged the end of the bench a little farther out, to give herself more room to move, and sat down. As she did, she let her hand brush the hilt of her knife for reassurance.

"Come closer, please," Jonystra said. "You must be able to see the cards, and I must see you."

Eleret slid along the bench. Now her back was to Daner,

and the candle at Jonystra's elbow threw light in her eyes. She could not see Mobrellan, either, but with the width of the table between them she would have plenty of warning if he tried to come at her. Eleret shifted again, as if trying to find a more comfortable position. Better, but not much. She still could not see Mobrellan or Daner, and the candle still made watching Jonystra's face difficult, but at least now she did not have to stare directly into the light each time she looked up from the table.

"Are you ready? Good." Jonystra's voice was soft and soothing. "Think of a question for the cards, something about your future that you wish to know. Don't tell me what your question is, just think about it. Do you understand?"

"Yes." The only questions Eleret could think of at first had nothing to do with the future: What was Jonystra hoping to do? Why were so many people interested in Tamm's kit? Who had told the Syaski who she was and how to find her? Why did the raven ring seem so important, and how many people knew about it? Finally, she settled for wondering what effect the raven ring would have on her future. The way things had been going, it was sure to have some.

"You have your question? Hold it clear in your mind." Jonystra stretched one hand out imperiously. "Mobrellan! The cards."

A white blur appeared in the darkness on the far side of the table and floated toward Jonystra's hand, becoming squarer and more solid-looking as it drew nearer. The effect was impressive; with the candlelight in her eyes, Eleret could barely see Mobrellan's hands deposit the packet in Jonystra's outstretched palm. Jonystra drew her arm back slowly, then turned. "Think once more of your question, and turn back the covering," she said, offering the packet to Eleret. "Be careful not to touch the cards."

White silk slid smooth and cool under Eleret's fingers, and fell away from a stack of cards with gilded edges. Jonystra smiled. "Study the cards that will tell your future and think, for the third time, of your question."

She did not seem to mean that Eleret should hold the cards herself, so Eleret continued to look at them. The top card showed a symmetrical maze of dark red lines on a black background. Bloodred, thought Eleret, like blood on a battlefield, except that spilled blood was never so neatly arranged.

Jonystra's hands moved under the silk that lay between them and the cards. The cards stirred and shifted, separating, turning, and mixing together once more in a pattern as intricate as the maze painted on their backs. As they lifted to glide past each other, Eleret glimpsed fragments of the pictures on their other side: a hand holding a teacup, an outstretched wing, a Shee woman's startled eyes, half a skull. With a start, she remembered that she was supposed to be thinking of her question. *The raven ring,* she reminded herself. *What should I do with the ring?* It wasn't exactly the way she had put it the first time, but Eleret did not really care. If the change confused Jonystra's cards, that was Jonystra's problem.

"Enough." Jonystra pulled the cards back, flipping the silk up to cover them once more. Her eyes were wide, and her breathing was a little fast, as if she had just climbed a steep slope or finished splitting a pine log. Closing her eyes, she bowed her head over the packet.

Eleret darted a look across the table. Mobrellan was a motionless shape, a place where the shadowy gloom thickened into darkness. From the corner of her eye, she saw Daner nod once; then Jonystra raised her head and Eleret's attention snapped back to her.

"Now, Freelady, as I lay out your chart, think for the fourth and final time of the question you would have answered."

As she spoke, Jonystra unfolded the silk and set her fingertips against the top card. Eleret did not see the point of thinking about her question now; it was too late to change the order of the cards, even if thinking could influence the way Jonystra shuffled them. Still, there seemed no harm in following this direction, so once again Eleret concentrated on the raven ring.

"First comes your past, from support to opposition," Jonystra said. She turned the first card face up on the table.

Snow gleamed on the top of a rocky gray mountain. Halfway down, a shadow cut across the stone; a road circled the base of the mountain. Jonystra nodded in satisfaction. "The Mountain is the base of your support; it stands for security, but also for unused potential." She laid another card to the left of the first.

Eleret barely stifled a gasp. A woman warrior with chestnut hair stood proud and wary in the center of the card, a glowing sword in her right hand. At her feet, a white leopard crouched as if preparing to leap at whatever danger faced the two of them, while behind them a curtain of fire blocked their retreat. A second, more careful look told Eleret that the woman's resemblance to her mother was limited to her hair color and profession, but the shock of recognition, however mistaken, stayed with her for a moment longer.

"The Lady of Flames," Jonystra said, oblivious to Eleret's reaction. "Also called the Swordswoman. It is a powerful card, and a good one, but the position it holds is weak. She has helped you in the past, but you cannot expect her to do so in the future."

It's meant to be Mother after all. Eleret swallowed hard and tried to concentrate as Jonystra placed the next card to the left of the Lady. This one looked safer: an empty birdcage hung in a room with stone walls. Brightly colored feathers lay scattered on the floor beneath it.

"The Seven of Feathers. A card of obstacles, in the position of the beginning of obstacles. Temptation and illusion lie in your past."

Again, Jonystra turned up a card. As she laid it in place, completing the row of four, her face paled and Eleret felt the raven ring tighten against her forefinger. The card showed a tall, indistinct form standing beside a long table, on which lay a shattered diamond, a broken feather, a burned-out candle, and a cracked crab shell. It was impossible to tell where the form ended and the shadows around it began; the only clearly visible portion of the figure was its hand, reaching toward the table. A wisp of black smoke trailed from its fingertips.

"The Mage Trump," Jonystra whispered. "The source of opposition, the hidden threat rooted in your past." She glanced up, as if she expected to find the anonymous shape reaching toward her from the shadows. On the far side of the table, Mobrellan shifted. Jonystra raised her chin defiantly and turned back to Eleret. "The Mage is dangerous and powerful, but it—he—is not an *immediate* threat to you. Your other cards will tell us more."

Quickly, Jonystra laid two more cards just above the first two she had set out. "These cards are in the nearer past, though like the Mountain and the Lady of Flames they, too, support your desires. Ah, the Priest of Flames and the Two of Stones. A man of good intent and some potential, and a balance of opposites. Good cards, but not strong. Your recent opposition . . ."

The card was upside down, so it took Eleret a moment to make sense of the picture. A man robed in red stood at the top of a short flight of stone steps. Fire shot from his outstretched hand to a hearth below, sending flames roaring up a chimney. At the foot of the stairs, the ghostly outline of a white cat contemplated the dangling ends of his belt.

"The Mage of Flames, reversed," Jonystra said in a voice that shook slightly. Eleret looked up in time to see her glance across the table once more. "A powerful and intelligent man, who is and will be your strongest opposition." She hesitated, then pressed her lips together and reached for the next card.

Behind her, Eleret felt Daner shift, and then Jonystra laid the final card in the second row. "Three of Shells, reversed. Loss and emotional pain, which may cloud your judgment. Be wary, and think carefully on your decisions."

Jonystra paused, her fingers touching the next card. "The next two rows will tell your future, advising what you should do and what people will help or hinder you. Listen closely, and remember. This is the beginning of your future."

As she spoke, she laid the first card in the next row. She stopped, frowning. Eleret looked at the card: a jester juggling three flaming torches.

"Well?" Eleret said after a moment. "What does it mean?"

"Three of Flames," Jonystra said automatically. "Surprise or unexpected actions. It is . . . an odd position to find such a card."

"Really?" Eleret thought of all the surprises she'd had since she picked up her mother's kit—had it only been that morning? She still didn't understand most of what had happened; it seemed almost reasonable to expect more surprises in the near future. "I don't think so."

"It should not be there," Jonystra said, half to herself. "Perhaps the next— The Demon? No! That isn't right. How—"

Jonystra broke off, her face white and her hands shaking visibly. Simultaneously, the raven ring tightened on Eleret's forefinger, and a sharp prickling sensation ran around the finger below the band. Her left hand dropped to the hilt of her dagger and drew it without conscious thought, just as Daner gave a wordless exclamation and surged forward.

"What do you mean by using spells in my household, Luck-seer?" Daner demanded.

"I can't . . . I'm not . . ." Jonystra swayed where she sat, her eyes fixed on the stack of cards in her hands.

"Luck-seer!" Daner took hold of Jonystra's shoulder and shook her, none too gently. "Explain yourself." His eyes were narrowed in concentration, and the air around him had the faint but unmistakable smell of the high meadows after a thunderstorm. Eleret slid away from the two of them, reaching right-handed for a raven's-foot as she did. If there was magic going on, she wanted as much space between herself and it as she could conveniently manage.

"I can't . . . can't hold," Jonystra gasped. "No!"

Blue fire flared ceiling-high from the cards she clutched. Daner staggered back, his hands raised to shield his face. The raven ring pricked Eleret's finger once more, hard and sharp. On the far side of the room, something made a pinging noise, as if a coin had just fallen on the stone floor.

The fire burned brighter, fanning out from the deck and lighting every corner of the room. Eleret had just time to notice that Mobrellan had disappeared; then, with a cry of pain and horror, Jonystra tried to throw the flaming cards from her. As they slid reluctantly out of her hands and scattered across the cloth-draped table, the blue flame vanished.

Jonystra's elaborately arranged hair was burning in a frizzle of fire and an acrid smell. Without thinking, Eleret leaned toward her. Her right hand jabbed the raven's-foot into the table, then grabbed the unlit portion of Jonystra's hair and pulled it taut, while her left hand rose and swung. Her knife sliced through the piled-up coils, cutting loose most of the burning section and sweeping it forward onto the table. Eleret slapped at the bits of flame that remained on Jonystra's head. She didn't have much time, she knew. The falling cards had tipped over the candle, and odds were that either the tablecloth or the cards would catch fire in a minute or two.

Suddenly the light grew stronger, and Eleret knew that her time had run out. She threw herself sideways off the back of the bench, away from the burning tabletop, her right arm sweeping Jonystra along with her. Jonystra cried out again, and struggled weakly, but Eleret was too strong for her. As they crashed to the floor, Daner's voice shouted a single word, and the light vanished.

Eleret kept a grip on Jonystra, who sobbed once and then was quiet. As she pulled her knees up, disentangling them from the bench, Daner's voice came out of the darkness above her. "Eleret? Are you all right? Where are you?"

"Here. Don't step on me."

The faint rustle of movement stopped. "Where?"

"On the floor. Can you give us some light?"

"Making light is more difficult than—"

The door burst open, spilling lamplight into the room around the outline of a man with a drawn sword. Immediately, Eleret let go of Jonystra, shifted her hold on her dagger, and rolled out of the triangle of light. She came to her knees, poised to throw.

"Daner! What's all the noise? Loren's Luck, what a mess!" Baroja said.

With a tiny sigh of relief, Eleret lowered her arm. She glanced around the room once more, then resheathed her dagger as Daner said tiredly, "Baroja, what are you doing here?"

"I was just coming to see what was taking you so long, and I heard shouting. What happened? Didn't your Cilhar lady like what my Luck-seer told her?"

"Later, Baroja. Right now, just bring us a lamp."

"Oh, very well, but I want an explanation, mind."

"So do I," Eleret muttered as Daner's cousin retreated into the hall in search of a light. "Most definitely, so do I."

FIFTEEN

Eleret had just time to climb to her feet before Baroja returned, carrying a hanging lamp filched from one of the wall sconces outside. In Baroja's hands, the lamp lit barely a quarter of the room and cast long black shadows across most of that.

"Where's Mobrellan?" Eleret said, peering uneasily into the gloom on the far side of the room.

"Who?" Baroja swung the lantern, sending shadows dancing and making it impossible to tell if anyone was hiding. Fingering the hilt of her dagger, Eleret backed up, closer to the door.

"Baroja! Give me that." Daner took the lamp away from his cousin and looped the chain over a bracket near the door. As the shadows steadied, Eleret looked around again. There was no sign of Mobrellan, but now that there was better light, Eleret could see a second door, in the far wall.

"Good idea," Baroja said to Daner. "Now, you've got your light. What happened?"

"In a minute. Eleret, are you all right?"

"I'm fine. Jonystra's been burned; I'm not sure how badly. Mobrellan got away." When Daner frowned, plainly puzzled, Eleret added, "Jonystra's porter. He probably dodged through there in the confusion." She waved at the far door.

Daner hesitated. "Baroja, would you check?"

"What for? He's just a porter."

"He might know something we need to hear."

"You chase him, then." Baroja flicked an invisible dust mote from his shoulder.

"I should stay here, in case your precious Luck-seer tries another spell."

"I don't think she can, right now," Eleret put in. Jonystra lay curled in a wretched ball beside the overturned bench, hiding her face and moaning softly to herself. The ragged, half-burnt ends of her hair stuck out in all directions. Eleret suppressed a wave of sympathy.

"Even so, I want to stay here," Daner said. "Baroja . . ."

"*Another* spell, you said?" Baroja raised his eyebrows. "This explanation is going to be worth a week's profit from the long docks." He studied Daner's expression for a moment, then gave a lazy shrug. "As you'll have it, Cousin. But you owe me for this."

"Not much," Daner replied. "And you owe me far more for bringing a spell-caster into my home to attack my guests. Go, Baroja."

Finally, Baroja went, stepping cautiously around the end of the table and across to the far door. Daner snorted softly, then turned and knelt beside Jonystra. As he reached for the Luck-seer's shoulder, Eleret sighed, pulled out her dagger once more, and said, "Daner."

Startled, Daner looked up. "What?"

"Don't block my throwing lines."

Daner blinked, nodded, and shifted his position. Then

he reached out and gently pulled Jonystra out of her protective ball.

"There's nobody in the back room, Daner," Baroja announced. "And no other door, so the porter couldn't have gone that way after all. Are you quite sure— Loren's Curse! What happened to her?"

Jonystra's eyebrows and eyelashes were gone, and her eyes had swollen shut. Her hairline had been scorched back half an inch, leaving twisted black stubble over angry red burns. Most of her face was bright pink, and long whitish blisters marked her chin, cheeks, and nose. She moaned and raised her hands as if to hide, and Eleret swallowed hard. The Luck-seer's hands looked worse than her face: the backs were giant blisters, and blood oozed from several places where the blackened skin had split open across the palms.

"Get a healer," Daner said over his shoulder. "One who knows how to treat back-flow burns."

For once, Baroja did not argue. Face pale, he vanished through the outer door, leaving Eleret and Daner alone with Jonystra. Daner shifted his grip to Jonystra's wrists and began muttering a strange, liquid string of unfamiliar syllables. After a moment, Jonystra stopped pulling away, and her moans ceased. Slowly, Daner loosened his hold on her, but he continued muttering steadily, his face a mask of concentration.

Uncertainly, Eleret backed away, hoping her movements would not distract Daner from his spell-casting. He went on murmuring without a blink. Reassured, Eleret crossed to the wall and lit three of the unused lamps from the one Baroja had brought in. She righted the overturned bench, then looked for and found the raven's-foot she had thrust into the table. Finally, she satisfied herself that the connecting room really was unoccupied. As she finished her inspection, Daner stopped muttering. Lips tight, he looked down at Jonystra's unconscious form, then sat back with a sigh.

"That should hold her until the healer gets here, as long as no one moves her," he said. "At least, I hope so. I've never seen back-flow burns this bad before." His face was several shades paler than normal, and his expression was grim.

"What are back-flow burns?"

"Burns caused by losing control of certain spells at a critical point. The energy that's supposed to go into the spell snaps back at the magician instead."

"Like a bowstring snapping against your arm if you aren't holding the bow right?"

Daner nodded. "It happens when someone tries a spell that's too difficult for him. Most of the time the results aren't much worse than a bad sunburn; if you're going to lose control, you tend to do it before you've built up much energy. This kind of thing . . ." He looked down at Jonystra and shuddered. "I didn't know she was so close to the edge. I didn't *know*." His voice was full of guilt.

"How could you tell?"

"I should have known! But I wasn't thinking about back-flow. I must have distracted her at a critical moment, and—"

"Daner." Eleret waited until he looked up, then repeated patiently, "How can you tell if someone is close to losing control of a spell? What are the signs—what do you look for?"

For a moment, Daner just stared at her. Then he said in a more normal tone, "It's in the feel of the power. Spells give off bits of power the way a fire gives light and heat, and the bits feel differently when something is going out of control. It's hard to explain."

"Is it something you would notice if you weren't looking for it?"

"A spell large enough to do this kind of damage should have practically slapped me in the face." Suddenly, he frowned. "When did she set it up? I don't remember seeing her do anything unusual. The whole spell was just *there* all of a sudden."

"You said that charting cards could take magic."

"Not like that. Card-charting is a delicate spell; it takes skill, not power. That's why someone who's a bad magician can still be a good card-charter."

"Well, if she wasn't charting cards, what *was* Jonystra trying to do with all that magic?" Eleret asked.

"I haven't the slightest idea." Daner blinked, then scrambled to his feet. "Maybe I can tell from the cards."

"Are they safe to touch?"

"I'll know in a minute." Daner bent over the table, his eyes narrowed to slits and his hands hovering a scant three inches above the scattered cards. *"Iffura nor amini—* No, there's no residue left, at least, not that I can find. We'll have to wait until Dame Nirandol here is in a condition to tell us." He shook his head in disappointment and began picking up the cards.

Eleret hesitated, then shrugged and joined him. "Why don't more of them have burnt edges?" she asked after a moment. "It looked to me as if the whole deck was on fire."

"Most of your cards must have come from the middle of the deck," Daner said, then frowned. "No, these aren't scorched, either, but this one— Eleret, sort out the ones that are burned."

In a few moments, they had a small pile of charred cards and a large stack of unmarked ones. Daner picked up the smaller pile and riffled through it. "I still don't see what . . . Wait a minute. Two, three, five, six, nine— Ha! Eleven cards." He looked at Eleret triumphantly.

"So?" Eleret said.

"Don't you see? Jonystra was half done with your pattern when she lost control. Eleven cards would finish the chart." Daner shuffled through the cards once more, and his frown returned. "Silence, War, Night, Death, Despair, Chaos, Betrayal . . . I don't like this at all."

Judging from the names, Eleret didn't think she liked them, either. "They're just cards."

"Sometimes." Daner tapped the cards against his palm. "But they really can tell you something about the future, in the hands of a good magician. And Jonystra was casting a spell, a powerful spell—too powerful to be a simple foretelling. What if she was trying to *influence* the future?"

"You mean, trying to make things come out the way she wanted them to?"

Daner nodded.

"Could she really do that with a bunch of *cards*?"

"She could certainly try. I'll have to check with Climeral to see how possible such a spell is. If it can be done at all, it's Adept-level work."

Eleret stared uneasily at the cards in Daner's hands. "Is it safe for me to look at them?"

"Of course. There's nothing particularly magical about the cards themselves; they're just a tool, really, something to focus a magician's spell." Daner glanced involuntarily in Jonystra's direction. "Without a magician, nothing can happen."

"Give them to me, then," Eleret said quickly, hoping to distract him before he started wallowing in guilt again.

Daner turned and handed her the cards. As her hand closed around them, the raven ring pricked gently at her finger. She let go of the cards at once, and they scattered across the table.

"Eleret!" Daner sounded exasperated. "They're just cards; you said so yourself."

"No they're not," Eleret said. "There's something wrong with them, or about them."

"I checked them myself," Daner said, bending to pick up two of the cards that had fallen to the floor. When he straightened, his expression was more thoughtful than annoyed. "What do you think is wrong with them?"

"I don't know. I'm not a magician."

"Then how can you tell?" The exasperation was back, stronger than before.

"Because Mother's ring pricked my finger when I took them," Eleret said, nodding at the cards. "It's the second— no, the third time it's done that. I think it's a warning."

"What ring? What—" Daner stopped short and took a deep breath. Then he set the little pile of cards in a neat stack, seated himself on the end of the bench, and said, "Tell me about the ring, and the warnings, from the beginning."

"This is the ring," Eleret said, twisting it around her finger so that the raven seal faced outward as it was meant to do. She held out her hand so that Daner could see it, and was relieved when he did not ask her to take it off so he could examine it more closely. "It's a family heirloom. Mother must have taken it with her the last time she left the mountains; I found it in her kit. I've been wearing it since then, to make it harder to steal."

"It doesn't look valuable, but if it has magic—"

"I think it must. It pricked my finger in the alley, just before you stumbled, and again when Jonystra's spell went wrong. And it pricked me just now, when you gave me those cards."

"It sounds like magic." Daner stared at the ring, frowning. "But I don't feel a thing. Would you mind if I did a few tests?"

"Not as long as I don't have to take it off."

Daner looked startled, then nodded. "Hold your hand steady. *Ri thala lac il nobra shavazist—*"

Something pushed Eleret's hand downward. At the same time, Daner's head snapped back as if he had been struck, and he broke off in mid-sentence. He shook his head as if to clear it, then looked ruefully at Eleret. "It's magic, all right. I can't tell exactly what it does, though; it seems to have a strong resistance to outside spells. Don't you know *anything* else about it?"

"My many-times great-grandmother, Geleraise Vinlarrian, brought it to the mountains seven hundred and some years ago, and it's been in the family ever since. Mother used to call it our good-luck charm, because of the raven."

"Ravens mean good luck? I didn't know that."

Eleret shook her head. "Ravens are for protection, at least among the Cilhar."

"Protection," Daner muttered, feeling his chin. "Of course."

"The black stone is for night and shadow," Eleret went on. "I can't remember what the silver means."

"Magic." Daner stood up cautiously, as if he were not quite sure he would be able to keep his balance. "Silver is for magic. At least, it is in most color systems."

"That doesn't sound quite right."

"Well, if you think of something that does, tell me. It could be important." He scowled down at the two stacks of cards. "I wish I knew what made it prick you. If it's some sort of magical residue in the cards, it's too faint for me to find."

"Why does it have to be magic that sets the ring off?" Eleret asked, fingering the hilt of her dagger. "Couldn't it be something else?"

"I suppose so, but I can't think what. The ring is very sensitive to spells." His hand went to his chin again.

"It didn't prick me when you tested it, or when you were busy with Jonystra."

"It didn't?" Daner's eyes narrowed. "Did you feel anything when you picked up the rest of the cards?" He leaned forward and tapped the larger, unscorched stack of cards as he spoke.

"No, and it didn't bother me to handle those one at a time," Eleret said, waving at the smaller pile. "It only pricked when you gave me all eleven at once."

"Generally malefic, or specifically directed?" Daner muttered. "Or maybe both together."

"Daner, what are you talking about?"

"The exact type of spell that sets off your ring. If it's meant as a warning—"

"We don't know for certain that spells set it off," Eleret pointed out. "It could be something else. And I don't think this is a good time for experiments. I—"

The sound of voices in the corridor outside caused Eleret to break off and turn toward the door. A moment later, Baroja, Lord tir Vallaniri, and three nervous-looking servants carrying knives and torches entered the room.

"Don't touch her!" Daner said sharply as the newcomers crowded around Jonystra. "Stand back, or you'll upset the protective spell. Blast it, Baroja, I asked for a healer, not a mob."

"The healer is on his way," Lord tir Vallaniri said. "The 'mob' was my suggestion. When Baroja told me that someone had blown up your charting, and that he might still be running loose in the house, it occurred to me that you might find a use for a few extra knives."

"You did say Jonystra's porter was missing," Baroja added, smiling at Eleret.

Eleret nodded, her opinion of Baroja rising. The problem of Mobrellan's whereabouts had been nagging at the back of her mind, and it was good to know that someone else had thought to deal with it.

"He's not here, and we haven't seen a trace of him," Daner said. "How soon will that healer arrive?"

"As soon as he can," said Lord tir Vallaniri. He gestured, and two of the servants bowed and left. "Now, before he gets here, please tell me what has been going on, so that I have some idea what, if anything, still needs to be done about it."

"Yes, Cousin," Baroja said with a wicked grin. "It's time for that explanation you owe me."

SIXTEEN

Daner's summary of the card-charting and the spell gone wrong was brief and accurate. Baroja and Lord tir Vallaniri listened in silence until he finished, and the questions they asked afterward were clear and pointed. To Eleret's relief, Daner did not go into the possible reasons behind Jonystra's actions, nor did he mention the raven ring.

"I'll arrange to have the woman questioned when the healer is done with her," Lord tir Vallaniri said at last. "My apologies, Freelady Salven; this should not have happened in my house."

"I am the one who should apologize, for bringing this trouble on you," Eleret replied, but she was warmed by his evident sincerity.

"I suppose it was *you* she was interested in, Freelady?" Baroja studied his left sleeve as he spoke.

Daner frowned. "It certainly looked like it to me. What are you getting at, Baroja?"

"Only that it seems a little odd for someone to get inside

a noble household, associate however briefly with the family, and then attack a relatively unimportant visitor."

"Jonystra followed us from Eleret's lodgings."

"Nonsense." Baroja waved a hand in careless dismissal. "I found her myself, down in the Orphan's Market."

"Did you? Or was she the one who found you? Just how *did* you get hold of her so conveniently, anyway?"

Lord tir Vallaniri stepped forward, and was instantly the focus of attention. "A telling question, Daner, but one that will have to wait. I am more concerned about your sisters. This woman charted cards for all three of them, as I understand it. Are you magician enough to tell whether she cast any spells on them, or should I send for a wizard?"

Baroja's eyes widened and his jaw went slack with surprise, as if he had not thought out all the possibilities before he had made his remark and was now almost regretting having spoken. Eleret wondered what he had been trying to do and why, and whether she would ever understand the way these incomprehensible people behaved.

Daner pursed his lips, then nodded at his father. "I think I can spot anything major, but if you're worried about subtle effects, you'd better send for Fenutiol. It would be easier if I knew what she was trying to do with Eleret, but—" He shrugged.

"Can't you tell from the chart?" Baroja asked. "That *is* the whole reason for fussing with these cards, after all."

"She didn't finish Eleret's chart," Daner said. "We've got what we think are the last eleven cards, but you can't tell much from them without knowing in what order they'd have fallen."

"*I* can't," Baroja said. "But I know who can. Mother. She's been to so many card-charters that she knows the cards as well as they do, and she's always reinterpreting other people's charts out of order."

Remembering the conversations in the main hall, Eleret almost smiled. Baroja's description fit Lady Kistran like a made-to-measure breastplate.

Daner blinked. "I suppose it's worth a try. Eleret—"

"Not tonight," Lord tir Vallaniri said. "Speak with your aunt in the morning, Daner; I can't spare that much of your time tonight. Do what you can to check on your sisters, and I'll arrange for a more thorough inspection tomorrow. Freelady Salven, again, my deepest apologies for this incident, and forgive me, too, for keeping you standing here. After all you've been through, you must be very tired. Bresc! Escort Freelady Salven to her room, and see that she has everything she needs."

"Thank you, but I'd rather stay," Eleret said. She wouldn't learn anything stuck in her room, and she had a feeling she was going to need every shred of information she could scrape together in order to make sense out of the day's events.

"You needn't prove yourself to me, Freelady," Lord tir Vallaniri said. "Go on and rest. I'll send Daner up later to let you know if we've found anything." His tone was kind, but his attention had already shifted to Daner and Baroja.

Eleret hesitated. She did not want to offend Lord tir Vallaniri, but neither did she want to depend on his goodwill for the information she needed. From the look of him, he was likely to forget her existence the moment she was out of his sight.

"And I'll let you know right away if there's anything urgent," Daner said.

"Very well. Fortune favor you, my lords." Eleret bowed,

smiled at Baroja's startled expression (though she did not understand it), and followed the stony-faced guardsman out the door.

Bresc took a different route from the one Laurinel had used, and Eleret kept a closer eye than usual on the twists and turns of the hallways. As far as she knew, Mobrellan was still loose somewhere in the house, and that was cause enough to keep a hand near her knife. He might be the innocent servant Baroja and Daner seemed to think him, but until she had good reason to believe differently, she would assume that he was waist-deep in Jonystra's plots. *Better to be prepared for the rock that doesn't fall . . .*

Finally, Bresc paused. "Your room, my lady."

"Thank you," Eleret said. Keeping as far back as she could, she set a hand to the door and shoved it open.

Candlelight spilled into the hall. Eleret stepped sideways into the shelter of the wall and reached for her knife.

"Lorig has prepared your chamber for you, my lady." Bresc's voice was even more expressionless than usual, but there was a gleam of approval in his eyes.

"Oh." Eleret straightened. She should have guessed; an intruder would hardly advertise his presence by lighting candles.

"Will there be anything else, my lady?"

"No, thank you."

Bresc bowed and left. Still feeling edgy and vaguely disquieted, Eleret walked through the open door. Her kit bags had been moved to the foot of the bed; a candle burned on the table, the embers of a fire glowed on the hearth, and the room was uncomfortably warm and stuffy. Eleret sighed and crossed to the window. If she was going to get any sleep tonight, she'd have to air the room.

"Ahem."

Eleret spun, dropping into a crouch and reaching for her weapons as a man stepped slowly out of the deep shadow between the wardrobe and the far wall. His size and stance were faintly familiar, and he held his hands out to either side, fingers spread to emphasize the fact that they were empty. Even before he spoke, she suspected who he was, and his voice confirmed it.

"I come unarmed, and mean no ill to you or yours," Karvonen said in careful, barely accented Cilhar. "Quite the contrary, in fact, though I expect you'll take some convincing of that."

Eleret blinked in surprise. *So the thief speaks Cilhar and knows the conventions for safe approach.* She relaxed a little more; anyone so knowledgeable deserved to be treated accordingly, at least until she knew what he wanted and how he had gotten there.

"Come out where I can see you," Eleret said in Ciaronese.

"Will this do?" He stepped forward half a pace and leaned into the candlelight. Fox-colored hair gleamed briefly; then he pulled back into the shadows. "I'm not anxious to be noticed by anyone else, you see. Quite apart from the damage it would do to your reputation, think of what it would do to mine."

"Karvonen Aurelico." Eleret shook her head in wonder. "What are you doing here? How did you pick this room? And how did you get in?"

"I was waiting for you," Karvonen said promptly. "As for getting in—I'm a thief, remember?"

"You make it difficult to forget," Eleret said. "Be a little more specific."

"Why don't you close the door first? It's a long tale, and I'd hate for us to be interrupted in the middle. You might never hear the end of the story."

"I certainly wouldn't want that to happen." Keeping one hand on her knife and both eyes on Karvonen, Eleret edged toward the door and nudged it shut with her foot. "Now, try again. Why are you here?"

"I'm trying to retrieve my mistake this afternoon." Karvonen sighed and folded his arms across his chest. "Having scruples is such a nuisance. You wouldn't believe the trouble I get into because of them."

"You're right," Eleret said. "I wouldn't. For the third time, what is it you want? Or do I have to use the same method as I did this afternoon to get a reasonable answer? As I remember, you were much more talkative then." She slid two inches of her knife out of the sheath, turning slightly so that the candlelight glinted on the exposed blade.

"No, no," Karvonen said. "There's no need for that sort of thing, really. I just don't know where to start."

"You can start by coming out where I can see you clearly, now that no one can look through the door and ruin your reputation," Eleret said. Karvonen's expression might not give away much, but she wanted to be able to watch it anyway, just in case.

"That's easy enough." Karvonen slid out of the shadows and sat down on the edge of the bed. Leaning back, he said, "Will this suit you? It will take me a moment to get into position, if I want to try something; that should give you plenty of warning. Now, where were we?"

Eleret looked at him with the most skeptical expression

she could muster and slid another inch of knife blade free. "Try the beginning."

"The beginning," Karvonen said, and shook his head sadly. "Right to the beginning, with no lead-in, no setting the atmosphere, no background, no buildup of suspense. When am I going to meet a Cilhar who understands small talk? It begins with the twist."

"The what?"

"The twist. Snagging your boyfriend's bucket this afternoon."

"Stealing his purse, you mean."

"That's what I said."

Eleret gave Karvonen the look she usually reserved for her sister Nilly when Nilly brought home yet another orphaned fox cub or injured squirrel.

Karvonen sighed again. "Not one for colorful language, either, I see. Very well. In plain words: I thought something was odd about the job from the beginning, but I didn't worry about it until I found out you were Cilhar. When the Syaski showed up—"

"How do you know they were Syaski?"

"Their boots and their belts," the thief said without hesitation. "Syaski like wooden-soled boots with heels, and lace them up along the outside of their legs, and there's a fashion in Syaskor right now for braided leather sword-belts. Your average Syask in Ciaron will change the rest of his clothes to suit local styles, but he won't walk around in soft leather shoes and he'll keep his familiar, properly adjusted sword-belt unless someone cuts it off him." Karvonen gave Eleret a sidelong look. "The same way a Cilhar will find some way of carrying half an armory's worth of weapons no matter what she wears."

"Go on." Eleret kept her tone carefully neutral, but she pushed her knife back into its sheath. As long as Karvonen cooperated, she was willing to give him a little maneuvering room. A very little; she kept her hand near the hilt.

Karvonen made a show of politely ignoring the gesture, and continued. "When the Syaski showed up, I *knew* something was stranger than a Kith Alunel envoy without something to argue about."

"Why?"

"Because I'm not incompetent. You think I just decide whose tail to twist on the spur of the moment? I heard about you and your boyfriend—"

"Lord Daner isn't my boyfriend," Eleret said, annoyed. She'd let it go by once, but after two mentions, she had to correct him. Karvonen would drive her crazy if he kept referring to Daner that way.

"Huh." Karvonen pursed his lips skeptically. "I'll bet it's not because he didn't try."

"You'd lose."

"Then Daner's an idiot," Karvonen said with feeling.

"Let's get back to your long tale. You heard about Lord Daner and me—"

"—from a local acquaintance who lets me know now and then when he runs across a good thing. He said there were lots of rumors about you but no solid information, which usually means big money is involved. Being fond of money, I thought I'd just appropriate a little of it before some amateur loused up the whole thing."

In spite of herself, Eleret's lips curled in disgust. Karvonen spread his hands, a picture of apology. "It *is* my profession."

"Well, don't ever practice it near me again."

"I wouldn't have practiced it near you once, if I'd known

you were Cilhar. That's what I've been trying to tell you. None of the gossips know you're Cilhar, but those Syaski knew."

"So who do you think set them on us?"

"Brains as well as skill and beauty. Daner *is* an idiot."

"Leave Daner out of this," Eleret said. "Who was it?"

"A fellow by the name of Gorchastrin, Grand Master—"

"—of the Order of Tsantilar in Rathane." Eleret was surprised, but she was also relieved. At least she didn't have yet *another* unknown enemy lurking somewhere in Ciaron. "The Grand Master and I have met."

"No you haven't," Karvonen said smugly.

By an effort of will, Eleret kept her expression from changing. She wasn't going to give the little thief the satisfaction of showing surprise. "Explain."

Karvonen gave her an exasperated look. "You're no fun at all, do you know that? Anyone else, even a Cilhar, would have at least said something about not believing me. But you—"

"I have a lot on my mind." The success of her strategy pleased her, but she couldn't show that, either. "About Gorchastrin?"

"Oh, very well. Grand Master Gorchastrin of the Order of Tsantilar in Rathane died mysteriously some time ago. Possibly murdered, though no one seems quite sure. Sometimes it's hard to tell with wizards."

"But you're sure he's dead?"

"Absolutely. No mistakes, no substitutions, no secret revivals. He's dead, all right. And it gets better. The night before he died, Gorchastrin told his fellow Grand Masters that he had just made a discovery that would put the Order of Tsantilar at the top of the extremely messy heap of wizard's guilds in Rathane. How much do you know about Rathani politics?"

"Nothing at all."

"Then there's no point in confusing you with an explanation. Unless you want to spend the next three or four hours untangling the snakes' nest of factions they've accumulated over the years. I love Rathane," he added in a happy tone. "If you pick the right person and the right place, you can steal his purse, his sword, and the cloak off his back and stroll off admiring the scenery, because the locals will take two days to decide who's responsible for catching you."

"How long ago did this happen? The business with Gorchastrin, I mean."

"Two months ago, give or take a day."

"Two months ago?" Eleret frowned. Her mother had still been alive then. "Where was he killed?"

"In his bedchamber in Rathane. And you really should say 'died'; I did tell you I wasn't *sure* he was murdered."

Eleret shrugged. So long as Tamm Salven hadn't been involved in the fellow's death, Karvonen's hairsplitting wasn't important. "If Gorchastrin's dead, who tried to persuade the City Guard to arrest me this morning?"

"How should I know?"

"You seem to know an awful lot of other things."

"There is that." Karvonen looked thoughtfully at the ceiling. "Put it down to an inexplicable gap in my otherwise vast fund of knowledge."

"Karvonen . . ."

"I'm serious. Well, almost. When I found out that a dead Rathani mage was wandering around in Ciaron, I asked a couple of people who should have known who he was, really. Nobody did. Inexplicable."

Eleret snorted. "How do you know all the rest of these things?"

For the first time, Karvonen looked uncomfortable. "Family connections. I'm afraid I can't say more than that."

"Very well." Eleret forced her frustration down. After all, family matters were for family. She was surprised that a thief appreciated that; then she remembered that Charis had said the Aurelicos held to some honor code of their own. Evidently, the City Guardswoman had been right. The thought made Eleret feel friendlier toward Karvonen.

Karvonen looked surprised, then grinned. "For the first time all day, I'm glad you're a Cilhar, Freelady. Most Ciaronese wouldn't let go of it that easily."

"Then they have odd ideas about proprieties."

"Not odd, just different. If I said I was connected with the Imperial palace, a Ciaronese would nod and say no more. You don't ask awkward questions about one of the Emperor's spies."

"No one would believe you were one of the Emperor's spies."

"But if they did, they'd stop asking questions." Karvonen rubbed his nose, looking thoughtful. "And you'd be surprised at the tales people will swallow, if you put them right."

"Maybe." Eleret frowned. Karvonen had not acted as if he knew any of this earlier, so he must have gone out looking for it after their encounter that afternoon. Why? And why was he telling it to an almost-stranger? To her surprise, Eleret found that she wanted to believe him, but she had to consider the possibility that it was some sort of trap. She sighed. "Why are you telling me all this?"

"Would you believe me if I said I was smitten by your

beauty and couldn't think of any other way to see you again?"

"No."

Karvonen sighed again. "I didn't think so. Well, if you must know, it's because you caught me snagging your boyfr—Lord Daner's bucket this afternoon."

"So?"

"So if I don't do something to make up for it, I'm in big trouble. This is all I could think of."

"If you came to make up for picking Daner's pocket, what are you doing in my chamber?"

"Because he's just a wizard. You're Cilhar."

Eleret shook her head. "That doesn't explain anything."

With an air of resignation, Karvonen said, "Family policy. You don't mess with wizards, and you *really* don't fool with Cilhar. The difference is, not messing with wizards is just a good idea. Basic good sense for anybody, but especially for a thief. Fooling with Cilhar . . ." His voice trailed off and he shook his head.

"Yes?" Eleret prompted.

"It's hard to explain. Look, there are certain people that the family never, *ever* crosses. Not under any circumstances, or for any reason. Most of them are people who are connected with the family in one way or another."

That made sense; an honorable thief wouldn't rob his kin, even distantly connected kin. Eleret nodded.

"There are one or two people who've done favors for someone in the family at one time or another, and a few we don't bother out of professional courtesy. And there are some families we don't bother with because of things that go back centuries. The Kyel-Semruds, for instance." He shook his head admiringly. "I think we wouldn't bother *them* even if it weren't for the tradition. They're the trickiest bunch I've ever heard of. Outside of us, I mean."

Eleret frowned. "I thought the Kyel-Semruds were Kith Alunel noblemen."

"Those are the ones. You wouldn't believe some of the things they've done." Karvonen smiled reminiscently at the corner of the ceiling, then glanced at Eleret and cleared his throat. "Yes. Well. Cilhar are the only people who are on the list as a group—not one family at a time, but the whole blasted country at once. The ban on stealing from them goes back almost as far as the one on the Kyel-Semruds; they both date from before the Wars of Binding, anyway. *And* there's an aid-in-distress clause. So you see my difficulty. When Grandfather finds out I bungled a snag on a wizard, he might be willing to pass it off as stupidity. But when he finds out I put the twist on a wizard with a Cilhar body-guard—"

"You've got it backwards again," Eleret said absently. She found Karvonen's explanation almost as disturbing as the information he had given her about Gorchastrin. "Daner was supposed to be guarding me."

"What?" Karvonen's face went completely blank. "Why would a Cilhar need a bodyguard?"

"Wizards." Eleret tapped her fingers absently against the hilt of her dagger, thinking of Jonystra. "I don't suppose—"

A knock at the door interrupted her, and as she broke off, Karvonen stood up in an economical movement. "Beg pardon, Freelady," he said in a voice just above a whisper, "but as I said earlier, I'd rather not be seen. Though I'm sure the residents are charming people." Bowing, he stepped back into the shadows, and a moment later Eleret had to squint to see him, even though she knew exactly where he was.

The knock came again. "Eleret?" said Daner's muffled voice. "Wake up; I want to talk to you."

SEVENTEEN

Eleret glanced once more at the dark corner where Karvonen stood, all but invisible, then put a hand to the door. "What have you found out?" she asked, swinging it partway open. "Has Mobrellan turned up?"

"Mobrellan?" Daner's eyebrows flew up in surprise; then he smiled. "Oh, yes, the Luck-seer's porter. He's long gone. We think he had help from one of the servants." He pushed the door wide and stepped past Eleret, then paced over to the window and looked out, his shoulders stiff with tension.

Quietly, Eleret eased away from the door, to a spot from which she could watch both Daner and Karvonen's shadowy corner without being obvious about it. She wasn't sure whether she wanted to protect Karvonen from Daner or Daner from Karvonen, but she hoped suddenly and profoundly that she would not have to do either. If Karvonen had told her the truth—and, apart from an ingrained distrust of thieves, she had no real reason to think he hadn't—he had done her a service of considerable proportions. Whatever his motives, she owed it to him to respect his wish to avoid discovery. Her debt did not extend, however, to letting him pitch a knife into Daner's back. She raised her left hand to the quick-throw position and held it there, hoping Karvonen had enough knowledge of Cilhar customs to recognize the gesture.

Daner hadn't moved or spoken. "Well, what is it?" Eleret said at last.

"The Luck-seer's talking."

"Already? That healer of yours must be very good."

"Of course she's good," Daner said impatiently. "She works for the Vallaniri." He turned, frowning into the middle distance. "I wish we knew as much about that wretched Luck-seer."

"Daner, you're not making any sense. What's happened?"

"I told you, the Luck-seer's been talking. Not much, of course, not with injuries like hers, but enough so we could figure out what she was after."

"Which was?" With an effort of will, she kept herself from looking directly at Karvonen's corner, but the knowledge of his presence was a continuing distraction.

"You."

Eleret made an irritated noise. "We already knew *that*. Either stop being mysterious and let out what you know, or go away so I can get some sleep. Your father was right; it's been a long day."

"I'm sorry," Daner said at once, but the smile that accompanied the words looked a little stiff at the corners. "I wasn't thinking. Of course you're tired, after all that's happened." He moved away from the window as he spoke.

"So tell me what Jonystra said." Eleret shifted, drawing Daner's eyes toward her and away from Karvonen's corner.

As long as Daner was watching her, he was unlikely to notice the thief standing motionless in the shadows. *Not too much,* she cautioned herself. It would be ironic if, after all the fuss she'd made about it, *she* maneuvered *Daner* into blocking her throwing lines.

Daner hesitated. "It has to do with a ring," he said at last.

"Yes, but *what* does it have to do with my ring? If you can't make sense, I'll go find your father. I'll wager I can persuade him to give me a full report."

"No, don't," Daner said quickly, stepping between Eleret and the door. "He can't tell you anything more. He—we don't know any more."

"You got Jonystra to say that she wanted my ring, but you forgot to ask her why?" Eleret did not bother to hide her skepticism, though she could not imagine why Daner would lie.

"You saw how badly she was injured. We had a hard time getting as much information as we did."

"None of which is new." Eleret frowned. Daner was behaving very oddly. "Why are you here?"

"Now that we're *certain* Jonystra was after your ring, we should make sure no one else gets a chance at it before we find out why."

"What do you mean?" Eleret asked warily.

"There's a strongbox built into the wall of my father's study; it's been spelled against every kind of interference anyone could think of. The ring will be much safer there than here."

"I'm sure you think so." Eleret had to struggle to keep her tone neutral, because she was not at all sure. Everyone else seemed to want the raven ring; perhaps Daner, too, had succumbed to its lure. The thought made her feel alone, as if a comrade she'd depended on had deserted her. Why? Daner wasn't Cilhar. Before that morning, she hadn't even known he existed.

"Come, don't be foolish," Daner said with a touch of impatience. "This is the best way, I promise to the land's end. Give me the ring." He held out his hand toward Eleret.

Behind him, Eleret saw the beginning of movement in the shadows. "Daner!" she shouted, and jerked a raven's-foot free of the strap that held it against the padded shoulder of her vest. Daner whirled, raising his hands in an unfamiliar motion. Eleret's arm whipped down, and in the moment of release, her wrist flicked infinitesimally to one side. An instant later, as Daner finished his gesture, the raven's-foot struck his shoulder. Simultaneously, the raven ring stabbed Eleret's forefinger.

As she pulled another raven's-foot loose, Eleret's mind caught up with her body. Something was wrong with Daner's reaction, his timing, his stance—that wasn't Daner at all!

"Don't move, you," she said. "Karvonen? Can you get his dagger?"

The door swung open. "What dagger?" Daner's voice said from the hall outside. "Eleret— Stars!"

A second Daner stepped through the open door, stopped short, and reached for his knife, his eyes wide with astonishment. The set of his shoulders and the way he held his knife fit Eleret's memories of the fight in the alley. Eleret smiled slightly, and kept her eyes on the false Daner and her raven's-foot raised to throw. "Stay where you are, Daner," she said to the newcomer. "I don't want to get you mixed up. Karvonen! Hurry it up."

"Small chance of that," the false Daner said. He straightened, clutching his left shoulder, and bowed sardonically in

Eleret's direction. "Fare ill, Cilhar girl, until we meet again, and do believe I'll try my best to make it so. *Ilmora!*"

Between one eyeblink and the next, he vanished. The candle flames bent briefly toward the empty space as Eleret stood frozen, staring. Then, weapon poised, Eleret advanced, while behind her Daner muttered rapidly.

"No good; he's gone," Daner said, sheathing his dagger. "Who— Eleret, look out!"

As Daner spoke, Karvonen half stumbled, half fell out of the shadows toward Eleret, his face twisted and his eyes wild. Both hands clutched at his throat; it looked as if he were trying to strangle himself, and more than half succeeding. Eleret slid her unused raven's-foot back into place and took three quick steps forward. Her hands closed around Karvonen's wrists and she threw all her strength into a quick push-pull. There was a moment's resistance; then the opposition ended abruptly. Karvonen fell against her, choked, and began breathing in great gasps.

"It's the thief!" Daner's knife was back in his hand. "What in the Emperor's name is he doing here?"

"He came to talk to me." Eleret helped Karvonen over to the bed and let him drop to a seat on the edge of it. He was laboring for breath and unable to talk, but he responded with a wave and an exaggerated nod which Eleret interpreted as thanks.

"You can't be sure of that," Daner said. "He might have come to rob you. For all we know, he might be in league with that woman downstairs."

Karvonen frowned and tried to say something, which set off a coughing fit.

"That's not what he told me," Eleret said, shaking her head at Karvonen.

"*Told* you?"

"He was here when I came up. We talked for a while before you—I mean, he—I mean, that other Daner came in." Without thinking, she glanced at the place where the false Daner had disappeared, and suppressed a shudder. "I thought shapeshifters were just a story."

"They aren't, more's the pity," Karvonen said. His voice sounded hoarse and he still breathed heavily, as if he had been running, but at least he wasn't gasping for air like a drowning man. "And they're worse than wizards. Shit a two-by-twenty-weight of iron through the bottom of a badly patched canoe. *What* have I gotten myself into?"

"A cell in the Emperor's dungeon, if I have anything to say about it." Daner glared at Karvonen and shifted his grip on his dagger. "What are you doing here, thief?"

"Sitting on the Freelady's bed, getting my breath back, after we saved each other's necks," Karvonen answered. He took another deep breath, then looked up to meet Eleret's eyes. "For my half of which I thank you most profoundly, Freelady. I owe you my life."

Eleret blinked, surprised again by Karvonen's familiarity with Cilhar customs. Daner frowned. "Saved *each other's* necks? I saw Eleret save yours, but when did you do anything for her?"

"When I realized your shapeshifting double was a fake," Karvonen said, then glanced doubtfully at Eleret. "At least—"

"I knew he wasn't Daner when I saw him move to attack you," Eleret said. "And not until then, so yes, you did something. But how did *you* know he wasn't Daner?"

"His phrasing. 'I promise to the land's end' is a Rathani saying, and it isn't used often enough for most foreigners to pick it up on a casual visit to the city. Add to that the fact that the Vallaniri trade interests are mostly in the south and east, and the way he was urging you to give him that ring—"

"What?" Daner looked from Karvonen to Eleret with an expression of outrage. "And you were going to do it?"

"Of course not," Eleret said. "Look, it'll make more sense if you hear it in order." She gave a quick summary of events, finishing, "Now you know what he told us. How much of it was true?"

"About Jonystra? Nothing." Daner fingered his dagger as if he was not sure whether he wanted to keep it in hand, put it away, or throw it at someone. "She's not capable of talking yet, and the healer said she wouldn't be until tomorrow afternoon, at the earliest. Once he finished with her, he hauled me over the starboard yard and back; apparently when it comes to taking care of burns, I did almost everything wrong except put her to sleep." He shook his head. "Why do healers always expect people to know as much about their business as they do?"

"They don't." Karvonen shrugged expressively. "They're just like most people—they hate it when some amateur makes their job more difficult. As long as we're explaining things, would someone mind telling me what this ring is that almost got me killed?"

"Yes, I mind," Daner said. "Eleret, watch him for a minute while I call someone. As soon as he's locked up, we can—"

"No."

Both men looked at Eleret with surprise, Karvonen's mingled with dawning delight, Daner's with irritation. "He's a thief and a sneak," Daner said angrily. "You can't trust him!"

"Maybe not, but I owe him something." Eleret looked at Karvonen. "I won't say that I owe you my life, but you've taken risks twice for me. Once to bring me your information, and once to let me know about the shapeshifter."

Karvonen cocked his head to one side and studied her.

"You know, I have the melancholy feeling that neither one was really necessary."

"There's no telling now," Eleret said. "In any case, I won't help Daner lock you up. But I won't help you get away, either. You're on your own, thief."

"Eleret, you can't mean to say that you believe him! He's an admitted thief—"

"And good at it," Karvonen murmured. "Don't forget to say 'good at it.' "

"—and an intruder," Daner continued determinedly. "The sea lords alone know how he got in here."

"Well, I know, too," Karvonen put in. "But I can't say. Professional secret," he added with relish.

"You don't even know that he told you the truth—"

"And *you* don't know that I didn't," Karvonen said smugly.

Daner glared at him. "Whatever his claims, you don't owe him anything but a cell. Which is where I intend to put him as quickly as possible, whether you agree or not."

"That's called the watch in," Karvonen said, shaking his head. "You'll never get her to help now. Oh, and by the way, I didn't make any claims. I acknowledged a debt. Another one," he added in a gloomy tone. "Why these things always happen to me . . ."

"Go ahead, then," Eleret said to Daner.

"I thought you'd see it my way," Daner said with a triumphant glance at Karvonen. "I won't be long; keep him here—"

"No."

"What?"

"I won't keep him here," Eleret said calmly.

Daner transfered his glare from the thief to Eleret. "Why not?"

"Because she already said she wouldn't help you lock me up," Karvonen said, grinning broadly. "You don't know much about Cilhar, or you wouldn't have wasted your breath arguing. So what are you going to do now, my lordly Ciaronese friend? The minute you're out that door, I'm gone. And believe me, once I am, you won't catch me."

"I won't have to," Daner snapped. "Because you're not getting away, no matter what you think."

"I got in here, didn't I?"

"Stop it, both of you." Eleret made her voice as commanding as she could, hoping that surprise would make them listen even if nothing else did. If they kept to the path they were traveling, there'd be blood on someone's dagger before morning.

"Eleret, can't you see what he's doing?" Daner said. "This is all some sort of trick. He's probably after the ring too, just like everyone else."

"I'm never like everyone else," Karvonen objected, and paused. Then, too casually, he asked, "What ring?"

"This one," Eleret said, holding out her right hand. She kept her fingers curled into a fist, just in case.

"Eleret, are you crazy?" Daner demanded as Karvonen studied the ring with an expression of casual interest. "What do you think he came here for?"

"I came to give her some information," Karvonen said patiently. "I've told you that several times."

"I don't believe you."

"I do," Eleret said, surprising herself as much as Daner. "But if you won't take his word for it—"

"Take his word? He's a thief!"

"But the City Guards said the Aurelicos were honorable ones," Eleret said uncomfortably. She couldn't bring herself to say aloud that she rather liked Karvonen. In the past, when she had needed to know whether to trust someone, she had relied on the knowledge and experience of her family and friends, as most Cilhar did. Here in Ciaron she had little to depend on but her own instincts, and she couldn't hold those up to Daner as a reason to believe Karvonen.

"An honorable thief is a contradiction in terms."

"Well, Karvonen seems pretty contradictory to me."

Karvonen's eyes widened; then he grinned and bounced to his feet. "A fairer compliment has never been paid me, Freelady," he said in Cilhar, bowing with fluid grace.

"What was that he said?" Daner asked suspiciously.

"He thanked me," Eleret told him, allowing some of her irritation to show. "Daner, do you intend to stand there all night? Because that's what you'll have to do, if you won't trust at least one of us."

"It's not a matter of trust."

At least he didn't sound quite as determined as he had a moment earlier. "Then what is it a matter of?"

"Pride," Karvonen suggested with an air of innocent interest.

"Keep out of this," Eleret said, exasperated. Karvonen was behaving like the kind of person who'd poke a willow wand into a wasp's nest for the fun of watching, never mind the stings. And just when she was starting to get somewhere with Daner, too.

"I can't," Karvonen said even more innocently than before. "I'm what you're arguing about, aren't I? So I'm in the middle whether I want to be or not. I'm just trying to enjoy myself a little."

"If you're not careful, you'll enjoy yourself right into a cell."

"All right," Daner said abruptly. "He can go, but only because you say you owe him a favor. And this cancels it." Setting his knife back in its sheath at last, Daner looked toward Karvonen. "Don't come anywhere near Eleret again, or I'll hand you over to the Emperor's Questioner. Understand?"

Karvonen blinked, then looked reproachfully at Eleret. "I thought you said he wasn't your boyfriend."

"What?" said Daner, completely at a loss.

"He isn't," Eleret said. "And you'd better leave while you have the chance."

Daner glared at Eleret. "What did he mean?" he demanded, jerking his thumb at Karvonen.

"That little speech of yours sounded an awful lot like a fit of jealousy to me," Karvonen replied. "I'm sure you'd agree, if you could consider the matter rationally."

"Karvonen you idiot, get *out* of here," Eleret said as Daner's face reddened and his right hand dropped to his dagger's hilt once again.

"Sorry, no." Smiling, Karvonen sat deliberately down on the bed and swung his feet up on the covers. Clasping his hands behind his head, he leaned back against the nearest bedpost, a picture of casual relaxation, and said, "Think it through, Freelady. When you owe someone a favor, you don't get to decide how to pay it off."

Daner growled and started forward. "Don't worry, Freelady," Karvonen said without moving, as Eleret caught at Daner's arm. "He's not likely to kill an unarmed, unresisting man, or even wound him, particularly not on top of your bed."

"You—" Daner stopped short, staring at Karvonen, then began to laugh. "You're right."

"Well!" Karvonen sat up and returned Daner's stare, then gave him a half-bow that managed to look graceful in spite of Karvonen's semi-reclining position. "I underestimated you, my lord. Or perhaps 'misjudged' is the better word; what do you think?"

"Oh, misjudged, certainly," Daner said, still laughing. "Since it seems I did the same to you. That way, we're even."

Eleret looked from one to the other, baffled by the sudden air of amity. "If that's settled, Karvonen had better leave now."

"Oh, no." Karvonen leaned back against the bedpost once more, looking stubborn. "I'm not going anywhere, not for a while, anyway."

"Why not?" Eleret and Daner said together.

Karvonen favored them with a charming and impartial smile. "Because I want to collect on that favor first. Tell me about this ring of yours, and the lady downstairs who can't talk yet, and whatever brought you to Ciaron in the first place. It's a fair trade, information for information, and when you're done we'll call your side of the debt canceled. Agreed?" He looked at them expectantly.

EIGHTEEN

Eleret stared at Karvonen in disbelief. Beside her, Daner stirred, and she realized that she was still holding his arm. She let go quickly, too quickly, and Karvonen cocked an eyebrow at her. Her face warmed, but she forced the muscles to remain still, refusing to acknowledge it. Karvonen's expression grew more sardonic, and he gave Daner a sour look.

"I don't think 'contradictory' was the right word for him, Eleret," Daner said, frowning. " 'Audacious' would be a better term. The idea of trading information with a thief—"

"Well, I can't steal it out of your head," Karvonen said, with the air of a man trying to be reasonable. "And it works the same for you, my lord, unless the Adepts of the Island of the Moon know a spell that tells you what people are thinking *and* have taught you how to use it. So we don't have much choice, do we?"

"You've already told us what you know," Daner pointed out.

"Some of it." Karvonen smiled blandly. "There might be more. You can't say for sure."

"What do you want us to tell you?" Eleret didn't believe that Karvonen had anything else useful to say, but if he decided to follow her around in order to satisfy his curiosity, it could cause problems. "Keep in mind that there are limits to that favor I said I'd do you. And you've already admitted that you owe me more than I owe you."

Karvonen grimaced. "I'm not likely to forget it. Tell me about this ring with the raven on it."

"Eleret . . ."

"Don't start again, Daner! I've had enough argument for one night, and I'm tired."

"So am I." Stretching his legs across the bed, Karvonen wiggled his shoulders into a more comfortable position against the pillows and gave Daner another too-sweet smile. "And the sooner you tell me what I want to know, the sooner we can all go to bed." He paused for a quick glance at Eleret. "And—eventually—to sleep."

Daner clenched his fist around the hilt of his dagger, but had the wit not to respond in words.

"What exactly do you want to know?" Eleret asked Karvonen with determined calm. A matter-of-fact, stick-to-the-strategy approach seemed the best way of dealing with the thief's deliberate outrageousness.

Karvonen gave her a reproachful look, then shrugged. "Why does your *friend* there think this ring of yours is too important to talk to a thief about?"

"Because so many people seem to want it," Eleret said. "You saw one yourself—the shapeshifter who was pretending to be Daner. And don't ask why they're interested; if we knew that, we might not be in such a mess."

"Mess?" said Karvonen, looking pointedly down at the silk-embroidered coverlet and then around at the rest of the room's furnishings.

"Appearances are deceiving," Eleret said.

Karvonen cocked his head thoughtfully. "Not yours."

"Perhaps not at the moment," Eleret said, thinking of the problems she'd had with the skirt she'd worn most of the day. Then she snorted softly. Maybe Karvonen was right; the disguise apparently hadn't deceived anyone. "Is that everything you want? Because if it is—"

"Nowhere near," Karvonen said. "You wouldn't think it to look at me, but I'm an ambitious man. I want to be wealthy, talented, and four inches taller. I want to be the first man to steal the Emperor's crown and scepter in full view of the court—"

Daner raised an eyebrow. "*That* isn't why you're in Ciaron, is it? To steal the Emperor's crown?"

Karvonen's eyes grew large in a parody of surprised innocence. "Heavens no! I was speaking of the Emperor of *Rathane*. I thought that was obvious."

Eleret almost laughed at the blend of suspicion and annoyance on Daner's face. "Why should it be obvious?" Daner demanded.

"Because the crown of the Emperor of Rathane is far more impressive." Karvonen's eyes went out of focus, as if he were gazing at something in the middle of the room that only he could see, and his voice took on a dreamy quality. "Three flawless blue-white diamonds, each the size of a hen's egg, and a good two dozen more as big as my thumbnail; six matched rubies and eight sapphires as big as a dove's egg; four big square emeralds that would fill a child's palm; and enough smaller gems to stock a jewelsmith's shop for at least four years. Plus a goodly amount of gold and silver to hold them all together, of course. Tasteless, but immensely valuable. The scepter—"

"I don't believe it," Daner said.

"Oh, that's right. You've never been to Rathane."

"Neither have I," Eleret put in. "Nor do I intend to go there. So this whole discussion is beside the point as far as I'm concerned. If you two want to continue it, go out into the hall so I can get some sleep."

"But you haven't told me what I want to know yet," Karvonen said plaintively.

"I've told you as much as you've asked," Eleret said, trying to be patient. "If you *will* keep wandering off the main trail—"

Karvonen sighed. "Oh, very well. The ring. Everybody wants it, you say. How did *you* get it?"

"It's a family heirloom."

There was a moment's silence; then Karvonen shook his head. "Getting information out of you is like trying to take a toy from a toddler," he complained. "So you inherited the thing. How long ago? From whom, exactly? Under what circumstances? How many people knew about it? And how many of *them* know the ring is magical?"

"No one," Eleret said, frowning. "I didn't know it myself until today. So how do *you* know?"

Karvonen sighed again, this time with more sincerity. "My big mouth. I guessed."

"Did you?" Daner said skeptically. "Or did you know before you came here looking for it?"

"If I'd known, I wouldn't have come, Cilhar debt or no Cilhar debt. I don't fool around with magic." Karvonen paused. "If I can help it."

"How did you guess?" Eleret asked.

"It was the way you saved my life a minute ago," Karvonen said reluctantly. "You're no magician, so whatever broke the choking spell—"

"What?"

Karvonen looked from Eleret to Daner and back. "You didn't realize, either of you? The shapeshifter threw a choking spell at me just before your raven's-foot hit his shoulder. Eleret broke it when she grabbed my hands. If she hadn't— Anyway, there aren't many Cilhar magicians, so the odds were good that she had something with her that neutralized magic. When you said everyone was after that ring, it seemed obvious."

"The ring neutralizes magic?" Eleret stared down at her hand. "I thought it just warns me whenever there are spells nearby."

"Warns you?" Karvonen sat bolt upright, his studied air of casualness completely gone. He leaned forward, every fiber intent. "How does it warn you, Freelady?"

"It pricks my finger."

"But not always," Daner pointed out. "It didn't react to my probe." He rubbed his chin. "Not in any way *you* could feel, at least."

"Well, that part fits with what Karvonen just said about neutralizing magic." Eleret frowned, struggling to explain clearly what she wasn't sure she quite grasped herself. "And I think it only warns me when I need warning."

"Then why didn't it let you know about Jonystra?" Daner asked.

"Who's Jonystra?" Karvonen asked. "And how and why did she try to get hold of the ring? And don't ask me how I know that, because you've mentioned the name several times already, and it's fairly clear she's not trying to help out."

Eleret looked at Karvonen in mild exasperation. "You ask

all the right questions, thief. Trouble is, we don't have the answers."

"Start at the beginning, then. It makes for a more organized tale."

Frowning indignantly, Daner opened his mouth. Then he closed it again and sighed. "It's your choice, Eleret. I'm still not sure it's a good idea."

"What can we lose?" Eleret said. Tactically, they were in a strong position; she had the ring, she had allies, and she was in a safe place. Relatively safe, she amended, remembering the shapeshifter. In terms of long-range strategy, however, things were more precarious. She didn't know enough about the ring, about who wanted it and why. Without more information, she couldn't plan an effective defense. On the other hand . . . She turned to Karvonen.

"Information for information, you said. What have you got to trade that might be useful to us?"

"I won't know until I hear your story."

"You'll have to do better than that," Eleret said. "I won't pay in advance for arrows I haven't tried. Give me an idea of what I'm buying, or take your wares to someone else."

"And people say the Cilhar are too insular to bargain well." Karvonen shook his head sadly. "They ought to meet you, Freelady, and readjust their ideas."

"Your information?"

"Mmmm. I've already told you about Grand Master Gorchastrin's death, but I could add a fair bit about him and his order. Your not-so-friendly shapeshifter seems to be Rathani; I can tell you about their customs, habits, and so on."

That might be useful, but she wanted more. Eleret gave Karvonen a neutral nod. "Go on."

"I can tell you a good bit about Ciaronese politics. And a lot about the, er, foibles of the nobility." Karvonen gave

Daner a deliberately guileless look. "Some of it might be quite instructive. I can tell you a few things about shapeshifters that you may not know. And of course, I can always take an order."

"What does *that* mean?" Daner said.

"What does it sound like? You tell me who or what you want to find out about, and I'll set the family on to it. In a day or two, you'll know as much about 'em as can be known."

Daner snorted. "Then why are you asking *us* about the ring, instead of this miracle-working family?"

Karvonen pursed his lips and stared past Daner's left shoulder. "Well now, I had thought of that. But I'm not sure they'd tell me."

"Then what good will it do us to ask you about the ring?" Eleret said, frowning.

"Oh, if *you* ask, Freelady, they'll give you whatever you want to know. I thought I'd mentioned that there's an aid-in-distress clause for Cilhar." Karvonen leaned back against the headboard, a picture of innocence. "So tell me, Freelady: what do you want to know?"

As Eleret hesitated, Daner's lips twitched. Then he shook his head with reluctant admiration. "You're a rare catch indeed, thief. You're setting the younger son against the elder so you can walk off with the family fortune."

Karvonen smiled smugly. "I told you I was good."

"I don't quite follow you," Eleret said.

"If he's telling the truth, he's wiggled himself into a position where we're going to make it possible for him to get what he wants to know," Daner said. "On his own, he can't find out anything from us or from his family. But if *we* ask, his family will tell us whatever they can dig up. And now that we know that, we have to ask."

We? thought Eleret. *It's my ring!* But all she said was, "Why?"

"Because *somebody* out there knows more about that ring than we do, or they wouldn't want it so badly."

"Several somebodies, by the look of it," Karvonen muttered. "Cilhar never do things by halves."

"The only way to find out what his family knows is through him," Daner continued, nodding at Karvonen. "And the only payment he seems interested in is our information."

"Well, if you offered me the crown of Rathane, I wouldn't turn it down. The object, that is, not the position."

"So we tell him what *we* know. Then he talks to his people, they tell him what *they* know, and suddenly he's the only one with both pieces of information."

"Until he passes it along to us," Eleret said.

"Assuming he does."

"Of course I will!" Karvonen said indignantly. "The family would throw me out for sure if I didn't."

Eleret considered briefly. "All right, information for information. But you won't get everything you want, not before you fill your half of the bargain."

"Or after," Karvonen muttered, giving her a sour look. "Well, I suppose it's my own fault for sticking my fingers through the wrong knothole. Agreed, Freelady. What do you want to know?"

"Quite a lot." Eleret frowned, trying to decide what would be most useful. "How many people have heard the same rumors you did, and will act on them? How many other thieves will be after my ring?"

Karvonen winced. "There shouldn't be any. Nobody's going to waste time on a wild rumor when there are over a dozen targets in Ciaron with a sure payoff. Nobody but me, that is."

"Then where did all these other people who're trying to steal Eleret's ring come from?" Daner demanded.

"What can I say?" Karvonen spread his hands. "They're not thieves."

"Then what are they?"

"Amateurs."

Daner laughed. "All right, I'll stop fishing in Eleret's waters. He's all yours, Eleret."

"Actually, that was going to be my next question." Eleret looked at Karvonen. "You know about Gorchastrin, or whoever is pretending to be Gorchastrin, and you've heard us talking about Jonystra. If they're not professional thieves, what are they? And how did they find out about my ring?"

"I don't know," Karvonen said. "But I can probably find out. It would help if you'd give me a little more to start with."

"Such as?"

"Such as Jonystra's full name, where you met her, and how she got hurt badly enough for him"—Karvonen nodded toward Daner—"to call in a healer. And if you want to know why she wants your ring or how she found out about it, it would help if you told me more about that, too."

"It would help if we knew more," Daner muttered.

"Jonystra followed me to the inn the day I arrived in Ciaron," Eleret said. "She told me her name was Jonystra Nirandol, that she was on her way to Kith Alunel, and that she collected small, old things like brooches and rings. She's probably the person who searched my room while I was out, though I haven't any proof of that. When Daner came to the inn to accompany me out of Ciaron, she was talking to me, which is how she met him. Daner's cousin, Baroja Vallaniri, brought her here to . . . to amuse people after dinner; he said she was a Luck-seer and would chart cards for everyone. He told us later that a Trader had recommended her. Jonystra charted cards for Daner's sisters; when she tried to do mine, the cards exploded in the middle of it and burned her."

"Not quite," Daner put in. "Fire certainly did shoot out of the cards, but Jonystra's injuries were back-flow burns."

"Terrific." Karvonen rolled his eyes. "Another wizard."

"I'm not sure." Daner hesitated, glanced at Eleret, shrugged, and went on. "You don't get burns like hers from a minor spell-casting. If she'd been doing anything major while she charted Eleret's cards, I should have felt it, but I didn't."

"So?"

"So she may have been using someone else's magic, not her own."

"That's supposed to make me feel better? I assume you don't have any idea who it could have been."

"I still think it was Mobrellan," Eleret said.

Daner shook his head. "If Mobrellan had that kind of power, he wouldn't have been working for Jonystra."

"Why not?" Karvonen asked. "And how do you know he was? Who is this Mobrellan person, by the way?"

"Jonystra's porter," Daner said with a hint of impatience. "He got away in the confusion after the cards exploded."

"He vanished," Eleret corrected. "The same way the shapeshifter vanished from this room a few minutes ago. I think Mobrellan is the wizard who was helping Jonystra, and I think he's the shapeshifter who pretended to be Daner. He's probably the person Karvonen says was pretending to be Gorchastrin, too."

"A wizard *and* a shapeshifter rolled up in one?" Karvonen ran a hand through his hair, thoroughly rumpling it. "This gets worse and worse."

"I suppose it's possible," Daner said, frowning. "But I still don't see why he'd have bothered playing porter for Jonystra. If he has that much power—"

"Maybe it was easier to hide behind someone else," Karvonen said. "A lot of shapeshifters work that way; it seems to come with the ability to get inside a different skin. Maybe he wanted someone else to take the blame if things went wrong; maybe they're old friends or partners; maybe she owed him a favor, or he owed her one. Having power doesn't mean you have to be right out in front where people can shoot arrows at you all the time."

"No, but—"

"It's possible," Eleret broke in. "You said so yourself. We don't *know* anything about Mobrellan, and until we do we shouldn't waste time arguing about whose guess is going to be the right one."

"So you want to know about Jonystra Nirandol and her porter Mobrellan," Karvonen said. "Anything else?"

"No." There was the obnoxious Birok Maggen from the Imperial Guard, of course, but Commander Weziral could tell her what she needed to know about him. It wouldn't hurt to find out a little more about Gorchastrin, just in case Karvonen was wrong about his being dead, but she'd do better to get that information, too, from other sources. Eleret swallowed a yawn. "That's all I want, and I want it as soon as I can get it. So you'd better get started."

"That," Karvonen said sagely, "was a hint." He rose smoothly and bowed. "Never let it be said that an Aurelico doesn't know when to take a hint. It's been an enlightening evening, Freelady. My lord."

Daner's eyes narrowed; then he smiled slightly and returned Karvonen's bow with a flourish. "That it has. Fare you . . . well."

NINETEEN

I t wasn't that easy, of course. Despite the promising beginning, it took another fifteen minutes to get both Karvonen and Daner out of the room. Neither seemed willing to be the first to go, and in the end Eleret had to threaten to summon a servant to get rid of them. When they left at last, she sighed in relief and began preparing for bed, hoping there would be no more unexpected visitors that evening.

She considered the possibility as she unbraided her hair. Sleeping armed was nothing new, though it was a shame she wouldn't be able to enjoy the full comfort the bed promised. The room's physical entrances were easy enough to shield; Eleret tilted the table against the door and balanced her mother's whetstone against the window shutters, where the slightest jar would send it clattering to the floor. A double handful of raven's-feet set out in the Heron's Dance pattern on the floor around the bed took care of the possible return of the shapeshifting wizard, or at least it was the best she could do. She wished briefly that she had thought to ask Daner for a spell to keep the shapeshifter from reappearing as quietly and inexplicably as he had vanished. Then she smiled. Daner was no fool, and neither was his father; once they knew someone could pop through their guards like that, they'd take some sort of precaution to protect the whole house. She shouldn't have to worry about the shapeshifter popping back. For a long moment, she stared down at the raven's-feet; then she left them where they were.

Eleret expected to fall asleep the moment she lay down, but her mind was too full to let her rest. With a resigned sigh, she opened her eyes and began setting her thoughts in order.

She couldn't go back to the mountains now, not with so many unknown enemies interested in her and her mother's ring. Pa would still be laid up with his broken leg, and Nilly and Jiv couldn't face down the kind of trouble Eleret had run into in Ciaron. Shapeshifters and wizards and government officials would be a handful even for Pa. The neighbors would help out, of course, if they knew there was trouble, but you couldn't go shooting every stranger in the mountains full of arrows anymore. In some ways, the old days had been simpler.

Listen to me, Eleret thought. *I sound like one of the old folks down at Raken's place, going on about the way things used to be.* She snorted softly and turned her mind back to her problems.

First among them was the raven ring. She thought she knew, now, why Tamm had taken it with her to the wars. A ring that warned of hostile magic would be exceedingly useful to a soldier, and one that broke spells would be invaluable. But Tamm was too canny to have talked about the ring, or even worn it openly. She'd have turned the seal to her palm, as Eleret had, and worn it on her off hand to make it even less noticeable. So how had Jonystra, the shapeshifter, Maggen, *and* Gorchastrin all found out about it?

And did the ring have anything to do with Tamm's death? Eleret frowned. According to Karvonen, the real Gorchastrin had discovered something important, something that would be a great help to his order of Rathani wizards. Could his discovery have been the raven ring? The Rathani often used battle magic, and if Gorchastrin had cast a spell and the raven ring had bitten him back, the way it had bitten Daner when he tried to find out more about it . . .

Eleret made a rude noise in the darkness. The shapeshifter was a wizard, too, and Jonystra must have at least a little skill or she couldn't have tried to enchant Eleret's cardcharting. The real Gorchastrin was certainly a wizard, and the false one she had met in Ciaron was probably the shapeshifter. Maggen was the only one of the people after her ring whom she didn't *know* was a wizard, and she supposed that it was quite possible that he knew some magic as well. It looked as if she could stop wondering how they had all found out about her ring. The wonder was that every wizard in the city wasn't chasing her.

No, that wasn't reasonable, either. The ring didn't announce its presence; Daner hadn't noticed it at all until she'd mentioned it to him. So if she was right about how all the wizards had learned of the ring, each of them must have cast a spell at the ring or at someone wearing it. Why? One Rathani wizard—Gorchastrin or the shapeshifter, perhaps— might have been involved in the skirmishes around Kesandir, but what about the rest?

Eleret scowled into the darkness, then shrugged. Her problem was still the same: she didn't know enough. There was no point in making wild guesses, especially when tomorrow she'd learn more. Even if Jonystra still wasn't fit to question, Commander Weziral would have news of Maggen and his noble relations. Until then, Eleret should concentrate on general plans and what little she *did* know about the raven ring.

Start at the beginning, Karvonen had said, *it makes for a more organized tale.* Well, he was right about that at least. But what was the beginning?

Many years ago, when the mountains were young and the Cilhar lived in peace, Geleraise Vinlarrian came to live among us. The memory of her mother's voice, blending with the crackle of a winter fire and the roof creaking in the bitter wind outside, was so vivid that Eleret's eyes prickled. She turned her head into the strange smoothness of the bedclothes and fought a losing battle against the dammed-up tears. When they broke through at last, so did other memories, each as precise and clear as the first: Tamm aiming an arrow for a difficult shot, her eyes narrowed in concentration and wisps of chestnut hair escaping from her braid; Tamm showing Eleret how to hold her first sword and later sparring with her; the sunny spring day they had climbed together to the top of the lookout peak and undone their braids to let the damp wind fill their hair with the smells of earth and new growth. Tamm in marching dress, her kit slung across one shoulder, her face expressionless, saying, *I have to do this, Eleret. All my life, there has been war, and I don't seem to be able to do without it. You're young enough to adjust; I'm not, though Morravik knows I've tried. I'll be back in a few months, if all goes well.* And she had been, that time, and six other times since. Until now.

I should have stopped her, Eleret thought, but she hadn't been able to stop Tamm the first time, nor any of the other times. *If I had said it out loud, maybe she'd have stayed this once. Maybe she wouldn't have died.* But she hadn't needed to say it. Tamm had known how she felt, how they all felt, and she had gone any-way.

She died with honor, Eleret reminded herself, and almost stopped weeping until a treacherous voice at the back of her head whispered, *but still, she died.* Even the thought that it had been Tamm's choice brought only anger and renewed tears. The friends and relations who had died in the old wars had been defending the mountains, protecting their homes and families. Tamm had been fighting for others, for money, for the love of the fight itself, or perhaps for some other reason Eleret could not even suspect. It was too late now to ask, and the part of Eleret that understood without the explanation was washing away in the flood of tears.

"Why?" Eleret cried aloud to the darkness, and the single word encompassed a multitude of questions, some with an-swers and some forever unanswerable: why had Tamm died, why hadn't her formidable skills or the raven ring been enough to save her, why had she had to leave the mountains and her family, why was it Eleret who had to face the tangle Tamm had left behind, why did she have to stay another day in this confusing, complicated city, why was it *Tamm's* ring so many people wanted? The stone walls of the room swal-lowed Eleret's cry and gave back only a faint, wordless echo. Eleret buried her face in her pillow, hiding from the dark and the questions and the unwanted responsibility of the raven ring, cold and close around her finger. Gradually, her tears ceased, but it was a long time before she slept.

She woke at dawn, with sticky eyelids and a mouth that felt as if she had been eating sand. The remnant of last night's wash water was still in the jug; she picked her way to it between the raven's-feet on the floor, her bare feet finding the clear path through the pattern without conscious thought. Once she had washed properly, she felt much better.

A faint jumble of far-off city noises drifted through the shutter slats. Eleret retrieved her whetstone and raven's-feet and replaced the table in its proper place, pleased that her precautions had been unnecessary. As soon as she had checked her weapons and straightened her clothes, she left the room in search of breakfast and a place to go through the basic drill. The previous night's succession of argument, thought, and unbridled emotion had left her with a need for some simple, straightforward physical exertion. Besides, she hadn't practiced for two days, not since she'd arrived in Ciaron, and with wizards and shapeshifters and Morravik knew who else after her she couldn't afford to lose her edge.

Her footsteps echoed dully along the empty hallway, though she stepped as softly as she could. She turned left at the end of the hall, then right, looking for the stairs Lady Laurinel had brought her up the previous evening. As she rounded the second corner, she heard a door open behind her. She whirled, to find herself facing the disapproving glare of Jakella, the gaunt serving woman who tended Laurinel's son, Drioren.

"What are you doing here?" the woman demanded before Eleret could speak.

"Looking for the stairs."

Jakella folded her lips together in a thin, disapproving line. "Indeed. I fear you've made a mistake. The stairs at the end of this hall don't go up."

"I don't want to go up," Eleret said, puzzled. She couldn't imagine Lord tir Vallaniri setting up a drill area on his roof. "I'm trying to find the guards' practice ground."

Surprise and consternation flashed across the gaunt

woman's face and were gone. "I wouldn't know about that." Her eyes narrowed, and she added, "You won't find my lord Daner there, not at this hour."

"I'm not looking for Lord Daner. I'm looking for the practice ground." And she'd wasted enough time talking. Jakella was plainly determined to be as unhelpful as possible. So Eleret nodded and turned away. At the stair door, she glanced back. Jakella still stood watching, her face stiff.

Eleret met no one on the stairs, and the long room with the spindly chairs was unoccupied when she entered. There was no one in the room where they had eaten the night before, and no one in any of the halls she was familiar with. In front of the wall chamber where Jonystra had done her card-charting, Eleret paused, trying to decide whether to begin wandering through the house at random. Just as she was about to retrace her steps, the chamber door opened and Daner came out.

He had dark circles under his eyes, and when he saw Eleret, he paused and blinked at her. "Eleret! What are you doing up at this hour? Is something wrong?"

Eleret hesitated, then called, "Behind you!" as she shifted her weight to a fighting stance.

Daner ducked and spun, reaching for his dagger. When he realized that there was no one else in the hall, he straightened and looked at Eleret indignantly. "What was that about?"

"I apologize for startling you, but it was the only way I could think of to make sure you were you."

"Oh, yes, the way I move. Amazing what a false fright will do for you. Five minutes ago, I'd have sworn I was too tired to jump like that." He settled his dagger back in its sheath as he spoke.

It wasn't just the difference in Daner's stance, she realized. The shapeshifter's automatic reaction had been to throw a spell; Daner reached for a weapon. She said as much, then added, "I hope that doesn't mean he's a better wizard than you are."

"Probably. I couldn't have vanished the way he did." Daner looked at her thoughtfully. "You don't have to do that every time we meet, you know. From what little I know of them, shapeshifters don't heal any faster than other people, and the fellow that was here last night left with a hole in his shoulder."

"Not a very big one," Eleret said. "Still, it should make using that arm a bit uncomfortable for a day or two." And now that she had something to look for, she was sure that she could spot any signs of stiffness in a false Daner or Lord tir Vallaniri if she had to. If she had to . . . "If he's a better wizard than you are, can you keep him from coming back the same way he left?"

"I've spent all night trying." Daner rubbed the back of his hand across his eyes. "I don't know how he did what he did, so I couldn't just counter it. I had to set up every warding spell I know, and hope that one of them will keep him out, or at least give me warning enough to try something else."

"You did them alone?"

"Father wants all of this kept as quiet as possible, especially the shapeshifter. Actually, I'm not certain he quite believes that part. Anyway, it won't stay quiet for long if we start calling in wizards, so I had to cast the spells myself."

"I see." Eleret thought Lord tir Vallaniri was arming himself to hunt a fox when it was a mountain lion that had been at the hens, but then, she'd seen the shapeshifter and Daner's father hadn't. "How long will your spells last?"

Daner shrugged. "A few hours, half a day—I'm not sure. I've never tried anything like this before. The spells should give me time to consult Adept Climeral, though, and that's all I really want from them."

Looking at the tiredness on Daner's face, Eleret felt guilty. "You may only need a few hours. I doubt that the shapeshifter will have much interest in your household once I've left."

"You can't leave until we're sure it's safe." Daner sounded slightly shocked by the very suggestion. "You're a— You're our *guest*."

"Granted," Eleret said, frowning in turn. "And as your guest, I have an obligation to see that I don't bring harm upon your household."

"Baroja is the one who dragged Jonystra in here," Daner pointed out. "You didn't have anything to do with that."

"Didn't I? Do you really think she'd have agreed to chart cards for your sisters if she hadn't thought I'd be here, too?"

"She might have."

Eleret shook her head. "You know better. And the shape-shifter was after me. The sooner I'm gone, the sooner you can stop worrying about wards."

For a minute, Daner looked as if he wanted to argue; then he sighed. "Let's talk about it after breakfast. Even if I agree with you, the wards are up now, so you might as well stay safe for as long as they last. We've got all morning to talk about it. Maybe even all day."

Which wouldn't be the best strategy, in Eleret's opinion. She'd do better to leave Daner's house at a time of her own choosing, well before circumstances forced her out. Besides . . . "I was hoping to do a few drills before I ate. Where's your practice ground?"

"Down and out," Daner said. "And it's in the center court, so it's even warded. I'll show you. If it please you, Freelady?" He extended his arm with exaggerated courtesy.

Eleret chuckled and laid her hand on his elbow. "Indeed it does, Lord Daner."

The practice ground was a neat square of packed sand in the corner of what Daner referred to as an open court. Eleret would have described it as a large, walled yard. The Vallaniri residence rose on all sides, shutting out the world. Only the square of gray clouds overhead and a faint sense of movement in the air let Eleret know she was out-of-doors. Daner made sure the guard at the inner door knew she was a guest, then left her to her practice.

She began with a series of controlled stretches, holding each position for a long moment before moving fluidly into the next. She repeated the sequence four times, increasing her speed slowly with each repetition, then went on into more strenuous moves. Sand crunched under her boots as she kicked and leaped and spun. The three days since her last practice had allowed her muscles to get a thorough rest without beginning to grow soft, and everything felt deceptively easy. Though she knew she would regret it next day if she pushed herself too hard, Eleret could not resist doing a few combinations—leap and roll, fall and rising punch, spin-kick and drop-dodge. It felt good to work; her only regret was her lack of a sparring partner.

Around her, the household began to stir. A window scraped open above her; Eleret spun and ducked as if it were a known threat. Two women carrying water jars walked across the yard and gave her curious, sidelong glances. They, too, became an unwitting part of Eleret's drill. She kept on until she felt herself beginning to slow. Although she could have continued for another ten or fifteen minutes, and would have, had she been at home, she reduced her efforts. There was no sense in working herself tired when later in the day she might be attacked by the shapeshifter, or Maggen, or more Syaski.

As she started into her closing stretches, Eleret saw Daner watching her from the near doorway. How long had he been there? She dismissed the thought and concentrated on her work; the ending stretches were as important as the opening ones. Finally, feeling loose and pleasantly tired, Eleret brushed the dusting of sand from her clothes and stepped off the practice ground.

Daner came forward at once. "Impressive," he said as he reached her side. His eyes were admiring, but all he said was, "I don't have to ask whether you've caught yourself an appetite."

"Yes, I was just going to ask about that breakfast you mentioned."

"It's ready and waiting upstairs. Along with Aunt Kistran; she was up early, so I thought I would hook her now, while there aren't a lot of people around to ask awkward questions."

Eleret did a quick mental review of the previous night's events. "That's right, your cousin suggested we talk to her about Jonystra's cards. Do you think she'll mind?"

"Mind? She's happier than an oyster-fisher with a bucket of pearls. She loves giving advice."

"Good." Eleret smiled at Daner's expression. "It's always good to have information, and I don't *have* to follow the advice."

Daner nodded and smiled warmly in return. "Very true, Freelady. And you have an advantage over us relations: you won't have to explain later why you didn't do as she suggested. Shall we go?"

TWENTY

In spite of the fact that there were only three of them at the long breakfast table, Vallaniri meal-servers descended on them in hordes the moment Eleret took her seat. Their offerings included a large bowl of steamed clams, a platter of soft white cheese mixed with herbs, hot bread, plums preserved in wine, cold sliced beef, and several things Eleret did not recognize. Sternly suppressing an unexpected longing for a plain bowl of porridge, Eleret took a little cheese and some bread, and what her mother had called "tasting samples" of the other foods.

Lady Kistran had already heaped her plate with clams and a thick green paste studded with chunks of something white. As Daner and Eleret finished choosing their meals, she smiled at Eleret and said, "Daner tells me you have some questions about your cards, Freelady."

Eleret nodded. "Especially since the charting was . . . interrupted so spectacularly."

"Yes, Baroja told me." Lady Kistran separated one clam

from the rest and inspected it. "How far into the chart did the Luck-seer get?"

"She was just starting on El—Freelady Salven's future," Daner said. "That's what is worrying us. There were eleven cards left to turn, and after things calmed down we found eleven with singe marks. We think Jonystra was trying to influence what is going to happen, and I was hoping you could give us an idea what she had in mind."

"Possibly." Lady Kistran sounded as if there were not a shred of doubt in her mind. "Since all of the cards involve the future, I should be able to get a general sense of where the reading was going. They would have more significance if you could determine their intended order, of course."

"I think I already have a general sense of the reading," Daner said. Eleret frowned, mildly annoyed by the way Daner had taken over the conversation. *Lady Kistran is his aunt*, she reminded herself, but could not keep from adding, *Still, it's my cards they're discussing.*

"The singed cards were all bad ones," Daner went on. "Silence, Death, Despair, Chaos, War, Night—"

Lady Kistran snorted expressively. Daner broke off and gave her an inquiring look. Caught in mid-mouthful, his aunt could only make a disapproving face and shake her head.

"I assure you, Aunt, I'm not mistaken." Daner frowned uncertainly. "Would you like to see the cards?"

Shaking her head again, Lady Kistran swallowed. "No, that's quite unnecessary. Unless it was an unusual deck?"

"I don't think so—"

"Then it doesn't matter. What I was attempting to convey is that the cards you named are *not* necessarily bad cards."

"Well, I'm sure Jonystra didn't intend anything good," Eleret said.

"That's as may be, but if she meant you ill, she chose an odd set of cards." Lady Kistran set down her eating knife and tapped the table with her forefinger. "If you'd ever bothered to study their meanings, Daner, you'd have seen it yourself. Silence, for instance—that's for waiting, preparation, and possibilities. Or Chaos. Only an amateur would deliberately include Chaos in a chart she was trying to influence. Chaos is a card of complete unpredictability and uncontrolled change; it would be just as likely to disrupt the charter's plans as help them. And Death is for an important choice—something life-changing, but not necessarily bad. Some of the cards you named are unfavorable ones, certainly, but not all by any means."

"I think I see," Eleret said. "They all *sound* sinister, though."

"Maybe that's it," Daner said, frowning. "Maybe Jonystra chose them by their names, to intimidate you, instead of by their meanings."

"That doesn't explain—" Eleret stopped. Daner's theory didn't explain the warning she had received from her ring, but she didn't want to mention that in front of Lady Kistran. Too many people knew about the ring already.

"It's also possible that the woman was not as good a Luck-seer as she pretended," Lady Kistran said. "What did she tell you about the cards she *did* chart?"

"I don't think we need to go into that," Daner said as he cut one of the plums into small pieces. "If she was no good, the chart won't mean anything anyway, and—"

"No, no, the competence—or incompetence—of the *Luck-seer* has nothing to do with the accuracy of the *cards.*" Lady Kistran shook her head. "Really, Daner, I'm surprised at you. With all the interest your sisters take, I'd expected you to be better informed."

"I've been busy with other things, Aunt."

Lady Kistran sniffed. "I can imagine. Fortunately, it is never too late to learn. If you'll tell me what you remember of your chart, Freelady Salven, I can—"

"Excuse me," Daner said, rising. "Father wanted me to let him know how the spell-casting went last night. He'll be up now, and I shouldn't keep him waiting. My apologies, Freelady, Aunt."

It sounded like a thin excuse to Eleret, but Lady Kistran only nodded. "Apology accepted. Another time, have a better memory for your duties."

Uncertainly, Eleret pushed her seat away from the table and stood up. Daner shook his head at her. "There's no need for you to come with me, Freelady. Father and I will be discussing . . . technical details. I'm sure you'd prefer to stay and talk to my aunt."

It's definitely an excuse, then, Eleret thought as she resumed her seat. *He doesn't want to sit through his aunt's scolding, even if she has something to say that's worth hearing.* She couldn't blame him, though. She'd felt the same way about Uncle Arlim's lectures on the virtues of Sadorthan dual-weapon fighting. Well, if Lady Kistran's explanations became too irritating, Eleret could find her own excuse to leave.

"Now, Freelady, can you remember the cards of your chart, in order?" Lady Kistran said as Daner bowed and left the room. "And what the Luck-seer told you?"

"Do you want her exact words, or would you prefer a summary?"

"As exact as you can manage, Freelady," Lady Kistran said with a small smile.

Eleret considered for a moment. " 'As I lay out your chart, think for the fourth and final time of the question you would have answered.' "

Lady Kistran blinked. "What?"

"It's what Jonystra said. And then, 'First comes your past, from support to opposition,' and she turned up the first card. It was a picture of a mountain with a road at the bottom. She said, 'The Mountain is the base of your support; it stands for security, but also for unused potential.' The second card—"

"A moment." Lady Kistran shook her head as if to clear it. "Security and unused potential—that's all she mentioned?"

"I gave you her words."

"Yes, yes, you have a remarkable memory. It just . . . if the Mountain was your first card . . . But perhaps it was because of the position."

"I'm afraid I don't understand."

"Every card has many meanings, and every card influences the others in a chart. A good card-charter will choose the meanings that fit best with the other cards in a chart, but it's very unusual for a charter to be selective with the meanings of the first card. Since there are no other cards, as yet, to influence it."

It took a moment for Eleret to absorb Lady Kistran's meaning. "What did she leave out?"

"The Mountain also means 'a difficult but rewarding task.' Of course, it usually turns up closer to the center, or in the quadrants of the future, and—"

Lady Kistran went into an involved explanation of the significance the Mountain generally had in other positions and the various ways it could be modified. Since Eleret had no interest in any of them, she listened with half her attention and devoted the other half to her breakfast. "A difficult but rewarding task" certainly fit her reason for coming to Ciaron, but she could not think of any sinister motive that might have led Jonystra not to mention it.

Eventually, Lady Kistran finished and asked about the

next card. "The Lady of Flames," Eleret said, and a shiver ran down her back. It had looked so like her mother. . . . She pulled herself together and recited Jonystra's interpretation. Lady Kistran nodded approval and asked for the next card.

" 'The Seven of Feathers. A card of obstacles, in the position of the beginning of obstacles. Temptation and illusion lie in your past.' "

Lady Kistran frowned. "That's all she said?"

"Yes. Did she leave something out again?"

"Quite a lot, I would say. The Sevens are all cards of temptation, illusion, and obstacles, but the Seven of Feathers specifically relates to lack of information. It is inexcusable for her not to have mentioned that, since this is one of the cards at the base of your difficulties."

Lack of information had certainly been one of Eleret's biggest problems since her arrival in Ciaron. "She said that was in the past. . . ."

"The cards of the past affect the cards of the future," Lady Kistran said sharply. "Unless of course you do something to change the situation, which is the whole point of reading a chart. And if you haven't been given a proper interpretation, you may very well do more harm than good when you try to change things."

Eleret held her face in an expression of polite attention, though she felt like rolling her eyes in exasperation. So far, neither Jonystra's original interpretation nor Lady Kistran's revised version had provided her with grounds for action— at least, not for any action she would not have taken anyway. Lady Kistran studied her for a moment. Then, satisfied that her words had struck home, she said, "And the last card of the first row—what was it, and what did she tell you?"

" 'The Mage Trump. The source of opposition, the hidden—' "

"The Mage *what?*" Lady Kistran broke in, frowning.

"The Mage Trump," Eleret repeated. "Is something wrong?"

"There's no such card," Lady Kistran said. "Not that I've ever heard of, not even in the Western Hand variation of the deck. What did it look like?"

Eleret pictured the card in her mind. "A . . . person in a hooded robe, standing in the shadows beside a table. On the table there was a broken feather, a burned-out candlestick, a—"

"Oh, of course," Lady Kistran said. "The Shadow-Mage." She looked at Eleret curiously. "You must have a serious difficulty indeed, to have *that* card turn up as the source of your opposition."

Shadow-Mage . . . no, don't jump to conclusions. Carefully, Eleret set down her eating knife, and in a voice she hoped sounded normal she said, "Tell me about this card."

"It's one of the sixteen Major Trumps, and therefore very powerful," Lady Kistran said. "And it's not just a bad card, like Betrayal or the fives in the suits. The Shadow-Mage is one of the few cards that can represent something *evil*, though it's relatively rare for that to happen. Still, even the usual meanings—"

"Why is it called the Shadow-Mage?"

Lady Kistran gave her a reproving look, but answered. "I believe the name comes out of a group of old stories—ancient, actually, they go back to before the old Estarren Alliance was even founded, or so the minstrels say. They refer to evil creatures called Shadow-born, and— Good heavens, you've gone white as a slice of boiled cod! Is something wrong?"

Eleret hardly heard the question. *Shadow-born.* The nightmare creatures that haunted the oldest Cilhar tales and lurked at the root of their darkest fears. *Shadow-born*. The insubstantial, deathless things that stole others' bodies and consumed them from inside. They had been confined for all time in secret places at the end of the Wars of Binding, so the tales said, and nowadays few Cilhar would openly admit to believing in their existence. But the tales continued to be told and retold, and no one tolerated the smallest change in their wording. *And I thought the Shee were legends, before I came to Ciaron and met Climeral. If the best things from the old tales are real, why not the worst as well?* But what could she do if the Shadow-born were behind her troubles?

"Freelady Salven! Are you unwell?" Lady Kistran's insistent voice penetrated at last, and Eleret shook herself.

"I'm . . . all right."

"You don't look it. I should have warned you about the clams, they sometimes give me a turn this early in the day." Lady Kistran paused. "Would you prefer to continue our discussion later?"

"No!" Seeing Lady Kistran's startled expression, Eleret forced a smile and said in a more moderate tone, "I don't think I want any more to eat, but I would very much like to just . . . sit and listen for a while." If there were any more surprises in her chart, she wanted to know about them *now*.

"As you will have it." Lady Kistran sat back, studying her. Then she gave an approving nod. "Yes, I think you're wise. Bad enough that your Luck-seer was misinterpreting your cards; worse yet to have your charting broken off in the middle. There's certainly no need to compound matters by stopping our discussion now. What was your next card?"

"The Priest of Flames," Eleret said automatically. "And then the Two of Stones. Jonystra said—"

"Just tell me the cards, Freelady," Lady Kistran said. "Spare me the Luck-seer's distortions. The Priest of

Flames—a good card, but not a strong one. He supports you, but he does not realize his own power to help." She closed her eyes, as if trying to picture something in her mind. "And he is in the cross-diagonal position from the Lady of Flames, so he does not work actively with her. A pity; they would make a good combination.

"The Two of Stones represents opposites in a stable balance, or evenly matched. Since it's in a supporting position, it may refer to differing advice, or two actions that cancel each other out."

Or two people who are opposites? Eleret thought of Daner and Karvonen, and almost smiled.

"The next card?" Lady Kistran prompted.

"The Mage of Flames, reversed."

"Unusual to have so many court cards of the same suit, so early in a chart," Lady Kistran said, frowning. "The Mage of Flames, reversed . . . a man of power and intelligence, who uses both for destructive ends. And the power of the Shadow-Mage supports him. That is an *extremely* bad combination. I would be very careful, if I were you."

"I'm always careful." Eleret hesitated. "The Mage of Flames and the Shadow-Mage—could they be the same person?"

"Unlikely." Lady Kistran tapped her finger on the tabletop, as if she were tapping the face of a card. "If they were the same person, I'd expect them to be stacked, one above the other, not on the close diagonal. Also, the outer cards, like the Shadow-Mage, represent influences, not necessarily direct involvement. The Mage of Flames is an inner card, so he's probably someone you've encountered recently."

Mobrellan, Eleret thought. "The last card in that row was the Three of Shells, reversed."

"Unexpected loss and emotional pain. You must be careful not to let it influence your decisions too closely."

That was more or less what Jonystra had said. "The last two cards were the Three of Flames and the Demon," Eleret said. "Then the Luck-seer . . . broke off the charting."

"Three of Flames—unexpected actions. Something surprising will happen, which may lead to an opportunity for you. The Demon—" Lady Kistran shook her head. "Generally it refers to limitations, particularly unexpected ones, but it can also mean a surprise that leads to loss. That would cancel out the Three of Flames, which makes very little sense." She tapped her fingers against the table again. "I wish we knew the rest of your chart. I don't suppose . . ."

"What?"

"Laurinel has a charting deck somewhere, I think. I could lay out a new chart for you; perhaps that would clarify things."

"I'd like to think about what you've told me first," Eleret said. "I—"

The far door opened and the serving man entered. Bowing, he said, "Lady Kistran, Freelady Salven, pardon the intrusion. There is a messenger here to see either Lord Daner or the Freelady, and he says it is urgent. Since Lord Daner has—"

"Yes, I know, he's with his father," Lady Kistran said, waving the man to silence. "You did quite right not to interrupt them. Show the man in." As the servant bowed again and left, Lady Kistran turned to Eleret. "If the message is truly urgent"—her tone said she did not believe it could be—"you can send word to Daner once you know."

No reply was necessary, for the door opened once more and the serving man bowed as a small man in a bright blue, gold-trimmed tunic entered. "Karvonen?" Eleret said in disbelief.

"At your service, Freelady Salven." Karvonen bowed with a flourish. Apart from the attitude, he bore very little resemblance to the scruffy thief who had accosted Daner the day before. His hair was carefully combed, his clothes looked both new and expensive, and he even stood differently. *More confidently,* Eleret thought, *not as if he's nobody, hoping to be overlooked. Well, an official messenger would be that way.* And there was certainly no stiffness or hesitation in the way he used his left arm. Still, she felt a twinge of uneasiness.

"You know this man?" Lady Kistran said.

"Yes, he's . . . brought me a message once before." Eleret rose as she spoke. "Whatever news he has, I think it's safe to say Lord Daner will want to hear it. If you would take us somewhere we can talk, and then send word to him—"

The serving man looked unhappy. "I'm sorry, Freelady, I'll be happy to show you to a private room, but I'm afraid I don't know where Lord Daner went."

"He's with his father," Lady Kistran said. "Really, Henwas, I don't understand why you're having such a problem."

"No, Lady Kistran." The serving man's expression grew even more troubled than before. "That is . . . Lord Daner saw Lord tir Vallaniri for a few moments before he left, but that was at least half an hour ago."

"Left?" Eleret said.

"Yes, Freelady," the servant said patiently. "Lord Daner left the house half an hour ago, and has not yet returned. If you wish, I can ask the man at the door when Lord Daner said he would return."

"Do that." Eleret hoped her voice did not sound as angry as she felt. "In the meantime, I'll talk to this . . . messenger in that private room you mentioned."

"Very good, Freelady. This way, if it please you."

TWENTY-ONE

To Eleret's surprise—and considerable relief—Karvonen did not say anything more
until they had reached the private room and
the door had closed behind the servant. Then he dropped
into the nearest chair—a heavy, high-backed oak frame with
wide arms and several large pillows—and sighed. The movement, the pose, were pure Karvonen, and Eleret's doubts
vanished.

"Looks like Lord Daner has run off on you," said the
thief. "Any idea where?"

"If I had to guess, I'd say he's gone to see Adept Climeral
at the magic school. He wanted to ask about spells to keep
that shapeshifter from coming back."

"Not a bad idea, actually." Karvonen sounded almost
disappointed.

"No, it isn't. What brings you back so soon? Surely you
haven't answered all my questions already."

"Even Aurelicos have limits. No, I came to let you know

that somebody seems to have put the chain back on the Syaski."

"I don't understand."

"Put the chain on them, called them off, sent out word that you're not the one they're looking for." He frowned, displeased by her lack of response. "I *thought* it was good news. Yesterday you weren't safe on the streets; now—"

"I'm no safer than I was then." Eleret shook her head at his expression. "Do you really think the Syaski will stop looking for me just because some mysterious person says not to? And even if they did, would that stop them making trouble if they happen to run into me?"

"I see your point." Karvonen grimaced. "I don't suppose I could talk you into running away, could I?"

"Why should I?"

"Oh, for a start, there's a shapeshifting wizard who seems to want you dead, and about a hundred Syaski in town who you've just said won't hesitate to oblige him even if he's told 'em not to."

For a brief moment, Eleret allowed herself the luxury of picturing herself somewhere else, away from the city and all the complex problems that had developed since she arrived. Then she shrugged. " 'Trouble always runs faster than you do.' I don't think the shapeshifter will give up just because I've left town. At least here, I have some allies."

"You could still try it."

"No. And why are you so anxious for me to leave, all of a sudden?"

Karvonen raised a hand as if to run it through his hair, then stopped at the last minute and let it fall. "Because the more I find out, the less I like the look of the whole mess, and some of the rumors . . . Never mind. But with the Syaski off the streets, even a few of them, even just for a while, this is probably your best chance to jump ship. I didn't really expect you to, but I figured it wouldn't hurt to point it out."

"Well, now you have, and I've said no, so let it be. Is that all you came for?"

"I—" Karvonen stopped, frowning. Then he leaned forward and gave her a searching look. "All right, what's wrong? And don't say 'nothing,' you stubborn Cilhar, because I can see that something's bothering you. Is it the shapeshifter again?"

"No." Eleret paused, unwilling to admit that she had been unsettled by finding a legend in a pack of cards. *The Shadow-born are only an old tale,* she told herself, but part of her did not believe it.

"What is it, then?"

"Daner's aunt just finished going over the cards Jonystra was charting for me." She hesitated again. "One of them was a card called the Shadow-Mage."

"I didn't think a Cilhar would take card-charting so— The what? What was the card?"

"The Shadow-Mage."

Karvonen looked sick. "Shadow-born. I knew I shouldn't have gotten mixed up in this. Are you *sure* you won't run away?"

It was comforting to have someone else react the same way she had, even if his automatic response was to suggest flight. Eleret shook her head. "If there are Shadow-born involved, I don't want them following me home." Her voice quivered on the last word.

"It might not be that bad." Karvonen did not sound as if he believed what he was saying. "After all, the only evidence you have that there's a Shadow-born stirring the soup is one card in a chart that never got finished." When she did not respond at once, he frowned. "That *is* the only evidence you've got, isn't it?"

"Yes."

"Good. For a minute, there, I thought maybe . . . Anyway, if it's only the card—"

"I won't take chances with my family." Cilhar folk had more than enough problems to contend with, even in times of peace, without bringing something out of nightmares down on them.

"I suppose even Cilhar would have trouble dealing with Shadow-born," Karvonen said, and again the echo of her own thoughts disturbed and reassured her at the same time. "Well, if you're not going to run, what are you going to do?"

"I don't know. Let me think." Her instincts told her to handle things alone; one person was enough to risk against such a powerful opponent. But it was too late to keep Daner out of it, and Karvonen— "Why don't you take your own advice?"

"Run away?" Karvonen's face went blank of expression. "And leave you and his most noble lordship like a couple of babies playing at cliff's edge? It's a tempting thought, but no. Not just yet." His tone was a fair approximation of his usual bantering, but Eleret could hear the strain underneath. Her opinion of him rose tentatively. Whatever his motives—and he still had not explained them, she reminded herself—he was plainly as determined as any Cilhar to face possible dangers in spite of his fears.

"All right." Eleret did not even try to sort out the confused mixture of emotions she felt. She had more pressing problems. *Lay it out like one of Raken's tactical problems. Who are my most powerful enemies?* The shapeshifting wizard, and, possibly, the legendary Shadow-born. Compared to them, the

Syaski rated a distant third, despite their numbers. *Who opposes them?* Herself, armed with her skills, her daggers, and her ravens'-feet. Daner, with his swordsmanship and spell-casting. Karvonen, still largely an unknown quantity. *What other resources do I have?* The raven ring, which she didn't know how to use. Her mother's back pay and death fee, which would be an enormous sum in the mountains but which might not be so startling in Ciaron. *Think of things that are not so obvious. What's the terrain?* The twisting streets of Ciaron, which both Karvonen and Daner seemed to know well. And the equally twisting maze of people and privileges and customs in the city, which Daner navigated without even thinking. *Other possible allies . . .* Commander Weziral had offered his help, and so had Climeral. Lord tir Vallaniri might also be willing; Jonystra and the shapeshifter had disrupted his household and threatened his family, and a common enemy made good grounds for alliance.

Eleret began to feel less unsettled. But for the possibility of Shadow-born, the situation was not so bad as she had begun to fear. And as to the Shadow-born . . . *Set a legend to defeat a legend.* She smiled slightly, and looked over at Karvonen, who immediately assumed an expression of exaggerated patience.

"Thought it all out at last?" the little thief asked solicitously.

"Not all of it, just the next step. We're going to see Adept Climeral." From the look of relief on Karvonen's face, he'd expected her to offer an open challenge in the market at midday to any Syaski, shapeshifters, or Shadow-born within hearing. Eleret felt her smile grow. "Come on. No sense in wasting time."

* * *

After offering her regrets to Lady Kistran, Eleret led Karvonen down the narrow front stair to the outer door. The guard on duty was the same one who had let her and Daner in the night before, and she nodded a greeting as she approached. To her surprise, he stepped in front of her, blocking the door.

"Give you good day, Freelady." The guard's words resonated against the stone walls. He eyed Karvonen briefly, then shifted his weight forward and moved his hands a fraction farther apart, where he could more easily reach his weapons if they should be needed.

"Good day return to you, Bresc." Eleret paused uncertainly. Was there some unfamiliar protocol for leaving a Ciaronese nobleman's home? "The messenger and I have to find Lord Daner. Will you open the door?"

"I'm afraid I can't, Freelady." Bresc's tone was polite, but with an undercurrent of implacability. "Lord Daner's orders were very clear."

"Lord Daner's orders?"

"No one is to come in or go out until he returns." Bresc's eyes flicked to Karvonen once more. "And no one has." Karvonen was back in his role, his face was a mask of professional politeness and unconcern, but beneath it he was taut as a new bowstring.

Eleret shifted, and Bresc's eyes snapped back to her. She felt more than saw Karvonen relax, and shifted again, so that the thief was very slightly behind her. "Keeping people out makes good sense, under the circumstances," she told Bresc. "But keeping people in—"

"His lordship was very specific about that, Freelady. No one leaves without his express permission."

"Which we can't get, because he isn't here." She could, of course, try to fight her way out. Bresc was no Cilhar, and his reflexes were unlikely to be a match for hers; on the other hand, experience would make up for some of the speed that age had robbed him of. With regret, Eleret set the idea aside. She couldn't start a fight in her host's home, especially since Bresc was only doing his duty, nor could she challenge the guard simply because Daner had been thoughtless again.

Behind her, Karvonen cleared his throat. "If the Freelady feels the matter is of sufficient urgency, perhaps Lord tir Vallaniri . . ."

"I believe Lord tir Vallaniri is aware of Lord Daner's commands, and agrees with them," Bresc said. "If he gives you permission to leave, I shall, of course, obey."

"Then I will no doubt see you again soon." Eleret bowed, turned, and, with Karvonen two steps ahead of her, headed for the stairs.

"Do you really think Lord tir Vallaniri is going to let you out of here?" Karvonen asked as soon as they were out of the guard's hearing.

"Why shouldn't he?"

"Because you're a guest who's been threatened and he thinks you'll be safer here, or because you're a suspicious stranger he wants to keep an eye on, take your pick. Ciaronese take both their host-duties and their families very seriously."

"So do Cilhar. And speaking of suspicious strangers, how did *you* get in?"

"Ummm—the love of your bright eyes made my heart so light that I flew over the wall?"

Eleret snorted. "Let's go talk to Lord tir Vallaniri. Whatever he says, he'll make more sense than you do."

* * *

"Leave? No, no, Freelady, there's no need for that," Lord tir Vallaniri said. "The house is perfectly safe now; Daner's seen to that."

"Yes, he told me." Eleret frowned. "But you don't win wars by sitting in a safe-hole waiting for your enemies to come to you, and there are things I should be doing."

"I'm sure they can wait until Daner returns," Lord tir Vallaniri said. "He shouldn't be away much past noon." He looked at her face and added, "I appreciate your position, Freelady. I hope you appreciate mine. You are my guest, and you have already been attacked once under my roof. It would be far worse if you should be injured or killed through my carelessness."

"I understand." At least, she understood that Lord tir Vallaniri was not to be persuaded, any more than Bresc had been. It looked as if she would spend her morning sitting home whittling tent stakes, whether she wanted to or not. Smothering her irritation, she gave a formal half-bow. "Good day to you, then, my lord."

Outside the study, Eleret turned right, toward the staircase that led up to her room. "Not that way," Karvonen said. "This way. Unless you want to waste the morning admiring Lady tir Vallaniri's taste in furnishings."

"You have an idea?"

"I have a way out." Karvonen hesitated. "It'll unwrap a few family secrets for you, though, so if you use it you'll have to promise not to tell anyone how you did it."

"I give you my word," Eleret said at once. Her duty as a guest prevented her from fighting her way out, but it did not forbid her use of other means to escape her hosts' overprotectiveness.

"Then follow me."

Two flights of stairs and three narrow hallways later, curiosity about Karvonen's "way out" had given way to amazement at how well he knew his way around the Vallaniri house. Only once did he pause and motion for Eleret to stop and be silent. Slightly puzzled, she did so, and heard footsteps growing fainter down a branching hall. She looked at Karvonen and raised her eyebrows.

The footsteps faded into nothing. "I didn't want to be seen," Karvonen said softly. "This way, Freelady."

"Seen by whom?" Eleret asked. "And why do we have to go up two floors to get to your 'way out,' when all the doors are at the bottom of the stairs?"

Karvonen peered cautiously around the corner. "We're meeting some— Hsst! Jaki! Over here. Help for the family."

"What— Karvonen?" It was a woman's voice, familiar but changing tone and timbre so completely between the two words that Eleret could not be certain who had spoken. A moment later, Jakella rounded the corner. For a moment, the two women stared at each other in mutual astonishment; then Jakella spun on Karvonen, her whole body stiff with anger.

"Help for the family," Karvonen repeated in an insistent tone, as if the phrase was a password. "Come on, Jaki, you know the drill. Where can we talk?"

Jakella pressed her lips together, glanced back over her shoulder, then motioned them around the corner and through a door. The room beyond was small and clearly seldom used; the hearth was cold and swept clean, and the air smelled faintly of dust.

"Now you can talk," Jakella said. "And you, my *dear* cousin Karvonen, had better have a damned good reason for crying *family* to an observer on a job, and in front of an outsider, at that."

"It's all right, Jaki, she's Cilhar."

"I know that. So?"

Karvonen looked nonplussed. "She's given her word not to say anything about this to anyone. You haven't broken cover yet."

"That's a help, but it still leaves a little matter of—"

"Excuse me," Eleret said, laying her hand on the hilt of her dagger. She felt a little ill at what she was about to do, but duty to her host and her pledged word gave her no choice. "I won't tell anyone about you, but I have to stop you. Guest-service. I'm sorry."

"Wait!" Karvonen stepped between Eleret and Jakella, hands carefully out to the sides, fingers wide and empty. "Can't we talk first?"

"I don't think you want me to hear any more," Eleret said. "And you can't change my obligations. Lord tir Vallaniri is my host. Since I was foolish enough to pledge you my silence, I'll have to stop whatever theft you're planning myself."

Jakella made a small choking noise. "*Theft?* Karvonen, what have you been telling her?"

"*I* haven't told her anything," Karvonen said, sounding harassed. "Shut up a minute, Jaki. Eleret—Freelady Salven—what makes you think—"

"The City Guards told me that the Aurelicos are all famous thieves," Eleret said. "And you admitted as much yourself."

"Oh, no," Karvonen said, shaking his head emphatically. "Acquit me of that, Freelady. I said *I* was a thief, that's all."

"And a pretty poor excuse for one," Jakella said. "Which still doesn't explain why you dragged me into this."

Karvonen rolled his eyes, then twisted around to look at her. "I appreciate your impatience, Cousin, but please, do me the favor of waiting until I have talked her out of killing you. I find it difficult to manage two explanations at once."

"Maybe then we'll get more truth out of you," Eleret said.

"I'm *telling* the truth." Karvonen looked genuinely hurt. "Jaki's my cousin, umpty-times removed, but she's no thief and never has been. She follows the family's second profession, which is more respectable. She's . . . an information gatherer."

"A spy?"

Karvonen winced. "If you must call it that, yes."

"Karvonen—" Jakella's tone was full of warning.

"She won't tell anyone, Jaki! She's Cilhar!" He looked hopefully at Eleret. "You do see, don't you, that this changes matters?"

Eleret frowned, considering. The explanation fit neatly into all the bits and pieces Karvonen had let slip about his family. Too neatly, perhaps. On the other hand, he *had* never claimed that all his relatives were thieves, only that he was one. Eleret's lips twisted. She *wanted* to trust Karvonen, to believe him when he said he was telling the truth, but to trust a thief . . .

"I should also point out, Freelady, that I am in this household at this time merely by coincidence," Jakella said in the sour, overly formal voice she usually—usually?—used. "I am a servant in the household of Lord Domori Trantorino, and had Lady Laurinel not chosen to visit her parents while her husband is away I would never have set foot in this house. Nor is my . . . employer one who wishes harm to Lord or Lady Trantorino."

"Your employer?"

Jakella's lips thinned. "Who it is, I will not say, but I swear by the Cup and the Shield and the skill of the family that my activities have nothing to do with the Vallaniri. If this assurance will not satisfy you, I am sorry."

Eleret hesitated, then glanced at Karvonen.

"She means it, Freelady," Karvonen said. "That's an oath we take seriously."

With a nod, Eleret lifted her hand from her knife and turned back toward Jakella. "Very well. I will accept your assurances."

Heaving a sigh of relief, Karvonen lowered his hands. As he turned toward Jakella, Eleret thought she saw his lips twist in a brief, bitter smile, but the expression was gone too quickly for her to be sure. "Now, Jaki, about that help—"

"Explanations first, Cousin," Jakella said, dropping her sour nursemaid's voice. "And you'd best hurry; I have duties, too."

"The explanation's simple. Freelady Salven needs to get out of the house without being seen, and the doors are guarded."

"That's no explanation at all. You may owe her for something, but I don't. Begging your pardon, Freelady."

"Oh, come on, Jaki, she's Cilhar. The aid-in-distress clause—"

"—is something nobody takes seriously, unless he's looking for an excuse to poke his nose into— Oh, I see." Jakella shook her head. "Sometimes I wonder about you, Karvonen. Curiosity is all very well, but getting mixed up with a *Cilhar* . . . Are you planning to take up the Fourth Profession?"

"Do I look like a lunatic? I like my pieces right where they are, thank you, all together and reasonably undamaged, and I intend to keep them that way into a ripe and rotten old age."

"Fourth Profession?" Eleret raised her eyebrows and looked from Karvonen to Jakella.

"Our family has as much variety as most," Jakella said with a ghost of a smile. "But there are four occupations that are . . . traditional, though the fourth is seldom deliberately chosen. We tend to be thieves, spies, artisans—"

"Artisans?" Eleret said, surprised.

"Forgers and counterfeiters," Karvonen translated. "Some of our cousins can copy anything, from the portrait of the first Queen of Kith Alunel to that silly-looking broadsword with the gem-studded handle that the Emperor of Rathane uses when he's passing out titles."

"You're trying to change the subject," Jakella said. She turned back toward Eleret. "As I was saying, we're thieves, spies, forgers—and heroes."

"Heroes?"

Jakella smiled. "That's what I said. Hardly anybody realizes it, because those of us who take up the Fourth Profession generally change their names. The Aurelicos are too well known as thieves, you see."

It sounded like a joke to Eleret. Well, if Karvonen and Jakella wanted to see how much bait she'd swallow, it made no difference to her. She shrugged. "I suppose so. If we're going to leave, shouldn't we do it soon?"

Karvonen nodded. "Yes, Jaki, about leaving . . ."

Jakella looked at him and began to laugh. "All right! I'll never get rid of you otherwise, and then I really *will* break out of cover. Exactly what is it you want from me?"

TWENTY-TWO

Karvonen repeated his explanation of the problem, adding, "All we really want is a way out. If you know a door that wouldn't be guarded . . ."

Jakella shook her head. "Lord Daner's no fool. Your shapeshifter got in here once disguised as someone's servant, and he won't have forgotten that. You'll have to go off the roof."

"I was afraid you were going to say that. I *hate* rope work in Ciaron, especially on these old places." Karvonen made a disgusted face and looked at Eleret. "Normally, you can just loop a rope around a merlon and go, but the Ciaronese are nearly as paranoid as you Cilhar. At least one out of every three merlons is built to break away if anyone tries that. It's meant to make things harder for attackers, of course, but it's just as bad for . . . anyone who wants to get out unnoticed."

"Don't fuss, Karvonen," Jakella said. "Do you think I'm an amateur? I'll show you a nice solid spot to anchor your rope. And no, Freelady, my employer has no interest in the defenses of Lord tir Vallaniri's home. It's my own personal escape route. Not that I'm likely to need one, this job, but—"

Eleret nodded in understanding. She'd never done any reconnaissance work herself; there'd been less need since the Emperor forced his peace on the Syaski. But everyone still got basic training, and one of the first things Raken beat into his students was the need for a way out. *If not for you, then for the things you've learned,* the teacher's voice rang in her head. *What good is information if you can't get it home? Secure your way of escape, no matter how unnecessary it looks, and then worry about the rest.* Apparently Jakella knew her job.

Five minutes later, they were on the roof. Jakella provided the rope, as well as showing them where to anchor it. To Eleret's surprise, they had their choice of three possible spots, all of which would allow them to descend without being seen from the street in front of the house.

"Isn't this a little odd?" Eleret asked.

"Oh, the Ciaronese aren't worried about people getting *out*," Jakella said. "In fact, there are times when it might be convenient to slip someone down the side wall and away. It's people coming *in* that they fret over."

"Then why aren't there any guards or watchmen up here?"

"If there were a war on, or if the Vallaniri were in *orilista* feud with another family, there would be more than enough lookouts to satisfy your Cilhar caution," Karvonen said. "When things are quiet, they don't bother."

"I thought you were in a hurry," Jakella said. "And if you aren't, I am. I can't spend all day up here, you know."

With an apologetic nod, Eleret took a firm grip on the rope and slid over the edge of the building. The descent was smooth and easy. When she reached the ground, she shook the rope twice to let them know she was down. Karvonen's head appeared, checking; a moment later, he started after her.

He came down hand over hand without using his legs, a display of strength and skill that impressed Eleret in spite of herself. *He's showing off, but at least he's got something to show.* Amused by the thought, Eleret watched, taking pleasure in seeing something done well.

"That was easier than it should have been," Karvonen said as he dropped the last two feet to the ground. Looking up, he gave a low whistle. The rope trembled, then began to rise as Jakella reeled it in.

"Now, where did you— No, not that way!" Karvonen said as Eleret started for the main street. "Do you want Daner's overly enthusiastic doorman to see you? Not to mention any stray Syaski and shapeshifters and Shadow-born who might be keeping an eye on the place?"

"No, of course not."

"Then come *this* way."

Karvonen led her toward the rear of the house, then down a narrow alley to a series of dark, smelly back streets. Compared to the avenues she had traveled the day before, these were nearly deserted. An occasional barrow-man trundled by with his wheelbarrow full of trash, and now and then a second-floor window opened to spout dirty washwater or kitchen garbage, but that was all. Eleret attracted a few curious glances, but most eyes were drawn to Karvonen's uniform, not to her. No one approached or followed them, and within half an hour they had crossed the last avenue and reached the Islander's school.

Prill answered the door. When she saw Eleret, her eyes widened. "Oh! I . . . ah . . . Welcome, er, Freelady. Sir. What can I do for you?"

"I'd like to talk to Adept Climeral," Eleret said. "Is something wrong?"

"No, no, he's quite— That is, I'm sure he'll be surprised to see you. This way, Freelady."

Eleret frowned. "Has Daner been here?"

"No! That is, I don't know. I haven't seen him." Prill shifted nervously from one foot to the other.

"You aren't a very good liar. He's told you about the shapeshifter, hasn't he? And you think I'm . . . somebody else." Eleret's frown deepened. "That'd be a knot in the bowstring for certain."

"I'll vouch for you," Karvonen offered.

"I wouldn't know anything about that, F-Freelady," Prill said a little desperately. "If you want to see Adept Climeral—"

"More than ever." As they started down the hall, Eleret glanced sideways to make sure Karvonen was following.

Karvonen saw the glance and stopped. "Perhaps I'd best leave now. So you won't have to make any awkward explanations." His grin looked a little forced. "Arriving in the company of a thief won't do much for your credit with the Adept."

"How can you vouch for me if you aren't here?" Eleret said, unsettled by Karvonen's unexpected attitude. Then she remembered his aversion to wizards, and sighed. "I suppose I should have expected this, and you've already done a great deal. Though I don't see what difference one more wizard makes at this point."

"One more wizard— Oh. Right. I think—"

"Are you two *coming?*" Prill said in a tone much more like her usual one.

"On our way," Karvonen said. "Let's be off, Freelady. Mustn't keep the young woman waiting."

Eleret fell into step beside him, shaking her head. "I thought you were leaving."

"I changed my mind."

"You are the most inconsistent person I have ever met."

"On the contrary. I'm probably the most consistent person you've ever met. I only look inconsistent because you don't understand me." Karvonen made a lugubrious face. "Nobody understands me."

"Maybe they would if you stopped talking in riddles."

"Ah, but then I'd lose my air of mystery. An air of mystery is very important for those of us who lack Lord Daner's looks, money, and sense of fashion. It attracts the ladies." He gave her a sidelong look.

"You know some ladies?"

Karvonen blinked, then grinned. "*Armies* of them. Of course, none of them would ever admit it in public. . . ."

Just ahead, Prill stopped and threw open a door. "Freelady Salven's here, Adept Climeral," she announced, and motioned Eleret forward.

Warily, Eleret moved to the doorway. If Prill thought she was the shapeshifter then so must Climeral; and if the Shee Adept chose to do something about it . . . But Climeral stood, relaxed and smiling, beside a table piled with small brass bowls, pottery jars, and oddly shaped glass tubes. Eleret paused at the threshold. "Karvonen, come here. I want you to meet—"

There was a soft popping noise on her left, inside the room, followed by Daner's voice: "Ow! Blast that ring! Eleret . . . But this *can't* be Eleret!"

"Well, I am," Eleret said. "If you don't believe me, ask

Karvonen. Not even a shapeshifter can imitate two people at the same time."

"Karvonen?" Daner appeared, shaking his right hand as if something had stung him. "What are you doing with that—that—"

"Thief," Karvonen said blandly. "At least, I believe that's the word you're looking for. Though I suppose you might be thinking of something more specific, like 'cutpurse' or 'bandit.' 'Pirate,' on the other hand, would be completely inaccurate, since—"

"Will you stop your irrelevant babbling?" Daner said.

Karvonen looked thoughtful. "What are you offering? Babble comes cheap, I admit, but I think the unusual circumstances rate some sort of bonus, don't you?"

"No! That is— Eleret . . ." Daner stopped, torn between irritation and uncertainty.

"Eleret and her companion had better come in and sit down," said Climeral. He glanced at Daner, then looked away, the corners of his mouth twitching. "Prill, would you move that bench a little closer? . . . Yes, that will do nicely. Freelady Salven?"

Swallowing the remnant of her own amusement, Eleret seated herself on the bench. Prill gave her an uncertain look, glanced at Climeral, and with a farewell nod left the room. As she crossed in front of Daner, Karvonen slid sideways and sat down on the other end of the bench. Daner glared at him, then hooked a stool toward himself with one foot.

Climeral surveyed the group with some satisfaction and nodded. "Now, I think we had best begin again. Greetings and good day to you, Freelady."

"And to you also," Eleret responded, falling automatically into the familiar formal pattern for greeting and introductions. "I wish to present my friend Karvonen Aurelico, who has been of service and help to me. His knife is as my own." Then her mind caught up with her mouth, and she wondered what had possessed her to claim Karvonen as a trusted battle companion. Not that he didn't deserve it, in a way, but she hadn't intended to make a public declaration. Still, it was almost worth it just to see his face—from his expression, he understood exactly what she had just committed herself to, and he hadn't anticipated it any more than she had.

Climeral's eyebrows rose. "I am honored by the acquaintance. And what brings you here, Freelady?"

"Yes, and how did you—" Daner broke off at a reproving glance from Climeral.

"I have some questions that need answering," Eleret said. "I was hoping you could help."

"Your questions would appear to be urgent ones," Climeral said with another glance at Daner.

Eleret, too, looked at Daner. "I don't like being cooped up. And nobody asked for my parole."

"Parole?" Daner said, stung. "You talk as if you were a prisoner."

"Wasn't I?"

"I shut up the house for everyone's *safety!*"

"I know. And it was a good idea, certainly, to keep people out. Maybe even to keep some in; you know your folk better than I do. But I'm not in your command." Eleret shrugged. "You did what you thought you should; so did I. That's all."

"All *right,* then." Plainly, Daner wanted to continue the argument but was reluctant to do so in front of Climeral and Karvonen. "But how did you get *out?*"

"Down the north wall on a rope from the roof," Eleret said. "It wasn't bad."

"You could have been killed! Half the merlons will break away from the roof if you put any weight on them."

Resisting the impulse to glance at Karvonen, Eleret said, "Somebody mentioned that a while ago. I was careful."

"Which brings us back to the question of *why* you chose to take such, ah, unusual steps," Climeral said.

"Two things. First, I wanted to ask you about—about Shadow-born."

"Shadow-born?" Daner snorted. "Is *that* why you risked your neck—to find out about *nursery stories?*"

"Before I came to Ciaron, I thought the Shee were nursery stories."

"Which we are not," Climeral said. "And you are right to think the Shadow-born are as real as I. But they are bound, and have been for centuries. What cause have you to ask of them?"

"Did Daner tell you about the card-charting?"

Climeral nodded.

"Well, according to his aunt, Jonystra left a lot out when she did mine. There's a card called the Shadow-Mage—"

"*That* card turned up in your chart?" Climeral said, frowning. "In what position?"

"Lower left-hand corner," Eleret said. "And when Jonystra and Lady Kistran both said it was the source of opposition . . ."

"I can see why you would be concerned." Climeral's frown deepened, and he shook his head. "Yet the card has other meanings, or it would not have appeared in any chart laid out in over two thousand years."

Daner was staring at them as if they had both run mad. "Adept Climeral, are you saying that Shadow-born actually exist? That they're not just legends?"

"Most legends have some truth in them," Climeral replied. "This one, unfortunately, has more than most. Still, they've been bound so long that no one is even certain where they lie. I doubt that there's any real need to worry about them."

"All Cilhar have reason to worry about Shadow-born," Karvonen said unexpectedly. "The Cilhar played a big part in the Wars of Binding, and the Shadow-born won't have forgotten that, even if everyone else has."

"How do you know that?" Daner demanded.

"Family records." Karvonen gave Daner his most irritating smile. "I'd offer to show them to you, but I haven't got them with me, and besides, they're strictly confidential."

Climeral shook his head. "Even if you are correct about the past enmity between the Cilhar and the Shadow-born, I don't think we should assume, on the strength of an admittedly flawed card chart, that—"

"I'm not assuming anything," Eleret broke in. "That's why I'm here. I wanted to ask you if you know a way to find out for certain whether there's a Shadow-born at the bottom of things or not. One way or another, I'd like to know."

"Ah." Climeral's expression cleared. "I think I know how to reassure you. A scrying spell—and if I can find a deck of cards, I'll use one as the secondary enhancer. I wonder . . ."

"Nijole has a deck," Daner said. "I asked her about charts last year, when my sisters started getting interested, and she brought them out to demonstrate a proper, full-fledged chart spell."

"Good. I'll borrow them as soon as we're done here." Climeral looked at Eleret. "Two questions, I think you said. The second is . . . ?"

"It's about Ma's ring. Daner may have mentioned it—"

"Not specifically. He said the shapeshifter who attacked you appeared to be trying to obtain an item that had belonged to your mother, but he didn't go into details. I assume the ring is the source of your difficulties?"

Eleret nodded, pleased that Daner had, for once, been as discreet as she would like. "We think so. It seems to have some magical properties—"

"Seems to—hah!" Daner flexed his fingers. "It bounces spells better than a Major Ward. My hands are still stinging."

"What were you trying to do?" Karvonen asked. "Paralyze her? Melt her weapons? Turn off the magic she doesn't have? Or—"

"If you must know, I cast a spell to see whether she was the shapeshifter," Daner said. "Can we get on with things?"

"You were the one who interrupted," Karvonen pointed out. "Twice."

"The ring also . . . warns me, sometimes," Eleret said to Climeral. Briefly, she explained what she knew of the ring's history and summarized her own experiences with it. "I'm hoping you can tell me more, or at least untangle what we know already."

"I can certainly try," Climeral said. "May I examine it?"

Eleret twisted the raven ring so that the stone was no longer hidden against her palm, then rose and held out her hand to Climeral.

"Be careful," Daner said. "I tried to analyze it last night, and it threw the spell back at me before I'd even finished casting it."

"Mmmm." Climeral bent over the ring, his green eyes narrowed to slanted slits. "Probably a reflection spell. Varnan wizardry, you said?"

"It could be, but I don't know for certain," Eleret replied. "My multi-great-grandmother, Geleraise Vinlarrian, came from Varna, and the ring was hers."

"It would explain Daner's difficulties. If I might look at the ring more closely—"

As Climeral reached for her hand, Eleret pulled it back. The Shee Adept stopped at once and gave her an inquiring look. "I'd rather not take the ring off," Eleret said.

"I believe I understand." Climeral straightened. "If it's Varnan work, there'll be a mark on the inside of the ring behind the stone. Perhaps you'd prefer to look for it yourself."

Reluctantly, Eleret pulled off the raven ring. As she peered into the circle, she realized that it was the first time the ring had been off her finger since she had picked up her mother's kit from Commander Weziral. Her hand felt bare without it, as if she were going weaponless. *Tamm's ring—is this how Ma felt without it? Is that why she took it with her to the Emperor's wars?* Eleret blinked and shook away the thought, then forced herself to focus on the ring. "I think there used to be something here, but it might be just a scratch. It's very worn."

Climeral smiled. "Varnan markings don't depend solely on physical features. If you will hold the ring a little higher . . . *Thalana mec ticna!*"

Just above Eleret's palm, an image formed in the air, small but crystal-clear—a four-pointed silver star, crossed by a slim, double-edged sword with a plain hilt. Karvonen made a choking noise; Daner started, then turned to Climeral and said, "How did you do that without getting knocked halfway across the room, if I may ask?"

"By casting a general spell, rather than one aimed specifically at the ring or at Freelady Salven." Climeral looked almost smug. "Also, I wasn't fighting the ring's magic—Varnan markings are *meant* to be seen, under the right conditions."

"So you provided the conditions," Eleret said. The image was fading, but she held her hand steady until it had completely disappeared. Then, with an unaccountable feeling of relief, she slipped the raven ring back onto her finger. "Now we know that it's Varnan work."

"We may know more than that, if we can find out something about the mark." Climeral crossed to a small brass handle set in the wall and pulled. In the distance, something chimed; a few moments later Prill appeared in the doorway.

"Prill, I need a reference scroll from the library—the one that lists the marks that Varnan wizards used," Climeral said. "Bring it to my office; I don't think we're going to get any more done here today. And if you see Nijole, ask her to bring her charting cards as well." He glanced around and smiled. "In the meantime, may I offer you some refreshments?"

"We'd be honored," Eleret said for them all.

TWENTY-THREE

The next hour was not nearly so orderly as Climeral's plans had made it sound. Prill and the scroll arrived at the same time as did a skinny boy carrying a tray of glass mugs filled with a hot, herb-scented drink. While Climeral scanned the scroll, Prill handed the mugs around. Before she finished, Climeral asked for two books and another scroll. These appeared along with the librarian, who was plainly displeased by Climeral's departure from normal procedures. Climeral was in the middle of soothing the annoyed librarian when a tall, dark-skinned woman entered and demanded to know what foolishness Climeral was wasting time on now, and didn't he realize that some people had work to do? This prompted an outburst from the librarian and an argument from Daner, during which someone managed to upset one of the mugs over Climeral's desk. Prill snatched up the scrolls barely in time to keep them from being drenched, and the argument spread to nearly everyone as accusations, denials, and reassurances flew.

Finally, somehow, peace and order were restored. The librarian left; the tall woman, after another minute's discussion, pulled a small silver case from her pocket and handed it to Climeral. "Don't let them get wet," she said as she turned and left the room.

"I'll watch out for them, Nijole," Prill called after her. She turned and looked at Climeral. "If you're going to do a chart, Adept—"

"One thing at a time," Climeral said. "We were looking for that maker's mark—ah, yes." He set the silver case carefully to one side, then picked up the two books the librarian had brought in. Having given the first to Daner, he offered the other to Eleret.

Eleret shook her head. "I'm afraid I won't be any help with that. I'm no scholar."

"It doesn't take a scholar to skim historical summaries," Daner said, looking up with a puzzled frown.

"Only lots and lots of patience," Prill put in. "Some of them are so *boring*—" She caught Climeral's eye and subsided.

"You misunderstand," Karvonen said to Daner in a smug tone. "What she means is that she doesn't read Ciaronese." With a faint smile, he held his hand out to Climeral, who nodded and handed him the book.

"I—" Daner stopped and looked at Eleret, who nodded. Then he shifted uncomfortably and looked down at his book. "I'm sorry, Eleret. I didn't realize."

"It's not important," Eleret said. Daner was acting as if he had accused her of misinterpreting a battle map.

"Ah!" said Climeral suddenly and with great satisfaction. Smiling, he glanced up from the scroll, which he had appropriated for himself. "I believe I have it. Four-pointed star, crossed moonwise—that's from left to right—by a sword, simple, hilt down: maker's mark for Dara kay Larrian, registered in the fall of 1241 at the main League Hall in Ryshavey. Extremely rare; known pieces are minor work but highly specialized."

"That isn't much help," Eleret said.

"On the contrary. It tells us a great deal." Climeral turned the scroll sideways. "And there appears to be a later note in the margin—" He squinted at the faded letters, then read, " 'Pieces include Twis's Armband and the Serolissin pin. See the *Dark Men Compendium* for full descriptions.' "

"Back to the library," Prill said, pushing away from the wall with a sigh. "I'll only be a few minutes."

"No need," Climeral said. "We haven't got a copy. Imle borrowed ours because she has a particular interest in the subject and the Lesser Fraling school where she's stationed is too minor to have a copy of its own. I sent the scroll to her last month; it'll be six months more before her students have finished lettering and she can send it back."

"So we're in a blind canyon," Eleret said. "And even if you had the scroll, it wouldn't tell us anything about my ring, just that pin and armband."

"We don't require the scroll," Climeral said. "I told you, I looked it over only last month. And no, I don't remember the Larrian pieces specifically, but the mere fact that they're discussed in the *Dark Men Compendium* tells us something."

"It may tell *you* something," Daner said, "but my net's as empty as ever."

"I bet I can guess." Karvonen looked at Eleret, his face stiff. "I bet the *Dark Men Compendium* is all about Shadow-born."

"Goodness," said Prill. "Is *that* what all this is about? No wonder everyone's jumpy."

"Oh, not Shadow-born again," Daner said. "Really—"

"How did you guess?" Climeral asked Karvonen with considerable interest.

"The Wyrds call Shadow-born 'the Dark Men,'" Karvonen said. "Under the circumstances, it wasn't difficult."

"And how do you know what the Wyrds call Shadow-born?" Daner demanded. "No, let me guess—'family connections' again."

Karvonen stared at Daner for a moment, a picture of wide-eyed, innocent astonishment. "I'd hate to have to admit that you're right." He smiled. "So I won't."

"You're almost as bad as Nijole," Prill told Karvonen.

"Shadow-born," Eleret said, and swallowed. "So my ring does have some connection with them."

"I suppose you could put it that way," Climeral said. "Opposition is, after all, a kind of connection."

"Opposition?"

"The *Dark Men Compendium* is not exactly 'all about Shadow-born'; it is more limited in scope. To be precise, it is a catalog of various strategies, spells, and items that have been used effectively against them at various times. It includes nearly everything, from Elasien's Silver Tree and the Harp of Imach Thyssel to—well, to things like Twis's Armband."

Eleret's heart lifted; then she shook her head. "But the raven ring isn't on the list."

"Varnan wizards, with very few exceptions, tended to specialize," Climeral said. "If Dara kay Larrian made two pieces that work against Shadow-born—and work well enough to be included in the *Compendium*—then I doubt that her third has no relevance to Shadow-born at all."

"Yes, and I can think of at least two reasons why it might not have been included." Daner looked at Climeral. "You said the *Dark Men Compendium* only included things that have worked against Shadow-born. If the ring was made but never actually used—"

"Then it would not appear on the list," Climeral said, nodding. "And your second possibility?"

"That the ring was a family secret and the author of the *Compendium* didn't know about it."

"I thought you were going to say that maybe they tried it and it didn't work," Prill put in.

"That is unlikely," Climeral said. "An unsuccessful test would almost certainly have destroyed the ring, in which case we wouldn't be worrying about it now."

Daner turned to Eleret. "Your great-great-grandmother, who brought the ring into your family—she was Varnan, wasn't she?"

Eleret nodded. "Geleraise Vinlarrian—Vin*Larrian*! Do you think she was related to the wizard who made the ring?"

"Why not? It makes as much sense as the rest of this business."

"My, you're cranky today," Prill said. "I suppose it's because you didn't get enough sleep. Nijole says that's the usual reason, when people get snappish."

"Either maintain a suitable discretion, or attend to some of your work elsewhere, Prill," Climeral said.

"That means 'Hush up or leave,' " Prill said with an unrepentant grin. "But I promised Nijole I'd look after her cards, so—"

"Have you any objection to her presence, Freelady?" Climeral asked.

Eleret considered. Her instincts still cried for secrecy, but she had to admit that there were already far too many people involved for her business to stay secret long. One more would make little difference, and she had decided earlier that the islanders were trustworthy. She shook her head.

"I don't object, Adept." Eleret looked at Prill. "But you should know that this may be dangerous. Not just watching, but—"

"Talking about it after?" Prill said. "That's all right. I can keep my tongue tied if I have to."

Climeral raised an eyebrow. "Then prove it by being silent." He turned to Eleret. "We have learned all we can from these." He waved at the books and scrolls. "If you are agreeable, I think it is time to proceed to the next stage."

"You mean the scrying spell you mentioned earlier?" Eleret hoped she did not sound as nervous as she felt. Owning a ring of unknown magical properties was one thing; having a Shee wizard cast spells for her was something else again. It seemed . . . presumptuous. *He offered*, Eleret reminded herself. *I asked for information, that's all. He was the one who started talking about spells.* It didn't help. For the first time, she thought she understood Karvonen's attitude toward wizards, at least a little. But it was the only way to find out what she needed to know. . . . "What do you want me to do?"

"Stand here." Climeral gestured toward the near side of his desk. "Daner, have you ever assisted a scrying? Well, you're about to get a bit of practice. Prill, take these scrolls, please."

"Ah, if I'm in the way, I'd be quite happy waiting in the hall," Karvonen said.

"No, you're fine where you are. Just try not to distract any of us during the spell." Climeral reached down and from somewhere under the desk he brought out a small wooden box. Opening it, he removed four teardrop-shaped stones, each a different color. These he placed on the corners of the desk—red, white, blue, and green.

Daner blinked, then frowned slightly. "I didn't think scrying spells were supposed to be warded. Won't the wards interfere?"

"Not if they are carefully done, and focused outward," Climeral said. "And I would never consider working without wards when there's a good possibility that Shadow-born are involved." He snapped the lid of the box closed and bent to put it away.

"You're really taking these Shadow-born seriously." There was a hint of uncertainty in Daner's voice. "Even if they are real, they can't possibly be as awful as the stories make them."

"Want to bet?" Karvonen said.

Climeral straightened and laid both hands on the desk, palms down. He looked at Daner, his face expressionless. "If you refuse to recognize a threat, you cannot begin to deal with it. Since it is through my actions that you are involved in this matter, it is my responsibility to see that you recognize the threat. We will discuss this after I have finished the scrying for Freelady Salven."

"If you insist, Adept," Daner said stiffly.

"I do insist, Lord Daner." There was a brief, uncomfortable silence. Then Climeral went on. "First, however, we have the scrying spell to perform." He looked at Eleret. "There will actually be three spells: a protective ward, a spell for the cards, and the scrying itself. Since your ring is Varnan in origin, it would be unwise to use it as a scrying focus. The protective spells the Varnan wizards used are powerful and long-lasting. Thus the cards become more important. It would be . . . helpful if you laid out the chart yourself, as it will connect the spell more clearly to you and your ring."

"I'll do whatever is necessary," Eleret replied. "But I don't know anything about card-charting."

"I will direct you." Climeral turned to Daner. "Will you hold the wards after I set them? Use the technique I showed you this morning; it will be good practice."

Daner nodded.

"Very well, then. We begin." Climeral closed his eyes briefly, then lifted his hands and gestured, almost too swiftly to be seen. *"Lithkatri mec cebarat; ri becvaro lithsavar. Katri a!"*

The four stones on the corners of the desk began to glow. Climeral gestured again, and the glow grew stronger, spreading out from each of the stones like ripples in water. In an instant more, the arcs of light met and fused. The four colors melted into a single, golden radiance that expanded until it brushed the ceiling and the walls, surrounding the onlookers with shimmering light.

"The wards are raised," Climeral said. "Lord Daner, please take over monitoring them."

"Flashy, aren't they?" Karvonen muttered.

Silently, Eleret agreed. If this was typical of protective magic, she was not surprised that her father disdained it. It made her think of the castles the Syaski used—maybe you were safe inside, but your enemies knew right where to look for you. All they had to do was wait for you to come out. *Nobody ever won a war with a brilliant defense,* her mother's voice said in her memory. *Not the kind of war we're fighting, anyway.*

"Freelady Salven?"

Eleret came back to attention at once. "Yes, Adept?"

"Please remove the cards from the case. It will be better for my purposes if you are the only one who handles them."

Eleret stepped forward and picked up the silver card-case. To her surprise, the metal was warm to the touch. Cautiously, she removed the lid and shook the cards into her hands. They felt smooth, and they slipped against each other like the feathers of a bird's wing folding into place.

"Give the case to Prill," Climeral said, and smiled at Prill's surprised expression. "Since the cards are your excuse for being here, you may as well be useful. Now, Freelady, hold the cards here, over the desk, and try not to move them until I tell you."

As Eleret stretched her hands out over the desk, Climeral began speaking rapidly in the same strange language he had used before. This time the spell was longer, but Eleret kept her arms rock-steady. The cards grew warm, and the edges pressed against her fingers.

"You may pull your hands back now, but keep hold of the cards," Climeral said, and with a small shock Eleret realized that his spell was finished. "Stand facing me. Now find the Shadow-Mage card and place it on the desk, to your right. Try not to look at it too closely."

Eleret turned the cards over and began looking through the deck. At first the pictures seemed blurry, and she thought it would not be difficult to follow Climeral's instructions. Then, suddenly, one of the cards sprang sharply into focus: a woman with chestnut hair holding a drawn sword, her retreat blocked by a curtain of flames. The drawing was a little different from the one on Jonystra's cards, but Eleret still recognized the picture from her chart. It was the Swordswoman of Flames, whom she had taken to represent her mother.

"The Shadow-Mage," Climeral's voice prompted softly. "Let your other questions go, for now. Find the Shadow-Mage."

The drawing of the swordswoman blurred again, and Eleret went on through the deck. Another picture leaped out at her: a person in armor riding a black horse, face and head covered by an iron helm. This one was easier to pass by; it lost its sharpness almost immediately. A third picture snapped into clarity. This time it showed a couple sitting comfortably at a wooden table in front of a fireplace, and Eleret had to fight her desire to pull it from the pack.

"The Shadow-Mage," Climeral said insistently, and once again the picture blurred. Warily, Eleret kept on. Halfway through the deck, the Shadow-Mage sprang into focus. Mindful of Climeral's instructions, she tore her eyes away from the hooded figure and the enigmatic objects it seemed to contemplate. Pulling the card from the deck, she laid it faceup on the desk as Climeral had instructed. As the card touched the surface, violet light glimmered briefly around its edges. Eleret let go with more haste than she had intended.

"Excellent," the Shee Adept said. "This is the card of your quest, which is to know whether and to what purpose the Shadow-born threaten you and yours. Look at the card."

Reluctantly, Eleret let her eyes return to the drawing. A hooded figure stood beside a table bearing a shattered diamond, a spent candle, a broken feather, and a splintered crab shell. Behind it, the figure's shadow loomed against the wall, barely distinguishable from the figure itself. One hand reached toward the table, trailing a wisp of black smoke from its fingertips. There was menace in the gesture, and danger, and a deep hunger. *I'm imagining things*, Eleret thought. *It's only a card.*

And then the picture moved. The hand stretched forward, plainly reaching for the dead candle, but unable quite to touch it. Eleret thought she glimpsed a chain holding back the wrist beneath the sleeve. Black smoke collected around the outstretched fingers and rolled forward over the candle, which crumbled into powder. The hooded figure chuckled and began to turn toward Eleret. Automatically she reached for her knife. . . .

Abruptly, the drawing was as it had been, the faceless

figure frozen in mid-reach toward four broken, useless objects. Eleret looked up, shaken, and met Climeral's green eyes.

"Did you see . . . ?" Eleret found she could not finish the sentence, and waved the pack of cards toward the Shadow-Mage instead. She was careful not to look directly at the card.

Climeral shook his head. "What the cards show is for you alone. That is why this spell is so effective—when we finish, we will have two views of the chart, mine, which is an interpretation based on the meanings of the cards, and yours, which is more direct and personal." He smiled slightly. "I would caution you to remember what you see, but I have already had a demonstration of your abilities in that area."

"Then what does the card mean?" Eleret said.

"The first card is your question. Often, one sees nothing in it, but when one does, it indicates that the question is of immediate importance," Climeral said. "It seems you are right to worry."

"It was turning toward me," Eleret blurted out.

"What?" Frowning, Climeral glanced toward Daner. "Did the wards—"

"They are intact, and nothing has tried to breach them." Daner sounded edgy and uncomfortable. Then his voice firmed. "I'll tell you at once if anything happens. Go ahead whenever you're ready."

"Go ahead?" Karvonen said. "Why? If you know now that there are Shadow-born involved—"

"That is not the only thing we seek to learn," Climeral said. "Are you ready, Freelady? Then begin at the beginning of the deck, and find the card that is clear to you. When you have found it, place it directly in front of you, close to the edge of the desk."

If Climeral felt that it was important to continue, Eleret had to cooperate. She shifted the cards and began working her way through them once again, trying not to think about the Shadow-Mage. This time, the pictures were uniformly blurred until she was nearly at the end of the deck. Using her peripheral vision, she plucked the card from the pack and laid it on the desk.

TWENTY-FOUR

As Eleret laid the card on the desk, green light flickered around the edges. Eleret heard a soft intake of breath off to one side: Prill, probably. She kept her eyes on Climeral's calm expression, refusing to look at the card herself until he instructed her.

"This is the root of the matter, the role that your question card may play in your life," Climeral said. "It is a Major Trump: the Breaking Tower. Look at the card."

Eleret let her eyes drop. A tower stood at the edge of the sea, its top half broken off and toppling into the raging waves. Fire leaped from great cracks in the remaining portion, and wind whipped bits of debris into the air. Behind the tower, the slim red crescent of the moon Kaldarin hung in a purple sky; on the road below, three tiny figures cowered away from the havoc.

Again, the picture moved. The tower-top completed its fall, sending water high into the air. Stones crashed all around, some from the disintegrating tower, others from somewhere outside the picture. *The mountains themselves are crumbling*, Eleret thought, and did not know where the thought had come from. Fire, wind, stones, and waves combined in massive destruction, overwhelming the three struggling people on the road.

And the card was as it had been, the tower in mid-fall once more. Eleret raised her eyes.

"The Breaking Tower stands for disaster, conflict, and destruction," Climeral said. "It is not surprising to find it at the root of the matter when the question involves Shadowborn. Choose again, and lay the card in front of you, near the far edge of the desk."

Reluctantly, Eleret looked down at the cards in her hands once more. She found the card quickly and laid it on the desk in front of Climeral. White light flared, and Climeral said, "This is the peak of the matter, the role that you yourself play. A Minor Trump: the Mason. Look at the card."

A Shee woman in a gray smock crouched on one knee before a partly finished wall of rectangular gray stones. She held a trowel in one hand and a V-shaped mortar holder in the other, and she was frowning slightly, as if she had been interrupted at her work.

Eleret tensed as the picture began to move. The Shee woman shook her head, brushed a loose wisp of hair out of her eyes with the back of her wrist, and turned back to the wall. Her frown faded as she worked, replaced by a look of absorption. The soft scrape of her trowel against the mortar was oddly comforting. Before the card froze, the wall had grown by two more blocks.

"The Mason stands for patience and dedication to a constructive task, and for the power of perseverance in the face of great odds," Climeral said. "Not unreasonable, under the circumstances. Choose again, and lay the card to your left, on a line halfway between the other two but off to the side."

Feeling a little more comfortable, Eleret complied. This time the light was red-orange, and for a moment she was afraid the card had caught fire the way Jonystra's had. The light faded, and she breathed a sigh of relief.

"This fuels the matter," Climeral said with unruffled calm. "It represents the resources you have. Three of Stones. Look at the card."

A Wyrd stood in a dense forest, just placing the last rock on a three-stone trail marker. The picture remained motionless much longer than the others had; then, as the Wyrd straightened, an enormous pebble-skinned creature with large, dark eyes and long claws leaped out of the trees. Fast as thought, it swung at the Wyrd; simultaneously a flight of glowing arrows came out of the trees. The Wyrd dodged, barely in time; the arrows struck home; the monster collapsed; the Wyrd made a triumphant gesture at the unseen archers; and the card returned to its peaceful initial picture.

"The Three of Stones stands for unexpected action, particularly unexpected activity on your part," Climeral said, and Eleret choked on a laugh. "Unexpected" certainly described the scene she had just witnessed, but how it related to her and her problems was not exactly obvious. Climeral gave her a questioning look; when she did not respond, he went on. "Your primary resource seems to be surprise. Choose again, and lay the card to the right, next to your question card."

As she started through the deck for the fifth time, Eleret realized that this card, with the previous three, would form a diamond, with the Shadow-Mage off to its right. *We must be nearly finished*, she thought, and set the card in its place. Blue light flared, and she looked at Climeral.

"This drowns the matter; it represents the resources that oppose you. Mage of Flames, reversed. Look at the card."

A tall man in red stood on a staircase, pointing toward the hearth below; fire shot from his hand to the flames roaring up the chimney. Eleret recognized the card at once, even upside down. It had appeared in Jonystra's chart, and it had been her immediate opposition. *The shapeshifter*, she thought, *Mobrellan*. As if in response, the picture began to move. The man in red gestured, and more flames sprang up around him, driving back the ghost-cat that had been contemplating the dangling ends of his belt. The man's face twisted, and again he gestured, and again, until the whole card was enveloped in fire. From behind the flames came a laugh, the laugh of the hooded Shadow-Mage from the first card. Eleret jerked involuntarily, and the card returned to its original condition.

"The Mage of Flames is a man of power and intelligence, capable of using the abilities of others for his own ends. Since the card is reversed, his power is likely to be misused. Choose again."

"I thought that was the last card," Eleret said, surprised.

"One more," Climeral said. "Choose, and lay your card in the center of the diamond."

Eleret found the card almost immediately; it was the fourth from the front. She positioned it with a feeling of relief, and did not even start at the warm golden glow that briefly surrounded it.

"This is the crown, which opens the road to the future," Climeral said. "A Minor Trump: the Raven. Look at the card."

Before Climeral even finished speaking, Eleret's eyes dropped to the picture. A raven in flight filled the center of the card, its wings extended behind it in readiness for their next stroke against the air. Below stretched mountains, some bare, others covered with trees or dotted with tiny fields. *Home*, thought Eleret, and hardly noticed when the raven's wings began to move and the scenery below flowed past. The bird cawed once and beat the air with its wings, then stretched and soared higher on some invisible current of air. The mountains and everything in them fell away below it, until all that surrounded the raven was clear air and a sense of release.

The card froze. "The Raven is for freedom earned through personal effort, for release," Climeral said. "A hopeful sign, but not very helpful, I am afraid. Perhaps you will find the meaning clearer in the future."

"It stands for that ring of Eleret's, I'll bet," Karvonen said. "Are you finished?"

"The chart is finished," Climeral said. "The scrying is still to come." He looked at Eleret. "If you will remove your ring and hold it over the central card, Freelady—"

"I thought you weren't going to use the ring," Daner objected.

"I have no intention of focusing the spell on or through it," Climeral said. "However, Varnan magic is often powerful enough to influence the things around it. I hope that the proximity of the ring to the focus of the spell will have the effect we want." He smiled slightly. "I am depending on Freelady Salven's quick reflexes to break the link if something goes wrong."

"Break the link?" Eleret frowned. She was uneasy enough about having a Shee work spells for her like a common hedge-magician; she hadn't thought that Climeral might be risking any harm. Or at least, she hadn't thought he would be taking any more risk than magic normally entailed. "What do you expect to go wrong? And what do you mean by 'break the link'?"

Climeral's slanted eyebrows lifted slightly. "I do not *expect* anything to go wrong; however, caution is never a bad idea. In the unlikely event that something untoward were to happen, removing your ring from the area affected by the spell will be quite enough to break the link between it and the scrying spell."

"I don't like the sound of this," Karvonen muttered.

"If you're uncomfortable, you don't have to stay," Daner said in a tone that was only a little more polite than necessary.

"I wouldn't give you the satisfaction." Karvonen's voice was too sharp, without its usual teasing undercurrents. *He is nervous*, Eleret thought, and had to suppress a renewal of her own anxieties.

"Quiet," Climeral told them. "Daner, kindly keep your attention on the wards." He rose and pushed his chair to one side, then took up a position opposite the point of the diamond-shaped layout of cards. "Freelady Salven, if you are ready to begin?"

Half-done is worth none, Tamm's voice said in Eleret's memory. *You can't use a pot without a handle or a bow without a string. Finish what you start, or you'll have a house full of bits and pieces, and nothing in fit shape to use.* And a rebellious part of Eleret's own mind responded, *This is* her *job, not mine. Haven't we learned enough?*

The others were waiting for her. *Ma would have finished this if she could*, Eleret told herself firmly. *Since she couldn't, it's up to me, and I'd best make a good job of it.* She looked at Climeral, then slowly removed the raven ring from her finger once more and held it over the raven in flight. Climeral nodded and stretched his own hands out to either side. Bringing them together with a swooping gesture, he said softly, *"Aheltri varthal-srilreth."*

A pinpoint of clear white light appeared less than a finger's-breadth above Eleret's final card. Barely visible at first, it grew brighter and brighter until Eleret could not look at it even through slitted eyes, and had to turn her head away. Climeral had not moved, nor even squinted. *How can he stand it?* Eleret wondered. But nothing in his expression or actions hinted at a problem, so she kept her hand steady, holding the raven ring two feet above the brilliant, sourceless light.

At last Climeral lowered his hands and stepped back. *"Helpara mec,"* he said, and the light vanished. He looked at Daner, who echoed the phrase, and the golden glow of the warding spell disappeared as well. Eleret slipped the raven ring onto her finger and looked around. In the relative dimness of normal morning light, Daner stretched like a hunter who had been crouched too long in a blind and Prill shifted her weight as if she had not dared to move before. Only Karvonen remained tense and watchful, his shoulders forward and his feet apart in readiness for a sudden move.

Climeral blinked, then scooped the six cards into a pile and handed them to Eleret. "Just put them in the case with the rest of the deck," he said when Eleret hesitated. "The order doesn't matter; Nijole will shuffle them before she uses them again. Then you can give them to Prill to return."

"You're not going to send me away before you tell everyone what you saw, are you?" Prill said. "That's not fair!"

"Returning Nijole's cards is your responsibility," Climeral said. "You may fulfill it in whatever way you see fit. Bearing in mind the possible consequences."

"You mean Nijole's going to yell at me," Prill said cheerfully. "But she does that anyway. So *that's* all right."

"You are incorrigible," Climeral said.

"What *did* you see?" Daner asked.

"The details would be . . . confusing," Climeral replied. "I will tell you instead what I learned. To begin with, the Shadow-born remain bound, all of them, everywhere. You need not fear facing one of them directly."

"Well, that's something," Karvonen said.

"Your ring is indeed at the center of what has been happening," Climeral continued. "However, I am afraid it will not prove a major weapon. It warns the wearer when shadow magic is near, and it will provide you with protection from certain general spells, but a strong, direct attack will wear through in a matter of minutes. A direct attack with shadow magic . . . well, I suspect the ring could disrupt it briefly, but no more, and it would probably be destroyed in the process."

"I don't suppose she has any control of the process, either," Karvonen muttered.

Climeral smiled slightly. "It depends on what you mean by control. Since Eleret is not a magician, she cannot enhance the ring's abilities, though a direct effort of will could shut the spell off temporarily."

"Oh, now that's *really* useful." Karvonen snorted derisively. "Just what you want to do when the Shadow-born are after you—shut down the only thing you've got to protect yourself."

"Does the ring warn about other things besides shadow magic?" Eleret asked Climeral, frowning. "Because it's warned me several times, and if the Shadow-born are all bound—"

"That is the worst of my news. At least one of the Shadow-born has loaned a portion of its power to a human sorcerer, for what purpose I do not know. It is that power—indirect and filtered through another—that you have felt these past few days."

"Mobrellan," Eleret murmured. She was not really surprised.

"Are you sure this guy is a Human, and not a Wyrd or Neira or Shee?" Karvonen asked. "Because Human shape-shifters aren't all that common, and—"

"He is Human," Climeral said. "I doubt that he has been a shapeshifter for long. The talent probably woke in him when he began using the power of the Shadow-born, and that is a matter of months, at most."

"Well, no wonder . . ." Karvonen sat back, looking simultaneously enlightened and disgusted about something, but though Climeral waited a moment and Daner gave him a pointed look, he did not comment further.

"If this sorcerer is already using shadow magic, why does he want Eleret's ring?" Daner asked.

"That, I could not determine," Climeral said. "He guards himself well. Perhaps he thinks it more powerful than it is, or fears even a minor disruption of his new abilities. Or perhaps he has some use for it—someone he wishes to protect, for instance. Without knowing more about him, I cannot guess his purpose."

"Power," Eleret said, thinking of the leaping fires she had seen on the Mage of Flames. "He wants power, and more power—and the more he gets, the more he wants."

"How can you be sure of that?" Daner said. "Was it something he said last night, when he was pretending to be me?"

"No, it's the card, the Mage of Flames. It was in the chart Jonystra did, too."

"The Mage of Flames stands for power misused, certainly," Climeral said. "But your interpretation goes far beyond that." He leaned back, awaiting an explanation.

Eleret told them what she had seen in the card, finishing, "He'll never be satisfied, no matter how great he becomes. But how could my ring be of any help to him?"

"You must discover that for yourself," Climeral said. "And remember that the card, and what you saw in it, may bear other meanings."

"What did you see in the other cards?" Prill asked.

"Mostly just the pictures moving. The Breaking Tower fell into the sea, the Mason worked on her wall, the Raven flew."

"And the Shadow-Mage?" Climeral said gently.

"It touched the candle, and the candle turned to powder," Eleret said, trying to repress a shiver and not altogether succeeding. "And then it started to turn toward me. There was a chain on its wrist, I think, but I couldn't see clearly. And it laughed."

Climeral looked startled. "You *heard* something in the cards?"

"Wasn't I supposed to?"

"It is . . . a little unusual. You must have been concentrating very hard."

"Or else you had bad oysters at breakfast this morning," Karvonen put in. "Speaking of which, isn't it time for lunch?"

"We still have things to discuss," Daner said.

"Can't you talk and eat at the same time?"

"Prill can take you to the refectory," Climeral said, and smiled at Eleret. "Lord Daner and I will join you in a few minutes. We have a discussion on the reality of Shadow-born to finish."

Daner gave Climeral a look of mild surprise. "Do you really think it's still necessary—"

"It's necessary. Prill, see to our guests. And don't forget your other errands once they're settled."

"Nijole's cards and the scrolls from the library," Prill said, nodding. "Do I tell Nijole what happened, when she asks, or do I get yelled at?"

"Refer her to me," Climeral said.

With an air of suppressed glee, Prill nodded again and ushered Eleret and Karvonen into the hall. "This way, Free-lady," she said as the door closed behind them, and then skipped three paces down the hall to the left. Seeing Eleret's slightly startled expression, she stopped. "Sorry, Freelady, but I can't help it. The expression on Nijole's face . . . I can hardly wait."

"I understand," Eleret said, and smiled, thinking of the weaponsmaster in Calmarten who had trained her with the raven's-feet. Eleret had never had an opportunity to surprise him as Prill expected to surprise Nijole, but she would have thoroughly enjoyed doing so. "Go ahead and skip."

Prill grinned and started down the hall once more, not quite skipping, but very light on her feet all the same. "I'm glad someone got some joy out of all that," Karvonen said as they followed in a more decorous fashion.

"I know you don't like wizards, but—"

"It's not a matter of liking or disliking," Karvonen said in a patient tone. "It's policy. I *like* your Adept Climeral very well; I'd just prefer not to be mixed up in his business."

"It's not his business, it's mine," Eleret said. "And you don't seem to like Daner much."

"Tactful, aren't you? That's another thing entirely." Karvonen gave her a sidelong look. "That's not policy, it's personal. And anyway, he doesn't like me."

They turned a corner and crossed a large courtyard. "Well, do me a favor and stop sniping at him," Eleret said. "I have the beginning of an idea of what to do next, and it would be useful if you were cooperating with each other."

Karvonen's eyes went wide, and he stared at her for a moment. Then he gave her a smile that held not only all his usual careless charm but also an underlying warmth like glowing embers. "I'll do *you* all the favors you want."

"Um. Good. I think." Eleret looked away, unsettled and unsure of exactly what had unsettled her. *Karvonen certainly has a knack for throwing people off balance,* she thought. *Now, if he could just catch Mobrellan with his bow unstrung . . .*

"Here we are, Freelady," Prill said, pushing open a set of double doors. "Savrik, these are Adept Climeral's guests; he and Lord Daner will be joining them in a little while. Will you see that they're taken care of? I've got errands to run."

TWENTY-FIVE

By the time Daner arrived, Eleret and Karvonen were seated at one of the long tables,
their tin plates heaped with snowy chunks of
fish mixed with carrots and an unfamiliar gray-green vegeta-
ble. One of the servers appeared with another plate as Daner
slid onto the bench opposite Eleret.

"What kept you?" Karvonen said. "And why couldn't it
have kept you a little longer?"

Daner did not look up from his plate. "Climeral wanted
to show me a few things."

"And did he?"

"More than I wanted to see." Daner's expression was grim
as he looked at Eleret. "I don't suppose I can talk you into
staying here until we catch that shapeshifter, can I?"

"No," said Eleret. "Why should I?"

"Because the school is probably as close as we can get to
a safe place right now, as far as you're concerned. Even if
Mobrellan can get past Climeral's wards, the detection spells
will let you know he's here. And there are enough Adepts

here to take care of him, shadow magic and all. Are you sure—"

"I fight my own battles. And staying safe doesn't win wars." *Assuming that staying safe is possible,* Eleret thought.

Daner sighed. "I was afraid you were going to say something like that."

"Then why'd you bother asking?" Karvonen said.

"Karvonen." Eleret waited until the little thief looked at her, then went on, "You said you'd stop that."

"Not exactly. And it's a hard habit to break."

"Then work at it." She looked back at Daner. "Are you going to try to block my strokes again?"

"Block your— Oh, I understand." He looked down and shifted uncomfortably. "I'm sorry about this morning, Eleret. I . . . shouldn't have done it."

"And now?"

"I won't try to make you stay here. If I can't persuade you . . ." He shrugged. "I'll just have to be twice as careful when we're on the street."

"It's not just that." Eleret frowned, trying to put into words something that all Cilhar understood in their blood and bones. "An army or a battle team can only have one commander, or it doesn't work well. And you're not just acting as if you're the one in charge; you act as if you're working entirely alone. I don't know why—"

"I do," said Karvonen.

Eleret looked at him, but his expression was serious and his voice did not have its usual mocking edge. "Why, then?"

"It's because he's so used to being my lord Daner Vallaniri, second heir to Lord Breann tir Vallaniri of Ciaron."

"Bah!" said Daner. "That's absurd. I don't trade on my rank."

"No," Karvonen said, still seriously, "but you're used to

having it. When you ask about something, things get done your way, without argument. Most of the time, you don't even have to ask. So you don't think to find out how Eleret wants them done."

"He's probably right," Eleret said. "And you're going to have to stop. If it comes down to it, it's my ring and my problem, not yours."

Daner looked as if he had bitten into a sour apple. "This seems to be my day for lectures. Very well, I'll try."

"Good," Eleret said. Daner looked at her in some surprise, and she smiled. "I want your help, so it's nice to know I can have it."

Daner returned her smile. "You'd have it in any case."

"You don't understand," Karvonen said. "It's not a matter of your willingness to help, it's a matter of her willingness to have you. If you'd said you couldn't accept her command, she'd act without you."

Startled, Daner looked at Eleret, who nodded. "I see," he said, and for a few minutes everyone ate in silence.

"I'm almost afraid to ask this," Karvonen said to Eleret at last, "but do all these questions mean you've come up with a plan?"

"No," Eleret said. "I've got the beginnings of an idea, that's all. Daner, didn't you say that now you can tell whether or not someone is the shapeshifter?"

"Not exactly. Adept Climeral has taught me a spell that will detect a shifter, but I can't just walk out the door and cast it at the market crowd. It has to be directed at a specific person."

"Mmm." Eleret frowned. "It will have to do. Can you keep him from vanishing the way he did last night?"

"I think so." Daner shook his head ruefully. "An hour ago, I'd have said yes without question, but if what Climeral says about shadow magic is true, I can't be sure how long I'll be able to hold him."

"Assuming we can catch him," Karvonen said.

"Assuming we can catch him."

"That's what this is all about," Eleret told them. "Before I start setting traps, I want to know they're strong enough to hold my game."

"Traps?" Karvonen said in a wary tone. "I don't like traps."

"Climeral said my primary resource was surprise," Eleret said. "And what I saw in the Three of Stones was an ambush." *And a very effective one.* Eleret smiled slightly, remembering the glowing arrows winging out of the trees, and the monster falling.

Karvonen still looked doubtful. "It's too easy for something to go wrong."

"Things have been going wrong ever since I got to Ciaron," Eleret said. "Besides, it would be silly to ask for Adept Climeral's advice and then ignore it."

"Well, I don't like it."

"You don't like anything that has to do with magic," Daner said.

"If you've got a better idea, I'd like to hear it," Eleret said to Karvonen. "The only other thing I could think of is to wait for Mobrellan to attack again. The problem is, Mobrellan seems to like making other people do his work, while he skulks in the background. We have to make sure he doesn't send more Syaski or people like Jonystra instead of coming himself, or we'll never catch him."

"Sounds to me like a mouse trying to catch a tomcat," Karvonen muttered. "He's got a line into a *Shadow-born*, Eleret. Can't you just stay out of his way?"

"I haven't had much luck avoiding him so far."

"True." Karvonen sighed. "All right, then, how do you

plan to get him to show up himself, instead of sending some more henchmen?"

"The same way I make sure my snares catch rabbits and not weasels: use the right bait." Eleret raised her hand and wiggled her forefinger, making light glint on the raven ring.

"It might work, if we can put it to him the right way," Daner said thoughtfully.

"Yes, and how are you going to do that?" Karvonen said. "Send out a crier to shout your message on the street corners?"

Eleret smiled at him. "That's your job."

"My job? Look, I'm willing to help, I've told you that, but I'm not a wizard. I've been trying to find this guy since noon yesterday, and I haven't had a whisper of luck."

Eleret let her smile grow. "You won't have to find him. He'll find you."

"I have a feeling I'm not going to like this idea much." Karvonen sighed. "It's what I get for getting mixed up with Cilhar wizards."

"Eleret's not a wizard," Daner objected.

"Her umpty-great-grandmother was, wasn't she? That's good enough for me. Or bad enough. Well, what is it you want me to do?"

"Your family sells information, right?" Eleret said. "Offer to sell somebody information about where I'm going to be tomorrow afternoon. One way or another, that should draw him."

Daner choked on a spoonful of stew. "Eleret, are you crazy?" he demanded as soon as he could speak again. "I thought you were planning to use the ring as bait, not yourself!"

"It's the same thing," Eleret said. "I'm not taking this ring off again, no matter what."

"I knew I wasn't going to like this," Karvonen muttered.

"Eleret, you—" Daner stopped and closed his eyes as if he were in pain. After a moment, he opened them and looked at her. Eleret returned his gaze steadily, and at last he sighed. "I'm not going to be able to talk you out of this, am I?"

"No. You can refuse to cooperate, though."

"And you'll do something even crazier."

"She can't help it," Karvonen put in sourly. "She's a Cilhar."

Daner gave Karvonen a dark look, and turned back to Eleret. "All right. We'll do it your way. But how do you know this *thief* won't sell Mobrellan the truth and wreck your trap?"

"He won't." Eleret could not explain why she was certain, any more than she could explain why she had claimed Karvonen as her knife-friend in front of Climeral, but she was as sure of the little thief as she was of Daner. *More sure,* whispered an unfamiliar corner of her mind. *You won't ever catch Karvonen blocking your throwing lines. . . .*

"I may be a thief," Karvonen said to Daner, "but I would never sell up a friend." He paused, then shrugged. "In this case, there's no point to it. I'll get just as much money for what you want me to say, and as long as it's true as far as it goes, the family reputation won't suffer."

"Then you'll do it?" Eleret said.

"Under protest and against my better judgment," Karvonen said. "Where do you want me to tell him you'll be?"

"That could be tricky," Daner said, frowning. "I doubt that he'd be foolish enough to come here; the Island of the Moon has too much of a reputation for magic. And after what happened last night, he knows we'll be ready for him if he comes back to the house."

"He won't expect anyone to be particularly ready for him

at the Broken Harp Inn," Eleret said. "And I can't think of any reason he'd be reluctant to go there."

Daner nodded slowly. "It's a good idea. From what I remember, none of the rooms is too large for me to cover with a blocking spell."

"And there's room to maneuver, if we need to."

"I'll send Bresc over earlier with a couple of men," Daner went on, setting down his spoon to drum his fingers absently on the tabletop. "They can hide somewhere until Mobrellan shows up; that way, we won't have to worry about whether he's bringing some more of his hangers-on with him." He straightened suddenly and looked across at Eleret. "If it's all right with you, that is."

"I have no objection to making sure he's outnumbered," Eleret said. "It'll be a nice change."

"I'm glad to see you've got *some* sense," Karvonen said. "But I can hardly put out word that you're going to be waiting at the Broken Harp with a gaggle of guards, hoping your shapeshifter will show up. I need a good story."

"A story?" Daner raised his eyebrows.

"Some kind of reason why, after all that's happened, you've decided to spend the afternoon at the inn instead of under heavy guard or running for your life like a sensible person," Karvonen said. "What else would you call it?"

They spent the rest of the meal considering and discarding possible tales. At last they settled on one that everyone agreed was plausible: Jonystra had regained consciousness long enough to convey a piece or two of interesting information, and Eleret and Daner were returning to the inn to go through her belongings in hopes of finding out more.

"It's not a bad idea, you know," Daner said as the servers removed their empty plates. "We're fairly close. Why don't we head over there now, and—"

"No," Eleret said firmly. "You and I can't go anywhere near that inn until tomorrow afternoon. Mobrellan might have someone watching it, or us, and we don't want to scare off the game."

"I'll take a look, if you like," Karvonen offered. "It *is* rather more my line of work, after all."

Eleret nodded. "Send us word if you find anything interesting, but don't come yourself. You shouldn't be seen with us until after Mobrellan's got his teeth into the bait."

"If that's how you want to work it," Karvonen said. "I won't miss the kill, though. One way or another, I'll meet you at the inn tomorrow. Where will you be in the meantime?"

"The headquarters of the Imperial Guards," Eleret said. "Mobrellan won't try anything there, not with half an army watching."

"Are you sure? He's a wizard and a shapeshifter, and whatever else he is, he's not Cilhar. He won't have your respect for uniforms and swords."

Daner's chin rose. "*Nobody* would risk an attack on the headquarters of the Imperial Guard of Ciaron."

"Your shapeshifter doesn't seem to go in for frontal assaults," Karvonen said. "He's more likely to try a sneak attack."

Eleret shook her head. "Not with so many people around. Too many things could go wrong. He's tricky; he's not stupid."

"If you say so," Karvonen said with a shrug. "But wouldn't it be safer to go back to the Vallaniri keep and wait?"

"Probably, but Daner and I were supposed to talk to Commander Weziral this morning—"

Daner's expression turned apprehensive. "Ah . . . I hate to tell you this, but I sent a messenger to tell Weziral we wouldn't be coming. Since I needed to be here and I, er, didn't expect anyone else to be going out . . ."

"Somehow that doesn't surprise me. I still want to talk to him, though. Will the spells you put on your home hold a while longer, or do you need to go straight back?"

"I think they'll hold, but I'd feel safer if I made a few adjustments. Climeral showed me a more effective method of blocking, and if there are Shadow-born involved in this, I'd like my blocks as effective as I can make them."

"So you're taking Shadow-born seriously now," Karvonen said in a tone that was half question, half comment.

"Adept Climeral was very convincing."

"Good," Eleret said. She thought for a moment. "Mobrellan probably doesn't realize that I've left the house, so it will be best if I visit Commander Weziral before I go back. Why don't you go strengthen the spells and then meet me at the Guard headquarters?"

Daner frowned. "I don't like the idea of you running around Ciaron unprotected. I know you're a competent fighter, but anyone can be taken down by superior numbers. If Mobrellan sends out another batch of Syaski . . ."

"If the news Karvonen brought this morning is correct, he can't do that," Eleret said, and explained briefly. "Syaski don't like being ordered around by outsiders, any more than Cilhar do," she finished. "I don't think they'll listen to Mobrellan any longer, and they won't be quite as dangerous without him to direct them."

"They'll still be looking for you, though," Daner said, his expression unchanged.

Eleret shrugged. "Syaski are always on the lookout for Cilhar. We're used to it. Stop fussing and take care of your business. The sooner you're done, the sooner you can meet me."

* * *

Daner did not, of course, stop fussing at once. He argued all the way to the side door, and when he could not change Eleret's mind, he offered to escort her to the Guard headquarters himself. Eleret pointed out that she had arrived at the school without him and without incident, and added a sharp remark about his duty to his family, and in the end, Daner agreed to do things her way.

"He'll probably run all the way home," Karvonen said as the door closed behind them. He sounded almost wistful. "I wish I could watch."

"Daner's not that foolish," Eleret said as they turned toward the narrow, nearly empty backstreets.

"Foolish?"

"Running would attract a lot of attention."

"I don't think he'll worry much about that. He's got other things on his mind." Karvonen gave Eleret another enigmatic, sidelong look. "Want to bet he gets to Weziral's before we do?"

Eleret laughed. "Not when you're my guide. The way you pick a path, you could take me twice round the mountain and I'd never be wiser."

"Would I do that?" Karvonen gave her a look of totally spurious wide-eyed innocence.

"Probably. So I won't tempt you."

"As you wish. This way, Freelady." Gesturing extravagantly, Karvonen steered Eleret toward a dark and unpleasantly smelly walkway between two buildings.

I'm going to have a time cleaning my boots tonight, Eleret thought, picking her way over and around the larger pieces of garbage. But at least the alleys were all but deserted; if trouble headed for them, she had a good chance to see it coming.

The route Karvonen chose was even more circuitous than the one that had brought them to the school. It led past a half-broken courtyard wall, through a warped wooden gate to a dim storage area filled with broken barrels and out again by an unlocked door on the far side, along a slightly wider street to another narrow walk, and on to a maze of passageways that reminded Eleret of the Charileduk Caverns, only damper.

Gradually, the alleys widened and became lighter and less filthy. Finally, Karvonen paused beside a smooth wall of the ubiquitous gray stone. "This is the headquarters of the Imperial Guard," he said, patting the wall gently. "There's an entrance just around that corner. You'll pardon me if I don't accompany you farther, but I suspect that your solemn Commander has thought up a lot more questions for me since yesterday, and I'd rather not have to answer any of them. Particularly since I don't have Lord Daner's nobility to hide behind at the moment."

"I understand."

Karvonen started to turn away, then paused. "Eleret. May your knife do its work swiftly, and your raven's-feet fly true," he said in Cilhar. "And may we meet again in honor when this clash of arms is ended."

The words of the traditional Cilhar farewell before battle sent cold lightning down Eleret's spine. *May we meet again* . . . Generations of comrades, companions, knife-friends, and sword-mates had voiced that hope, knowing that the coming hours would be full of danger and death. For many—too many—the only meeting had come in the smoke of funeral pyres. For a moment, she could not move, but as

Karvonen began to walk away, she pulled herself together. "Wait," she croaked.

Karvonen stopped short. Slowly, he turned back, his expression both wary and questioning.

"You know a great deal about Cilhar customs," Eleret said, trying to think how to phrase her request.

"Studying interesting places is a nice, safe way of filling up my spare time."

"Do you know how to plait a battle-braid?"

"Yes, I—" Karvonen's eyes widened, and for a moment a confusion of emotions swept across his face, too many and too complex for Eleret to be certain of anything but the astonishment. Then he took a breath, and was in control once more. "Are you asking me to do one for you?"

"Yes," Eleret said firmly. They were heading into battle, no matter that they were the only ones who knew it. She wanted the comfort of knowing that she had done things right, that if Commander Weziral had to send her braid home along with her mother's, her family would see that she had died fighting. *And Karvonen knows how, and as comrade and knife-friend he has the most right of anyone here.* Then, as a reluctant and uncomfortable afterthought, *Even if he is a thief.* She shoved both thought and discomfort away, and looked at Karvonen expectantly.

"All right," Karvonen said. "All right, if you want it. Turn around and stoop a little so I can see what I'm doing."

It took less effort than Eleret expected to turn her back to him and crouch in an awkward, hard-to-defend position. His fingers felt gently at her hair, loosening the old braid and separating the strands, then rebraiding them. She had not realized how intimate a task the battle-braid could be; no wonder it was normally done only by family or the closest of friends. Her head was oddly light, as if the touch of his fingers and the familiar-but-strange pull and twist of the braiding had removed a weight, instead of merely reshaping her hair.

"There," he said. "I'm afraid I haven't any red cord to tie it with, so I reused the brown."

"The pattern is more important than the cord color," Eleret said, straightening. She felt the braid hugging the back of her head, and nodded in approval. "Thank you. I wish I could return the favor."

"Actually, I'd rather— Hold on a minute, there's a bit coming loose on this side." Karvonen frowned. "Bend over so I can tuck it in."

Obligingly, Eleret leaned forward. Karvonen reached up and brushed his fingers along the top of her hair, then set his hand against the back of her head and, without warning, kissed her.

Total surprise kept Eleret motionless for a long and rather pleasurable moment. Then her training surfaced belatedly, and she pulled back. Karvonen released her at once, and grinned crookedly at her expression.

"What did you expect?" he said. "I'm a thief, after all. Good hunting, Eleret." Before she could collect her wits, he had turned and vanished down one of the alleys.

TWENTY-SIX

Eleret stared after Karvonen, her thoughts skipping wildly from one spot to another like water-spiders on a still pond. *That's why he and Daner don't . . . That's what Daner meant when . . . Oh, Mother of Mountains, surely not both of them. Why didn't I see it sooner?* She felt like a fool. But how could she have guessed that anyone on active duty would try to start a courtship? Of course, Daner and Karvonen might not consider helping her as "active duty"; still, they should have seen that *she* was on watch even if she wasn't under orders. *Blizzards take these Ciaronese, they don't do anything like normal people. And now what do I do?*

The answer to the last question was immediately obvious, if not entirely relevant to her current puzzlement. Firmly, Eleret pushed the last few moments out of her mind and started down the alley. Daner and Karvonen might have other ideas, but she was a Cilhar preparing to confront an enemy. She would take time to consider things later, after the shapeshifter had been dealt with.

But the interesting problem with which Karvonen had

presented her kept creeping back into her thoughts as she explained her business to the doorkeeper at the central building and followed a dour guard to Commander Weziral's offices. The outer office was unoccupied today, and Eleret's escort crossed directly to the other door. "Wait here," he said, and vanished inside.

Eleret sat down on a long bench with her back against the wall. Try as she might to think of other things, Karvonen—and his kiss—intruded on her reflections. And Daner. She should be far more upset about Daner than about Karvonen; after all, Karvonen had never quite crossed the Cilhar boundaries for acceptable behavior . . . until that kiss. Now that she had the opportunity to recall things and examine them in an orderly fashion, she could see that Daner had been interested in courtship from the very first. *He just doesn't know anything about Cilhar. But Karvonen does. Karvonen . . .*

He's a thief. He's a coward—he says so himself. He's probably a liar. He can play-act a messenger or disappear into a crowd. I shouldn't trust him. Eleret sighed. *But I do.*

Unasked, he'd offered his help and information to a stranger. Eleret smiled. *Offered? He practically forced it on me.* More than once, he'd taken risks to help her. She'd named him knife-friend in public and asked him to plait her battle-braid. *What more do I want from him? What does he want from me? If that kiss was just another of his tricks . . .* But she did not really believe that. *Or do I only* want *not to believe it?*

The outer door swung open. Eleret straightened quickly, then relaxed as a dark-haired guard ushered Daner into the room. "If you'll wait here, Lord Daner, I'll tell the Commander you're here," the guard said, starting toward the other door.

"Eleret!" Daner said in tones of relief. "You did get here

safely. And a while ago, I see; you've done something different with your hair. It's charming."

"I haven't been here long," Eleret replied, thinking, *A battle-braid, charming?* She felt both irritated by Daner's interruption of her train of thought and glad of the distraction at the same time. "You must have hurried."

"I certainly did," Daner said. Eleret thought of Karvonen's comments and almost smiled. "There was no sign of the shapeshifter at home," Daner continued, "so I reinforced the wards and left without even talking to anyone. My father is going to be annoyed if he finds out."

Before Eleret could respond, the inner door swung open and the two guards reappeared. Eleret's escort looked, if possible, more dour than before; Daner's wore a smug expression. "My lord Daner, Freelady, the Commander will see you now," he said, and waved them into the office.

"Lord Daner, Freelady Salven, welcome," said Weziral as the door closed behind them. "I'm sorry you couldn't be with us this morning. Problems all settled?" He gave Daner a sharp look as he spoke.

"Not settled, but under control for the moment, I think," Daner replied. "I apologize for the inconvenience."

"So your man said." Weziral leaned back in his chair. "Find a seat, the pair of you, before I break my neck trying to talk to the crow's nest. Just dump something on the floor. It won't hurt the floor, and I can't remember what most of the papers are anyway."

"I trust our absence this morning did not cause any great difficulties," Daner said.

Weziral snorted. "Maggen caused the difficulties. It's as well you weren't here, my lord; I'd have felt guilty about wasting your time."

"Maggen didn't tell you anything, then?" Eleret said.

"Oh, he told us plenty. The problem is, it's all lies, and I know it. But he won't admit he's been weaving the wind, so he sits in a cell and I sit here, and neither of us gets any further." Weziral shook his head. "I don't understand the man at all."

"What did he tell you?" Daner asked.

"A lot of nonsense," Weziral said. "The short version is that his noble cousin Lord Ovrunelli put him up to pulling these tricks—all of 'em, from trying to buy Freelady Salven's kit to abusing his authority to have her arrested and brought in."

Daner frowned. "If Lord Ovrunelli is behind Maggen's interest in Eleret—"

"That's just it," Weziral interrupted. "He isn't. Not only does he deny it, it's flat-out impossible. Ovrunelli was in council all day yesterday. He couldn't possibly have visited Maggen's office at the times Maggen claims he was there."

Eleret and Daner exchanged looks. "Lord Ovrunelli talked to Maggen *in person*?" Eleret said.

"That's what Maggen claims. He won't back down, either. The poor fool thinks Ovrunelli is going to use his influence to have him released." Weziral scowled. "If he were under my command, instead of merely in my employ, I'd have him court-martialed. After all I've done to keep the Guard out of politics . . . As it is, all I can do is keep him locked up for a few days and then fire him."

"I think perhaps we can explain Maggen's misplaced confidence," Daner said with another glance at Eleret. "There's a shapeshifter in Ciaron who seems to be impersonating people by the boatload."

"A shapeshifter?" Weziral said skeptically.

Both Daner and Eleret nodded. "He tried being me last

night," Daner said. "Fortunately, Eleret saw through him before he did any damage."

"I see." Weziral frowned. "You're certain it wasn't merely some actor's trick, my lord? They can do some remarkable things with a little gum and horsehair."

"There is no question of trickery," Daner said firmly. "El—Freelady Salven talked with him for several minutes, and I was face-to-face with him myself at the end. He's a shapeshifter."

"Even so, do you seriously think he'd try to impersonate one of the Imperial Councilors?"

Eleret saw what was disturbing Weziral, and said, "I doubt that he's learned any state secrets or given the Emperor bad advice. He relies on his appearance, and doesn't bother trying to move or act like the person he's imitating. That's what made me suspicious of him last night, and I've only known Daner for a day. He couldn't fool anyone who knows Lord Ovrunelli well."

"Then how could he have fooled Birok Maggen?"

"Maggen doesn't necessarily know Lord Ovrunelli well just because they're related," Daner said. "They may not even have met. Maggen's father or brother may have been the one who requested Lord Ovrunelli's patronage, and as long as he wasn't asked to provide an important post for Maggen, Ovrunelli might not have bothered to make his acquaintance."

"That would explain a lot," Weziral said sourly. "I suppose we'd better have another chat with him. If you'll come with me, my lord, Freelady . . ."

Weziral led them out of the office and through the maze of hallways to the courtyard. Their progress was interrupted repeatedly by various guards and officers who politely insisted on speaking with the Commander about one thing or another. Weziral dealt with most of the reports quickly; still, it was nearly half an hour before they reached the guard-house where Maggen was being held.

"I'm sorry about this, my lord, but it's something of a custom here," Weziral said, turning back from yet another messenger. "As long as I'm in my office, they don't worry me with the little things, but outside I'm a fair catch no matter who I'm with."

"Don't let it concern you," Daner said, grinning. "My father has the same problem."

"And if this happens all the time, you can be sure the shapeshifter wouldn't get far imitating you," Eleret said.

Weziral threw her a startled look and led them into the guardhouse. Inside, a heavyset officer took down their names before handing them over to another guard for escort to the cells.

The four cells had been built in a corner of the guard-house, two against each wall. The open area in front of them was small and bare; apparently the questioning of prisoners was done elsewhere. A heavy oak shutter covered the top half of each door. Surprised, Eleret studied the shutters more closely, then nodded in understanding and approval. A small window would allow a single guard to pass food to prisoners with no chance of being overpowered. She would have to remember to mention the idea to Raken when she returned home. All of the shutters were closed, so it was impossible to tell how many of the cells were occupied.

The guard paused in front of the second door. "Just the shutter, sir?" he asked Weziral.

"No, open the door. It will be crowded enough with three of us to ask questions, without having to peer through the grille as well."

"Yes, sir."

As they entered the cell, Maggen rose from a straw pallet

in one corner. A chamber pot sat next to the door; otherwise the room was bare. Maggen scowled at Weziral. Then he saw Daner, and his expression brightened. "Welcome, my lord! I knew Cousin Ovrunelli would send someone, even if he couldn't come himself. I knew—" He broke off as Eleret moved into view. "What is *she* doing here?"

"That is my affair," Daner said. Maggen snickered, and Daner gave him a quelling look. "You had best concern yourself with assisting me in clearing up the lamentable confusion you have created through your carelessness. Lord Ovrunelli is *not* pleased."

"I did what he told me to," Maggen said sullenly.

"That," Daner said loftily, "remains to be seen." He turned to Commander Weziral. "Have you anything to add to your previous comments?"

"No, my lord." Weziral's voice was grave, but his lips twitched as he spoke. Fortunately, Daner was between Maggen and the Commander, and by the time Daner moved, Weziral had his face back under control.

"And you?" Daner asked Eleret. His back was to Maggen, and he raised his eyebrows inquiringly, his expression a little doubtful.

Eleret thought she understood. "I've nothing to add. You may proceed, my lord."

Relief flashed across Daner's face, then he smiled warmly at Eleret. "Very well," he said in the same imperious manner, and grinned before schooling his expression to match his tone of voice. Turning back to Maggen, Daner studied him as if he were an improperly fletched arrow that Daner was deciding whether to salvage. "You had best begin at the beginning," he said at last.

"Aren't you going to get me out of here?" Maggen said.

"In due time," Daner replied, so coldly that Maggen

flinched. "Provided I am satisfied that you fulfilled your instructions. Proceed."

"My cousin, Lord Ovrunelli, came to see me—"

"Without informing you first?"

"No, there was a note—"

"I believe I told you to begin at the beginning," Daner said in a tone that was, if possible, even colder than before.

"Sorry, my lord. I didn't think it was important."

"You didn't think at all," Daner said. "Describe the arrival of the note, and what it said."

"A messenger brought it to my office," Maggen said. "It said that my cousin, Lord Ovrunelli, wished to speak with me on a matter of great importance. I was to meet him at an inn; I forget the name."

"And you didn't think it strange for Lord Ovrunelli to come to you in such a place?" Commander Weziral asked.

Maggen shrugged. "Everybody needs to relax a bit now and then. And we're cousins. Why shouldn't he?"

"You are third cousins, once removed," Daner said. "And you had not met Imperial Advocate Lord Ovrunelli before. Never mind. Go on."

"What was I supposed to do, quiz the messenger? He was just a hireling. Cousin Ovrunelli hadn't told him anything."

"Lord Ovrunelli," Daner corrected with dangerous gentleness. "And it is obvious that you did, in fact, 'quiz the messenger,' or you would not have known he was a hireling."

"I just wanted to make sure my cou—Lord Ovrunelli was being well served, that's all."

"Commendable, I'm sure. Continue."

Under Daner's persistent prodding, Maggen's story slowly emerged. He had met "Lord Ovrunelli" at the inn. Ovrunelli had been alone, without guards. No, Maggen had not thought that strange. Ovrunelli had asked Maggen to obtain the contents of a kit bag that had accidentally fallen into the hands of Commander Weziral. The bag contained an object vital to the security of the Ciaron Empire. Maggen would be well rewarded for returning it to his cousin; the exact nature of the reward had not been specified.

Maggen had attempted to break into Commander Weziral's office without success. At a second meeting with "Lord Ovrunelli," he had been forced to confess his failure. Ovrunelli had been furious. Maggen had tried again, with no better results. This time, Ovrunelli had been less angry, and had told Maggen to wait for the person who would be picking up the kit bag. Once the kit was away from the security of Imperial Guard headquarters, it would be much easier to retrieve.

The day before Eleret's appearance at the Commander's office, a note had arrived giving her name and warning Maggen to watch for her. He had found various excuses to loiter near Weziral's office for the rest of the afternoon and most of the following morning, but when Eleret showed up at last he had been unable to persuade her to give up the kit.

Frustrated, Maggen had returned to his own office, dreading his "cousin's" rage. To his surprise, another note had arrived less than an hour later, instructing him to use his position in the City Liaison's office to have Eleret—and her kit—brought to him when she tried to leave Ciaron. This he had done, and though the attempt had been even more spectacularly unsuccessful than his try at burglary, he fully expected Lord Ovrunelli to reward him for following instructions.

"These notes," Commander Weziral said when Maggen finished. "Did you keep them?"

"Ah—" Maggen looked at Daner uncertainly. Daner nodded, and Maggen said, "They're in my storage chest at home."

"Good," Weziral said. "If that is all, my lord Daner, perhaps we should be going."

"Are you satisfied as well, Freelady?" Daner said.

"You've covered everything pretty thoroughly. I don't have any more questions."

"Then we are at your disposal, Commander." Daner bowed and stepped aside to let Weziral leave the cell before him.

"Wait! What about me?" Maggen said. "You said you'd get me out of here."

"I said that might happen in due time, *provided* I was satisfied that you had followed instructions," Daner said. "You were told to destroy Lord Ovrunelli's notes, were you not?"

Maggen blanched. "I— But—I didn't—"

"Yes. You didn't." Daner frowned. "I shall do my best to explain matters to Lord Ovrunelli, but under the circumstances I can do nothing for you now. Commander, Freelady, if you will join me?"

They left Maggen sputtering in the cell and started back toward the main building. As soon as they were out of hearing, Weziral laughed. "Neatly done, my lord. I must confess, I wouldn't have thought of trimming sail to fit his mistake, but you changed course as smoothly as you please. You got twice as much out of him as we did this morning."

"Thank you, Commander," Daner said. "It seemed the best thing to do at the time, but I wasn't sure you'd approve."

"I might not have, if it hadn't worked so well. Success is hard to argue with."

The walk back was as slow and full of interruptions as the walk over had been. Eventually, they reached Weziral's office. As the Commander reached for the door, another aide came hurrying up.

"Two seconds more and I'd have been safe," Weziral said resignedly. "Ah, well. What is it, Vardon?"

"There's a messenger here looking for Freelady Salven," the aide said. "He just arrived. I thought all of you were still over in Building Four, so I put him in that empty room just down the hall."

Eleret frowned. It couldn't be Karvonen; they'd agreed he would avoid Eleret and Daner until they sprang their trap. Of course, he might have found something important in Jonystra's rooms. . . . Or perhaps it was someone from Climeral's school? She shook her head. "Daner, can you work that spell from here? The one to see if whoever is in there is the shapeshifter?"

"I can cast it here, but it won't tell me anything unless I can see the person I'm trying to test," Daner said. "It'll have to wait until we're in the room with him."

"What about the spell to keep him from vanishing?"

"That one takes a lot of energy, Eleret. I'd rather not cast it until I need it."

"And I'd rather not let Mobrellan slip my snare again. Do it."

Commander Weziral looked from Eleret to Daner with a slightly startled expression. Daner smiled and shrugged. "As you wish, Freelady."

As Daner began muttering the spell, Weziral turned to his aide. "Go get the Inner Watch. They're to accompany Freelady Salven and Lord Daner, and arrest whoever is inside that room if Lord Daner gives the word."

"Yes, sir."

"Wait," Eleret said. "Commander, I'd welcome the help, but it might be better if your men didn't come in with us."

"Why? From what you've said, this fellow is dangerous enough to warrant it."

"Yes—*if* it's the shapeshifter in there. I may be shooting my arrows at a patch of mist. But if it is Mobrellan, we don't know who he'll look like. Would your men arrest Imperial Advocate Lord Ovrunelli on Daner's say-so?"

"Sir, I'd have recognized Lord Ovrunelli," the aide put in. "It isn't him."

"Then if Freelady Salven opens the door and finds Ovrunelli waiting for her, we'll know it's the shapeshifter, won't we?" Commander Weziral said. "Still, I see what you mean, Freelady. I'll make sure the guards have clear instructions." He nodded at the aide, who left at a brisk walk.

"Done," Daner said.

Eleret turned. Daner's eyes looked tired and his face was drained. Before she could voice her concern, Daner went on. "The only way anyone can get out of this building for the next hour is to walk, run, or be thrown out a window. I hope you're not in a hurry to see who's waiting for us, Freelady. I'm going to need a little rest before I can cast another spell."

"It will take a few minutes for the Commander's guards to get here." Eleret hesitated. "Will that be enough? Is the next spell as . . . demanding as this one?"

"A few minutes will be plenty of time," Daner said reassuringly. "And the test for shapeshifting ability is a relatively easy spell. It doesn't have to hold anyone, you see, or last any length of time."

"Good," Eleret said with a confidence she did not feel. But by the time Weziral's aide returned with two quiet, efficient-looking guards, Daner's face no longer looked tired and drawn.

"Go ahead, Freelady," Commander Weziral said. "We'll be here if you need us."

"Thank you, Commander," Eleret replied. As she opened the door the aide had indicated, she said to Daner, "You know, I'm going to feel a little silly if it's only Karvonen after all."

"Why?" said Karvonen's voice from inside the room.

Daner let out an explosive breath. "Karvonen, you idiot! Why didn't you leave your name with Weziral's guard?"

"Because he's a thief," Eleret answered. Stepping into the room, she looked to her right and saw Karvonen lounging on a bench. Benches lined the wall opposite her as well, below three narrow windows. At the far end of the room from Karvonen stood a stack of boards and several trestles. As the door closed behind Daner, Eleret returned her gaze to the thief and said, "The real question is, what are you doing here? We had an agreement, if you remember."

"Ah, yes, the agreement." Karvonen pushed himself to his feet. "What you're really after is the password, of course."

"Passw—" Daner broke off abruptly, even before Eleret's warning nudge touched his side. "Yes, you'd better give us the password before you forget it."

Karvonen smiled. In careful, clearly memorized Cilhar, he said, "Karvonen says to tell you I'm the shapeshifter."

TWENTY-SEVEN

Eleret's blood sang in her ears, and for an instant she was blinded by rage. *How dared he steal Karvonen's shape? And what has he done with Karvonen?* Instinctively she reached for the raven's-feet at her shoulders, and the movement brought her back to herself. Hands poised, she stopped. *He doesn't realize yet that I know he's not Karvonen.* Close on the thought came another. *Daner is suspicious, but he can't be sure, because he doesn't speak Cilhar.*

With that, the surge of emotion ebbed, leaving only clear, cold reason behind. Eleret turned slightly toward Daner, so that her shoulder blocked the shapeshifter's view of her hands, and said in what she hoped was a normal tone, "It's him, all right." As she spoke, she pointed her right forefinger and tapped the raven ring with her left.

Daner's eyes dropped to her hands and he nodded. "I'll just go tell the Commander, then. There's no sense in letting him worry."

"I disagree," the shapeshifter said. "This won't take long."

Eleret moved farther into the room, where an unexpected spell would be less likely to catch both her and Daner at once—and where she could get a clear throw at "Karvonen," should she need it. "Let be, Karvonen," she said, wondering as she spoke that she could say his name to this creature without choking. "You still haven't said why you came."

"No." The shapeshifter smiled, and if she had not already known it was not Karvonen standing at the other end of the room, she would have realized it then. There was none of Karvonen's wry humor or cheerful irreverence in that smile, and very little pleasure of any kind. He raised a hand and gestured. *"Behtha."*

Before the shapeshifter finished speaking, Eleret had thrown two raven's-feet and was reaching for two more. In mid-reach, she stopped, staring, as the raven ring pricked her finger in unnecessary warning. Her weapons had halted two feet from the false Karvonen's face, and now hung motionless in midair, as if someone had suspended them on strings. She threw two more anyway; they'd give him something to walk around if he started down the room.

The shapeshifter finished his gesture, and the door of the room shimmered and began to glow a poisonous green. Daner, who had been reaching to open it, jerked his hand back and spun to face "Karvonen." His sword rang as it came free of the scabbard. Faintly, through the wall, Eleret heard a sudden commotion in the corridor outside.

With a faint smile on his lips, the shapeshifter studied Daner's sword. *"Zyrimi sal."*

"Nor hanri darvaria," said Daner almost at the same time.

The raven ring tightened uncomfortably around Eleret's forefinger. The light from the windows dimmed briefly and then brightened once more, as if someone had drawn a curtain and then opened it again. Daner smiled and lifted his sword briefly before lowering it to guard-position once more. The blade shone as if they stood in a battle ring at noon instead of indoors in half-light.

The shapeshifter's eyebrows rose. "Not bad, for a beginner. But you can't keep it up."

"Neither can you," Daner said.

"Now there, you are wrong." The shapeshifter grinned, and Eleret shuddered to see Karvonen's smile go so subtly awry. "I have help." He gestured again and rattled off a long, complex phrase.

"Nor hanri darvaria," Daner repeated, but this time the dimness did not vanish entirely. It hovered against the ceiling and filled the corners of the room, withdrawn but waiting. From the shadows behind the shapeshifter, Eleret heard a soft chuckle, and the ring pricked again, emphatically.

Displeasure mingled with surprise in the shapeshifter's expression. "Where did you learn that?"

Slowly, quietly, as if she had sighted a deer and were circling for a better shot, Eleret moved sunwise and forward. Her raven's-feet still hung frozen in mid-flight; Daner's counterspells had not allowed them to move even an inch. But the shapeshifter's magic had not yet affected her, or Daner. If she could get close enough . . .

"I learned it in the same place I learned any number of other things," Daner said. "Why don't you give up now, and save us both some trouble?"

"You must think I'm a fool," the shapeshifter said, and smiled his disconcerting, not-Karvonen smile once more. "I'm here for that ring of hers. Give it to me, and I'll go."

As he glanced in her direction, Eleret stopped moving and slid her knife out of its sheath. "Why should we believe that?"

Anger twisted the shapeshifter's face. "I suppose you don't think a bastard is as honorable as someone who's true-born. Well, my word is as good as anyone's, and better than some."

"No doubt," Eleret said noncommittally. She had no idea why he had reacted to her question so strongly, but she did not want to provoke him into an attack just yet. Not until she was near enough for her steel to touch.

Daner snorted. "You can have ten fathers, or you can be the legitimate son and heir of the Emperor himself; I don't care. After what we know you've done, we wouldn't believe a thing you say."

"Then there's no point in talking, is there?" said the shapeshifter, and raised his hand.

"Wait!" Eleret said. "Why do you want my ring?"

"Does it matter? You won't believe me, and if you did, you still wouldn't give it to me." His voice was bitter, and he glared in Daner's direction, but he did not move to complete his spell.

"Daner doesn't speak for me," Eleret said. "I might believe you. What harm can it do?" She wasn't close enough for a lunge, and there was no point in throwing the dagger, not with the spray of raven's-feet still hanging uselessly two feet in front of his face. And he looked so much like Karvonen . . .

The shapeshifter studied her as if he had never seen her before. "I want the ring in order to discover where the Shadow-born have been bound," he said at last, and Eleret was sure that he spoke the truth. "Make of that what you will."

"What are you going to do when you find them?" Daner asked. "Release them?"

The shapeshifter hesitated. "I'm not a fool," he said at last. "I would never unbind a Shadow-born I could not control."

A shiver ran down Eleret's spine, and she remembered the Mage of Flames calling fire, and more fire, until the flames consumed everything, including himself. *He thinks he's found a way to control a Shadow-born. Once he has the ring, he'll unbind one, and try. And fail—nobody can control a Shadow-born. And then there'll be a Shadow-born loose in the world. . . .*

"I'm glad to hear that you aren't a fool," Daner said dryly. "Eleret, he's going to—"

"I know. I'm not a fool, either." She looked at the shapeshifter. "You were wrong, and you were right. I believe what you said, but I won't give you the ring. Not for that. No Cilhar would."

The shapeshifter turned his head toward her. "Then I'll have to take it."

As the shapeshifter's eyes left him, Daner moved forward with the swift, practiced grace of a swordsman closing on an opponent. He was not swift enough, or else the distance was too great. Before he reached striking distance, the shapeshifter turned and snapped a single word.

Something chuckled again, the same chuckle Eleret had heard from the Shadow-Mage card during Climeral's charting, and from the corners of the room, the darkness surged forward. Daner gasped, and his movements slowed, as if he were wading through knee-deep mud. *"Nor hanri darvaria,"* he repeated for the third time.

The darkness retreated fractionally, but Daner's progress remained impossibly slow. "Eleret! I can't hold this for long."

"I shouldn't think so," the shapeshifter said in tones of detached interest. "It will be interesting to see how much difference your spells make. Last time, it only took a few minutes to kill, but last time there was only the ring to keep it at bay."

He killed Ma. Eleret took an involuntary step and discovered that she, too, had been slowed to a crawl. Apparently the ring could only handle one spell at a time.

"Of course, it was my own fault," the shapeshifter continued. "I wasn't using the full strength of the spell then, so I expected it to take hours to work through the ring's defenses. I thought I'd arrive just as it took effect, but . . . If she hadn't died so quickly, I'd have had the ring, and all this would be unnecessary."

Eleret froze. In her memory, Climeral's voice said, *. . . but a direct effort of will could shut the spell off temporarily,* and suddenly she was positive that she knew what had happened. *Ma called for the healers and then shut off the ring, so that by the time he got there, her things were sealed up to send home. She must have figured out what he wanted, the way I figured it out, and that was the only way she could be sure he wouldn't get hold of the ring.*

"She must have been weaker than I thought," the shapeshifter finished. "You two are certainly doing better than I expected, though."

Again, Climeral's words came back to her: *It will provide you with protection from certain general spells, but a strong, direct attack will wear through in a matter of minutes.* How long had it been since the spell had been cast? Eleret forced her feet forward, but her best effort made little progress. She would never reach him in time.

Her arms were free; she could throw more raven's-feet, or her knife. But while the shapeshifter's warding spell stopped them in midair, throwing things would be useless. Unless she threw the right thing.

On the card, the painted raven's wings began to move. The bird cawed once and beat the air with its wings, then stretched and soared higher on some invisible current of air. The mountains and everything in them fell away below it, until all that surrounded the raven was clear air and a sense of release. Release . . .

Eleret stared at the raven ring. *Climeral said it could disrupt shadow magic, but it might be destroyed in the process. And it was Mother's. He killed her for it. He'll use it to free the Shadow-born. I can't give it to him. I can't take the risk. If it doesn't work, I'll have lost everything Mother fought for. And if it does work, I'll lose the ring anyway. I can't do it. No Cilhar could.*

Her own thought reverberated in her mind. *No Cilhar could. No Cilhar would. Ma was Cilhar, she spent her life fighting, she taught me the old tales. She couldn't stop fighting. She couldn't let go of the ring—but she could die for it.*

She glanced up. Daner's face was shiny with perspiration, but he had managed another step. The shapeshifter watched his efforts with the air of a drill captain observing a raw recruit at weapons practice. In the corners of the room, the shadows had thickened, swallowing the light. Eleret winced. *I'm not Ma. And if I don't try now, it will be too late.*

The shapeshifter turned and looked at her out of Karvonen's eyes, and renewed rage swept Eleret's doubts aside. "You want my ring?" she said. "Take it." She pulled it from her finger and tossed it underhand in a high arc.

"Eleret, no!" Daner said, but the ring was already in the air, a gleam of silver in the dimming half-light. *Take this, too,* Eleret thought, *from me and Ma.* And threw her mother's knife after the ring.

The shapeshifter's eyes widened in an expression of puzzled surprise, and then the ring struck his chest, unslowed by his spell of warding. His hands came up and caught it in automatic reflex—and abruptly the light in the room brightened.

The shapeshifter's cry of astonished dismay changed—

first to a scream of pain as four razor-sharp raven's-feet struck his face, then to a cry of agony as lightning exploded inside his closed hands, then to a choked gurgle as Eleret's knife, Tamm's knife, buried itself hilt-deep in his throat.

Eleret stumbled forward as the force holding her back vanished. Before she could reach him, Daner's sword slid over the shapeshifter's charred, half-raised arm and into his chest.

Karvonen's features blurred—no, his whole form blurred and altered, stretching and twisting his clothes, until it was no longer Karvonen's shape bleeding and choking in front of them, but Mobrellan's. His dying hands clenched convulsively around the remains of the raven ring, and he toppled.

As the shapeshifter fell, the last of the unnatural shadows fled, leaving only the normal variation of light and shade. An instant later, the door burst open and half a dozen soldiers with drawn swords charged into the room. The swords glimmered faintly with the light of some protective spell, and so did the soldiers' breastplates. Eleret smiled faintly. Commander Weziral would be a good man to serve under.

"My lord!" one of the men said to Daner. "Are you all right?"

Daner pulled his sword free of the body, turned, and began answering questions. Eleret left it to him; her mind was occupied with other things, and Daner would make a better job of the explanations in any case. The last of her smile faded as she stepped forward to stare down at the shapeshifter.

She felt no triumph, only relief that she did not have to retrieve her weapons from a body that still resembled Karvonen. If this was her revenge on her mother's killer, it was not worth having. *But it's more than revenge*, she reminded herself. *He won't be after me or any other Cilhar, ever again, and he won't be letting Shadow-born free to trouble the world.* It still did not feel like a victory, only like the absence of defeat. But she could not take the time to ponder now, not while she still was unsure where Karvonen was and what had happened to him.

Carefully, so as to avoid the spreading pool of blood, she crouched beside the body. The raven ring was a worthless chunk of metal, embedded in the blackened flesh of Mobrellan's palm. She shuddered and left it there, reaching for one of her raven's-feet instead.

"Ah, milady, should you be doing that?" one of the soldiers said.

Eleret looked up, uncomprehending. "He's not my first battle kill, by any count. And who should clean my weapons, if I don't?"

"Let her be, Captain," Daner said, and there was a rueful expression lurking at the back of his eyes. "It's all right. She's a Cilhar."

"I've heard about them," the soldier muttered, backing away. "Well, if you say so, my lord."

Quickly but methodically, Eleret picked her raven's-feet out of the wreckage of Mobrellan's face and cleaned them on his shirt—Karvonen's shirt, actually, but it was ruined in any case and she doubted he'd want it back. Assuming he was still in a condition to care about such things. She shut off the thought and made her fingers work faster. Two of the raven's-feet had to go into her pouch; when she'd pulled them free, she'd split the thong that held them to her shoulder. Well, that was what the thongs were for. She still had a row and a half at each shoulder, if she needed them again.

She yanked her knife free and wiped it clean, then rose. As she turned, she heard Daner saying, "—quite definitely the same shapeshifter. I doubt there was more than one, so it's over."

"No it isn't," Eleret said. She nodded to Commander Weziral and said, "I'm sorry, Commander, but I've a friend in trouble to see to. If you need more explanations, they'll have to wait."

Daner frowned; then his eyes went past her to the shape-shifter's body and widened slightly, as if he had only just noticed that Mobrellan had been wearing Karvonen's clothes. "I think the Commander is finished with us," he said. "Where do we start looking?"

"Karvonen was going to Jonystra's room. He was either waylaid there or on his way there; the timing is too close for anything else." Eleret started purposefully for the door.

"If it would be any help, Freelady, I could send some men—" Commander Weziral began.

"Send them to the inn called the Broken Harp," Eleret said without pausing, and an instant later she was in the hall outside.

Daner caught up with her halfway down the corridor. Neither of them said anything until they were almost out of the building; then Eleret glanced over at him and said, "Good job."

"That last sword-thrust?" Daner shrugged. "It seems to have been unnecessary."

"That, yes. Unnecessary or not, it's best to make sure. And if you hadn't done whatever you did to stop his magic, I couldn't have thrown anything—ring or knife—once the ring was off my finger. But that wasn't what I meant." Eleret hesitated.

"Well?" Daner said after a moment. "What did you mean?"

"This time, you didn't block my throwing lines."

TWENTY-EIGHT

When they reached the streets, Eleret chose the most direct route to the Broken Harp and set a brisk trail-pace in spite of the crowds. There was no point in trying to track Karvonen through the alleys from the point where they had parted; if he had been waylaid before he reached the inn, the quickest and surest way to find out was to determine that he had never arrived there.

Daner did not object to her hurry, though he looked as if he would like to. Eleret suspected that he'd have preferred to wait for Weziral's men to accompany them, but that would have meant another five or ten minutes' delay while the soldiers were assembled and instructed, and she could not have stood it. She needed work, or action, or perhaps merely movement—something to release the tension she felt, or at least to distract her from it.

It occurred to her that she had never translated the shapeshifter's Cilhar "password" for Daner, so, as they crossed the broad avenue toward the area where the inn was located, she did so.

Daner's expression went grim. "I wondered what that was about, but when you tapped the ring . . ."

"You thought I knew it was the shapeshifter because the ring had warned me?" Eleret shrugged. "It was a reasonable guess. And it really doesn't matter; the important thing, then, was that you were sure it wasn't Karvonen."

"I wish I knew how Karvonen persuaded him to say something he didn't understand," Daner said. Then he closed his mouth abruptly and his expression changed from grim to bleak. "I was going to ask if you were sure you didn't want to wait for the Commander's men," he said after a moment, "but now I don't think *I* want to wait for them."

"Wait? Why?"

"That shapeshifter—Mobrellan or whatever his name really is—had a tendency to get other people to do his dirty work for him. If he's left someone at the inn—"

"Then we'll deal with them."

They turned the last corner, and Eleret saw the splintered harp above the inn's door. Her stride lengthened further, even as her stomach clenched. She found herself almost hoping Mobrellan *had* left someone on guard. With Daner half a step behind her, she pushed open the door of the inn.

The transition from the near-noon light of the street to the smoky gloom of the public room blinded Eleret to detail for a moment, but she heard a startled exclamation as she entered, and then a muttered *"Hoy! Oransk voyi Cilhar,"* and the scraping of benches being shoved back from tables.

"Syaski!" Eleret called the warning to Daner, then drew her knife and moved left, out of the light spilling through the open door. *I should have let Daner come in first,* she thought. *It would have given us another second or two; they couldn't have identified* him *as a Cilhar from looking at his clothes.*

Steel rang against leather as Daner drew his sword. Five figures converged on them, their expressions indistinct but their intentions clear. Near the back of the room, the proprietor of the inn pushed his wife into the kitchen, then discreetly followed her out of harm's way.

Eleret flipped a raven's-foot at the nearest Syask, expecting him to dodge. He did, but not far or fast enough. Clutching his left eye, he tripped over a bench and temporarily disappeared from sight.

One out, four to finish. Eleret dropped into a crouch as the first man came at her. His movements lacked edge—*he's probably been drinking. Stupid thing to do, if you're expecting a fight*—and she closed with him, ducking under his descending sword to slide her knife between his ribs. *Two out.* As she pulled her knife free, she shoved, hard. The man fell backward into his compatriots, entangling their swords and slowing their advance.

Backing away, Eleret circled sunwise. Off to her right, she heard the clash of sword against sword. *Daner has one. Two left for me.* The nearer man turned to face her and found her knife waiting. *One for me, one for Daner.*

The last man was ready for her. His sword licked out, and she jumped backward, barely avoiding it. The Syask smiled and lunged again. Eleret took the cut across the fleshy part of her right arm—not deep enough to cut muscle, but painful. Ignoring the pain, she caught at his wrist and pulled him toward her, bringing his throat within reach of the knife in her left hand.

As she jumped back to avoid the spurt of blood, she heard a strangled cry to her right, and the sound of a body falling. *That's all of them.* Automatically, she bent to wipe her knife.

"Eleret! You—" Daner stopped.

Looking up, she found him staring at her with an astounded expression. "What is it?"

"You killed *four* of them?"

"No. Two. That one will probably live." She pointed her knife at the man she had sliced between the ribs. "And the one over there is sure to survive." She gestured in the direction of the man she had blinded with her raven's-foot.

Daner shook his head. "You're amazing."

"Not really. The innkeeper's in the kitchen; go ask him which room is Jonystra's. If I ask, he'll want explanations, but if you do it—"

"He'll be happy to tell Lord Daner Vallaniri whatever he wants to know." Daner was heading for the kitchen door before he was quite through speaking.

Eleret finished cleaning her knife and sheathed it, then pressed her hand against the sword cut for a moment to reduce the bleeding. By the time she had retrieved her raven's-foot, Daner was back. "First door on the left, upstairs," he said, then, "You're hurt!"

"Not enough to matter." The cut was messy and needed bandaging, but though it continued to ooze, the bleeding was not bad enough to worry about weakness or blood loss. A few more minutes would make little difference in its eventual healing.

"I begin to understand Karvonen's attitude toward Cilhar," Daner muttered. "A few minutes won't—"

"—make enough difference to be worth the time," Eleret said from the far door. "Be quiet. There may be more of them upstairs."

"I think they already know we're here," Daner said, glancing pointedly back at the overturned bench, the two injured Syaski, and the three bodies.

"Probably, but they don't need to know to the second when we're coming through the door."

Without waiting to see whether Daner was following, she started up the stairs. She moved quickly and quietly, as she did when she hunted in the forests at home, her ears straining to catch any whisper of sound that might betray the presence of enemies above. In the hall by Jonystra's room she paused, suddenly reluctant to face whatever waited inside. Her slight hesitation allowed Daner to catch up with her. At his inquiring look, she whispered, "Spells?" and gestured at the door.

Daner's eyes narrowed and he muttered something indistinct. Then he shook his head. Eleret took a deep breath, nodded once, and pushed open the door.

No Syaski burst out to attack them. What she could see of the room was empty, save for a wash table very like the one in the room she had had downstairs. Eleret frowned; then, dagger ready, she leaped through the open door and whirled, scanning the room. No one crouched against a wall or lurked behind the door. Satisfied, she sheathed her dagger and looked around more carefully.

Two wooden trunks sat against the wall beside the door, each closed with an iron lock. The bed was in complete disarray; the blankets had been pulled off and dumped in a heap on the floor beside it, leaving the straw pallet bare. No, not pulled off, dragged. And even half-blocked by the pile of blankets, there was something odd about the shadow under the bed. . . . Stepping forward, Eleret jerked the straw pallet off the bed, and found herself staring through the rope webbing into Karvonen's terrified eyes.

Relief made her dizzy. "It's all right," she said in Cilhar. "It's really me." Switching to Ciaronese, she called to Daner, "I've found him."

"Is he all right?"

Only then did the swellings and the lacework of fine cuts on Karvonen's face register. "No," Eleret said. "Give me a hand with this frame, so we can get at him."

Karvonen's eyes closed, and his head dropped back to the floor with a thud. He did not move as Daner and Eleret lifted the wooden bedframe and moved it aside. With the frame out of the way, it was easy to see the marks of a thorough beating on his naked body, as well as the threads of dried blood that marked the path of a knife. His hands and feet were bound tightly enough that his fingers were blue and swollen, but he had not been gagged. Daner made a sickened noise and turned away. The thief neither moved nor spoke.

Frightened by Karvonen's stillness, Eleret knelt beside him and reached for the pulse point at his throat. Her fingers tingled as she touched him, and she pulled away. "Daner, I think there's a spell on him."

Daner was beside her in an instant, muttering incomprehensible words as his hands hovered over Karvonen's chest. "You're right; it's a silencing spell. No wonder nobody heard him while they were . . . Never mind. This will take a minute." He frowned in concentration and began murmuring once more, his hands making odd plucking gestures in the air above Karvonen. *"Halkana wilinin sala; valyra wilme sal,"* he said at last, and sat back.

An instant later, Karvonen gasped, coughed, and said in a raw, hoarse whisper, "E-Eleret?"

"It's me," Eleret said in Cilhar.

"Did—did—shape—" Karvonen broke off, coughing painfully.

"I got your message," Eleret said. "The shapeshifter is dead."

"Thoroughly dead," Daner put in. "And if I'd known he'd done *this*, I'd have twisted the sword as it went in."

Karvonen's cracked and puffy lips curved very slightly. "Good."

"Don't talk." Eleret studied Karvonen's bonds for a moment, wincing in sympathy, then drew her dagger. "And try not to move. I'm going to cut the thongs around your wrists, and I don't want to slip."

"You . . . won't."

"Quiet." Carefully, Eleret stroked the knife point across the taut leather. She counted under her breath, two, three, four times, each stroke slicing a fraction farther, until the thong parted at last. Working as gently as she could, she unwound the leather from the swollen flesh. Karvonen sighed as his hands came free at last, then shivered.

Eleret looked dubiously at the rough blankets, but there was nothing else to use. As she reached for the top blanket, Daner undid the clasp on his cloak and swung it away from his shoulders. Leaning forward, he draped it over Karvonen's recumbent form. Karvonen tried to raise an eyebrow, winced, and took a deep breath.

"I told you to be quiet," Eleret said before he could speak. "You can tell Daner 'thank you' later."

"What makes you think he was going to thank me?" Daner's tone was bantering, but his expression was concerned. "It's more likely he was planning another insult."

"Whichever it is, it is going to wait," Eleret said firmly. She threw a grateful smile at Daner, and slid down to undo Karvonen's feet.

The sound of footsteps on the stairs outside drifted through the door. Eleret shifted to face the entrance, and Daner readied his sword. An instant later, they both relaxed as the innkeeper's worried face appeared. "My lord? Lord Daner? I— Death storm on the open sea! What *happened* here?"

Eleret turned back to her task, leaving the explanations to Daner. He gave the innkeeper a succinct and considerably edited story focusing mainly on Karvonen's rescue and leaving the distinct impression that it had all involved a plot against the Emperor. The innkeeper, while impressed, seemed far more interested in who was to pay for various damages and what he was to tell the City Guards when they arrived.

The last thong parted, and Eleret looked up. "Daner, settle this outside. Karvonen needs a healer; failing that, he needs quiet."

"I'm . . . not—"

"*Quiet!*" Eleret said. "Daner, go away. And when you come back, bring a healer."

"An unnecessary stipulation," said a new voice. "Livarti! Double time; you're needed." And a stocky man in the uniform of the Imperial Guard stepped through the door. Bowing to Daner, he said, "I'm Captain Sheverin, at your service by Commander Weziral's order and with his compliments, my lord, Freelady. Some of my men are cleaning up downstairs; do you require any additional assistance?"

"Not at the moment, Captain," Daner said. "Your arrival is very timely."

Another uniformed man appeared in the doorway. "Captain, I hope you've got a good reason for dragging me up here. There are two men downstairs who need my attention."

"The man up here not only needs it, he deserves it," Daner said. "That is, if you're the healer Captain Sheverin called for a minute ago."

"I'm Livarti." The man eyed Daner suspiciously. "You're not injured."

"Over here," Eleret said. "Daner . . ."

"Perhaps we should continue our discussion in the hall," Daner said to the innkeeper. "I'm sure Captain Sheverin will want to join us."

"Indubitably." The Captain bowed, Daner bowed, and between them they shepherded the awed innkeeper out of the room.

The healer was already shaking his head over Karvonen's condition. "Close your eyes and try to hold still," he told the thief. "This shouldn't hurt, but it may feel a little strange. If it *does* hurt, tell me immediately."

"Yes," Karvonen rasped, and Eleret had to repress another automatic command for him to be still. Karvonen must have realized what she was thinking, because he caught her eyes and winked very deliberately before following the rest of the healer's instructions.

Livarti folded Daner's cloak back, then began muttering rapidly, while his hands wove through the air above Karvonen's body. Blue light sprang up and faded almost at once, first around Karvonen's head, then his chest, then each arm and leg in turn. Eleret watched in worried fascination. She hadn't realized how different a practiced healer's work would be from the tests Gralith had run on her father the day before she had left the mountains.

At last the healer paused. "A cracked collarbone, two broken ribs, and a damaged kidney, plus an amazing assortment of bruises, sprains, and cuts. What happened?"

"I . . . was—"

"Tcha," said Livarti. "A moment, please." He laid his right hand against Karvonen's throat and made a series of strange gestures with his left. Orange light bloomed around his hand. Frowning, the healer made another complicated gesture and began muttering under his breath once more. Slowly the light changed color, fading from angry orange to clear yellow and then to white.

Finally, Livarti stopped muttering and let the light die. When the last glimmer was gone, he lifted his hand from Karvonen's throat and flexed the fingers. "How's that?"

"It's . . . much better." Karvonen's voice was still slightly hoarse, but he no longer sounded as if every word were painful.

"If you didn't have so much else wrong with you, I'd have pushed a little further, but under the circumstances it wouldn't have been wise. You're going to need the rest of your energy for more important repairs."

"You're the healer."

"Now, then—what happened?"

Karvonen started to shrug, winced, and stopped short. "I ran into a man who wanted some information. The only way to convince him that he was getting what he wanted was to let him . . . persuade me to give it to him."

"But the silencing spell . . ." Eleret said, then stopped, uncertain how to continue.

"He put it on and off like a gag. Very effective. It'd be a useful trick to know, under some circumstances."

"This, I take it, represents the fellow's means of persuasion," the healer said with a disapproving frown at Karvonen's injuries.

"Not all of it. Some of the bruises are from rolling off the bed." Karvonen gave Eleret an apologetic look. "I couldn't get loose, but I thought I could make it look as if I had. So I rolled off, and sort of slid underneath, and pulled the blankets down. It was the best I could do."

"You must have either an iron constitution or an iron head," Livarti said acidly. "With a damaged kidney, that kind of movement—"

"It . . . wasn't one of the more pleasant things I've ever done," Karvonen admitted.

The healer snorted. "You're luckier than you deserve. About this man you met—the Commander will want details. The Emperor frowns on incidents like this; whoever did it—"

"The Commander already has details, and the man who did it is dead," Eleret put in. She looked at Karvonen. "Are you sure you weren't a little *too* convincing?"

Karvonen smiled very slightly. "Now that you mention it, I think maybe you're right."

"Next time, don't overdo it," Eleret said, and touched his shoulder lightly, careful not to add to his pain. "Or Jaki will be convinced you've taken up that Fourth Profession of yours."

"There had better not *be* a next time," Livarti said. "I don't like patching people up twice."

"Don't worry," Karvonen told him. "I never disobey a healer's orders."

"Then you're the first patient I've ever had who doesn't. Quiet now. I'm going to do some preliminary work on that kidney, and set a few binding spells to hold the rest of you together until we get you to the infirmary. Freelady, would you tell the Captain to send two men up with a litter in about half an hour? I'll tend to that arm of yours as soon as I'm finished here."

That was a dismissal if she'd ever heard one. Reluctantly, Eleret rose and left the room. As the door swung closed behind her, she heard the low murmuring of the healer's spells begin once more.

TWENTY-NINE

For the next two days, Karvonen lay in a small room in the infirmary of the Imperial Guard of Ciaron, tended alternately by Commander Weziral's healer Livarti, and the Vallaniri healer, whom Daner insisted on sending over the moment they returned to his home. Eleret was impressed by the speed with which Karvonen's bruises purpled and faded; in the mountains, he'd have rivaled a rainbow for a week. The cuts, too, healed unnaturally fast. By the evening of the second day, there was only a network of darker skin to show where they had been, as if someone had painted a diagram of Ciaron's streets across his face and chest in walnut juice.

We need someone at home who can do things like that, Eleret thought, watching Karvonen devour a dinner large enough for three men. Such rapid healing, the two physicians had explained, made unusual demands on the patient's physical reserves. Until he was well enough to leave, Karvonen would spend whatever time was not occupied by the healers' treatments either eating or sleeping. *Maybe Climeral can send a teacher to the mountains next year, or maybe he'll let Orimern or Calla come to school here. I'll have to ask him before I leave.*

Finally, Karvonen pushed the tray away and sat back with a sigh against the pile of pillows at the top of the bed. Daner frowned. "Are you sure you've had enough? You've left half the fish paste."

"I'm sure," Karvonen said. "Anyway, they'll be back with another load in two hours. If I've missed anything, I'll make it up then."

"Livarti says—"

"Livarti can go shovel fish-heads. I'm not eating any more tonight, and that's that."

"I'm pleased to see that you're feeling better," Commander Weziral said. As one, Eleret and Daner turned to find him standing in the open door of the room. "And since you're all in one spot, perhaps you can fill in a few details in regard to this shapeshifter of yours. I've put off making my report as long as I can."

"What do you need to know?" Daner asked.

"What that shapeshifter was after, for a start," the Commander replied promptly. "After that—well, it would be nice to know exactly what happened before my men got to that inn, and why."

"I usually charge for this, you know," Karvonen muttered.

"No you don't," Eleret said. "That's a different branch of your . . . family business."

"Ah? What business are you in?" Weziral asked.

"Oh, my family has broad interests," Karvonen said. "I'm sure you wouldn't be interested in the details. I'm in the acquisitions end of things," he added blandly.

Daner made a choking noise.

"I thought what happened at the inn was fairly obvious,"

Eleret said quickly. "Mobrellan left some Syaski there in case we came before he found us, and we had to fight our way through them when we arrived."

Weziral sighed. "Yes, but *why?* Posthumous revenge is well enough in minstrel's tales, but—"

"He didn't expect it to be posthumous," Daner said. "And— Well, it will be easier if I start at the beginning."

"I've been waiting for someone to say that. Hold on a minute." Weziral went out, returning almost at once with another stool. He sat down and looked at Daner expectantly. "You were saying?"

"Mobrellan was the bastard son of a Rathani wizard," Daner said. "Illegitimate offspring aren't highly regarded in Rathane, so even though he had his father's magical abilities, he didn't have much of a future to look forward to."

"Until he got himself hooked by a Shadow-born," Karvonen said.

"Exactly. I don't know whether he tried to summon the Shadow-born, or whether the Shadow-born felt some of Mobrellan's more . . . unusual magical experiments and reached out to him without being called, but it doesn't matter. Mobrellan—"

"How did you find out all this?" Eleret asked, frowning.

Daner gave her a guilty look. "Jonystra Nirandol has recovered enough to talk. My father and I spent the afternoon asking questions. You were busy with Adept Climeral, or I'd have asked you to join us."

Ciaronese have no sense of priority. "I see. Go on."

"Jonystra really was a Trader once, but the caravans threw her out. I think she was cheating the customers."

"All Traders cheat their customers," Karvonen said.

"Then it must have been for getting *caught* cheating the customers," Daner said with exaggerated patience. "Anyway, she and Mobrellan have been together for a long time, so she was able to tell us a lot.

"Mobrellan learned how to draw on the Shadow-born's power—that's where his shape-changing ability came from—but it still wasn't enough to get him accepted by the Rathani wizards' guilds. Then Grand Master Gorchastrin announced that he'd discovered something that would put his particular guild at the helm, and Mobrellan went a little crazy. He thought, you see, that Gorchastrin had hooked his own Shadow-born, which would mean that the guilds wouldn't need Mobrellan's borrowed abilities at all.

"What Gorchastrin had really discovered, of course, was the existence of Eleret's ring."

"But my ring wouldn't have been any help to a Rathani wizard," Eleret objected. "Would it?"

Karvonen grinned. "It bounced spells, didn't it? The Rathani wizards' guilds have such a complicated stack of spells and counterspells and counter-counterspells among them that all it would take is one little disruption to bring the whole mess down around their ears."

"That's what Jonystra said." Daner threw an annoyed look in Karvonen's direction. "Mobrellan went to see Gorchastrin the night he died. Jonystra doesn't *know* that Mobrellan killed him, but . . . In any case, Mobrellan came back determined to get his hands on the raven ring. He thought he could use it to control a Shadow-born completely, instead of having to accept whatever dribbles of power it chose to offer him."

"The more fool he," Karvonen said, shuddering.

"Mobrellan and Jonystra left immediately for the border, which was where Gorchastrin had detected the magical disturbances that led him to the ring."

"Ma must have been wearing it in a battle," Eleret put in.

"If a Rathani tried a battle spell, the ring would deflect it, and from what you've said, the wizard would notice for sure."

Daner nodded. "It took them a while to track your mother down. When they did, she was recovering from wounds. Mobrellan used his shape-changing to slip into the infirmary tent and try to talk her into giving him the ring. When she wouldn't, he used his shadow magic. Someone interrupted him before he finished, and he left, planning to return the following night."

"But by then Ma was already dead," Eleret said softly.

"Yes." Daner gave her a sympathetic look. "He'd overestimated her strength, or the ring's, or underestimated the power he'd put into his attempt at persuasion."

No, he underestimated what Ma would do to keep him from getting hold of what he wanted, Eleret thought, but she did not say it aloud. After all, she had only her own inner certainty as evidence. Pa would understand, but not these Ciaronese. *Well, maybe Karvonen . . .*

Daner glanced at Commander Weziral. "Mobrellan had also underestimated the effiency of the Ciaronese army. By the time he came back, Freelady Salven was on her pyre, and her personal effects had been sealed to send home."

"I suppose Mobrellan was responsible for the various attempts to get at the effects afterward, as well," Weziral said.

Daner nodded again. "He heard someone talking about Eleret one day when he was here looking for a way to get at them. That's how he found out she was coming to pick up her mother's things."

"Rathani are idiots," Karvonen said disgustedly. "With a little practice and a bit more common sense, that man could have made a fortune as a spy, but did he even think of it? No. He was too busy haring off after Eleret's ring on the chance that it would get him into that rat's nest the Rathani call guild politics."

"It's as well that it didn't occur to him," Weziral said, frowning. "The chaos he could have caused doesn't bear thinking of."

"Sorry." Karvonen shrugged. "I just hate to see talent go to waste, that's all."

"The rest of the story you already know," Daner said to Weziral, pointedly ignoring Karvonen. "Mobrellan couldn't get at the ring while it was in your office, so he got Maggen to try for it here. He also planted some rumors among the Syaski, because he'd heard they disliked Cilhar, and even tried to get hold of the ring himself by posing as Gorchastrin. When that didn't work, he and Jonystra tried the cardcharting."

"So it was just a trick to get into your house?" Eleret said.

"Not entirely. They *were* trying to manipulate your future, but Mobrellan didn't know enough about the cards, and he didn't realize that since Jonystra was doing the chart, she would have to control the spell and whatever power he fed into it. She's nowhere near the magician he was, so she lost control fairly quickly. At that, she's lucky. If she'd hung on for another card or two, she'd probably be dead now.

"When the spell went wrong, Mobrellan abandoned Jonystra and ran. Later, he tried to trick Eleret out of the ring by pretending to be me, but it didn't work. After that . . ." Daner shrugged. "You know as much as we do."

"After that, he went back to Jonystra's room at the Broken Harp to try to think of something else," Karvonen said. "He was still thinking when I got there to search the place. Apparently my arrival gave him all sorts of brilliant ideas."

"No need to go into detail," Weziral said. "I think Livarti

has given me a fairly good picture of all that went on." He looked at Eleret. "It's a good thing that ring of yours was destroyed."

"What?" Eleret stared at him in surprise.

"If you still had it, I would be forced to confiscate it," the Commander said. "The Emperor has placed rather specific limits on the types of magical objects that his subjects may hold, particularly within the city of Ciaron. I am sorry for your loss, but I confess that I am pleased to be spared an unpleasant necessity."

Karvonen looked at the Commander, started to say something, and then closed his mouth and shook his head. From his expression, Eleret thought she knew what he was thinking. *It wouldn't have been that easy to get Ma's ring from me, Emperor's law or no. Just as well we don't have to worry about it.*

"Speaking of which, I have a . . . memento for you, Freelady," Weziral went on. "That is, if you wish to take it."

Eleret looked at him in surprise, and he smiled and pulled a small object out of his pocket. When he held it out to her, she saw that it was the melted remnant of the raven ring.

"We . . . retrieved it from the shapeshifter's body after you left," Weziral said. "It retains no magical properties, and no traces of shadow magic or the Shadow-born; that's been checked, several times, in as many different ways as we could think of. A sufficiently expert wizard might be able to enchant it again, but there's no hope of reproducing the original spell. Varnan magic is beyond most of us, I fear."

"The magic was never the important part," Eleret said, taking the silvery lump from Weziral's hand. "Not to us. I'm glad to have it." She looked down, studying it. The silver had melted and run into a flattened blob, partially covering the raven stone. Only the raven's head and upper wings were still visible. *The raven is for protection, the stone is for night and shadow, and the silver . . . the silver is for sacrifice. I should have remembered that sooner. I bet Ma did.* She blinked back tears and looked up. "Thank you, Commander."

"What will you do with it?" Daner asked. "It's not big enough for a paperweight."

Eleret stared at him, then smiled suddenly as the answer came to her. "I'll have it set in something—a wristband, I think. There's time before I head home, if you can recommend a good jewelsmith."

Daner bowed. "I'll be happy to, Freelady."

"I believe that answers most of my immediate questions," Weziral said, rising. "If I need to know more, I'll talk to you in the morning." He looked across at Karvonen. "You'll be pleased to know that your healers think you're well enough to move to the main room in another two days."

"You've no notion," Karvonen murmured. "Fare you well, Commander."

Eleret spent the following day cleaning up the last of her business in Ciaron. Daner's jewelsmith produced a striking wristband of twisted copper wire, with the lump of silver held firmly in a sort of cage, so that the visible part of the raven stone showed clearly. Afterward, she stopped to see Climeral, to ask about training Cilhar healers and to say farewell. On her way back to the Vallaniri household, she visited Karvonen, who was much better but very restless.

So she was not surprised next morning when a note arrived from Weziral, saying that Karvonen had disappeared during the night, and asking that she and Daner come to his office at their earliest convenience.

"I don't know how he got out of the compound," the Commander said, "but he seems to have done it. The night guards will be up for discipline."

"Don't be too hard on them," Daner said, and the corners

— 343 —

of his mouth twitched. "Karvonen is . . . something of a specialist when it comes to this kind of thing."

"He left this, but I have no idea what it means." The Commander pushed a scrap of paper toward Eleret. "Maybe you can make something of it."

Eleret glanced at the scrap and smiled involuntarily. It was one of the symbols Cilhar drew on rocks or trees to mark changes in a trail or to let other Cilhar know which fork they had taken. This one meant, roughly, *I'm going this way; it's safer.* "It's Karvonen's way of saying good-bye," she said. "I don't think he was . . . comfortable with so many soldiers around."

"He could have said something."

Daner snorted. "Karvonen? He could have, but he wouldn't. It would make things too easy for everyone else."

"If you say so." The Commander still looked disgruntled.

Eleret laid the scrap of paper on Weziral's desk and looked across at him. "While I'm here, Commander, I'd like to make my farewells in a more formal manner than Karvonen did."

"You're leaving soon, then?"

"Today, as soon as I pick up my kit at Daner's. I said good-bye to Adept Climeral and the people at the school yesterday, but I wanted to thank you, too, for all your help."

"You're welcome, though most of it doesn't seem to have been needed. Safe journey, Freelady."

As they left the Commander's office, Daner frowned at Eleret. "I didn't want to say anything in front of the Commander, but we can't leave today. I've promised Father to look over the wards on one of the warehouses with him this afternoon. If you'd said something—"

Eleret sighed, knowing he was right. "I'm sorry. I *should*

have said something earlier, but there never seemed to be a good time."

"You don't *have* to go home right away anymore, you know," Daner said persuasively. "You could stay here for a week or two, and see more of Ciaron. Of course, if you really want to leave, I can be ready by tomorrow or the next day, but you should at least consider—"

"Daner."

Daner stopped and gave her an inquiring look.

Eleret sighed again and shook her head. "You're very kind, but I've seen as much of Ciaron as I want to see. And I'm not waiting until tomorrow, or the next day. I'm leaving this morning. I only stayed this long to make sure Karvonen was going to recover, and now that he has . . . Anyway, with Mobrellan dead I don't need a wizard bodyguard any longer."

"I was hoping you might think of some other reasons to bring me along . . . or to stay in Ciaron."

In spite of herself, Eleret smiled. "No you weren't, not really. Karvonen's right; you're just used to having your own way about everything." She let the smile relax into nothing, and said seriously, "I don't belong in Ciaron, Daner. Especially not in your part of it."

"If Metriss and Raqueva have done something to make you uncomfortable—"

"It's not your sisters, Daner. It's the buildings and the smell and the crowds. It's the clothes I'd have to wear if I stayed, and the manners I don't know, and the things people fuss about that I don't think are important. I don't fit here."

"I think I see." Daner looked down, then said quietly, "I could still come with you to the mountains."

Eleret shook her head. "You couldn't stay; you have responsibilities. And you'd be as bad a fit there as I am here. We might as well admit it now, and save ourselves some time and trouble."

Daner was silent for a moment—a long moment. Then his lips quirked. "Even though I've finally learned not to block your throwing lines?"

"There is that," Eleret said, trying to keep her relief from showing. "I suppose that with another fifteen or twenty years of training—"

"All right!" Daner held his hands up in mock surrender, laughing. Then the laughter faded. "I understand. I think. You never do things the way I expect you to, you know."

"That's part of what I'm talking about."

"I said I understood." He looked down the street, as if he were studying the people and the buildings for the first time, then shook his head. "Ah, well. Nijole will probably tell me it's good for me not to have exactly what I think I want all the time."

"She'll be right."

Daner shook his head in mock sadness. "You two have the same attitude. You'll forgive me if I say good-bye here? I'd rather not drag it out, and if I'm not going with you I may as well see if Nijole can give me a few more tips on checking ward spells before I have to demonstrate for my father this afternoon."

Eleret agreed readily, pleased by Daner's return to a good humor, though she suspected that he was more interested in avoiding his sisters' questions than in reviewing magical procedures. She herself had little difficulty in collecting her kit and thanking her hostess, possibly because Daner's mother was too polite to rack a guest.

As she turned away from the gate of the Vallaniri home, Eleret felt lighter. Her last obligation in Ciaron had been met, and she was free to go at last. *Like the raven in Climeral's cards* . . . She started back toward the east side of Ciaron and the gate through which she had entered.

"Leaving already?" said Karvonen's voice at her side.

"Shouldn't I be?" Eleret said cheerfully. "I've done what I came for, and Pa and Nilly and Jiv can't get on without me forever."

"Families do tend to be very demanding," Karvonen said. "Mine, for instance, has been demanding that I lie low for a while. Thieves are not supposed to get themselves quite so . . . noticed."

"That's what happens when you get mixed up with Cilhar and wizards." Eleret gave him a sidelong look. "Of course, if you've changed your mind about Cilhar, the Mountains of Morravik are a good place to stay out of sight for a while."

"Cilhar aren't bad," Karvonen said much too casually. "But I can't say I've developed much of a fondness for wizards. So I think—"

"Daner's not coming with me," Eleret broke in bluntly.

"What?" Karvonen stopped walking, forcing Eleret to stop as well, and face him. "I thought . . . Did he change his mind, or is it his family?"

"Neither. I told him I didn't need a wizard bodyguard any longer, so there's no point in his making the trip."

"No *point?*" Karvonen stared at her. "Eleret, he's good-looking, he's rich, and he's noble-born. He's intelligent, well-spoken, and he's a reasonably skilled wizard. He's *tall.* He's a magician with a sword, which ought to appeal to your Cilhar sensibilities even if none of the rest does. And you say there's no point in taking him back with you?"

"Are you finished? Because if you're not, I recommend you find some nice Ciaronese girl to spout your nonsense at.

I don't need a lover who has to be taught not to block my throwing lines, who forgets to mention important things because he doesn't think I'd be interested, and who's surprised every time I turn out to be worth something in a fight. In Ciaron, I'm a fish trying to fly. Daner would be the same back home, so we decided the trip wouldn't be worth the effort."

"You decided. Both of you?"

"Well, I decided. But Daner agreed with me."

"Ah." Karvonen looked obscurely satisfied. "Well, I'm too short to block your throwing lines, and while I may be intentionally obscure, I don't *forget* to mention important things. As for fights, I try to stay out of them as much as possible; you're more than welcome to my share. Would you perhaps be willing to have me as a companion on your road home?"

"It would please me enormously," Eleret said gravely, though a bubble of laughter was lodged in her chest, threatening to burst at any moment.

Karvonen let out his breath in a soundless whistle of relief, then grinned. "In that case, Freelady, the sooner we're out of Ciaron, the happier I'll be. May I suggest we turn here? The North Gate is only a few blocks down, if we cut through the alley . . ."